Ain't Nobody's

WHEN WE HURT

Book 2

By

Tracey Gerrard

Copyright © Tracey Gerrard 2019
This book is sold subject to the condition that it shall not, by way of trade or otherwise, be lent, resold, hired out, or otherwise circulated without the publisher's prior consent in any form of binding or cover other than that in which it is published and without a similar condition including this condition being imposed on the subsequent publisher.
The moral right of Tracey Gerrard has been asserted.
ISBN-13: 9781082234453

This is a work of fiction. Names, characters, businesses, organizations, places, events and incidents either are the product of the author's imagination or are used fictitiously. Any resemblance to actual persons, living or dead, events, or locales is entirely coincidental.

CONTENTS

Chapter 1	1
Chapter 2	12
Chapter 3	20
Chapter 4	30
Chapter 5	39
Chapter 6	45
Chapter 7	54
Chapter 8	62
Chapter 9	75
Chapter 10	87
Chapter 11	99
Chapter 12	112
Chapter 13	123
Chapter 14	134
Chapter 15	143
Chapter 16	153
Chapter 17	164
Chapter 18	176
Chapter 19	195
Chapter 20	207
Chapter 21	216
Chapter 22	226
Chapter 23	230
Chapter 24	235
Chapter 25	241
Chapter 26	249
Chapter 27	254
Chapter 28	261
Chapter 29	273
Chapter 30	280

Chapter 31......287
Chapter 32......298
Chapter 33......304
Chapter 34......309
ABOUT THE AUTHOR......*313*

ACKNOWLEDGMENTS

I would like to say a huge thank you to my family and friends who have supported me through this journey, your kind words and enthusiasm has driven me to keep on writing. It came as a big shock to a lot of people when I had my first book WHEN WE DANCE published back in March, but those people have encouraged me and have waited patiently for WHEN WE HURT.

However, I do need to give an even bigger thank you to Charlie, Lisa, Millie and Little Charlie as always, your love and support overflows.

Sharon my twin sister and Sarah my niece for reading chapter after chapter, your opinion always overwhelms me which gives me the strength to continue.

Serena, working with you gave me the skills I needed to bring out my creative side, so thank you, matey.

Margaret and Catherine, you have both been there from day one pushing me to continue with something that was a real challenge for me. The help and support you have given freely spending time reading my work and giving advice where needed. Thank you so much I couldn't have done it without you all.

Chapter 1

Vlad

Staggering through my bedroom door, out onto the rooftop patio, the afternoon sun singes my eyes. Shielding them from the light threatening to blind me, I lean down to pick up my sunglasses that I had left on the sun lounger this morning. My balance isn't good, well it wouldn't be, due to the whiskey I consumed for breakfast and lunch. I'm an old pro now; falling on to the luxurious soft cushion has become an everyday occurrence. So has drinking cheap old whiskey. It's not my usual tipple but then again, I'm not my usual self.

Out here, listening to the rustle of the leaves and the tweeting of the birds that nest high up in the lofty trees, lulls me. It's the only place out here that I'm not scowled at. My sons, all of them, look at me with disgust in their eyes. Nag at me to leave the bottle alone and fix the hurt I have caused, and I would if I knew how, but I don't. I'm not the man I was a couple of weeks ago. The family man who relished in having them around. I want to be on my own. I deserve to be alone with no one to care for me, only they do care, and I cannot bring myself to even look at my sons without feeling guilty. Guilty, that I let them down, let myself be consumed by the love of a good woman, a woman that I worshiped and would have given my life for. In the short time we were together, she became my everything. Obsessed by her beauty, I brought my past into our present and our future, destroying the loving relationship we had together and the hero status my family had bestowed on me.

Taking a large mouthful of the amber liquid, I sink further into the comfy mattress of the lounger. The sun warms my cold core and the drink helps me sleep.

Natural sleep has deserted me. Leaving me no choice but to sink further into the bottle to aid my tortured soul. Dreams of my past haunt me. The darkness I evaded for so long ago, back to remind me I haven't let go. Sleep is what I need. Sleep that isn't tormented by my demons. Ever since that night, when I showed Holly who I really am, I realised I am still plagued by my younger years.

"Happy Birthday, Vladimir," my father greets, smiling as he hands me a blue wrapped box that he had hidden behind his back.

"Thank you, Papa. What is it?" I ask, jumping from one foot to the other, excited to be ten years old. My father says that I am growing up quickly and will soon be a man. I love making him proud of me. He doesn't smile a lot; I think his job has him stressed. I'm not even sure what he does but there's always a lot of men in suits who carry big guns. Sergei, one of my father's employees, stays at our home day and night. He's a mountainous man with a bald head, and grey cold eyes. He seems to organize the other men that are always hanging around our home.

My mother and brother, Sasha, sit at the breakfast table watching me open my gift. Sasha is ten years older than me and works for my father. Although, I get the impression he doesn't love our father like I do, they're always arguing and fighting.

I hear a gasp from my mother when I pull out the gun from the box that my father has bought me. Looking towards her, she has one hand on her chest and the other one is covering her mouth. Her face pales as her soft blue eye stare unblinking at my father. "Don't give me that look, it's not real," my father says, shaking his head. Sasha rises like a god from his chair. His jet-black hair and tanned skin enhance his blue eyes that are always dark and intense when my father is around.

"So, it begins," Sasha spits out at my father, glaring at him like a wild animal.

"It has to happen sometime, Sasha, it's in his blood," my father states as he drinks his tea, without taking his focus off my brother. Sasha curses, knocking over his chair and slamming the door with such force on the way out, the kitchen

2

windows shake. My mother stands quickly, gathering the breakfast plates.

"Leave them," my father's tone harsh as he waves his hand around, getting up from his seat. I look at them both, not sure what is going on between them.

He moves to my mother's side and kisses her cheek, "We have Christina to take care of the dishes," my mother places them back on the table and sits back down. "Do you like your present, Vladimir?" he asks, turning to me with a smile on his face.

"Yes, Papa. Thank you."

"Come," he puts his hand out. "Let's go and see if we can teach you to use it."

I'm so excited that my father wants to spend time to show me how to use the present he bought me. We don't spend enough time together. My school friends get to spend lots of quality time with their fathers, going to sports events in the week and on the weekend. My father is always busy. I hurry towards the door where he places his hand on my neck and we head out together. We stroll silently into the woods that surrounds our home, Sergei and two other suited men follow close by. My father's smile lets me know that he is pleased with me. All I ever want to do is make him proud of me.

My eyes snap open and I'm greeted once again by the fiery sun. The sunglasses I had put on are lying on the floor along with the empty whiskey bottle. Standing on shaky legs, my whole body aches along with my heart. I need something to numb the pain, so I make my way indoors in search of my new friend. Sitting on the bed, I find another bottle on my bedside table sat behind a framed photo of Holly and me. Happy and in love.

Laying back on my bed, I take a mouthful of the burning fuel and run my fingers over Holly's angel smile. Her sapphire eyes call to me, calling for me to pull myself together and be the man I was. Only, I don't know where to start.

After my jealous rage in the club, losing my mind over some fucking chancer trying to make a move on Holly. Putting his dirty fucking hands on her. Holly laughing at him or, so I thought. If I'd have looked close enough at the grainy image on the CCTV, I would have seen the anguish in her eyes that she was just tolerating him, so he didn't cause trouble. Watching him put his arm around her shoulder and Holly pushing him away, smiling. Playfully slapping his arm had me raging to the point I found myself hitting the bottle.

I wasn't even planning on going back to the office that night. I planned on waiting outside in the car to give her and her friends a lift home. I'm not even sure why I went in, but I did, switching on the CCTV as soon as I sat down. Seeing him grab her waist and twirl her round rattled the demon in me, causing me to drink more. Half an hour later and half a bottle of Sebastian's Vodka gone, I saw only what I wanted to see.

Images of my dead wife flaunting herself around any man who was interested. Sneaking off to the ladies to snort shit up her nose with her friends. Night after night of arguing and fighting to the point I just refused to care anymore. I could see clearly, she didn't want to be in this marriage, but she was stuck. Just like me. So, when she would let men lead her off the dance floor to the dimly lit corridors, I stopped reacting and focused on getting home to my little boys. They didn't understand that their mother didn't love them, that their father would do anything to protect them and keep them safe from the evil of the world. Even if it came in the image of their mother and grandfathers.

When Holly sashayed off the dance floor towards the bar area that night, with the little prick following closely behind, I couldn't help but react. Blood rising to boiling point. Rage, exploding within me. With no other explanation than the one I'd concocted in my frenzied brain; I was tearing through the bar like a rabid dog.

After that night, I tried to reach out to Holly, only she wouldn't return my calls. And I don't blame her. Apart from taking my rage out on the man who was all over my woman and his two mates, I was callous and spiteful towards Holly. Putting her in the same category as the woman who tortured me for years. Deciding I needed to give her a few days to calm down, I stopped bombarding her phone begging her forgiveness and I stopped banging on her door pleading with her to talk to me. I was then informed by Sebastian that Holly had gone away for a while. How long? He didn't know. Where to? He didn't know that either. Her friends refused to tell me. Saying give her time, she's hurting. Knowing I was the one that had caused the hurt through my insecurities, I turned to the bottle to numb the pain.

Taking another swig from the neck of the bottle, I pick up Holly's pillow and inhale the faint scent of her. I still haven't changed the bedding, not wanting to lose her sweet smell of strawberries. She'd fucking kill me if she knew. A smile crosses my lips and it's the first one in a long time. Thoughts of her stripping the sheets after every night she stayed over. Just in case one of my brood descended on us, which they had on more than one occasion. Seeing her, tangled up in the super king size duvet cover, brought tears to my eyes because I laughed so much. Her little tantrums, the hands on her hips and the stamp of her foot had me laughing harder which had my little minx launching pillows at me. This then led to both of us tangled up in the sheets.

On occasions she had seen my mood darken. At the night of the auction in the golf club. Andrew, one of the members, drunk and handsy, nearly had me up out of my seat throttling him. Only, Sebastian was quick to pick up on my change of state and led me outside before I had time to get to him. Holly saw it too. One rub of delicate hand on my arm and the whisper of her soft tone, *whatever it is that darkens those eyes we will get through it together, but you need to talk to me.* But I never did.

When we all went to support Daniel and his band at the local pub. He asked Holly to sing with him. I couldn't have been prouder of my son and of the woman who would be coming home with me that night and every other night after, if I had my way. Yet again, I saw red when her ex-husband took it upon himself to put his hands on her when she headed for the ladies. This time it was Jack and Holly that stopped me from doing something I would regret. And again, Holly asked me to let her in. I promised I would. But when it came to it, I froze. Telling her what I had done, the man I grew into to protect my family, got stuck in my throat.

After taking another drink from the bottle I relax into my bed, holding the framed picture of Holly and me to my chest and snuggling into her pillow. Hoping my dark dreams will stay at bay and the light of my world will sooth me into a peaceful sleep.

"Come, Vladimir. I have a surprise for you," my father says, sitting on the end of my bed. I jump up, wiping the sleep from my eyes. It's my thirteenth birthday and I know my father will have something special for me.

Over the last three years, my father has taken time out of his busy working week to help me practice my skills in shooting and knife throwing. Three times a week we practice in the woods that surround our home. I have become excellent in both, hitting the bullseye on stationary objects as well as any moving targets my father throws into the air. We even practiced on rabbits once. My father would throw something into the grass so that when they moved, I was able to shoot at them. I didn't really like to hurt them, but father said that they were too many of them. They ate the vegetables that grew in our garden, so we were helping the cook who was not too happy about them.

"Quick get dressed, we have a job to do," he says as his tall figure gets up from my bed and leans against the door. He's wearing a black suit today with a crisp white shirt, looking like one of the top businessmen you see on TV.

"What are we doing?" I ask, hurrying into the bathroom to wash and brush my teeth.

"Meet me in the kitchen, I'll have your breakfast ready," he states, walking out of the door.

When I arrive in the kitchen there's just my father. "Where is mama and Sasha?" I ask, taking a seat opposite him. There's a plate of scrambled egg and toast which I tuck into straight away.

"Mama is not feeling well, she is still in bed," he says after having a drink of his tea.

"Oh, maybe I should go up to see if she needs anything before we go out."

"No need, son, Christina is taking care of her, it's nothing serious," he assures me.

"Where is Sasha?" I ask, finishing my meal and placing my knife and fork on my plate.

My father shrugs his meaty shoulders, "I don't know he did not come home last night."

"Okay," I nod. It's nothing new. Sometimes he doesn't come home, I think he has a girlfriend.

My father stares at me intensely. I'm not sure what's wrong with him this morning but he does not have that smile he normally wears when he is taking me out. "Are you okay papa?"

"Yes, Vladimir I am fine," he answers, leaning down and picking something up from under his chair. He places the box wrapped in blue wrapping paper on

the table. I know it's for me, he always wraps my present in the same colour paper. "Happy Birthday," he says with a smile that doesn't reach his eyes. "Today you become a young man, ready to make me proud," his eyes are darker than normal and there's a smirk on his face that reminds me of a reptile on one of those nature programs I watch. One where the reptile is ready to snap at its prey.

Cold sweat creeps down my back making me shudder.

"Open it," my father says, his voice is low, and eyes are wide.

I take the parcel and slowly unwrap it. There's a brown box and when I open it, it is filled with polystyrene balls. I feel around inside.

My fingers land on something cold and metal and I peek inside to see what it is. A gun. A real gun, for three years I have practiced and never used a proper gun.

"I'm sure your mama and Sasha will have something for you once we get back from our little job," my father says.

"Thank you," I utter, placing the gun on the table, nervous and unsure about using a real gun. I've shot at rabbits and small creatures, but this gun has the potential to kill and it has me scared.

Sergei appears in the doorway and nods his head at my father who is taking a sip of his tea. He nods back and places his cup on the saucer in front of him then pushes it to one side.

"Ready?" Papa asks, as he stands from the table, straightening his tie and running his hands down his suit jacket.

"Where are we going?" my voice is shaky.

"I've told you; we have a job to do," he snaps. "Bring your gun, Vladimir," he turns and strides out of the door, pulling at his cuffs.

Picking it up, I test the weight in my hands. It's heavier than I'm used to, and I find my hands tremble as I hold it.

My father holds the car door open for me as I approach the shiny black Mercedes. Once I'm settled in the middle, two of my father's employees climb in at either side of me. Sergei climbs in the driver's side and another man holds the passenger door open for my father.

We set off down the winding gravelled road and out onto the main road from our home. The car is quiet, so I play with my hands nervously.

Old buildings with broken windows and missing slates pass us by as we tear down the road at speed. Where we are and where we are headed, I haven't got a clue. My father's dark stare meets mine through the rear-view mirror and he gives me a small smile It's not the one I'm used to; I think he's as nervous as I am. I don't like it.

A sense of danger overcomes me when the area we drive into is full of old abandoned warehouses and two sleek black Mercedes are parked outside one of them.

Our car pulls up and everyone climbs out, I'm the last. There are more men in suits, some of them I've seen visiting my father, but some of them I don't know and don't want to. I stand at the side of Sergei, his towering six-foot-six body hiding me. My father rounds the other side of me. "Come," his tone is firm. My legs are shaky, but I follow anyway.

Entering the building, six men greet my father, he nods at them and continues through the building. The rotting smell curls my nose and has me retching, I think it must have been an abattoir at one time. Rubbish line the floors as well as a couple of old sleeping bags and I see a rat scurrying out of the way. Dank water drips from the walls as the old fluorescent light fitments hang slanted and flicker on and off.

We round into a longer corridor which has a closed door at the end of it. My palms are sweating, and my heart is pounding in my chest. When we are halfway down, I'm stopped in my tracks when a blood-curdling scream pierces my ears. It almost sounds like a wounded animal that has been caught in a trap. "Papa," he stops too, placing his hands on my shoulders. He eyes me nervously.

"Vladimir be strong my boy," he smiles. "This is what you have trained for the last three years," he states, still smiling at me, the one that says make me proud of you. And I want to, I really do, but something is not right. I can see it in the darkness of his eyes. His body language is not the same as it is when we go out shooting targets, playful and fatherly. No, it's as if he is going into work to…. I don't know what it is but it's not right.

The door opens, and we are greeted by a heavily tattooed man. He doesn't smile he just holds the door for us. Sergei enters first then I'm next, my feet not wanting to move. I can feel my knees shaking and I stop, not wanting to move any further. My father's hand is on my back and I'm pushed forward into the dark room. There are no windows. No natural light.

Rusty chains hang from the ceiling and murky water pools at our feet, the smell makes me want to vomit. I hear a low groan and when I turn my head to the side, I wish I hadn't.

Sergei stands just in arms way and I find I need to grab him to stay up straight. "Papa," falls from my mouth as I take in the scene before me.

The six men stand on either side of a set of rusty chains that hang from the ceiling. Suspended from the chains, hangs a man, motionless. With his head bent down towards the floor; blood drips from him into the dank water. Slash marks and bruises mar his semi-naked body. He has no shirt and his black suit trousers are ripped. Feet bare.

My father pushes me further into the room until we are about six feet from the man. I want to run. I don't want to be here. I'm not sure why my father has brought me to this torturing hell, but I have a good idea. The man's head lifts and his dark eyes seek out mine, even though he's been tortured I can see the evil that lives within him. My body trembles in fear as his head falls again. "Father?" I whisper, but he doesn't hear me, he just strides towards the strung-up man, lifting his head for all to see.

"Ivan," my father says calmly but with an arrogance about it. That must be the man's name. "You see that boy there?" He points to me and my heart beats out of my chest. "My son," he smiles. "Today he becomes a man," he smiles again as the man struggles in his chains. "Today he will end your life," he nods, pulling the man's head further back. Ivan moans and shakes his head, trying to rid the grip my father has on him.

My head shakes too and "No," slips from my lips, no one hears me because I've suddenly lost my voice.

Uncontrollably, my whole-body shakes. My father's eyes flick from the man to me then back to the man. "You dare to betray me and expect no repercussions, Ivan!" my father's tone borders on psychotic. There's no response from the man, he just stares at me with the same darkness on his face as my father.

"Take out your gun, Vladimir," my father commands.

"No, papa," I utter, shaking my head and wrapping my arms around myself. I'm cold and scared and there's no one here I can trust. All these years I've wanted my father's attention and all this time he spent with me was leading to this. I'm not stupid, I've seen films on TV. I might not have known what my father did for a living, but I do now.

Tears threaten my eyes and I see the curl on my father's lip; the snarl that says do not defy me. "Vladimir take out your gun," he commands again. I'm not strong enough to do this but I'm not strong enough not to do what my father wants. So, I take out the gun that my father gave me for my thirteenth birthday. It feels heavy and I fumble with it, almost dropping it on the floor.

One of the men that is stood at the side of my intended target sniggers at my clumsiness. Sergei, who is still at my side, takes out his gun, points at the man who had laughed at me, and shoots him in the foot. I know it's a warning not to disrespect the boss's son. The man lets out an ear-piercing scream.

"Fuck Sergei, I didn't mean anything!" he cries.

"Next time you disrespect I will blow off your balls," he says calmly then tucks his gun back in the holster under his jacket. With my gun in my hand I stand there shaking, cold and alone.

"Aim it at his right kneecap, Vladimir," my father says, his voice firm and controlling.

"No, papa," I whimper as bile rises into my throat.

"Vladimir look at…"

"I don't want to," I stutter out, stopping my father from what he was going to say.

"Vladimir Petrov don't you dare wimp out on me now," he states, and I can see the anger brewing in him.

"No, papa, please," I beg. Tears stream down my face, mixing with the snot from my nose that I can taste on my lips. Swiping it away with the sleeve of my jacket, my body quakes.

"Vladimir focus on your target. You're going to shoot the man who has turned against your father and you're going to do it now!"

"No, no, no," I repeat, shaking my head. My knees give out and I collapse on to them.

"Get up!" he roar,s making me jump. I place both my hands onto the floor, soaking them and my knees in the stale water. Trying to push myself up from the stench, I don't have the strength and I'm sinking into the pit of hell, crying like a baby. "Up!" my father's voice cuts through the pounding in my head as I see his dark figure standing over me. He puts his hand on the back of my neck and lifts me until I'm stood on my feet.

I stare into this man's eyes, the man I call my father and I see no love for me, just pure darkness.

I try to plead with him again. "Please, papa, don't make me do this."

"You will kill this man," he says while he strides back to the man hung up by chains. The man I see in front of me is not my father, he is someone I don't know.

Someone who wants to take the innocence from a boy. Someone who gets his kicks from seeing another man suffer. Anger erupts inside of me.

"*No, I won't!*" *I scream, tossing the gun on to the cold wet floor as I take a step back.*

There's a pop of a gun that echoes off the walls and I see the man in chains slump forward, dead. Vomit sprays from me and I feel the warm sensation down my legs letting me know that I have wet myself. All eyes are peering over my head and I'm struggling to understand. That's when I feel the warmth of a hand on my shoulder. No one moves as Sasha, my brother, takes my arm and turns me round to him. The menacing look and the gun in his hand tells me he killed the man. He did it for me.

He doesn't speak, just glares at my father, shaking his head. Sergei moves by my father's side, ready to protect. Sasha takes another look at these men as he spits on the floor and picks me up, carrying me out of the hell I had been in.

Sweat soaks through my shaking body as I wake from another dream of my past. This needs to stop. I stagger into the bathroom passing the rows of Holly's clothes still hung there. All her creams and perfumes still in their places at the side of my aftershaves and toiletries. And that's where they will stay. I need her back here with me to bring her lightness and take away my darkness. After relieving myself, I stare at my image in the mirror. Bloodshot dark eyes greet me and the smile I usually wear is gone. Hidden amongst nearly two weeks growth, I don't recognize the man looking back at me. Lost and alone. I know I need to fight for what I want. Turning from the mirror, I turn on the taps of the bath, ready to get rid of this man and bring back the one that Holly and my family wants.

Chapter 2
Vlad

Icy cold stagnant water claims me. Beneath the dark swirling pools, I'm drawn into the pits of hell. I know that's where I'm bound for, I can see the devil himself grinning at me. There's no point in trying to fight my way out, everyone here belongs amongst the depths of the abyss. Including me.

Deathly screams pierce my ears while the blood-soaked faces remind me of a past life that's come to reclaim me. Cruel, callous, greedy men merciless on their mission to snatch the light from the weak. Ridding the world of these wretched bastards was my goal.

Bloodless veined hands wrap around my stilled body, dragging me further into the darkness.

His crazed glare bores into my skin, seizing my blackened soul. Relentless, he nods his head while he roars out a blood-curdling laugh; taunting, teasing, knowing I don't have the will to fight.

Immoral faces come closer, snarling as they remember the man that eradicated them. Darkness deceives me. Trapped in the shadowy putrid place, I'm pulled deeper among the ghostly shadows. My name "Vladimir," chanted repeatedly. At the head of them, he waits to greet me. My father.

I can't let the wickedness of the demonic one win. I'm not a young boy anymore, scared of him. I'm not the man who believed his threats to take my sons from me or the man that needed to watch every move my wife made while having no choice but to work for my father. I beat him once. Defeated him while playing his game.

A stream of light appears through the thickness of the murky water and I pull my shackled arms to try and reach for it, with my mind and body weak and weary, it's a struggle.

"Vlad, Vlad," I hear through the haze, but it's not chanted. The English accent I know. "Dad, Dad," franticly called. These I know too. My boys, Sebastian, Nicholas and Daniel, call to me with panic in their voices. "Vlad," I hear called again. Tom, my housekeeper's husband and good friend. I need to get to them, there's no place for them in this hell hole. I don't hear Lucas, my youngest, the one I nursed as his premature body fought to stay alive.

I try to reach out to them, but my chest burns and I'm fighting to breathe. My shoulders, arms and legs are gripped tightly as I'm yanked out of the vile, vicious pit. Coughing, I wheeze out a roar while my eyes are pricked with a sudden bright light but refuse to open. My skin burns at the feel of harsh slaps to my face and chest as they continue.

"Dad," my son's voices surround me, I want to reach out to them, but I struggle to get to them. Warmth starts to seep into my cold shaky body, and I can feel the blood pump faster through my veins, bringing me back to my sons.

Focusing on the tiny bit of strength I have left; I use it to prize open my eyes. The outline of four men, knelt surrounding me, is cloudy. Pushing further to gain some sight, I see the solemn faces of three of my sons and it's a sight I never want to see again.

Dizziness and nausea overcome me as I try to sit up and before I have time to react, the contents of my stomach violently spill onto the marble floor. A damp towel sweeps across my chest and face, bringing Tom's concerned face into view. He lifts my shoulders and sits behind me so I'm resting on his legs. That's when I take in that I must have fallen asleep in the bath with taps running. Water covers the bathroom floor where I lay covered with just a towel.

Sebastian speaks first. "What the hell were you thinking?" his overly concerned voice says while he holds up an empty bottle of whiskey.

"Not now, Sebastian," Tom says as he tries to help me to my feet. "Let's get him in the bedroom and this mess cleaned up," he tells them. Nicholas and Daniel are quiet and that's a first for them. Nicholas would normally have some smart-arse comment to throw at me, making a joke out of any situation and Daniel always in on it with him. Lucas is a lot like Sebastian, sensible but he has time to fall into his own, he's not even a teenager yet. Wanting to know where he is, I call out, "Lucas," my voice but a croak. Coughing to clear it. "Where is Lucas?" I ask. I don't want him to see me in this state. I know what it looks like.

"Let's get you up and into your room," Tom suggests, ignoring my concern.

The four of them help me to my feet, I'm a dead weight at six-foot-three weighing ninety-six kilos. They lead me into my bedroom and sit me on my bed. Looking around I can see countless empty bottles that's accumulated over the last ten days. Well I think it's ten days but I'm not sure what day I'm in. I don't even know what time of day it is with the blackout blinds closed, shutting out the outside world. "What day is it?" I ask, my voice still croaky.

"Wednesday," Tom answers. I place my head in my hands, twelve days since Holly walked out on me and the last two days, I don't remember a dam thing.

"What time is it?" I ask lifting my head out of my hands. It's no use looking at my alarm clock, it's in pieces on the floor.

"Nine-fifteen," Nicholas tells me. I nod my head in a thank you to him.

I'm aware my sons are not happy with me. Fucking hell, I'm not happy with me. I've been a bastard these last couple of weeks. Not being able to handle the breakup with Holly, I chose to wallow in my own self-pity and drink myself into a coma every day. She wouldn't answer my calls or return my messages, I know I have fucked up, but I need her to forgive me if nothing else.

I watch Tom and my sons clean up the mess I have made, Daniel comes out of the bathroom. "All tidy in there now. It's a good job you have marble flooring otherwise that amount of water would have seeped through into downstairs," he says while drying his hands on a towel and tossing it into the washing basket. My eyes meet his and I give him a silent thank you. Tom brings me some clothes to put on.

"Go put the kettle on, Sebastian, and we will help your father downstairs," he points around at my sons.

"I'm fine to walk," I tell him, knowing full well I feel as weak as a kitten. Before I have time to get up, Tom reacts.

"No, you are not. You look like shit. God knows when you last ate anything, you've lost weight and we don't know how long you've been under that water," he says, shaking his head and I consider myself told. "We need to get you warm and some food because I'm telling you, you are no good to anybody in this sorry state," his eyes soak up the wreck before him. This isn't me. I don't get in these states, I'm a proud man. My hand runs over my face again and I can feel a good growth going on and I'm sure my usual short cropped hair will need a trim too.

Gingerly, I stand on shaky legs, wobbling from weakness. I need to get myself together.

Twenty minutes later we're sat in the kitchen around the island. I have a glass of juice and a black coffee. My boys are giving Tom a conspicuous look, maybe they are not sure what to say after finding me in such a state. Nicholas places scrambled egg and toast in front of me, I'm not sure I want anything to eat but I'll give it a go. Surprisingly, it goes down easily, and I could eat it again. Daniel stands by the grill cooking bacon, when he finishes, he puts a crispy bacon sandwich in front of me. As soon as the salty taste hits my taste buds, I devour every morsel. I can't remember the last time I ate anything, so no sooner it's in my mouth it's gone.

My eyes travel from my plate and I thank Daniel for my sandwich, that's when I'm drawn to Sebastian. His eyebrows are low, and his dark blue eyes are narrowed on me while the whites of his knuckles show as he grips the island. "Have we finished pussy footing around him now?" he growls.

"Stop it," Tom says as he glares at Sebastian. Looking at my sons and Tom, I know they're concerned; I can see it edged on their faces. I wipe my hands on the towel and toss it on to the breakfast bar. Pushing the stool behind me, I stand to my full height. I'm feeling a little more myself after eating. I face my troubled son Sebastian.

"What's wrong?" is all I manage to say before I'm bombarded with his anger.

"WHAT'S WRONG?!" he bellows, jabbing me in the chest with

his finger. My shocked face must say everything because I can't think of a time when one of my sons have raised their voice in anger to me let alone jab me in the chest with a finger. My lip rises at one side, amused that Sebastian dares to challenge his father but I'm shot down quickly with his next statement. "While you have been wallowing in your own self-pity, drunk every night for nearly two weeks, our little brother," his finger has moved from jabbing me in the chest to pointing at Nicholas and Daniel. "Our brother Lucas, you remember him? The one you've neglected. Did you not think that your break-up with Holly wouldn't hurt him?" he yells. "So, while you have been in your own pathetic, sorrowful little world, Lucas has gone missing!" he rages at me.

The shock of the swift short jab connecting with my left brow and the painful jolt to my ribs as I stagger into the kitchen island doesn't hurt as much as the words I've just heard. I don't hear what else he spits out at me as he storms off, shaking the hand that's just hit me in the eye.

Lucas is missing. This whirls around my head and my heart breaks for a second time in two weeks.

Tom rushes to my side with a towel to stop the blood running into my eye. I try to bat him away, but his overprotectiveness beats me, and I sit back down in my seat.

"What does he mean Lucas is missing?" I question, the firmness of my voice lets them know they need to tell me the truth.

Nicholas informs me that they haven't heard from him since this morning and now his phone is switched off. He goes on to say that Monday evening Lucas had phoned Sebastian to tell him he would get the bus to school on Tuesday morning and home again. Apparently, he and a school friend Martin were supposed to be working on a science project together, so he would eat at his house as well. Sebastian believed him; he had no reason not to. This morning Daniel was supposed to drop him at school, he told him the same, that he was catching the bus with Martin. Again, this wasn't questioned until this evening when Daniel was pulling in the drive and Martin was on his way to see why Lucas hadn't been to school for two days.

My stomach flips as I place my heavy head in my hands. He's been missing since Monday and nobody knew. I can't believe I didn't think of how it would affect Lucas. He's got close to Holly, the three of us spending a lot of time together. Drinking every day to help take away the pain and guilt I felt after my raging outburst towards Holly, left my youngest son to fend for himself and witness his father at his worst.

"Fuck," I bark out as I search the kitchen for my mobile. This is vain because I find it in pieces under the dining room table. Reaching in one of the many drawers in my kitchen I take out one of my old ones and put it on charge then I wait to get some life into it.

As my phone springs to life, alerting me to a text message, Sebastian strides back into the kitchen with his phone to his ear. "Oh, thanks Holly," he says, relief on his face. "We're just glad he's safe and well," it's those words, Holly and he's safe and well, that has me up out of my seat ready to put my trainers on to go to them. "Yes, that's fine. I'll tell everyone," then he glances towards me. "Yes, he's here. His phone was flat, it has just charged," he can see my phone laying there, so I quickly pick it up to read the message that arrived the same time as Sebastian walked back into the kitchen. It's from Holly.

Hi Vlad. Just letting you know Lucas is safe at my house. I arrived back from Jay and Ivy's cottage to find him here. He had taken the spare key that hung in your kitchen. I glance towards the shelf and see that it's missing from the hook. I should have known that's where he would go.

Reading the rest of the text my eyes fill up.

Lucas doesn't want to speak to you because of your vicious tongue. You really know how to hurt the people who love you. Don't you, Vlad? Anyway, I know you will all want to see him, but could you PLEASE leave it until the morning. He's gone to bed and I don't think he needs disturbing tonight. I'm also dead tired so please leave it until the morning. If you text me when you're on your way, I will go out and give you some time to right the wrong you have done.

My heart fucking hurts and I find myself placing my hand on it, rubbing at the pain. I'm so fucking relieved that Lucas is safe and at Holly's but I'm aware her message suggests she doesn't want to see me. Sebastian speaks but I don't quite hear what he says. "What?" I ask.

"I said don't go over to Holly's tonight."

"Mmmm…"

"Father, Lucas is safe at Holly's and she's asked that we leave it until the morning. He's in bed and Holly is tired so do the right thing and leave it until then," he says, pointing his mobile at me with a look that says you might be my father, but I'm pissed at you. I don't blame him.

If Lucas was anywhere else, I would be on my way now to bring him home, but he's safe, warm and well at Holly's who loves him like her own. My face drops into my hands when I remember my last words to him, no wonder he wanted to get away. Telling my twelve-year-old son that his dead mother was a drug-taking whore wasn't one of my finer points at being a father. I know I'm going to have to explain to Lucas what his mother was like now, his brothers have always known but we've managed to keep it from him, I haven't even told Holly anything about her.

That's why I flipped that night at the club, watching Holly dance. Men a lot younger than me ogling her, trying to put their hands on her, reminded me of my dead wife.

How she would be the centre of attention on the dance floor and let any man claim her, not bothered that she had a husband and sons at home? Holly is nothing like her and I can't believe I was foolish enough to let my past wreck my future.

"Will you be ok?" Daniel asks. "Or do you need us to stay at home tonight?" I glance up at Daniel who is leaning against the island arms folded. Nicholas stands there with his hands in his pockets looking like his mischievous self and my eldest Sebastian has that worried frown going on as he stares at me from the other side of the kitchen. Tom sits at the side of me, concerned. He would have made a fantastic father if him and Mary could have had children, unfortunately they couldn't conceive but he's been nothing short of a father figure to me since we met. It's a shame my own wasn't like him.

"I'll be fine. I'm going to clean this mess up," I point round the kitchen.

Tom jumps in, "Leave it, Vlad, Mary will be over in the morning to clean up...."

"No," I snap, sounding ungrateful. "Sorry. It's my mess I need to take care of it. Thank you for your help and I will thank Mary when I see her, but you've all done enough." The mess isn't just the house, it's the fucking big mess I've made of the relationship I have with Lucas and Holly.

I tell them they can all leave, and Sebastian hesitates as if he has something to say. I give him a tight smile and a nod of my head just letting him know we will be okay. I've already forgiven him for the split eye and bruised ribs, and I know he will forgive me for my behaviour over the last couple of weeks if I make things right with Lucas and Holly. Sebastian says goodnight and tells us he is going home to his children and heavily pregnant wife. This puts a smile on my face because I can't wait for the new arrival to the Petrov family.

Nicholas and Daniel grab me in a bear hug, making me wince when they squeeze me too tight and my ribs cry out in pain. They both find it funny and inform me that I did deserve what Sebastian dished out to me. They both leave with Tom, Nicholas shouting over his shoulder, "See you in the morning old man," he chuckles as he walks out of the door. Cheeky bastard, I'm only forty-five.

"Fuck off," I yell back, and I can hear him laugh harder because that's him and me. He takes the piss and I curse.

Chapter 3

Holly

I can't sleep, I've tried. Since coming to bed at eleven thirty, I've thrown myself around my king size bed.

Spending nine relaxing, peaceful days at Jay and Ivy's cottage on the Northumberland coast gave me time to reflect. I've gone over and over what happened in the club that night. The violence, the hurtful, cruel words that were spat at me and how I was manhandled. I know Vlad didn't mean to hurt me, but he did, more emotionally than anything else.

Then the three days that followed, I was bombarded with text messages, my voicemail full of pleading messages for me to hear him out and forgive him. I know he's sorry and heartbroken just like me, but it doesn't help the fact that his actions caused a lot of hurt and pain.

On the second day Sebastian, Nicholas and Daniel called to see me, Lucas was at school and I was missing him already. Pleased to see them I let them in and made them welcome. I could see they were as upset as I was. They practically begged me to hear their father out and give him a chance to explain himself. Nicholas let slip that he thought his father was paranoid about any man coming near me which was due to their mother. When I tried to get any more information out of him, he clammed up. Sebastian told me it was their father's place to tell me anything that had to do with their mother and their lives back in Russia. Although they never revealed any information on their mother, they did mention that Vlad's upbringing had not been normal, and he was forced to deal with things that any average teenage boy would not. They also said he had to carry out a role in life that he didn't want but had no way of ending it until six months before they came to live in England. The few titbits of information they gave me, although cryptic, told me enough.

Telling them I needed some time away and I would speak with Vlad when I returned was enough for them. After they hugged me and said bye, I packed a suitcase ready to set off early the following morning to get the keys for the cottage from Olivia and Jack.

Nine reflecting days with plenty of sleep due to the sea air, I had concluded that I would hear him out. And although I have it in me to forgive him for his actions, if he couldn't enlighten me to what his boys had said or what put the darkness in his eyes, then our relationship couldn't be saved. He needed to trust me, and I needed an explanation to what turned my handsome man with an enormous heart into someone vicious and angry. Almost animal-like.

Returning home at eight o'clock to find Lucas had set up camp in my home shocked me. Apparently, his father's vicious tongue wasn't just lashed out at me, but at his youngest son as well. Lucas told me that his dad had started drinking heavily when he couldn't reach me and had become unbearable. He hadn't been into work since he erupted and spent most of the days in his own room and out on the patio adjacent to his bedroom. His sons had decided to leave him be, hoping he would come around in his own time. Only, two days ago Lucas had asked him about going to parents evening and they had fallen out when Vlad told him he wouldn't be going and staggered off to his room. Not interested.

Lucas got upset and told him he wished he was dead and that his mother was here. He didn't mean it. That's when Vlad flipped and told Lucas that his dead mother was an evil witch who was only happy when she was drugged up and was being fucked by any man who would have her. To say the boy was upset was an understatement. What was the man thinking telling his son that?

I spent over an hour consoling him. Explaining to him that

sometimes adults say things they don't mean and I'm sure that his mother was a lovely woman. But Lucas was sure it was true. He told me that he had never seen a photograph of his mother and was told that any photographs they had were lost in the move here. He went on to say that they never spoke about her and when he had asked questions, his father barely told him anything. Sebastian and Nicholas were the ones to tell him what she looked like and how she had died. They told him she had been in a car crash which caused her to go into early labour and Lucas had to be delivered by C section. Then she died a couple of hours after. Lucas thought that it was too painful for his father to talk about, so he stopped asking questions. But after Vlad's spiteful words two days ago, his son wanted answers.

Thinking about what Sebastian, Nicholas and Daniel had told me before I went away and how he kicked off in the club, I think he was speaking the truth about their mother and he's going to have one hell of a hard time explaining how sorry he is that the truth about her came out in such a hurtful way. Bloody hell!

Once Lucas had cried in my arms, he went for a shower and I made us both something to eat. We played on his game that he had brought with him then he went to bed a little happier. That's when I text his father. What an idiot he is. I knew they would be panicking as to where Lucas was, so I let Vlad know he was with me. When I didn't get a reply, I telephoned Sebastian who was relieved to know his brother was safe and well and would inform his father. He still hadn't text me back, but Sebastian did say his phone was flat and that he had just charged it. The thing is I don't want to hear from him. I've got myself worked up and I could slap his face.

He's not only upset his sons but compared me to his wife. His words, *you're just like her*. How dare he.

It's one o'clock in the morning and I'm still no nearer to falling asleep. I sit up and throw myself back down, turning on my side coming face to face with the photo of Vlad and me. I could smash it into pieces.

Still angry with him, I contemplate getting up to have a cup of chamomile tea to try and relax me. I could do with some more of that sea air, it knocked me out most evenings. As I pull back the covers my phone comes to life, I don't need to look to see who it's from; it's playing our song.

Reading the message, I shake my head and chuckle in disbelief. Cheeky bastard.

Are you awake? Is all it says.

Am I awake? It's like the sun is up and holding my eyelids hostage. And this is curtesy of the twat that's just text me. I want to ignore his text. I know I should ignore it, I'm angry with him even though I've missed him. I've seen the nasty side of him and heard his vicious words. But I've also seen a loving man whose words melt my heart and make me feel cherished and loved. I've listened to Lucas upset at his father words, but I've listened to his other sons pleading with me to give him a chance and I've also witnessed how he dotes on his family. He would do anything for them. I know he will be sorry for upsetting Lucas and will do anything to mend the hurt he has caused.

My fingers betray my head and side with my heart, texting him just one word.

Holly: Yes

Vlad: Fancy a coffee?

I can't believe he thinks this can be fixed over a cup of coffee. Well yes, I can, because he knows once he gets his foot in my door then I won't be able to say no to him. And maybe if it was just me and him then he would be right but there's a twelve-year-old boy who is hurting and we need to put him first. Needing to get to the bottom of why he would say such a thing I text him back.

Holly: I'll put the kettle on

Vlad: I'll be round in ten

Comes back straight away. And I'm a mess.

Quickly I scramble out of bed, grabbing my dressing gown and making sure it's wrapped around me, fastened tight. I don't trust that he won't try with his wicked ways in trying to seduce me or is that me missing them? Skidding into the kitchen to switch on the kettle, I prepare two cups for when he arrives. I keep the lights dim and make sure that the door that leads to the bedrooms is closed, I don't want to wake Lucas. Thinking of the poor kid I get rattled again that Vlad would hurt him like that and that he would think I'm anything like his dead wife. If it's true that she took drugs and slept around then he doesn't think highly of me and as I hear the buzzer of the intercom sound, I tremble with anger.

I open the door and leave it ajar as I return to the kitchen to make our coffee. It's not long when I sense him in the same room, I can also smell that smell that normally would have me flinging myself at him but this time, I stay strong and turn slowly.

Shocked to see he has lost weight and the cut with bruising to his right eye along with them being blood shot makes him look vulnerable. I want to go to him, my heart is telling me to, but I don't. I need to stay strong. My body trembling has him closing the gap between us. He stills when I put my hand up to stop him. I see the torment in his eyes, he doesn't know what to do. We don't speak, and I don't think I can. I'm angry with him but my body wants to hold him. His eyes call to me, pleading for me to let him come near. "Holly," he puts out his hand for me to take and I shake my head. I'm a mess and any minute now I will burst into tears, I can feel them threatening to break out. I can also feel the velvety touch of him saying my name stroke over my skin and I'm in a turmoil.

Angry, upset, wanting to slap him but wanting his strong arms around me has me shaking my head and stepping forward. He steps in closer and tries to take my hand. This time I snatch my hand away from his then bring it up so fast I don't just shock him, I shock myself when it connects with the left side of his face.

Slap!

While my hand goes straight to my mouth, alarmed that I have hit him, he stands there nodding, knowing he deserved it. Tears pool in my eyes and before I can stop him, he has me wrapped in his arms with his face in my hair. "I'm so sorry, Holly," he breathes into my hair, over and over he repeats the words while his large hands, one of them cradling the back of my head and the other rubbing my back.

I sob into his shoulder for the hurt he has caused, knowing he didn't mean any of it.

When we break away, I move out of his arms, instantly I feel cold, missing the warmth of his embrace. I know I need to keep him at arm's length until he has made it up with Lucas and answered some of my questions and it's far too late to do that tonight. He knows it too. Feeling a little stronger now I reach for our coffees, handing him one. He takes his and makes his way over to the couch. I join him, choosing to sit on the opposite one rather than next to him. He breathes deeply and shakes his head not liking my choice on where I am sitting. Well he wouldn't would he because I normally sit at the side of him or on his knee. I don't like it either, but this is how it's got to be for now.

Vlad breaks the silence that surrounds us first, sitting on the end of the settee with his elbows resting on his knees. "How have you been?" Looking at him, seeing the hurt and anguish on his face, the bruising and cut to his eye and how for the first time he looks his age. I think I've coped better than him.

"Better than you by the looks of you. What the hell did you do to your eye?" I ask a little bit too abruptly.

"It's nothing. I deserved it," he says shaking his head then rubs his hands up and down his face.

"I didn't ask whether you deserved it, I asked what you had done," again my tone a little curt. This happens all the time, he never gives me a straight answer. It's not that he lies to me he just doesn't tell me anything. He must grasp that I am not going to put up with his vague answers because he nods his head keeping his dark blue eyes focused on me, he takes a drink of his coffee then places his cup on the table. "Sebastian...."

He doesn't get to finish when I jump in. "What? Sebastian hit you?" I can't believe his number one fan has given him a black eye. "What did you do to him?" I ask, wondering what his vicious tongue has said to upset Sebastian.

"I think upsetting Lucas, causing him to run off was a good enough excuse for Sebastian to let me know that he wasn't happy with me," he says pointing to his eye.

"Yeah, not one of your finest moments telling your son that his dead mother took drugs and slept around."

"I know," he winces and puts his head in his hands again.

I feel for him; I really do but he's got to sort his head out and start letting me in before I can help him.

"Vlad, Sebastian and Lucas love you; they will forgive you, but you need to handle Lucas delicately. Telling him about his mother, saying those things have hurt him. You're the one person he trusts not to let him down and I'm afraid he thinks his father and brothers have kept things from him that he should have known," I shift in my seat, putting my feet up and lean against the arm of settee. It's late and I'm shattered.

"What about you, Holly?" he asks, getting up off the settee. Crossing the short distance between us he crouches down in front of me. "Can you forgive me?" His hands reach for me and I don't move. They cup my face as he strokes my cheeks with his thumbs. Leaning into one of his strong, warm hands; I've missed his touch. I place mine on top of his and the connection brings back the love we hold for each other, not that it had ever gone. The desire and need to be together, stronger than it ever was but I know we have a long way to go before we can be together again.

Him being a father and taking care of Lucas comes first. Once their relationship is back on track then we can talk. I move his hands off my face and hold them in mine.

"Vlad we can't do this now," I whisper, looking into the dark blue eyes that hold nothing but love for me. I can see how much he needs me. How sorry he is for his actions and how he wants to right his wrong. He closes his eyes and lightly squeezes my hand, nodding his head at my words. I separate our hands and lift one of mine to his face stroking over his bruised eye, his eyes stay closed as he relishes in my soft touch. "Vlad," I say quietly.

"Hmmm..."

"Our priority is Lucas; we need to take care of him and do what we can to rid the sadness and hurt he is feeling at the moment."

"You're right," he shifts suddenly and winces, his hand going straight to the right side of his ribs. He takes a deep breath and returns to his seat on the other settee, wincing again when he sits down.

"What's wrong?" I ask, concerned for him.

"Fell into the kitchen island when Sebastian laid one on me," he divulges with no hesitation.

"Ouch. Do you need some painkillers?" I ask, it must have been one hell of a punch to knock him into the kitchen island. He's built like a brick wall.

"No," he says, rubbing his ribs. "I'll be fine."

"Okay. So, you think I'm right about Lucas?" I ask, as he fiddles with the corner of one of the scatter cushions. He's nervous, I can tell, but I'm not sure if it's the thought of explaining to his son about his mother or if it is about him and me, it could be both.

"Yes. I'll speak with him in the morning, it's time he learnt the truth about his mother. I never meant to keep it from him, and I never meant to blurt it out like I did. I was not in a good place," he says, shaking his head. His eyes look sad as if he's lost something precious to him.

"I know and I'm sure he will understand," I tell him. I know Lucas is a bright boy and I'm sure he will understand that some things are not easy to explain to a young boy. He loves his father dearly, which gives me hope that he will forgive him.

Vlad gets up from his seat and takes his cup into the kitchen then comes back in and sits on the same settee as me. We're not touching but my feet that I have up on the cushions are close to him. "I always wondered how I would tell him about his mother," he says quietly, putting his hand on my foot and running his thumb over the instep. I don't move it, I can't. The heat that travels through my body has me wanting to jump into his lap, letting him take his time caressing my skin with his soft lips and strong hands. So, I stay still and let him continue.

"He's asked questions over the years and I've fobbed him off, leaving it to his brothers to answer his questions. They knew how far to go without relaying the truth," he sighs, taking my foot and placing it in his lap. Once again, I don't move it. I just listen, letting him get off his chest whatever he has to say. "And I never wanted to lie to you," he turns to face me, leaning sideways on the settee so his shoulder and head rests on the back of it. "And I haven't lied to you. I just evaded telling you anything that would bring up my past," his eyes close as he takes a deep breath then lets out a heartfelt sigh as his eyes open again.

I mimic him leaning against the settee and lean forward so I can reach him. My hand comes up to stroke his face, I feel for him even though he's hurt me. "Vlad whatever it is we will deal with it after you have spoken to Lucas," I tell him, trying to reassure him that I will listen to what he has to say before I decide whether we can continue with our relationship.

I'm not ruling it out, I know I want to forgive him, but I need to make sure that his violent rage isn't going to become a regular occurrence.

When my ex cheated on me it never entered my head to give him a second chance, not that he wanted one, but he did want my forgiveness. Then again, I didn't love him like I do this man who is sitting here wanting a second chance.

"I have so much to get off my chest," he says, shaking his head. "Sometimes I feel as if it's going to choke me," he rubs his hands up and down his face then quickly stands looking like he has the world's troubles on his shoulders. "Be back in a minute," he says then strides off towards the bathroom.

I take my cup into the kitchen and rinse it out, yawning as I do. I need to sleep, and Vlad needs to go home. Sitting back on the settee, I get myself comfy again stretching out and resting my head on the cushion. When Vlad returns, he sits opposite me, plumps the cushion and puts his feet up.

"Shouldn't you be going home to get some sleep? You're going to need to be level-headed when you speak to Lucas in the morning," I tell him.

Wide dark eyes glare at me as if I'd just killed a puppy, talk about overreacting.

"What's that look for?" I ask.

"Holly, you're here, Lucas is here, I'm not going anywhere," he says, shaking his head. "Wherever you two are then that's where I am," his voice is low but firm, and I know there's no point in pushing him on it, so I don't.

"Fine, but your sleeping there," I point then I grab the throw over off the back of the settee, cover myself with it and close my eyes. I'm not going to bed, I'm sure he'd follow me and that would lead to something that we both want but can't have until everything is cleared up.

Before I fall asleep, I hear him moving around, opening my eyes I see he has stripped down to his boxers and his laid out on his back with his arm covering his face.

"Goodnight, Vlad," I whisper, turning over to get comfy.

"Goodnight, Holly," I hear him say, his voice but a murmur.

Chapter 4

Holly

Hushed voices wake me from my slumber as I unfold myself, body aching, that's when I remember I slept on the two-seater-settee while leaving Vlad to sleep on the three-seater.

The hushed voices turn into light laughter and I sit up quickly to see the chuckle brothers and Sebastian filling my kitchen area.

"Morning," Daniel says and gives me a little wave. He's leaning against the sink unit facing towards me while Sebastian and Nicholas are sat on the breakfast stools with their backs to me. Simultaneously they turn, giving me one of their wide smiles. Nicholas is off his stool in an instant and sat by my side before I have time to check if I'm decent.

"Good morning," he greets then kisses my cheek. "Come join us for breakfast Holly before Daniel devours the lot." He throws his eyes towards his brother who is presently tucking into a full English. I let out a chuckle at the three men who have set up home in my kitchen and have me wondering how long they have been here.

"Morning. It's good to see you, Holly," Sebastian says, hugging me. He gives up his seat and puts a plate in front of me.

"Morning. What time did you three get here?" I ask, inspecting my kitchen that was nice and tidy when I fell asleep but looks like the bloody Greasy Spoon builder's cafe now.

I wave my hand around my work tops that they have cluttered, lifting my eyebrows to them.

"Sorry for the mess," Sebastian says. "We let Daniel cook, he's not the tidiest of people as you know." Yes, I do know. I've seen the mess he makes in their kitchen when he cooks but one thing about these men, they always tidy up afterwards.

"It's fine," I say, adjusting my dressing gown that has tangled up around me. Can't believe I slept in the bloody thing last night.

Daniel gives me a sheepish look, shrugging his shoulders as he stands there propped against the sink unit with a plate in one hand and the other shovelling a forkful of bacon and eggs.

"The big man text us to bring breakfast, we got here about an hour ago. We didn't want to wake you," Daniel tells me when he's swallowed the forkful of food.

"We are so glad your back, Holly," Nicholas says, squeezing my shoulder. "He's been a sodding nightmare without you," he flicks his head towards the door that leads to the bedrooms, I'm assuming that is where Vlad is. Daniel puts down his plate and attends to the bacon that's sizzling away in the frying pan, he goes to place a few slices on my plate which I cover with my hand. I'm not hungry, nervous yes. Not knowing what is being said between Vlad and Lucas has my stomach flipping.

"How was your dad this morning?" my eyes search Sebastian because I know he will be feeling all kinds of hurt for the way his father reacted that night in the club. For his father's heavy drinking and cruel words towards Lucas. Then for his own actions towards his father. He's so much like Vlad, very protective of them all so I can only imagine the last couple of weeks have been hard on him.

"His black eye has come on a treat through the night," Daniel sniggers, still cooking away.

"Daniel," his big brother says in a chastising tone.

"What? Oh, come on he deserved it. You know it," he points at Sebastian. "We know it and he does too," he plates up two breakfast which I'm assuming are for Vlad and Lucas.

Sebastian nods at his brother. "You're right but it doesn't stop me from feeling guilty though does it?"

"I wouldn't worry too much," Nicholas intervenes. "He seemed happy enough this morning. Just thank yourself lucky that he's a good dad because if he had hit you back," he stops and gives a low whistle. "He'd have knocked you into next week."

"Yeah," Sebastian grins, rubbing his face.

"Have you spoken to him?" I ask Sebastian. He nods at me and takes a drink of his coffee as Daniel heads towards the bedroom.

"He apologized for his actions and said he would sort out the mess he has made with Lucas and you."

"I'm sure he'll do his best," I tell him, and I know he will, he loves his sons and he loves me. In Vlad's world that counts for everything, I just hope when it comes to it that he can convince me that it will never happen again.

We stop talking when the door that leads to the bedrooms open and we hear Lucas and Daniel laughing as they come through. "You are disgusting," Lucas says to his brother, screwing up his face and shaking his head as he digs him in his arm. He looks a lot happier than he did last night, whatever Vlad has said to him it seems to have brought the smile back to his eyes.

Daniel returns to where he was stood, propping up the kitchen sink and Lucas comes and stands between me and Sebastian.

"You ok?" Sebastian asks as he ruffles his sleepy hair.

"Yes," he nods, giving his brother an impish grin as he looks up at him. "I can't believe you smacked dad in the eye," he chuckles.

"Fuck sake, I'm never going to live this down," he grumbles, running his hand through his hair.

"Where is the twat anyway?" he laughs, looking behind him towards the door that they had come through. I let out a chuckle too because it's hard to believe that Lucas was so upset last night, he looked lost and afraid when I got home. Now it's like nothing happened. Having his father back to something resembling normal and his brothers here has perked him up.

"He's in your bedroom, Holly," Daniel answers Sebastian

question. "He said he was having a shower and if you were awake to ask if he could have a private word with you," he tilts his head raising one of his eyebrows at me, "Apparently, we're a pair of nosey bastards," he points between himself and Nicholas who is being quiet for once, fiddling with his phone.

"Yeah, he knows us well," he says without lifting his head.

"Are you alright?" I ask him, giving him a tap on his arm to get his attention. Nicholas is not a quiet man and would jump at the chance to pick fun at his dad and his brothers.

"I am now," he smiles while slipping his phone back in his pocket. Whatever had his attention is now gone.

"Please go speak with the ogre, Holly," he points over my shoulder, giving me his best pouty look. "I can't cope with his crankiness any longer. He needs you to take him in hand, just go kiss and make up, so we can all have some peace," he states with his usual cheeky grin. The rest of them chuckle at Nicholas.

"It's not funny and it's not that simple," I say, speaking to all four of them. "You all seem to forget that three men got hurt that night, granted they were being annoying, but it could have easily been your father who was hurt." A chuckle slips from Nicholas and all eyes look at me as if I've grown an extra head. I know what they find funny. It would take more than three average men to bring him down. "What?" I question, not happy that they are amused at what's happened over the last week or two.

"Holly," Nicholas says, turning his whole body, so he is facing me. "We're not laughing at the situation," he stops and thinks for a moment, "We're happy because it's been a hell of a few weeks, we've never had to deal with our father being out of control but he's on the mend. Lucas is safe and well and you're home, everyone is happy."

"But me and your father are not back together. I let him stay overnight so he could speak to Lucas first thing this morning," who am I kidding, I might have been angry with him, but I was just as pleased to see him.

"Yes, we know, but he will put things right, Holly. Before you went away, you said when you came home you would hear him out. Please give him a chance to try," he pleads.

There's nothing I want more than to be back in his arms, in his home as part of the family. I've missed him, and I've missed his sons, they all mean so much to me.

Standing from my stool, I place my hand on Nicholas' arm. "We'll sort it," I tell him, it might take time for him to let me in fully, but I'll be waiting for him whenever he is ready. With that in mind I turn and make my way to my bedroom to find the man who drives me bloody crazy.

My bedroom is empty when I enter, but I can hear Vlad showering in the very small cubicle. Sitting down on my bed, I smile at the struggle he must be having in there. There's not enough room to swing a mouse round in there never mind a cat and with Vlad's large build I'm surprised we don't have to phone the fire brigade to prise him out. He's used the shower in there before but always moaned about knocking himself on the door.

I lay back on my bed, resting my head on the soft pillows. I'm not there long when the bathroom door opens, and I feel my bed dip. Sitting up so I'm leant on my elbows, my breath is stolen from me and my stomach summersaults when I take in the man before me. His freshly showered scent along with his bare chest and huge strong shoulders call to me. I want to hold him. His muscles flex when he shifts further up the bed, placing his hand on my knee. The heat from him causes electricity to travel straight to my core and I swallow hard trying to calm my racing heart. The delight in his eyes twinkle and his lip lifts at one side giving me that flirty smirk, he knows I'm affected.

"Like what you see angel?" his husky voice strokes over my skin as he moves further up the bed. Of course, I like what I see, he's sat there in a pair of boxers with his muscular body on show, even with his bruised eye and ribs he's a sight to behold.

"Hmmm," is all I manage to let out, knowing fine well that I need to shake off this spell he has me under. If I take him back now, I will never get to the bottom of why he went into such a violent rage, beating the shit out of three men, verbally abused me and then went on to upset his son which caused him to run away.

"Don't worry sweetheart, I'm not about to try and take advantage of you," he says as he lifts his hand from my leg, getting up to pick up his jeans from my bedroom chair. I watch his fine physique as he dresses wishing he would but knowing he won't. As much as we both want each other, we need to sit down and talk. I made that clear last night and by the looks of things he is respecting my wishes and so should I. I need to be strong.

"Lucas seams a lot happier this morning," I say, trying to take my mind off the urge to drag him onto the bed and give him no choice but to wrap himself around me, I'm also hoping he will divulge a little bit of information into what he said to him. He won't lie to his son, so he must have told him something about his mother.

"Yeah, that was Daniel's doing. He's still mad at me for keeping him in the dark about his mother but he knows I did it to protect him," he slips his T-shirt on, wincing when he stretches. He takes a deep breath to combat the pain. I cringe myself, thinking about him being in pain.

"Do you need some painkillers or a heat pad?" I ask him, getting off the bed, so I can get him something from the bathroom. I don't wait for his response as I make my way past him to get some tablets from the cabinet.

"Thanks," he says when I pass them to him. He takes the two tablets and swallows them without water as I turn from him, he quickly grabs my hand and pulls me into him. His head rest on mine as his eyes search mine for forgiveness. "I will fix this," his voice is low and determined.

"I hope so," I tell him as his hands that are placed on my waist, warm my insides. Having Vlad hold me and look at me like I'm his world gives me hope that he will do just that.

Once we're back in the kitchen, Vlad grabs a cup of tea and quickly eats the breakfast that Daniel has kept warm for him. Sebastian and Vlad seem to be getting along fine, any upset between them forgotten. Nicholas and Daniel are being their normal loud selves while Lucas closely watches his father.

I'm distracted from them when I notice I have had three missed calls from Olivia while I was in the bedroom. I know I'm going to get the wrath of her tongue for not calling her when I got back last night but, in my defence, I did have other important matters to deal with. I decide I will call her once I have got rid of the men that have taken over my home.

"Holly?" Lucas says, getting my attention. He's now stood at the side of his dad, leaning on him.

"Yes?" I answer him as I move through my living room into the tight space of the kitchen. God knows how they have all squeezed into here, I know they like hanging about in the kitchen at home but mine is a fraction of the size of theirs.

"Would it be ok if I stay with you today?" Lucas asks, his face heating up a little. The boy has no need to be shy around me and he knows that. I don't mind if he stays, he's not going to school today but it's up to Vlad to make that decision.

"Hmmm," I glance at Vlad who seems lost in his own thoughts. "It's fine with me if it's ok with your father." Vlad lifts his eyes to mine and nods his head letting me know it's ok with him, he must have heard what Lucas was saying even in his trance-like state.

"Ok then," Sebastian says as he moves towards the sink. "Let's get Holly's kitchen cleaned up then we can go get some work done," he orders. I'm just about to tell them to leave it when he directs his orders at me to go sit down then his brothers jump to attention and do as they have been told.

Vlad joins me in the living room, opting to leave it to his brood to clean up.

"Thank you, Holly," he says.

"No thanks needed, I don't mind," he nods his head at me, picking up his phone and car keys off the table.

"I need to go into work and will be there most of the day, I have a lot to do." I nod at him this time, remembering I need to get in touch with Izzy. I left her in the lurch when I took off to the coast, but it couldn't be helped, I'm sure she'll understand. I hope she has been able to organise the bands she wanted while I was away. I know I could ask Sebastian, but I decide to call her later to see if she still needs my help.

"I'll pick Lucas up when I have finished work," I hear Vlad say as my mobile rings. By the time I get to it, it rings off then starts to ring again. It's Olivia and I know if I don't answer it, she'll be over here kicking my door down, in fact I'm surprised she hasn't been over already.

"Olivia…"

"Don't you Olivia me," she screeches, making me hold the phone away from my ear so I don't end up tone death. This amuses Vlad as he throws his eyes up and that cheeky smirk appears on his face, obviously he's heard her screech. He saunters back to his sons while I prepare to get a right royal roasting.

"Why the hell didn't you phone last night when you got home? You could have sent a text and why is your apartment full of the Petrov men?" she sounds exasperated but what I want to know is how she knows they are here.

"How do you know who I have in my home?" I ask.

"Never mind. I have my sources," she says and it's then I realise that Nicholas must have been texting Lucy, Olivia's daughter. They've become good friends over the last month, not sure if there's anything going on with them. I will have to keep an eye on them.

I chuckle down the phone because I can't keep anything from this nosey mare. "What's going on Holly?" her tone not as irate.

"It's a long story."

"Well get your arse over here and I'll put the kettle on, or shall I come to you?" she asks.

"I'll come to you. Give me an hour, oh, I'll have Lucas with me," I forgot Lucas was staying with me. It won't matter to Olivia; she'll probably make him something to eat and let him play on the PS4.

"Not a problem, he can help Jack and Jackson, they're clearing out the garage."

"Ok, give me an hour."

"Ok, see you then."

"Bye."

I put my phone on the table and join Vlad and his sons in the kitchen who are all ready to leave.

Nicholas and Daniel slap Lucas on his back and ruffle his hair then give me a hug before they leave. Vlad watches his two sons closely, noticing that whatever it is that we are going through it doesn't stop the friendship that his sons and I have. Sebastian is the next one to take off, picking up his car keys from the breakfast bar he gives Lucas a hug and kisses my cheek. This leaves an awkward silence between Vlad, Lucas and me which seems so strange as we would normally spend a lot of time together and always have lots to do and say.

"I better go," Vlad says, breaking the silence. He doesn't hesitate when he takes hold of Lucas, giving him a fatherly hug and kissing the top of his head. "I'll pick you up when I finish work," he tells him as he lets him go then passes by me. He doesn't go to hug me or kiss me he just tells me he will phone me later and strolls past me. The lump in my throat threatens to choke me as I hear him breathe in deeply through his nose and feel his fingertips touch mine ever so lightly then I watch his back as he walks out of the door. I bite my lip to stop from bursting into tears in front of Lucas and I'm thankful that a text message comes through on my phone. Quickly, I turn towards the living room to retrieve my mobile phone and hide the sadness that's edged on my face. Looking at the text I see it's from Vlad. *I love you,* it says, and those three little words alone cause a tear to roll down my cheek. It must have been as hard for him as it was me when he left not to give each other a good-bye kiss and cuddle. My fingers type three little words back, *Love you too*. As I wipe the tear away, I know I'm going to struggle without having his strong loving arms to hold me and his soft lips on my skin. I also know that having his sons at my home, spending time with them and working with Izzy our paths will cross often which means it's going to be harder to get over him if we can't get past his anger issues. He told me he would fix it but that means him letting me in to what causes him so much pain. If he can't then we can't be fixed and that's when we will hurt. All my ties with his family would have to be cut as much as I love them all because hearing or seeing him with another woman would be unbearable. I wouldn't cope.

Chapter 5

Vlad

"Where the hell did you get this chair from?" I rant at Sebastian as I fidget, trying to get comfy. I've been sat in front of my desk for the last two hours trying to catch up with paperwork and calls that I'd neglected over the last two weeks. My sons have done what they could but there's some things that can only be dealt with by me. Sebastian rearranged any meetings I had, hoping I would be back to my normal self after a few days. Well that didn't happen, did it? So, this week I have more meetings than I care to and a mountain of paperwork to catch up on. Anything to do with the restaurant is left to me and the new buildings that I am buying. I need to meet with Zach, my solicitor, and Alex, who I'm buying the buildings from, originally it was just the one building then he decided he would sell me another old building on the edge of the city centre. I'm waiting for planning permission to come through, so I need to give the council a kick up the arse or the building contractors won't be able to start the extensive work that needs doing on them. There's also picking out bathrooms, kitchens, tiles, fittings and colours which I'd hoped my Holly would have helped with. An ache grips my chest when I think of how much I've hurt her.

My hand rubs at it to try and sooth it but it doesn't work, there's only one thing that will. Holly; having her back in my arms, my home and my bed which isn't going to happen without me baring my soul to her. Hell, how am I going to do that without hurting her even more? This is one fucked up situation, the only reason she's spoken to me is because of Lucas. It nearly killed me last night, sleeping in the same room as her and not holding her in my arms. I hadn't seen or spoken to her in almost two weeks and it drove me crazy to sleep on the sofa opposite her and then to leave this morning without even so much as a goodbye kiss.

This morning was one of the hardest things I have ever had to do, telling my youngest son about his mother. Having him cry in my arms as I tried to explain to him that I'd kept these things from him because he was too young to understand didn't lessen his upset. Once he had calmed down, he never mentioned his mother again, he was more focused on whether Holly and I would be getting back together which had me thinking that it was our breakup that had upset him more. Not ever knowing his mother meant there was no bond there but having Holly around for the last couple of months he had grown attached to her. So, with our fall out and her not being around, me in my drunken pitiful state then lashing out at him in anger, could be the real reason he ran. Understandably, he felt something when he heard his mother was a drug-taking whore, but he was hurting more due to the two adults he cared so much about, letting him down. And I have to say both of us because as much as I was a bastard and wasn't there for him, Holly had taken off, not giving him a second thought.

"Ungrateful bastard," Sebastian curses, bringing me back to this fucking uncomfortable chair.

"Huh," I grunt out, not knowing what is wrong with him. He leans back in his chair which I'm sure is more relaxing than mine and shakes his head at me.

"I could have left you with the one that was in pieces," he grumbles. He's right. I should be grateful that he fixed up my office that I had ransacked when I went berserk. Throwing the chair at the CCTV screens, swiping everything off my desk including the photo of Holly and me then storming out when I couldn't find another drink wasn't something I am proud of.

I should be grateful that he cares enough to help clear up my mess. When we came to England, I made him promise that if I ever fucked up, he needed to do whatever he could to make sure I knew that I had. Him hitting out at me last night was him telling me that I had fucked up, big time.

"Thank you," I tell him, getting out of my chair to stretch my legs. "I am grateful for what you've done," I wave my hand around the office that he has had put back together, wincing as I do because my ribs have decided to start hurting again, the painkillers must be wearing off. God I'm getting soft in my old age, I've had stab wounds that hurt less.

"You okay?" he asks concerned.

"Yeah, just a bit sore."

"Sorry," he says getting up and standing in front of me. I shake my head at him, putting my hand on his shoulder. He has no reason to apologise, it's me who should be saying sorry to him for having to deal with everything while I was incapacitated.

"You have no need to be sorry, Sebastian. It is me who should be saying sorry and thanking you for everything you have done," I pull him in for a hug then kiss the top of his head. He might be married with children of his own but he's still my baby. I wince again as I'm moving my arm, causing Sebastian to raise one eyebrow at me.

"Do you think you have a broken rib?" he worries, chewing on his bottom lip. I chuckle and answer him.

"No son," I tell him patting him on the shoulder. "You hit like a girl," I scoot past him sitting down in his chair, getting myself comfy and hoping he takes it as a joke. Because I don't want another punch off him, truthfully it hurt like hell.

"I'm sure I do," he sniggers. "That's why I knocked you off balance, you're lucky I didn't really want to hurt you," the smile on his face tells me that all is well with me and my first born which is good because I just need to make sure that Lucas is ok then I can focus on Holly.

Sebastian grabs my chair and pulls it over to his desk, sitting opposite me. "How's things with you and Holly?" he asks, putting his feet up on the desk.

I shrug my shoulders. "Not sure. She wants answers to questions that I'm not sure I can't give her without hurting her more. She also wants to make sure Lucas is ok before she will even entertain my apology."

"Lucas will be fine. Why do you think he ended up at Holly's?" he questions, fidgeting in the chair he bought for me. I chuckle when he frowns, switching from one side to the other, trying to get comfortable. "You're not bloody wrong about this thing," he grumbles.

"I know why he went to Holly's, Sebastian. I'm not stupid or blind."

"Then you will know that it's not what you ranted at him about his mother that had him running to Holly's but that he had missed what the three of you had. He's only ever had two women around him, Mrs White, who fuses over all of us and treats us all equal. And Izzy who is more like a big sister to him." I nod at him, knowing what he is about to say. "Holly dotes on him like her own. She's spent time to get to know him and what he likes, and she hasn't just done it to get in your good books. She genuinely cares for him and I think he looks upon her as the mother he never had," he gets up out of his chair to grab a coffee, fetching me one. He also grabs a cushion off the settee, putting it on the bony chair before he sits down.

"Fixing your relationship with Holly will make him happy and I think answering any questions he has truthfully will put you back in his good books."

"To fix my relationship with Holly, I am going to have to tell her about your mother and in doing that I will have no choice but to tell her about your grandfather which...." He stops me by putting his hand up.

"Don't," he says, eyeing me cautiously. He knows the mention of them can send me into a rage, especially mentioning my father.

"Don't do it to yourself dad. They are dead and cannot hurt you or any of us anymore."

"But they can, don't you see? It's because of them that Holly and Lucas are hurting, and God knows what I put you Nicholas and Daniel through when I kicked off. I am sorry, God I haven't seen Izzy, Joseph and Rebecca in two weeks," I place my head in my hands, not sure how I am going to rebuild my relationship with Lucas and Holly. If I give Holly the answers she wants, which means revealing my past, she will hate me and that will be the end of us which will hurt Lucas even more. I'm fucked if I do and fucked if I don't.

"Paps," Sebastian brings me out of my wallowing. Narrowed dark blue eyes study me, he knows I'm in a state of unrest. My fucking headaches along with my ribs and my heart because of it all.

"You don't give Holly enough credit," he says. Not sure what he's on about, I ask him confused.

"What do you mean?"

"Well, Holly's mother was a drug addict who had wild parties and slept around a lot," I listen, not sure where he got that information from because I don't think Holly told him and I know I haven't. I don't have to wait long before he tells me his source. "She told Izzy. She was so overwhelmed the way you had cared for her when she broke down, I think she just wanted to sing your praises."

I smile remembering, although it was an emotional evening, it was the night we both admitted to one another that we loved each other. We also got pleasantly pissed and were at it like rabbits in this very office.

"What's that smile for?"

"Nothing, I just remember the evening well."

"Well, keep the details to yourself," he shivers.

"Go on. Finish telling me why I don't give Holly enough credit."

"Oh yeah. She understands a hell of a lot more than you think. She's not some young woman who hasn't seen life. I mean I know she was brought up in a family that went to church religiously, but that there shows you she was brought up to forgive. Do you see where I'm going with this?" he points at me, shifting his chair closer to the desk. I think I know what he's trying to tell me, however, I let him continue.

"Holly loves fiercely, anyone can see that in her. Fortunately, for you and us she has fallen in love with you and all your children. We also love her by the way," he gets me a little choked up with his declaration because he, Nicholas and Daniel, although they knew their mother they knew she had no love in her cold heart for them yet this woman they only met two months ago has shown more love in that short time than their real mother ever did.

"Go on," I tell him coughing to cover the lump in my throat.

"If you asked Holly what she would do to keep her children safe? I'm sure she would say the same thing as any parent would which would be anything. She might not have children of her own, but she loves Olivia's children, so ask her what she would do to keep them safe. Then ask her to multiply that love she holds for them and give her the same question again. What would you do to keep your children safe?" He sits back in his seat regarding me. I know what he means because I have, and I will do anything to keep my family safe, he knows that.

"That's all you did dad, you protected your sons," he gets up, picking up his phone and puts it in his pocket. "I need to go, I'm meeting Izzy," he says. But before he walks out of the door he turns. "Think about it. Give Lucas some time with Holly, spend time together, so he knows you're trying then when you think the time is right tell her everything. I'm sure," he chuckles. "It won't be pretty, and she may need time to come to terms with it. She may even look at you different for a while but if she has a heart she will understand." With that he leaves me sat there hoping he is right but not knowing how I would tell the woman I love that I have killed multiple times.

Chapter 6
Vlad

Laughter echoes around my home, breaking through the walls and seeping into my office where I am hiding. It's been two weeks since Lucas ran off to Holly's, needing the love of the woman he looks upon like a mother. He went back to school the following day and Holly went to meet Izzy at the club. While she was at the coast, Daniel took it upon himself to help Izzy out, so now the three of them are working together to change Aphrodite into a club with live bands and themed nights.

Sebastian told me he has put Holly on the books so that she will get paid each month even though she had said she didn't want to get paid and threatened to shave off his eyebrows if any money went into her account. He did it anyway.

Lucas stayed a couple of nights at Holly's and I invited myself to stay with him. Holly shook her head at me but offered me the settee to sleep on. I took up her offer but was not happy about not sharing her bed. After two nights I told Lucas he had to stay at home, I didn't give him a reason, but it was because I couldn't cope with being around Holly and not been able to hold her and sleep in the same bed. We saw each other every day, at my home, her home and the club where we spoke about work and Lucas, but not once did we talk about us. Sebastian keeps badgering me to tell Holly about my past but I'm afraid to, frightened I will lose her forever.

Over the last couple of days, the weather has been hot which had given my boys an excuse to barbecue. Of course, Holly was invited along with her friends and their children. Any other time I would have enjoyed having them all over, but with the way things are I couldn't get into the same summer spirit as the rest of them. This had me faking a problem at the restaurant two nights ago and staying late last night at the office just so I wasn't put through the torment of seeing Holly parade around my house in a pair of shorts and a bikini top. I couldn't get away with it a third night, Sebastian was on to me. An hour ago, I had tortured myself enough, telling everyone I had a phone call to make, I went to my office. I didn't need to call anyone but if I hadn't have gone when I did, I would have thrown Holly over my shoulder and took her to my room, I would have also spanked that fucking arse of hers for tormenting me the last few days.

Tap, tap, tap on the door brings me out of my thoughts that and the sound of giggling. I watch the door handle turn slowly then it flies open. Two little tornadoes terrorize my tranquil moment.

"Grandpa," Rebecca squeals as she skips towards me dragging her friend Megan along with her.

"Hi pip squeak," I greet, laughing as she tries scrambling up my legs, wanting to get settled on my knee. I help her along as Megan stands at the side of my chair, twiddling her fingers with a shy smile on her face as she watches her little sidekick jab me in the cheek with her chubby little finger and knee me in my bruised ribs. It might have been a couple of weeks since Sebastian took it upon himself to put me in my place, but the bloody things are still sore.

"Ow," I grimace playfully, rubbing the pain away which causes my little bully to giggle. She pats my other knee enticing her friend to climb up, once I put my other arm out for her, she pulls that little mischievous face and launches herself at me. When they both settled Rebecca grabs my face. "Dad said you have to get your..." she points to my bottom, "outside, or he will come and drag you out," she pulls at my shirt, imitating her father.

"You two were supposed to wait for me," lifting my head I watch as Holly sashays into my office and sits opposite me, shaking her head at the two little terrors that are now trying to scramble off my knee, eager to get to Holly. Our eyes connect causing the usual surge of heat to travel through me and my need for her grows stronger. So much for trying to hide away.

"You needed to pee, and we didn't want to wait," Megan tells Holly as she pulls her in and gives her a hug. Rebecca follows with the hugging of Holly and I sit there wishing it was me wrapped around her.

Holly's eyes look to me while the tornado two pull at her to go and play. My granddaughter adores her and, unlike Megan, who waited for me to give her the ok to climb onto my knee, Rebecca doesn't wait for a sign from Holly she just launches her attack, squeezing my angel tightly as she does.

Holly's been running around with these two for the last couple of hours, she must be knackered, but she won't say no to them, so I do it for her.

"Let Holly have a rest and go tell your daddy I will be out soon," I tell Rebecca who looks at Megan, hoping she will go with her. One thing about my granddaughter is she always does as she is told unlike her brother when he is with my youngest Lucas.

"Okay," she says and grabs Megan's hand as they both skip out of my office shutting the door behind them.

"Cute little buggers," Holly says as she stands and strolls to my side of the desk, perching her denim cladded bottom on top of it. Her beautiful bare legs stretch out while both her hands are placed on the desk at the back of her. She gives me a tipsy smile, I know she's had a couple of glasses of wine, I could see the little wobble in her walk when she rounded my desk.

"Hmmm," she muses as she chews on her top lip. "I've missed that," she says as she slides a little bit further across the desk, so she is practically between my legs. I make room by moving my feet, wondering what it is she has missed.

"What have you missed Holly?" I ask, tilting my head at her as I try not to touch the soft smooth skin that is taunting me. She licks her lips as her gaze falls to my knees.

"Sitting on your knee," she utters as her eyes sparkle like raindrops in the sun. I don't need any more confirmation that she is here because she is feeling the same as me. Lost and lonely. Craving what we had and needing to have that feeling we get when we are together.

Tapping my knee, she slides off the desk and sits in my lap, wrapping one arm around my neck. The other one goes straight for my chest as her head lays on my shoulder and my fingers immediately claim her skin.

They trail along the outside of her thigh and I hear her breath catch. I stroke up and down then travel further up until I reach her waist where my thumb makes tiny circles under the shirt she has open but tide in a knot at the front. Her head lifts and her eyes land on my lips, her fingers come up from my chest as her face comes closer to mine. I can't help but swallow and shift in my seat as I try to gage what she is going to do next.

"I've missed these too," her finger runs along my bottom lip then on to my chin before she's back again running her finger across my bottom lip, her eyes never leaving mine. Shifting her, so she is straddling me I place my forehead on hers, cupping her face in my hands.

"Where is this going Holly?" I ask, knowing I need her permission before I take this where I want it to go. It might be the last time we're together.

When I came into the office earlier, I booked a couple of nights stay in the hotel just half hours' drive from here, hoping Holly will meet me for dinner in their restaurant. Afterwards, and with a bit of luck, she will accompany me back to the room I have booked where we can talk without being disturbed either by one of my sons or by her friends.

"Wherever we want it to go," she breathes, answering my question as her hands trail up my shirt. And that is about as much as I can take. My lips smash into hers and without any hesitation from Holly she sucks in my tongue. Electricity surges through me, igniting every nerve ending while blood pumps fast around my body and travels straight to my groin. She grinds herself on the stiffness that lies between us, giving out a little moan as she tries to feed the want in her.

Breaking our kiss, I search her sapphire eyes for any reluctance to whether she regrets starting this. There's none. All I see is desire and want.

I'm up out of my seat carrying Holly with me. I swipe my phone off the desk as we make our way out of my office and through the kitchen area towards the staircase. I can hear the laughter and music from outside, but no one sees us. In seconds we're up the stairs and flying through my bedroom door. I slam it shut behind us and take Holly's mouth again. I know she wants this, and I have no qualms in giving us both this one night, to remember how good we are together.

Our hands roam, caressing and craving what we've missed for the last four weeks. Untying the knot of her shirt, I slowly push it off her shoulders, baring her smooth, soft skin. My mouth unlocks from hers as I trail kisses down her neck and along her collarbone. The swell of her firm breasts calls to me. My mouth travels to them as my hands make short work of unleashing them from the restriction of her bikini top.

Holly moans as I lap around her erect nipples, giving both the attention they deserve. One hand pulls at my hair while the other one unfastens my trousers, dipping into my boxers and taking hold of my hard length. I growl as I try to contain myself. Four weeks without her and I'm ready to go off like a rocket. Moving her hand, I pick her up and throw her on the bed, ripping my shirt off while she lets out a little squeal.

I know that no one can hear us, we could make as much noise as we like, and our friends and family won't hear a sound. My bedroom faces out onto the east side while my garden and patio face out west. Taking my phone from my pocket I send Sebastian a Do Not Disturb message then lock my door.

My trousers hit the floor as I take in the beauty of this woman before me. Climbing on the bed like a lion stalking its prey, Holly leans back on her elbows watching me. I send her a flirty wink and that addictive smile of hers, the one I haven't seen for so long, appears.

I kiss and nibble her ankle then continue up her long, tanned leg until I reach her inner thigh while she unfastens the button of her shorts and pulls down the zip. My fingers reach for them, peeling off the white denim that covers her. Tossing them on the floor then I rip off her lacy white knickers. Once I've placed a kiss on the apex of her heat, I carry on tasting her skin until I land on her lips. Her legs wrap around me and my hard dick rests at her entrance. I can feel she is ready for me and just to let me know she lifts her hips to spur me on.

Entering her, I'm home and so is she. We moan and groan as I move in and out slowly while our lips stay fused together. I savour every moment, knowing this could be the last time we make love. Over the next half hour, I keep us on the brink of ecstasy, appreciating Holly's soft moans, her teeth scraping at my skin and the passion of her kisses as they penetrate through me.

Feeling her tighten around me causes me to pick up my pace and as my heart races, my balls tighten then I erupt when I feel Holly's orgasm grip her.

I growl, and she calls my name as she squeezes every drop out of me leaving us both a mess of hot sweaty limbs, panting and fused together. We lay there while we claim our breath back, my face snuggled into her neck and her stroking her fingers in my hair.

"I've missed you so much angel," I murmur into her ear, knowing that this could be the last time we're together but hoping that she will understand why I did what I did. If there's any justice in this world then I have paid for what I did and should be able to live the rest of my life happy with this woman in my arms.

"I know, me too," she sighs, kissing my shoulder. "I love you, Vlad," she says, giving me hope that I might be able to get her to stay the night. Rolling off Holly and on to my side, my words fall freely.

"I love you too," my thumb strokes her cheek bone as I place a soft kiss on her lips.

"We should get cleaned up and back outside," she mumbles against my lips then as quick as I got her into my bed she's out, hurrying into the bathroom, leaving me to wonder does she regret what just happened between us.

I'm not left long to wonder when she steps back into the bedroom wearing a pair of clean knickers. She still has most of her wardrobe here and I'm praying that's where they will stay. She dresses quickly, and I watch spellbound by her beauty. Sitting on the side of the bed, she leans in and kisses me, gripping my face in her hands. Slowly lifting so I'm sat against the headboard, I place my hands on her hips, "Stay tonight," I speak into her lips, hoping she will but understanding if she doesn't want to.

I know she's missing what we had and that she is still in love with me. I know she came to my office to show me exactly that, but that doesn't mean I'm off the hook, she still wants an explanation. Pulling out of my hold she stands and takes a step back from me. Nervously, she bites her lip as her blue eyes gaze into mine. Her head nods slowly then she turns towards the bedroom door, when she opens it, she spins round. "I'll see you downstairs," she smiles, leaving me to get dressed and hopeful that I will be waking with my angel in my arms in the morning.

"That was one long fucking phone call old man!" Nicholas hollers as he shoves a plate into my hands. He's been the cook tonight and while everyone looks like they have already eaten he's kept the grill lit waiting for me.

"Thanks," I tell him as he piles my plate with peppered steak, a six-ounce burger and fried onions, he spoons potato salad and pops some cherry tomatoes onto my plate. I ignore his raised eyebrow and the smirk he has on his face and take a seat to tuck into my food, I've built up quite an appetite while Holly and I were getting reacquainted.

Holly's sat with Izzy and Daniel as they explain to Olivia, Lucy and Jack what bands and themed nights they have coming up. Jack tells them that the work he is doing at Aphrodite should be completed within a week.

From what Sebastian has told me there's not a great deal of work to be done. A few poles taken out, the stage lengthened and some lighting changes. Two of the poles that have been dismantled will be erected at either end of the new stage. Some new furniture will be brought in to accommodate the raised seating area at the far sides of the stage.

"I'm tired," Megan rubs at her eyes as she lays her head on Jack's shoulder then closes her eyes. Jack looks down at his granddaughter who's snuggled into him, "That's our cue to get going ladies," he says to Olivia and Lucy.

"Yeah, let's get her home to bed," Olivia strokes Megan's hair then gently places a kiss on her head. "You stay Lucy, we'll sort her out."

"No, it's ok, I'll come too."

Nicholas frowns and rubs his hand over his stubbled chin. Lucy passes by and mumbles something I can't quite hear but whatever it was it has him grinning now.

"I think we need to get the kids home to bed too, Sebastian," Izzy tells him. He helps her up out of her seat then gathers his son and daughter, telling them to say their goodbyes.

Jack comes and stands by my side, "How's it going?" he asks as he puts his chin out towards Holly. We both watch her as she gives the children a hug and then Olivia pulls her in, both whispering in each other's ear. Three days after I had kicked off at the club Jack came to see me, I wasn't in a good place and we nearly came to blows. Nick stepped in telling Jack if it had been Olivia who was being harassed by some idiots then he would have done the same thing. Obviously, they weren't given the full story from Holly, how I didn't just beat the shit out of the three men but was vile to Holly as well. Thinking about it makes me feel sick to my stomach.

She deserves better than me but I'm a selfish bastard where she is concerned, I couldn't stand not having her in my life. Maybe after tomorrow I won't have a choice.

"We're getting there, slowly," I lie, knowing what just happened between us might not ever happen again. My chest tightens at the thought.

"Good," he says, slapping me on the back. "Our families get along well, it would be a fucking shame if this had to stop," we both watch our grandchildren, children, his wife and Holly laughing at Daniel as he torments the very sleepy Rebecca and Megan. "Do I need to be concerned about them?" I follow his wide eyes that are glaring at his daughter Lucy and my son Nicholas. They're stood within inches of each other, having a very quiet conversation, both with want in their eyes. What gets my attention more is Nicholas' hand that is placed on Lucy's hip with his thumb stroking lightly up and down.

That's all I need, them getting together and him doing his usual love them and leave them trick. I'll have to have words with him, Lucy is a beautiful young woman with a heart of gold. She's also the mother of my granddaughter's best friend and she's Holly's goddaughter. Fucking hell, it will be a tossup who will skin him alive first; Jack, me or Holly.

"I think they're just mates," I try to play it down as I watch my son whisper into Lucy's ear and she playfully slaps his arm then walks away giggling.

"Hmmm," Jack muses, leaving me stood there while he goes to rescue his wife from Holly. He kisses Holly on the cheek and says his goodbyes to everyone else as he leads his family out of my home and leaving me feeling like the biggest twat that ever lived.

An hour later, the grill is put away and the patio cleaned up. Lucas has disappeared to his room for a shower and to pack his school bag. Nicholas and Daniel took off to meet a few friends for a couple of drinks which has left Holly sat in the kitchen, scrolling through her phone and me unsure whether to ask her tonight if she will meet me at the hotel restaurant tomorrow evening or to ask her in the morning.

Chapter 7

Holly

Seducing Vlad and staying in his bed last night was never my intention. I only planned on reminding him that I was still here. In the last two weeks, once Lucas had settled down, our interaction had become less and less, and I knew without a doubt that he had stayed away from the barbecues intentionally. He wanted me to give him a chance to explain himself and once I knew Lucas was okay, I was ready to hear him out, but he seemed to be staying out of my way.

When I entered his office dressed in white shorts, bikini top and an open shirt tied at the waist, I knew I would get his attention.

After the girls left the office, I saw my chance to remind him. Flirting with him was as far as I was going to go, but once I sat on his knee and felt his warm body around mine, I was done for. I couldn't resist his lips, tasting them left me wanting more. Vlad didn't complain and was only too eager to have me in his bed. When he asked me to stay the night, I was all in. It didn't feel awkward or wrong when we undressed and slipped into bed once everyone had left. In fact, snuggling up together had us both drifting into a peaceful night's sleep.

This morning when I woke, he was already up and dressed for work. Sat on the edge of the bed he asked me to join him at The Lion's Heart Hotel tonight. He had booked a table at one of the restaurants there in the hoping we could talk afterwards. I knew the hotel well. I had attended a wedding there a good few years ago and spent the whole weekend being pampered and wondering the extensive gardens that look out over the Yorkshire Countryside.

The hotel was an old thirteenth century castle that was renovated and turned into a five-star hotel; it houses many restaurants and each room has a four-poster bed. The entrance to the restaurant we will be dining in nestles on the outside of the hotel in one of the old battlements where soldiers from old would shoot their bow and arrows. The stone brick walls have remained and light up in the evening, giving it a warm glow.

The restaurant itself has polished wooden floors with about twenty tables placed in alcoves each table covered in white tablecloths. A small crystal teardrop lamp sits alongside a vase with red tulips and there's a small bar with a lounge area in the far corner. This part of the hotel caters to the public and not just its guests. Knowing this, I declined Vlad's offer to pick me up and told him I would meet him there. Taking the scenic route in the taxi, I wondered whether I should have driven in my own car and brought an overnight bag. It's one of those places that you want to explore what it has to offer. Its various restaurants and cocktail bars, its grounds and health spa. How the building lights up in the evening, is so romantic and the rooms are beautiful.

I arrive twenty minutes early but decide to wait inside for Vlad. I send him a text to let him know then make my way in giving the waiter Vlad's name then take a seat in the lounge, ordering a glass of wine.

Gazing around, I can see it hasn't changed since I was here with a couple of friends from the bar I worked at. Maria the chef was getting married and although Micky's had been closed for over three years, and I was married to Rob, we kept in touch. Rob refused to attend the wedding saying he wouldn't know anyone, so me and a few of the girls made a long weekend of it and booked a room from the Thursday to the Sunday. We took advantage of what the hotel had to offer and frequented the cocktail lounge often. The wedding was fantastic, and the bride and groom looked amazing and were very much in love. I get a sense of melancholy when I think how we all drifted apart after the wedding. We met up a few times for lunch but then lost touch.

"Hey," Vlad's low voice breaks my moment.

"Hi," I say as I look up at a man that could model a suit on the front cover of a magazine. Confidence oozes from him as he stands towering over me in his made-to-measure charcoal-grey pinstripe suit. His muscular thighs fit his trousers like a glove. The crisp white shirt opened at the collar shows just a glimpse of his tattoos and the sprinkling of chest hair. He has one button fastened on his jacket with one hand slipped into his trouser pocket. The smile on his handsome face makes my knees week and I let out a little moan when he bends down to kiss my cheek and his day-old stubble grazes over my skin. He knows I'm smitten.

"Shall I cancel the table and book a room?" he throws me a cheeky wink, chuckling while getting himself comfortable at the side of me.

"You're incorrigible," I say, shaking my head at him.

"Says the one who has just been undressing me with her eyes," he flirts.

"I was not," I lie. "I was just thinking how handsome you look," I wave my hand up and down.

"Yeah. Well we make the perfect couple then because you look stunning." He leans over and places another kiss on my cheek, and I inhale his scent.

"Can I get you a drink before you go to your table?" The waiter interrupts our little flirting game, making me blush, when the cheeky man smirks at me. I'm sure he just witnessed me sniffing at how manly Vlad smells.

"I'll have what the lady is having," Vlad informs the waiter. "Would you like another one?" he asks me.

"No, not yet. I'll wait till we eat," I say picking up my glass of wine that is still half full.

We chat for a few minutes about Vlad's day at work, once the waiter returns with his wine, we make our way to our table. The waiter leaves us while we study the menu. When he comes back, we both decide on the mussels in white wine and garlic for starters and I choose the pan-fried seabass in lemon and garlic with duchess potato and green beans for my main course, Vlad opts for the seabass with capers. He orders a bottle of Pinot Grigio and once the waiter has gone, I stare at my confident man that is looking anything but. One hand is playing with a serviette as the other one runs rings round the rim of his glass. His eyes are focused on the table where he seems to be lost. Lost in his own little world that only he can see into. I lean over, placing my hand on his, stopping him from picking at the serviette. His dark blue eyes meet mine; they hold so much emotion in them that he needs to let out before it eats away at him.

"Are you ok?" I rub at his hand, hoping he knows how much I care for him and whatever he divulges tonight won't ever change that.

"Yes," he answers, picking up his wine and taking a drink, his eyes never leaving mine.

"Vlad, we're here," I wave my hand around, "in this beautiful place. Let's enjoy it together before we get into any intense discussion." He nods his head while his fingers lace with mine and I can see the anguish lift from his face.

"You're right. It is beautiful here," his cheeky smile appears, and I show him one of my own, feeling weak at the knees as usual when his eyes rake over me in that way.

The waiter breaks the spell between us when he arrives with our starter. He gives us a smile as he places the mussels on the table, the poor man has caught us again. First me inhaling Vlad's scent and now us holding hands gazing at each other like two love struck teenagers.

We devour the mussels like it's our last meal, appreciating the flavours.

"Have you been here before?" I ask as I wipe my fingers on the serviette after dipping them in the finger bowl.

"No," he says once he swallows his last mussel. "But this is the hotel I had booked last month for us before our fall out."

My eyes light up, knowing we would have had one of the best weekends ever. I shouldn't be surprised by it though because he is a very passionate man.

"Wow, that is a shame," I laugh. "I might have forgiven you sooner if I'd have known you booked us a weekend here," I joke.

"So, I'm forgiven then?" he asks surprised.

"Oh, I think you're more than aware I have forgiven you for your little outburst," my eyebrows raise at him, hoping he remembers how I threw myself at him last night.

"Thank you," he says taking hold of my hand, he holds my gaze for a moment then asks, "What about you? Have you been here before?"

I nod my head, "Yes, I came here to a wedding a few years ago," I watch the transformation of his handsome happy face to one of a child who has just lost its pet dog.

"Please don't tell me you came here with that ex of yours?" his tone troubled.

"No," I say, watching as the relief of knowing I haven't spent time here with my ex-husband washes over him.

"Good, because I've booked a room for us angel," he says all matter of fact, throwing that sexy wink at me then thanks the waiter when he removes the bowl of shells from our mussels.

I wait to respond until the waiter walks away.

"That's very presumptions of you," I say light-hearted as I would love nothing else than to stay in one of the guest rooms here with him. Walking hand in hand through the scented gardens, sitting at the foot of the old oak trees and watching the transformation of this medieval castle turn into one of the most romantic buildings I've ever seen when the warm soft glow of the lighting illuminates the stone walls and the stained-glass windows.

"From the look on your face, I don't think it was presumptuous of me at all sweetheart," he says with that sexy grin of his just as the waiter returns with our main meal.

We both thank him for our seabass and Vlad pours another glass of wine. "I just thought that after last night, you wouldn't mind staying over with me. We have a lot to discuss and we won't be disturbed here."

"It's fine. I would love to stay here but I haven't brought anything to change into," I tell him, kicking myself for not forward thinking on the matter.

"Don't worry," he says as he tucks into his seabass. "I brought you a weekend bag from home."

"We're staying the weekend?" Shocked that he would leave Lucas for the full weekend then I remember that he had booked this place a month ago for us to have some alone time and Lucas was staying with Sebastian and Izzy then going to Olivia's to spend time with her sons. I also remember the real reason why we are here alone. His past.

"You must have a lot to get off your chest," I say chuckling, still trying to keep it light-hearted. I don't want to spoil this evening; I know he is nervous with what he needs to tell me. But for now, we can continue with our flirting and enjoying each other's company.

"So fucking much," he utters as he finishes his meal. He places his knife and fork on his plate then takes a large mouthful of his wine. I finish mine and Vlad asks me if I would like desert, I decline but accept another glass of wine. I've had three glasses but seem to be handling my wine a little better than I did a couple of months ago, when I'd get a little tipsy after a couple of glasses.

Once the waiter has cleared things away, we finish the bottle off and Vlad pays the bill. He collects our luggage from the car while I visit the ladies then we make our way through the main reception of the hotel to get booked in.

While Vlad speaks with the hotel receptionist, the porter takes our bags and I appreciate the beauty of this lavish place. Like the restaurant we just vacated, the wooden floor is highly polished. Its high ceilings are panelled and there's a grand stone-built fireplace. People mingle, sitting on the high- backed furniture, observing the artwork and tapestries.

We're led to a lift and on to a floor with a long corridor. We walk the full length until we meet a wide staircase. The porter leads the way up one flight where the landing is dimly lit and fitted with thick plush carpet. There's one door which Vlad opens with his key. The porter deposits the small cases Vlad had brought, tells us to enjoy our stay and just to ring reception if there is anything we need.

"Wow," slips from my mouth when the door clicks shut. This suite tucked out of the way on the west wing of the hotel with its own bloody landing and a living room fit for royalty, takes my breath away.

Taking off my shoes, I dig my toes into the thick piled carpet, marvelling how it has its own stone fireplace like the one in reception. The artwork on the walls are of knights in battle and there's a chandelier hanging from the ceiling. Walking into the bathroom, the snowy white marble sparkles in the light. It has a claw-footed bath, double sinks and a large shower cubicle.

Stepping into the next room, I let out a little screech and launch myself onto the simple but elegant redwood four-poster bed. The floaty voile drapes are pinned back, showing patio doors that lead out to a balcony. My fingers twirl round the slate grey embroider duvet as Vlad appears in the doorway. He chuckles at me as I bounce on the bed.

"Enjoying yourself?" he smirks as he rests his head on the wooden frame of the door.

"Come," I say, patting the bed at the side of me. He saunters over and sits down next to me. I bounce again. "Can you hear that?"

"What?" he lifts one eyebrow while he watches me bounce on the bed, that sexy smirk still imbedded on his handsome face. "I can't hear anything."

"Squeak free baby that's why," I say giddier than a child on Christmas morning. I might have led a sheltered life and had a boring sex life until I met my Russian man. But I've always wanted to make love in a four-poster bed with the man of my dreams. I don't need to enlighten him on my dreams because he must see it written all over me. With one swift movement, I'm pinned under him, our mouths fused together. My hands are clasped in one of his above our heads while his other strokes over my heated body.

His kiss is fierce and commanding. His tongue latching onto mine. His hand caressing the most sensitive parts of my body as I buckle underneath him. I moan, and he lapses it up. I want to touch him but his grip on my wrists is firm. Letting this powerful man control my body doesn't scare me in the slightest like it would have done just a couple of months ago and has me wondering whether I would trust him enough to blindfold me and tie me to the bed. Olivia and Sarah have mentioned it once or twice, that they really enjoyed it. I dismissed the idea but now maybe I want to try it.

Vlad's mouth breaks from mine, leaving me breathless. He kisses and nibbles at my neck and once he reaches my throat. I hear him curse. He lifts his head searching for my eyes and I see the torment in him. He wants to give me what I want but we have come here to talk. God what was I thinking. He releases my hands and places a soft kiss on my cheek. "Later," he whispers then climbs off me, sitting on the end of the bed. He rubs the back of his neck, stands and turns to look at me. "Sorry," he says. "I got a little carried away."

"Don't," I say, putting my hand up and moving towards him. "It's me who should be sorry, I was the one…"

He puts his finger on my lip to silence me. "Maybe we both got carried away," he shakes his head. "My angel has a little devil that wants to come out and play," he taps my nose and I chuckle at his comment because I think maybe I do. But it's something we will explore and enjoy together once we get over his past.

Our relationship could be so much more if he could only let loose what it his that has him raging with jealousy and has him wanting to rip apart any man that gets too close. He knows I've forgiven him for that night in the club and that I'm willing to move on. We both know we need each other and struggle when we are not together. But he must let me into the world that could make us or break us.

"Would you like a drink; I could do with one?"

"Yes, please," I answer, thinking he better make it a double because the dark intensity that has crept on to his handsome face tells me he will be baring his soul.

He stalks out of the room while I go in search of the case Vlad brought with him, so I can change into something more comfortable.

Chapter 8
Vlad

While Holly changes in the bathroom, I pour a glass of wine for her and a brandy for me then make my way out onto the balcony. I had booked us a romantic weekend here, with the hopes of having Holly all to myself but never got here due to our breakup. I was lucky to get the same suite when I phoned them yesterday, it's bigger than I thought it would be when I booked it. I wanted it to be out of the way of any other rooms, so when I saw that it had its own corridor with nothing adjoining it, I knew it was ideal.

The fairy lights give off a romantic glow and the view of the hotel grounds and the countryside which lies beyond is breath-taking. Being on the west side of the hotel, I'm sure the evening sunset will be something that Holly will appreciate.

Placing our drinks on the smoked-glass table, I take a seat on the three-seater wicker settee and place my feet up on one of the ottomans.

My nerves are shattered, thinking about how I am going to explain my life back in Russia to the woman I love. I know it will knock Holly for six and ruin the evening we have had so far, but if I don't do it now then I will never do it.

Watching her eyes light up as she took in the room I had booked and the mischief that crossed her face as she observed and bounced on the four-poster bed, snapped any restrain I had. Pinning her under me and devouring her, giving her what she wanted nearly had me throwing my plan out of the window. But I knew I had to stop before we went too far, going there would have kept us from the real reason we are here. Who knew my angel had a secret kinky side that she wanted to explore? I chuckle to myself. Well if we get through this, I'm more than willing to explore and encourage her wild side.

"Oooh, this looks romantic," Holly breaks my thoughts as she steps out onto the balcony. "Wow look at that view it's breath-taking," she pads along to the railings, so she can get a better look. Turning, she stands before me in a silky camisole which outlines her figure and shows off her smooth tanned legs. While her long wavy hair blows in the light breeze, her smile lights up the space between us. And it's the view of her that is breath-taking.

"Sit," I say, patting the seat at the side of me while I pick up our drinks. Holly is cautious, she's only too aware that what I have to say could end our relationship. She takes her drink from me and sips it carefully as her blue eyes gaze at me over the rim of the glass then sits down, putting her feet up on the cushions. I take a large mouthful and relish the burn I feel as it slides down my throat. I can't look at her knowing I'm going to hurt her, so I fixate on the small building in the distance and finish my drink.

"My father wasn't a good man," I begin. I need to get out where it all started, so I start with him. I keep focused on the point ahead of me but see her through my peripheral vision shift, so she is sat up, her feet tucked under her.

"He was evil, greedy, selfish and took whatever he wanted without a thought to who he hurt," I think back to the time when I was a young boy and didn't know what my father was. "When I was a young boy all I ever wanted was his attention, but he was always too busy. A businessman, as I thought." I shake my head knowing exactly what he was. "He always dressed sharp. His suits pristine, shirts starched to death. Cufflinks, tie pins and his watch, I'm sure they cost the price of a small house. Associates would call around, his home office always full of men of the same stature. Then when I was ten, I got what I wanted, he was there for me and I couldn't have been happier. My brother Sasha worked with my father, but they never got on…"

"Wait." Holly puts her hand on my arm. "You have a brother?" Holly asks, shocked that I have never mentioned him.

"Yes. He is my half-brother and is ten years older than me," I smile, remembering the last time we spoke on skype. My niece Lizzy drives him to despair. She is fourteen and wanting to wear make-up and talks about boys. I'm sure the first time she brings a boy home, Sasha will shoot him then lock Lizzy in her room until she's thirty.

"Nobody knew he had a daughter or even a girlfriend until after my father died, he kept them well hidden from the world we knew and my father's reach. The day after my father's funeral, Sasha came to my home carrying this little bundle of joy in his arms and this woman who wasn't the model type I normally saw him with but a petit thing with enormous blue eyes. Kindness oozed from them and when she smiled, I could see why he had chosen her and kept her hidden away from our father."

"Why did he hide them away?" Holly asks. I don't answer her question; I continue with what I want to say.

"I never understood why Sasha hated him until I was thirteen, that's when I saw who my father really was." My hand shakes when I think about what he wanted me to do at such a young age and bile burns my throat. Holly moves to the side of me and holds my shaking hand. Her touch soothes me.

"What was he?" she asks while her hand squeezes mine and she runs her other hand up my arm.

There's a cool breeze blowing, but I feel as if it's a hundred degrees, the thought of that morning. The stench, the noise. My father's dark dead eyes, the way he spoke and the gun.

"He was evil and the worse kind of man you could ever meet."

"What do you mean?"

I take a deep breath, knowing I need to spit it out quickly, "He was part of the Russian Mafia. A boss. My family was big in the underworld."

"What?"

I turn to Holly, keeping hold of her hand. She looks at me as if she hasn't quite heard right, so I say it again. "My father was a mob boss and when I was thirteen, he put a gun in my hand…"

"Oh my God. You mean he was like a Godfather?" her eyes are wide, and her hand covers her mouth. I nod my head at her, and she sits back on her heels.

"W…what did you do?" she stutters out.

I sit up, rubbing my hand up and down my legs, embarrassed with the thought of my reaction to what my father's intentions were. "My father wanted me to shoot a man and…" I stall when I hear Holly gasp. I can't look at her again or I will not be able to continue so I focus on the building that is disappearing as the sun starts to set. "I threw up, fell to my knees because I was so fucking scared my whole body shook and then I'm sure I wet myself. I remember the look he gave me as he grabbed me by my neck, forcing me to stand, and demanding I shoot the man that was strung up by rusty chains." Sarcastically, I let out a chuckle and lean my head back on the soft cushion. "He'd already told the man that had eyes darker than the night that I was going to kill him."

"What happened?" her voice is shaky.

"I remember shouting 'no, I won't do it'. Shaking uncontrollably. Feeling alone and terrified. Falling to the ground, the gun slipping out of my hands. I remember one of the men grinning at me because I struggled to hold the gun and Sergei shooting him the foot. My father cursing at me, bellowing at me to do as I am told. I was so fucking scared and then…. I heard the pop of a gun. All eyes were on me, but I knew I hadn't pulled the trigger. I looked at the man who was strung up, he was dead, then I felt a hand on my shoulder and when I turned Sasha was stood there with a gun in his hand. He glared at my father with so much hatred in his eyes, I'm surprised he didn't turn to stone. Sergei, my father's bodyguard and a few other men that I know were all my father's men stood in front of him, I think they thought Sasha was going to kill him, but he didn't. He picked me up and carried me out of that wretched place and drove me home," Holly throws her arms around my neck and I can feel the wetness from her eyes on my cheek as her hands come up to stroke my hair. She feels sorry for me. I don't want pity all I want is her forgiveness and love once I finish telling her the whole story.

I take her hands from my hair, kiss them then stand. "Where are you going?" she wipes the tears from her eyes, standing with me.

"I need another drink," I say then walk into our room to fetch the bottle of brandy that I had left in there. I also collect Holly's wine and a throw over from couch to keep my angel warm.

When I return, she's sat back down, her legs curled under her. I wrap the throw round her shoulders and pour another drink. Holly doesn't ask any questions she just sits there with her glass to her lips. Her blue eyes glisten like stars. I know she's upset but if I try and comfort her which I want to because it's killing me seeing her upset, I will never finish.

Sitting back in my seat, I finish my drink, pour another one and place it on the table for when I need it.

"Sasha told me never to trust our father, never underestimate what he is capable of and always stay one step ahead of him. He told me to remember he has eyes and ears everywhere. He promised me he would do what he could to try and stop him from dragging me into their world, but I had to be smart because he wasn't always around." I chance a quick glance at Holly and turn my head quickly back to the darkness that has descended on to us when I see the worried look on her face and how she is practically eating her fingernails.

"For over three years we managed to keep him at bay. I went to school and when my friend Dimitri moved here to England, we arranged I would come here as soon as I was eighteen."

"That didn't happen," Holly says as she moves to sit at the side of me and places her hand on my leg. My hand goes straight to hers, holding it, threading our fingers together.

"No," I say shaking my head. "Sasha had gone away on business; my mother was constantly suffering with migraines…"

"Did she know?"

"Know what?"

"What your father did when you were thirteen? That he was in the mafia?"

"She knew who he was, everybody did but we never told her about that day. Sasha didn't think she needed to know, and I agreed never to tell her."

"Was she a good mum?"

I nod my head even though I know she loved Sasha more than she did me, but I knew her reason why sometimes she struggled to look at me. "She tried to be, but my father kept her oppressed. I think she knew what he was capable of but remembered what he was like before Sasha's mother and twin sister were killed…"

"What!" Holly shrieks, jumping up from her seat and dropping my hand in the process.

"Holly," I stand and take her shivering body in my arms. She calms a little as we stand there holding each other.

"How did they die?" she utters. I sit us both back down because even I need to be sitting for this one. This time I don't focus on looking out into the distance. This time I focus on Holly because I need her strength to continue. She doesn't stop me when I sit her on my knee, she burrows her head into my chest, and I place a kiss on her hair.

"Remember when I told you my mother came to Russia when she was eleven to live with her aunt?" Holly nods her head but doesn't speak. She feels cold, so I pick up the blanket and wrap it round her.

"Well her aunt's husband had an older daughter; I think she was about seven years older than my mother. Eliza or Lizzy as everyone called her. She was engaged to my father and when she fell pregnant with twins, they got married. Apparently, they were very much in love, my father worshiped her and when the twins were born, he did everything he could to provide for them. They were happy.

"My father was only a soldier in the mafia, but he started to rise in the ranks and was getting his fingers into a lot of pies. Over the years he made a name for himself but was upsetting a few other families and gaining a few enemies.

"My mother was only young but loved Sasha and young Eliza as if they were her own, she'd babysit for them and took them out to the park and the zoo. Neither my mother or Lizzy realised just how dangerous things were becoming and always gave the guards my father provided them with the slip when they could.

"On the day they died, Sasha wasn't well, my father was away on business, so Lizzy asked my mother to take care of him while she dropped her daughter at school, only, they never got there. Her car was run off the road, killing both mother and child when the car flipped onto its roof and skidded into a brick wall." I can feel Holly's shoulders shaking and I hear a sob break out from her.

"Shush," I breath into her hair as I cradle her in my arms. She might not know these people but anyone with a heart would feel for them.

"Lizzy, Sasha's daughter. Is that why he gave her that name after his mother and sister?" she asks once her tears have subsided.

"Yes."

She nods her head then stretches out to reach our glasses, pouring us both a large one. She settles back into me, swirling the liquid round the glass. I down mine in one, at this rate I'll be pissed by the time I get to the main part. Maybe that would be a good thing at least I won't see the pain on my angel's face when her heart breaks.

"What did your father do?" she asks, once she's had a drink.

"What didn't he do. He was never the same again. Although he had killed before," Holly's eyes widen in shock at what I have just said. "That was the world he lived in Holly." I rub my thumb over her hand but don't dare look at her.

"I was told he was always a kind loving husband and father but that stopped the day they died. He couldn't look at Sasha without becoming angry, so my mother took him and cared for him. He went out for revenge and he didn't stop until he had wiped out two rival families."

"Oh my God," Holly breathes. "I thought things like that only happened in films."

So naïve. "No, sweetheart, some things are very much real life."

"What about the authorities, the police. Did they not do anything?"

"In his pockets."

"What does that even mean?" she asks, as she climbs off my knee. Straight away I feel cold and grab her foot so at least I can feel the warmth that radiates from her. She doesn't stop me but gets comfy on the seat next to me, resting her feet in my lap.

"It means he had the police, government officials and more men ready to lie and cheat for him so he could continue building his empire." She nods her head, taking in what I am saying.

"And your brother worked for him, but didn't want you to?" I nod my head agreeing because Sasha, although he did do my father's dirty work, would have given his life to keep me out of it.

"He had so much hatred in him after losing his mother and sister, he was only eight when they died. His father was never there for him that's when my mother moved into our home, so she could help take care of him. It was easy for my father to put a gun in his hand, but as he got older Sasha knew our father was psychotic and had gone too far. He grew to hate him.

My mother lived there about a year before…" I stop to remember the words my father spat at me on the day he died. I can't go into that with Holly, it infuriates me to think how he took advantage of my mother. Forcing himself on her and me being the product of him taking what he wanted when he wanted. I breath in deeply and finish with something that won't have Holly asking questions. "She lived there about a year before they got together, nine months later I was born." Holly gives me a tight smile and squeezes my arm.

"What happened when you were sixteen?"

"What?"

"You said that you were able to keep him away from you until you were sixteen. What happened then?" Concern edged on her beautiful face as she fidgets in her seat. Suddenly, my tongue is too thick for me to speak. I sit there, heart pounding and palms sweating, feeling like I could choke.

"Vlad," Holly's voice cuts through my torment, I feel her hand on my arm as she tries to bring me back to her but it's too late. I've gone back to the darkness that took so many years of my life where hatred and revenge got me through the day and the love of my sons washed my darkened soul in the evenings.

"Vlad speak to me," her voice is soft as her fingers stroke my cheek. Closing my eyes, I breathe in deeply and take Holly's hand in mine, lacing our fingers. I need her so much it is fucking killing me that my past might break us. I know our relationship was cracked but our night together last night and this evening up to now gave me hope that we can mend it. But I need to go on and let her in. Once it's out in the open, I will do anything to bring her back to me.

"When I was sixteen my father was having one of his lavish parties. Sasha was away, and my mother had been unwell for a few days with migraines, so she was on bed rest until her dizzy spells subsided. I never attended any of his over the top gatherings. I didn't want to be near him, and he looked at me as if I was piece of shit most of the time. But, with Sasha away and my mother not well he wanted me there. I argued that he didn't need me, my uncles and cousins were attending so there were plenty of family. Anyway, he wouldn't have it and I was summoned to attend.

So, there I was amongst the rich and powerful, hating every one of the arrogant bastards. Grown men sucking up to my father and women half his age flaunting themselves around him and my father loving every minute of it.

Within an hour, I'd had enough and was looking to exit the party when my father approached me with a middle-aged couple and their daughter. She was stunning, and I was infatuated the moment he introduced us. Her lips were warm and inviting and her eyes were like looking into the ocean on a hot summer's day. I got lost in them. Lust filled me and although she seemed to hang on to her father's arm as if the party was too big for her," I swallow hard remembering her smile as my father asked me to look after her. "She soon became relaxed once we left the party and went out into the grounds for a walk."

"What was her name?" Holly asks as she gets up to pour another drink. She lifts my glass, asking me if I want topping up and I nod knowing I could down the bottle and then some.

"Natalia," or she-devil I want to say but I don't. Holly, my angel, comes and sits back down, passing me the glass of brandy which I down in one. Her eyes widen at me as I lean forward and top myself up again.

"What happened next?" Holly asks on a slur. Wow my angel is getting a little pissed, maybe she will forget everything I'm about to tell her.

"We whipped a bottle of vodka from the party and went to my

room. Our home was huge, so having my room on the far side of the house had its advantages. Before the night had ended let's just say we had got to know each other a little better." I don't tell Holly how she seduced me and me being a horny teenager didn't object to letting her.

"You slept together?"

"Yes, several times. We met up secretly for a couple of months then she went missing."

"Missing?" Holly tilts her head, her eyebrows lowering at me.

"Yes. I went to our usual meeting places, but she never turned up. She'd left a scarf in my bedroom, so I turned up at her house on the pretence that I was returning it. I asked if she was in, but their housekeeper said she had gone away with her parents for a while. I was annoyed that she didn't tell me, but we weren't dating we were just fucking so there was nothing I could do.

She'd unleased the man in me and I found myself wanting to follow my big brother whenever he was going clubbing. For the next couple of months, I trained with him regularly and got laid frequently."

"So, you didn't love her then," I shake my head at Holly knowing the only woman I've ever loved is sat here with me.

"At first, I thought I did, but then realised I was just infatuated with her beauty and the way she made me feel. She was older than me by three years and I don't think I was her first. I was a horny teenager and loved the attention she had given me." Holly shakes her head at me, I shrug my shoulders and give her a little smirk.

"After a few weeks, I'd put her out of my head and was focusing on my goal to travel to England. I was happy, enjoying spending time with my brother and carrying on with my schoolwork. I knew I had less than two years to go before I could go to England and knowing I'd have a job in the restaurant that Dimitri's parents owned, then once I was twenty-one I would get my inheritance from my great-aunt which would pay for my business degree. Life seemed better than it had ever been," how wrong could I be.

"You seemed to have had it all worked out," Holly yawns out, covering her mouth. "Sorry, too much wine it's making me tired."

She puts her glass down on the table, "Be back in a minute, need the loo." I get up with her because I need the loo too. It always makes me smile the different names the English give to the toilet. I switch the coffee machine on, thinking Holly could do with one then follow her to the bathroom. Holly isn't shy when it comes to using the bathroom, she doesn't mind me wandering in while she's peeing. She's just flushing when I open the door, so while she washes her hands, I use the toilet. "I've switched the coffee machine on," I tell her. "Maybe a coffee might wake you up."

"Yeah, would you like one?"

"Yes, you go get yourself comfy, I'll make it," Holly vacates the bathroom and when I enter the living area she's brought in the glasses and the blanket. While I make the coffee, I watch her getting settled on the sofa.

"I thought we could sit in now, it's become a bit chilly out," she says as she stretches her legs out. Passing the cup of coffee to her, I lift her feet and put them on my knee when I sit down.

"You want to carry on?" she asks. No, I don't. What I want is to wrap her in my arms and forget all about my past life, but we've come here so I can bare all. Nodding my head at her I carry on.

"Like I said I didn't see anything of Natalia again until one day I had finished school and when I arrived home Sergei was waiting for me in the entrance hall. He told me that my father wanted to see me, so I went to his office to see what he wanted only when I walked in, he wasn't alone.

Sat on his leather sofas were Natalia and her father, looking very pleased with themselves, my father also had an unusual smile on his face. Both men had a glass of vodka in their hands and seemed to be celebrating something. 'What's going on?' I asked. 'Why did you want to see me?' Even though the questions were directed at my father my eyes never left Natalia's. I watched her eyes graze the floor and never once meet mine. She fiddled with the zip on her bag while my father dropped the biggest bomb shell on me ever."

"Come Vladimir. Sit. Join us in celebrating," he gushes. His face flushes with the alcohol he has already consumed. Standing up he pours me a drink.

"What celebrations?" I ask, confused.

"*Today you make me the proudest man in Russia,*" *he beams while slapping me on the back.*

"*Papa what are you talking about?*" *I question while locking eyes with Natalia's father who is grinning like a fucking idiot. Then my eyes catch hers as she sits up straight and proud giving me a sly smirk as my father's next words whirl around my head until I feel dizzy.*

"*Vlad good news. I'm overjoyed you have made me a grandpa. You're going to be a father. Natalia is pregnant with your child.*" *His words hit me like a vortex of violent winds so strong my head nearly explodes.*

My heart is beating so fast I could feel it trying to burrow its way out through my back. If I'd stood, I would fall because the feeling in my legs have gone and my throat threatens to choke me. My father passes me a glass, I manage to grasp it through my clouded vision and once I have it in my shaking hands, I gulp down the neat vodka. It takes a few minutes for me to gain some sense of what is happening.

"*No, I haven't seen you for two months. Tell him.*" *I all but shout at her to stop lying but she just sits there calmly while her father rubs her arm.*

"*I know Vladimir, but I am fourteen weeks pregnant with your child,*" *She says standing up, unfastening her coat so I can see the small bump that is holding my child.*

I step back from her, snatching my hand back that she has hold of trying to place on her stomach. The back of my legs hit the chair and I fall into it knowing this is it. He has me.

"Breathe Vlad," I hear my angel speak, as I struggle to get my breath. Just thinking about the cunning conniving bastards has me hyperventilating. I breathe through my nose until I can see Holly stood in front of me and I pull her into me. Her hands run through my hair as she tries to comfort me. "Are you alright?" she lifts my chin to look into my eyes. Somehow, she's ended up straddling me and my hands are on her hips. Without asking she places her lips on mine and it's the softest touch ever but it's all I need to calm me. She lingers there, our lips barely touching, soothing my soul.

"Sorry," I say once she breaks away. "Sometimes when I think too deeply about how they trapped me; it consumes me…"

"What do you mean trapped you?"

"It was a set up. A trap. A honey trap so to speak."

"Oh."

"Yes oh. I didn't know at the time; it was years later that I found out my father had paid her father a considerable amount of money for his daughter."

"Wow! Again, I can't believe things like that happen."

"Holly we could be here all weekend while I go in to how my father and his associates trapped me into working for him. How I was forced into a marriage I didn't want to be in. We didn't want to be in because I know she didn't want to marry me or anybody else. Jesus, she didn't even want children, so I'm going to try and get through what happened as quickly as possible because if I don't get it all out now I never will."

"Okay, but if you need to stop at any time then do so. I know this is painful for you, but I need to know what happened. What turns the kindest man with the biggest heart who loves passionately into someone I don't recognize." I know she's talking about the night I beat the shit out of those three guys and the way I viciously spoke to her. I may regret it until the day I die.

Chapter 9
Holly

Listening to Vlad divulge his past life in Russia unnerves me. Hearing he had a brother shocked me and had me thinking I don't really know him at all. There's so much I don't know about him and his family that every time he tells me something new, I struggle to take it all in. Shocked to say the least about his father being a mob boss. God I'm so inexperienced in this sort of thing. Honey traps, the mob, it all seems so farfetched, yet I know from looking at Vlad it's the truth. He's taken off his shirt showing his tattoos that I now know bare some resemblance to his life.

The colourful ink that mar his body tells a story. From the swirls and patterns to the various letters and stars that run up and down his arms and legs. Then there's the dagger and skulls on his neck and back. His chest showing a picture of a beast and jokers all make me wonder just what my man has done and why he had these disturbing tattoos on his body.

"Holly," his low husky voice strokes over my skin, his accent now thicker than usual making me want him more. He only has to say my name in that tone and I'm a mess but tonight I need to stay focused and not let him get to me.

"Hmmm," is all I manage as I watch him walk back from the bathroom. He stretches his hands above his head then cricks his neck. The muscles in his arms flex showing strength while the tattoos on his chest show sadness. As he comes closer, I can see the fading light colour of the bruises that were on his ribs and the bite mark that I made last night on his shoulder. A light sigh leaves my lips when I think about how he makes me feel. Vlad raises an eyebrow at me. He knows what I am thinking. "Sorry," I say on a flush, sitting up straight. He chuckles, and crouches in front of me. I want to run my fingers over his broad chest and bury my face into his neck. I don't get the chance because he takes my hands in his.

I can feel a tremble in them, so I scoot forward knowing the closer I am to him the easier it will be for him to disclose what hurts him so much. What it is that brings out a totally different man to the one that makes me feel loved and safe.

"Holly I'm going to ask you a question and I want you to think about it before you answer it. I also want you to keep that question and answer in here," he taps his head, his expression his serious, the chuckle now gone.

"What is the question?" He blows out a breath and stands quickly, releasing my hands. I watch his taut frame pace over to the window. One hand rubbing the back of his neck as he stares out into the night. He's struggling. Looking at the time on my phone, I see it's almost midnight. His past could take us into the early hours but that's what we're here for. Just him and me and no disturbances.

"Vlad," he turns to look at me unease written all over him. I pat the seat at the side of me. "Come and sit down. I'm here. I'm not going anywhere," I put my hand out for him to take. He holds it and sits at the side of me, our thighs lightly touching. "Tell me about your wife, Natalia. You said I was like her…"

"I shouldn't have said that. You are nothing like her. I was angry with you, I thought you had been leading that idiot on, flirting with him. Dancing with him, seeing you with him…"

"Is that what she did?" I cut in.

"Yes."

"Explain to me what she did. What she was like? Why she still has a hold on you." I squeeze his hand and he turns to me.

"What?"

"You were with her for fifteen years, you have four sons together, but something happened over those years that has you not trusting women. I know I was the first woman that you had taken home and introduced to your boys since you came to England, this by your own admission and your sons. You trusted me enough for that then suddenly I'm like your dead wife and if I'm right again by your own admission she was a drug taking whore, you're lucky I'm not slapping you round the face," I'm getting a little worked up now. "In fact, you're lucky I'm sat here at all…"

"You've already slapped me around the face but if it makes you feel better feel free to do it again, it's less than I deserve," he cuts in. Yeah, I did, and it hurt me more than him.

"Holly I thought you said you had forgiven me for my actions and words that night."

I turn to him, so our knees are touching, and we are holding each other's hands. His thumbs run over mine.

"Vlad, I love you so much," he breathes in deeply, closing his eyes at my words. "I want this to work, I don't want to walk away from what we have. I came to you last night to remind you that I was still waiting for you, it proved it last night for me that what we have is special and whatever it is that your past holds over you we can get through it." I stroke his cheek and his eyes open, showing me the love he holds for me. "I have forgiven you, but you need tell me why you react like that. Why you were sat watching the CCTV? Why you think when a man looks at me that I'm going to take him up on his offer? Although I get the feeling I know the reason to that, there's still a lot more I don't understand. You said your father was psychotic, but you border on that when you rage like a mad man, so I need to know all of it not just bits and bats."

He nods his head at me. "You know, getting to the root of the cause, letting it all out can help or you might need to see a therapist," he chuckles at me. "Just saying," I shrug my shoulders.

"I love you too," he says as he continues to rub his thumb over my knuckles. "I never thought I would meet anyone that could make me feel like you do but you're right, I do need to let you in to the world that controlled me for so long then maybe we can move on." He places a kiss on my cheek and whispers in my ear, "You are my angel," I know he calls me this all the time but this time when he says it the words hold so much more meaning to them.

"I wasn't happy when she claimed she was carrying my child and I certainly did not want to marry her," he continues while I sit there listening. "The chance that the baby she was carrying might not have been mine crossed my mind hundreds of times and to be honest I didn't want it to be mine. I argued with my father and hers that I would not marry her until the child was born. I wanted a paternity test and then if it was mine then I would think about marriage.

My father threatened to kick me out if I didn't agree to the marriage. I was disgracing the family. I told him to go ahead. I didn't want to be under the same roof as him anyway, I hated him, and I certainly didn't trust him. Anyway, he resigned to the fact that I was not going to back down plus I think it entertained him that I'd stood up to him. So, we waited till the baby was born. Only as soon as Sebastian kicked his way into the world, he came out legs first, I knew he was mine and I was smitten. I loved him straight away." Tears well in his eyes and he let out a shaky breath. Tears threaten mine too and I swallow hard to stop the lump in my throat.

"We married two week later, and she moved into our home. My mother loved Sebastian and didn't mind taking care of him. I took a job after school at the local supermarket and worked some weekends too. We didn't need a lot of money living at my parents, but I wanted them to know that I was willing to provide for my son and wife." He picks up his coffee that I'm sure must be freezing now and takes a drink. When he places it back on the table, he takes my hand again and turns to me.

"I was seventeen, married and a father. My plans to come to England were put on hold and I hatched a new one. I would work part time while I was still in education, do my degree in Russia than bring my family to England. I thought I had it all worked out, but Natalia didn't want that.

She wanted me to quit school and work for my father. We argued and argued all the time. Her screeching at me to man up and except responsibility for my family. She didn't want to live under my parent's roof and working with my father would give us enough money to move out and get a place of our own. Although I didn't love her in the beginning, I did have some feelings for her that I did mistake for love at the time, so I wanted to please her. She was the mother of my son and my wife, but I did not want to work for him.

One night, I think Sebastian was about four months old, I came in from work, I was tired, and I found Sebastian screaming in his crib. I quickly picked him up, he was soaked. His nappy was full, and he needed feeding. I set about cleaning him up and preparing a bottle, wondering where Natalia was.

I wasn't kept waiting long when she stepped into the room dressed to go clubbing. She was stunning. Her short fitted red dress left nothing to the imagination. With her thick dark hair pinned up, pouty lips and stripper heels she looked like she was on the pull.

I went ballistic about how she had left Sebastian while she got ready to go out. She just said she had had him all day and was off the clock, blew me a kiss and walked out of the door, leaving me with my son. I was on holiday from school and was supposed to be in work the following morning trying to earn extra cash, but she didn't come home all night, so I didn't go in.

The part of the house we lived in had been adapted so we had two bedrooms, bathroom, kitchen and living room. It was self-contained which meant nobody had heard my son crying.

My mum was pissed the following morning when I told her. She offered to watch Sebastian, but I wanted to stay at home and wait for her to come home. Eventually, she arrived home around dinner time and took herself off to bed to sleep off her partying. No remorse that she had left her son all night. No explanation to where she had been." I sit there listening knowing what was going to come next. I was only too aware of how some women prefer to party than care for their child. Just look at my mother.

"This started to happen regularly and when I pulled her up about it, she would scream at me telling me that she felt stifled living in my parent's home that she thought they were judging her all the time and that she was sorry for being a bitch. I'd feel sorry for her and tell her to go out with her friends and have a bit of fun and I would watch Sebastian.

I knew what it was like at home with my father and his cronies around plus the guards around the grounds. I was able to get out of there when I was at school or work, she wasn't.

A few times when she came home from the club, her eyes were wild and there was a distinctive smell of men's aftershave."

"Did you not go out together?" I ask.

"Yeah," he nods, biting his top lip. "We did. We would go out to a restaurant, a stroll in the park with Sebastian but she only ever wanted to go clubbing with her friends. One Friday night, Sasha asked me to join him and his friends at the Spinning Wheel; it was the top night club where we lived. My mother offered to take Sebastian for the evening, I was reluctant to leave him because I didn't want my father looking after him. She said she would stay in the spare room with him, so I agreed to go out.

The music was pumping so loud when we eventually got in the club, I could hardly hear anyone speaking. We had been to a few bars slamming shots and I was a little buzzed. Because of who we were the staff took us straight to one of the VIP areas that overlooked the dance floor and that's when I saw her.

She swayed in time with the music, her arms above her head, her thick long glossy dark hair hung in curls down her back. The dress she wore was so short you could almost see her knickers and some man had his hands all over her. She laughed at him, with him and practically fucked him on the dance floor. He stood there with his hands on my wife's ass rubbing up against her while she shimmied down him and then hung round his neck. I watched them leave the dance floor and join some friends in one of the booths.

Sasha saw what I was watching and shrugged his shoulders at me. He told me she came here all the time and got up to all sorts of shit and it was about time I knew about it. That's why he wanted me to join them. Apparently, she had even tried to come on to one of Sasha's mates."

Vlad's fingers run over the scar on his eye and something passes over his face. Darkness. Sorrow.

"What did you do?"

"I confronted them. I walked down to where they were seated. When I got there, they were just popping some pill into each other's mouth then went in for a full-on show with tongues and teeth. His hand up her dress and her enjoying every minute of it. I stood there a few minutes waiting for them to finish and when they did, they turned to look at me. I won't go into details but that's how I got this scar," I reach up and run my fingers over it then I lean over and place a kiss on it.

"He brought a knife out on you?"

"Yeah, but the idiot didn't know how to use it properly."

"What do you mean?"

"My father had shown me how to use a knife, he had trained me from ten years old up to the age of thirteen and even though I had not used one in a few years, it's something I hadn't forgotten. Sasha had also taught me how to fight from the age of thirteen and I often trained with him and his friends. That included disarming your opponent. So, when he brought the knife out on me, I was arguing with Natalia. He attacked me from the side, catching me here," he points to the scar above his eye. "He ended up with it stuck in his chest...."

"Oh my God," my hand shoots to my mouth. "Vlad you could have killed him," I say shocked.

"Yeah, if I'd have wanted to kill him, I would have slit his throat," his words come out harsh and have me wondering what I'm going to learn about my man. Do I really want to know?

I get up to walk to the window. I need a little fresh air; the room has become too warm and I can feel my skin overheating. Opening the windows, I let the cool air envelope me. My mind is whirling at what I have already learnt about Vlad's life and I have a feeling I'm not going to like what he is going to tell me next.

"Holly," I hear him speak, his tone firm and commanding. Turning to look at him I can see the dominant look on his face; the one that attracted me to him in the first place. He might have had one hell of a childhood, but I get the feeling that as he got older people did as he told them.

"Come here," he demands. I don't want to; I want to stay where the night air is cooling my heated skin. Where I don't have to listen to what he will tell me next. I might have wanted him to divulge everything but now I'm not so sure.

His dark eyes call to me, dragging me to him. His hands hold mine as I kneel in front of him, waiting for his next words.

"Holly don't fear me. Everything I have done was to keep my children safe. I didn't have a choice…" I don't fear him. I fear what he will tell me will end us.

"We all have a choice, Vlad, in what we do." He shakes his head at me, and sighs then joins me on the floor, so we're sat at the side of each other. He takes one of my hands and holds it in between his. My hand looks so small in his.

"I was going to ask you a question earlier but didn't," he says. "What would you do to keep your children safe? Think about Lucy and Megan and ask yourself that question before you judge me for my sins."

"What did you do?" I utter. Thinking about his question while I ask him mine, I'm not sure what I wouldn't do to keep my children out of arms way, if I had any. What wouldn't I do to make sure my god daughters were safe? Again, I can't answer that because I have not been in that situation. But if I was to guess, I would do anything to keep them safe.

"When Natalia fell pregnant with Nicholas, Sebastian wasn't even two. I'd forgiven her for her wild ways, and she seemed to settle down, although she still nattered at me to work for my father.

I'd thought about approaching him to see if he would let me work in the office. Even the head of the mob needed his books keeping. Anyway, once she found out she was pregnant again, she tightened the thumb screws and threatened to get rid of our child if I didn't go to my father for a job.

I didn't take her threat lightly; she had a nasty side to her, and I knew she would go through with her threat to prove her point." He shakes his head, blowing out a breath then chews on his knuckle, struggling with his next words. "I was eighteen, the youngest son of a man who wouldn't think twice about turning on one of his own. A wife who would manipulate me to get her own way, a son who I cherished more than anything else in the world. He was pure and unaware of the cruel world he was growing up in and I had another child on the way. My head was in bits. I wanted Natalia happy and I wanted my unborn child, so I bit the bullet and went to my father.

We spoke lengthily about what I would do in his organisation and in all fairness, he seemed to care. He was happy to let me work in the office and set me up in the room at the side of his.

Over the following year, Nicholas was born, Natalia and I went house hunting and we found the perfect home. My father bought it for us expressing how happy he was with my work and that it was also a belated wedding present.

Sasha seemed quiet and worried and when I spoke with him, he reminded me about his words to me when I was thirteen. I took them on board and carried on with my life. I still had plans to come to England, but I just didn't know when."

"What work were you doing for your father?"

"Ledgers. Anything to do with his accounts. Records of men who owed him money. Lists and lists of well-known people who were in his debt. Shipments of illegal drugs and arms…"

"It didn't bother you that you were contributing to your father's illegal activities?" He lifts my chin with his fingers and stares into my eyes, it's there for me to see before he speaks.

"Yes. Yes, it bothered me. It gave me nightmares that I was a part of it, I felt guilty, but I would go home to my boys and put all of it out of my mind until the following day. It was the only way I could get through it. Holding my sons, letting their innocence and love surround me, kept me sane." I chuckle at the thought of a Sebastian and Nicholas being toddlers, running rings around their father.

"I bet they kept you busy."

"Yes, they did," a wide grin appears on his face and it's the first tonight.

"Their mother wasn't good with them, all she wanted was to spend the money I was earning on hair, new clothes, nails. Going out to lunch with her friends, she didn't have the patience or time for them, so I employed a child minder. She was good with them. Took them out a lot. When I came home, they would charge at me like bulls and be hung round my neck for the rest of the evening. Even at bedtime they wanted to crawl into my bed, it didn't bother me. I would read to them, make up stories and sing to them until they fell asleep. Most of the time they would stay in my bed until the following morning. Natalia would rather climb into the spare bed than share her bed with her sons. It hurt me that she could dismiss them so easily, but it made me love them more." It hasn't gone unnoticed to me that his arm has slipped around me and his mood has lightened while he has been talking about his sons. I don't pull him up on it instead I rest my head on his shoulder and relish his touch when his hand plays with my hair.

"You're a fantastic dad, any child would be grateful to have a father as caring as you," I tell him.

"Thank you," he says. "Some fathers are not as caring and while you didn't know your real father Holly, I wish I hadn't known mine."

"That bad, huh." He nods his head, moving his arm from around me. He brings his knees up and rest his elbows on them, sitting forward. He then cups his hands over his mouth and nose before he speaks.

"One day I was in my little office, trying to calculate some numbers that wouldn't tally up. It looked like one of my father's associates were trying to pull one over on him. I didn't want to go to him with what I'd found, so I waited for Sasha. While I was waiting, I heard a very heated argument in my father's office. It was Sasha and my father. They didn't know I was there; I should have been home but had waited for my brother. The voices got louder and more aggressive, so I moved to the door to hear what was happening.

Sasha was bellowing at my father, that he could not go through with some plan and he was arguing back that it was time. I heard my father's hand hit the desk to show his authority and through the crack of the door I saw Sasha throw a chair at the wall. Then my father's words nearly put me in an early grave. *Sasha don't think I will not follow through with my promise if you stand in my way.* My father's words were harsh as he spat them out. *You cannot do this; she has done nothing wrong to you. All she has ever done is care for your sons and you threaten to kill her if I don't support you!* Sasha words shook the office and had me sliding down the door until I connected with the floor. They were speaking about my mother. My blood was boiling, I wanted to go in there and strangle him. He was bribing my brother with killing my mother, the woman who had cared for Sasha and loved him as her own. The arguing continued, and I soon found out why my father wanted Sasha's support.

My father knew someone was deceiving him and he knew who it

was, and he wanted him taken out. And the person he had chosen to do the deed was me."

Suddenly I can't move. I sit there frozen. Knowing, waiting for the words I think I always knew would come.

"I could hear drawers slamming, struggles. The sound of my father's office door being flung open, Sergei's booming voice. The cock of guns and that's when I couldn't hold back any longer.

I burst through the door yelling for them to stop. That I would do it. Sasha had stood up for me long enough, it was time for me to take my place within the family.

That evening I was driven to some building. My father stayed back in his office while Sergei drove, along with Sasha, Pete, Dominic and me. The gun was already in my jacket as I pulled it out, I didn't shake like I did when I was thirteen. I didn't feel sick or dizzy. I felt numb.

We pulled into the dark car park; Dominic was the first to exit the car then we all followed. As we approached the door to the old building, Sergei grabbed Sasha's arm and held him back. Sasha wanted to come in with me, but I gave him a nod and tight smile, letting him know that I was ok. That I could do this.

Pete opened the door and I stepped inside to the barely lit room. Stood there were two of my father's lackies holding some fat guy in dark grey suit. He was sweating profusely. A smirk appeared on his face when he saw that it was me standing there and one of the lackies commented on how my father had sent the boy to do a man's work.

I had no emotions when I lifted the gun and shot the man clean between his eyes and I had no regrets when I sent a warning shot to the man's balls who had disrespected me. My work was done, and I had sent a message not to underestimate me. Two men dead. Both associates of my fathers. The first of many to come.

I walked back to the car with my head held high, Sasha opening the door for me. The car was quiet when I puked into the bag that Sasha had waiting for me. Not a word was spoken, I thought I had gone deaf until Sasha spoke. *These men are no different to our father, they would sell their daughters to the devil and strangle their own wives for greed and power. Don't lose any sleep over what you did tonight."*

My stomach recoils as what I've just heard registers. I wrap my arms around myself to stop the shaking as blood pounds at my temples hard and aggressive, like a tide smashing against the rocks. A cold sweat washes over me and the bile that was settled in my stomach rises, burning my throat. My hand goes to my chest as the other one covers my mouth. Vlad's words plague me. *Two men dead. The first of many.* Men killed by the man's hands that sooth me, claim me, that hold me tight. That love me.

I can't hold it in any longer, I need to be sick. I scramble to my feet, batting away the strong hands that reach for me. Hands that would normally make me feel safe. I sprint to the bathroom, noise flooding my ears, a distressed cry calling my name. "Holly."

Chapter 10

Vlad

Two men dead. The first of many.

I felt her body jerk and shake as I revealed what I knew would be the one thing to cause my angel pain. I try to reach for her, hoping I can calm her but as she stumbles to her feet, I can see she's drained of colour. Her eyes pinched together in terror; she can't look at me.

I call to her as she heads for the bathroom, my voice tormented and in pain. I've broken her. Following her to the bathroom, I try to hold her hair from her face as she vomits the meal and wine we had consumed this evening down the toilet. She turns and knocks my hands away, her eyes wet and bloodshot and I die a little inside knowing I have caused the hurt and pain on her beautiful face.

Her body sinks to the floor once she stops being sick, her head on her knees sobbing like a child as she sits on the cold marble floor. My hand strokes over her back to sooth her but she flinches at my touch, bringing me to the floor. Fighting back the tears that want to erupt for bringing this strong woman, my strong beautiful angel to her knees. "Fuck," I curse as I watch her body tremble. I prop myself up against the wall, sickened with what I have done. This woman has come through so many obstacles in her life. Her birth mother preferring to shower herself in drugs and men than take care of her young child. Being adopted into a family that loved and treasured her then having them taken from her in her teens. Her husband who was supposed to love her till death us do part, crushed her with his betrayal and then me.

What have I done?

I've taken the strength that she had built up over the years and destroyed it in one night. Swallowing the lump in my throat as I watch Holly sob into her hands, I contemplate leaving.

She's better off without me, too good for me but I am a selfish bastard when it comes to her, I will never leave her. I can't be without her.

As her sobs slow to light sniffles, I stroke her hair hoping, praying she will accept my plea to comfort her. Her head still resting on her knees she turns and her red, swollen eyes blaze into me.

"Did you kill your wife?" she startles me, her voice quiet and croaky. Jesus what she must think of me. I wanted to strangle her many times. Shake her for hurting the sons she was supposed to love but no I didn't kill her.

"No," I say, shaking my head, moving so I am sat on the floor opposite her, my arms resting on my bent knees. Her hand wipes a lone tear off her cheek then she reaches for some tissue, wiping her nose on it. I want to wipe her tears and pass her tissues, but I know not to push my luck.

"Then tell me what happened between Nicholas being born and her dying when Lucas was born because I'm having a hard time believing that the car crash was an accident after what you have told me so far."

My blood rises at the thought that Holly would think I could do such a thing to the woman who was carrying my child. "Do you think I would try to kill my wife knowing she was carrying my unborn child, Holly?" My tone sharp, my eyes focused on hers. Her eyes give me a cold stare and have me believing that she really does think that I killed my wife. "Holly?" My eyes narrow, waiting for her answer. Then I see a bit of warmth come back to them when she shakes her head.

"No," she says, shaking her head again as she blows her nose on the tissue. Thank God because I couldn't take it if she thought I was that cruel.

Holly's arms rest on her bent knees, her head on them looking fragile and hurt while her intense stare bores into me.

"My wife liked to party and had very expensive taste. As the years went on, I got deeper into my father's business, wanting to end his reign as well as any associates, government officials, high ranking police officers, anyone that had connections with him. I had all the names and dirt on them that would either put them away or destroy their reputation if it got out. But I was only young and didn't know how to go about it. I'd spoken to Sasha who asked me to keep all the information safe until the time was right. So, while I was putting a lot of time in trying to bring down my father's organisation from under his nose, my wife was out constantly partying with her friends, spending the dirty money I earned on expensive clothing, jewellery and weekend spa trips.

Our marriage was not out of love but was forced upon us because of our fathers. In our world, families expect to marry off their sons and daughters to make their families stronger. My father knew I was opposed to this and that time was running out for him to get me to join his organisation because he knew as soon as I hit eighteen, I would be travelling to England. That's why he set the meeting up. Natalia and her father were only too willing to accept my father's money and his terms.

If she fell pregnant with my child, her family would benefit considerably, she would become my wife therefore she would have all the material things she wanted if she got me to work for my father. None of this was known to me at the time.

Anyway, she fell pregnant with my child, so I had to marry her. I made a lot of money working for my father even though he never knew what I was trying to do. Killing the men who were supposed to look after the people of our country but instead were taking from them. I hated them and my father. His threats were always in my head and I knew one day he would try to recruit my sons into this world that I had become a part of, and I could never let that happen.

Over the years, she got more dependent on drugs and loved to taunt me by flirting with other men. I cared for her as the mother of my children, so I kept her behaviour hidden from our fathers who would have had her killed if they had known.

For a few years we lived separate lives, lived in the same house but had separate bedrooms. She did her thing and I did mine. Until she came home one day and asked me if we could try again. She had come off the drink and drugs. She wasn't leaving the house to meet her friends and was trying to be a mother to our sons. Again, I forgave her and that's when she fell pregnant with Daniel. When he was born, Natalia nursed him and seemed to enjoy being a mother to all three of our boys. We still had the nanny to help her out, but I was the one who would read to them at bedtime and made sure they were always fast asleep if I had to go back out to do my father's dirty work.

My father was getting suspicious as to why men he had in his pocket were being killed off and shipments of arms and drugs were being contained by the authorities at either end of their destinations. I had sent a tip-off to the authorities in America which had caused my father to think someone in his firm had double-crossed him. Of course, this caused him to suspect anyone and everyone except his sons, so we were told to clean house. All his men were faithful to him and knew what happened to informers. Which meant Sasha and I had to come up with a cover story, it wasn't easy, but we managed to set up someone who we knew was into things that…"

I shake my head and gaze at Holly who is still sat there, her face pale as if all the blood has drained from her. I don't want to tarnish her with some of the sickening and disgusting men I have come across. "Let's just say he had it coming."

"What do you mean?" she asks, her voice still croaky from her crying. Her long hair is draped over one shoulder and I notice her fingers softly rubbing a piece between them. My heart shatters when I remember what she told me. Hiding in the wardrobe with her doll. Rubbing its hair to comfort her when her mother was drugged up, partying and arguing. Holly was scared and alone and that's how she feels now.

I move across the marble floor until I'm knelt in front of her. Taking her hands in mine, I place them on my chest with mine on top of them. She doesn't pull away, but her hands shake.

"Holly," I whisper. "Please don't be afraid of me. What I did was to make sure my sons didn't have to grow up the way Sasha and myself did. I wanted them to have a choice in what job they wanted. Who they married. I didn't want them to have to learn to shoot a gun. To be constantly watching over their shoulder. Ending up in prison or worse... Dead.

The men I chose to kill were evil men. Men who gave drugs to children, getting them hooked, so they could use them for their own gain. Young children, Lucas' age who were given guns and knives to use. Trained by men in my father's organisation until they were good enough to be put to work. These children were vulnerable and should have been cared for by the state, but the state turned a blind eye to what was going on. Because of greedy men who had the power to cover things up if my father lined their pockets.

My sons were not safe around their grandfather, he would have set them up like he did me. Found their weakness and trapped them so they could stand with him at the head of his firm."

I place her hands on her knees and sit down at the side of her. "I'm not afraid of you," she sniffles. I nod my head and continue to explain the best way I can about Natalia.

"Due to the shit storm I had kicked up when I'd informed on the shipment that was on its way across the waters, I wasn't at home as much as I usually was. But with Natalia devoting her time to my sons, I assumed they were safe and would be fine if I arrived home later than normal. Only I was wrong to trust my wife. To think she could be a loving, caring mother and a faithful wife... It was stupid and careless of me." I lower my head, regretting that I could have been so foolish. I feel Holly's cold hand take mine and when I look up, I see in her eyes that she cares.

"What happened?" I link our fingers together and continue.

"I'd had quite a few late nights but never suspected anything was wrong. The children were in bed and so was Natalia most nights. My routine was to jump in the shower and wash off the filth of the day. Some nights I'd stay under the shower until I couldn't stand the heat any longer, wanting to scrub my skin clean from what I had done.

This night when I pulled up in the car, I noticed all the lights on, usually Natalia left the outside lights on and the landing light. Jumping out of the car I raced into the house, finding Sebastian and

Nicholas huddled together crying on the staircase. Scooping them into my arms I charged up the stairs to Daniel's room, not listening to what they were trying to tell me. I could hear Daniel crying and my focus was getting to him. He stopped crying has soon as he saw me and put his hands out to be picked up once I had him cuddled into me that's when I heard what Sebastian and Nicholas had been saying. Their mother had collapsed on the bathroom floor, so settling Daniel with his brothers, I went to Natalia. She was sprawled out on the floor and I could see the remainders of the white powder she had shoved up her nose." I blow out a breath, remembering feeling guilty that I hadn't seen this coming and that maybe it was my fault for leaving her alone over the last few weeks.

"I checked her pulse which was faint, I phoned an ambulance then phoned Sasha. He arrived before the ambulance. The doctors took care of her and said she would be in for at least a week, not wanting to leave my boys too long with their grandmother, I went home. After my mother and Sasha had gone, I checked the CCTV, and what I saw left me knowing I'd been a fool."

"What was on it?" Holly asks me. Her tears have stopped now but she's still very vulnerable and delicate.

"The recordings showed that my wife had not just been going behind my back with the use of drugs but..." I let out a snigger of disgust, shaking my head. I can't believe I thought my Holly was anything like her, I should be ashamed of myself, and I am. "She had at least three different men in my house, dealers who were all on my father's payroll. They knew me. And even in the early years when I didn't have the balls of my brother, they knew I had changed and if I found out, their lives wouldn't be worth living. But that didn't stop them coming to my home to deliver her drugs when I wasn't at home, and it didn't stop them being seduced by her."

"Oh my God," I hear Holly gasp. "In your home with your sons in the house." She's shocked. Disgusted.

"Yes," I nod my head. "I watched over a months' worth of recordings that covered the boundaries of our home. The entrance, stairway and kitchen. Once she had been given her drugs, that's when they would have a couple of drinks, snort away and get it on in my fucking kitchen. They even used the staircase and the hallway. On one occasion I could see that one of my boys was sat on the landing,

Sebastian had seen everything."

"Fucking hell," Holly curses. She hardly ever swears, maybe a bloody hell or shit. She's angry.

Our eyes lock when I look up and I'm riddled with guilt for ever thinking this woman would hurt me in any way.

"I'm sorry, Holly," she nods her head at me, knowing why I am sorry.

"Carry on."

"She'd gone too far this time and I knew I had to put a stop to it. I wanted her out of our lives for good, I also needed to take care of the men she had invited into my home. That was easy, the following day I took care of them then when I knew she was able to come home from the hospital, I gave her an ultimatum. She went into rehab and then when she was clean, I would move her into a small apartment, or I would let our fathers deal with her."

"What would they have done?"

"My father would have killed her, no questions asked, and he would have probably tried to kill me for being weak and putting up with her. When she agreed to the little entrapment, she knew what it meant, being faithful to me and our family but it was kind of impossible for her. She was wild and couldn't give a shit about my father or her own who would have killed her."

"But you didn't let that happen," it's not a question. If nothing else I felt sorry for her. She had grown up with a father like mine, no wonder she had turned to drugs at a young age. She'd fallen for his manipulating ways and joined ranks with my father to trap me.

"No. I couldn't let that happen, so we fabricated what had happened. My mother came up with an idea to tell our fathers that she had been depressed since Daniel's birth and that she had gone to a clinic to recuperate, but it could take some time. With me being her husband, I had given instructions that she was only allowed my visitation until she improved."

"Would your father have gone to visit her?"

"No." I shake my head. "Her own father wouldn't have either, he was too busy with his own problems, but there was a chance one of her friends might. I didn't want them seeing her and them slipping up in front of someone that she was in a drugs clinic. Some people were only too eager to take back any information that might get them in my father's good books, and I wasn't about to let that happen.

She was in and out for a couple of years and then when she was clean, she settled in her little apartment. I set up a bank account for her, so she wasn't short of anything on the understanding she didn't come anywhere near our sons again. She agreed."

"How old was Sebastian when she overdosed?" Holly asks. I know she's not inexperienced when it comes to dealing with a parent who is addicted to drugs and the affects it can have on the children involved.

"He was nine. Nicholas was seven and Daniel was two."

"Poor boys," she says. "I know you tried to be the best dad you could be under the circumstances, and you are a devoted loving father. But you should have got them out of that horrible place sooner, Vlad."

"It wasn't for the want of not trying Holly. I was a young teenager when I became a father and a husband. I was thrown into a life that scared the shit out of me and it took me a long time to be able to deal with people that should have been locked up with the key thrown away. I had no other choice than to take on a role that no young man should ever have thrust upon him and I certainly wasn't going to let my sons fall into the same dark world my father had put his sons in." My tone is a little harsh which isn't directed at Holly, it's the situation we're in that is annoying the shit out of me.

"I know. I'm sorry, I didn't mean anything by what I said. I just feel for…"

I'm on my knees in front of my angel in a flash, taking her face in my hands. "You have no reason to apologise, sweetheart. None of this mess is your fault," I run my thumbs over her cheeks, wiping her tear stains away. Placing my forehead on hers I gaze into her sad, tired eyes.

"This is on me, Holly. You have done nothing wrong and I'm sorry with all my heart that I have made you feel this way." She places her hands on mine and nods her head, her eyes close as she leans into my hand. I hold my cheek to hers then kiss her softly before I break our connection. She wants to know the truth about my dead wife, so I need to carry on.

Sitting back down on the bathroom floor I wish I didn't have to tarnish my angel with my past, but it's the only way. To get to the root of my problem I need to let Holly see the torment my sons and I went through. I'm lucky that they were so young and that I'd talked to them over the years, getting them to open and discuss anything that troubled them. Because I'm sure they would have been as fucked up as me if they hadn't. I count myself very lucky that I have three grown up sons that will never have to do the things that I have done, and I know Lucas will grow up the same as his elder brothers.

"Natalia and I came to an agreement after her release from the clinic. She would live in the apartment and have no contact with our sons. She would no longer visit any of the clubs that were associated with my family and if she ever felt the need to resort back to drugs, she had to contact me. I would keep my side of the bargain and not let her ways get back to my father. She didn't need to work because of the money I was putting into her account every month. I knew she could easily slip back into taking drugs and I didn't want that for her that's why I told her to contact me if she couldn't cope." Holly listens carefully to every word I am saying but I can't read her. She's stopped playing with her hair, so I know she's no longer scared. Her elbow is leant on her knee and her hand is covering her mouth as she stares at me, her sapphire eyes that normally sparkle with so much life and love in them show nothing at all.

"Shall I continue?" she nods her head without breaking her stare.

"I didn't see anything of Natalia for years, I knew she was doing ok, I'd kept tabs on her for the first couple of years then stopped and focused on trying to bring the old man's business to an end. He was getting old and his men were wanting Sasha to take over. However, he wasn't about to let that happen, but he did pass over a lot of responsibility to him. Sasha and I were able to legalise the clubs and casinos my father had passed on without him knowing, it was big business and made a lot of money. What he didn't know wouldn't hurt him or anyone else. We struggled to get rid of the arms he dealt in because of who he was doing business with. We had managed to stop some a few years past without him knowing who it was that had informed the authorities. Although the names of the buyers were known to us, they seemed to evade justice just like my father.

My boys were getting older and were beginning to understand a lot more about the business I was in, frustration didn't come close to the way I was feeling. Unable to get them out and away from my father was very nearly killing me. At some point, I started hitting the bottle, going clubbing more often. I always made sure my sons were tucked up in bed when I left either the nanny or my mother to take care of them, and I was always home in the morning when they woke up. But I needed a release. Getting drunk and taking a woman back to a hotel became a regular occurrence."

"The same thing you did for twelve years here in England," she reminds me. She needn't have bothered. I'm more than aware of my actions and why.

"Yes," I agree. "I've never claimed to be a saint, Holly, but I never went with another woman while Natalia and I were together." I'm not sure if she believes me as she isn't giving anything away to how she is feeling, but she's listening, so I continue.

"One evening after I'd spent some quality time with my sons, I decided to hit the clubs. Once they were in bed, I headed out to meet Sasha and some of the men that were under him; he had his own men who he knew he could trust. We stopped at a couple of bars before venturing onto one of the casinos. I'd got bored and wanted to let my hair down, so I told them I would meet them at The Spinning Wheel, one of my preferred clubs. I went into the lounge there and sat watching the crowd while I downed more than my fair share of brandy. I don't remember getting home but when I woke the following morning, I was shocked beyond belief.

I knew I wasn't alone which alarmed me, I never brought a woman home. The scent of Jimmy Choo lingered in the air and all over my skin. Stretched out with her hand on my chest lay my wife, Natalia, as naked as the day she was born and so was I."

"Wow," Holly lets out a sarcastic chuckle and shocks me that she could find any of this amusing.

"Sweetheart, it was anything but funny."

"Isn't it? Oh, I think you will find that using women and booze to get you through, you were always going to find yourself in some trouble."

"I didn't use women. They wanted the same thing as I did, Holly."

"Whatever," she spits out and turns her head, so she doesn't have to look at me. A little childish but I don't say anything. "Then what happened?" she asks as she rolls her eyes at me. I don't know if I'm boring her or whether she expected to hear that Natalia ended back in my bed.

"I asked her to leave before the boys got up and told her that what had happened would not be happening again. She left, only to come back five weeks later to inform me I was going to be a father again." Holly doesn't speak, she just nods her head at the surprise Natalia hit me with.

"I had no other choice but to take her back. She was carrying my son and I wanted to keep an eye on her until she had given birth. The boys were wary of her and so was I. But she was adamant that she hadn't gone back to her old ways of drinking and drugs…"

"Did you ever take drugs while you were living in Russia?" Holly asks, cutting in.

"No. Never. I did all I could to help her get off them and to stop my father from dealing in them. I put my life on the line on numerous occasions getting rid of the middleman." I move towards Holly and lift her chin; I look her straight in the eye. "I have seen first-hand what they can do to people, the hurt it causes to families when loved ones use them. I ploughed money in to shelters for addicts because I felt guilty that it was my father that supplied the main bulk of the drugs that were coming into the city. My father had damaged too many lives including my mother's, Sasha's and mine; he needed stopping."

"How did Natalia crash the car?" Holly asks as she stretches out her legs and shifts side to side on her bum. I'm sure she's feeling uncomfortable; we've been sat here for well over an hour. She shivers a little and wraps her arms around herself. Getting up from the bathroom floor I wander into the living room to retrieve the blanket Holly had used earlier. Returning to Holly, I offer her the blanket, she takes it from me, and I sit next to her on the cold floor.

"Natalia slept in one of the spare rooms and I made sure I went to all her hospital and doctor's appointments. We knew that we were having another boy and he was a good size at the twenty weeks scan.

I was happy that she had kept to her word and laid off the drink and drugs, so I lightened up a bit on keeping tabs on her. Daniel seemed happy his mum was home but Sebastian and Nicholas not so much. They had heard and seen far too much of her wicked wild ways and understood that she had never really wanted anything to do with them.

When she was seven months, I noticed she was getting snappy with Daniel and the sarcasm she had always thrown at me was now directed at Sebastian and Nicholas. I spoke with her calmly, understanding that her hormones would be all mixed up, but my concern fell on deaf ears. The way she spoke and behaved had me believing she was using again. I couldn't prove it and I never mentioned my suspicions too her.

Having her every move out of the home watched was the only way I would find out, so I assigned Pete to the job. He had been one of Sasha closest friends within my father's firm, they had known each other a long time and his loyalties lied with Sasha. He'd shown over the years that whatever happened within the firm he would stand alongside Sasha and me and I trusted him to stay on task. They were a lot of men that worked for my father that hated him just as much as his sons did, they too had shown that they supported Sasha, but Pete was the one who would get the job done without my father knowing.

That afternoon my suspicions were verified when he telephoned me to let me know she had met up with one of the local dealers, he had videoed the exchange of the drugs on his phone, so I had proof when I confronted her." My blood pressure starts to rise when I think back to that afternoon, knowing she had scored a hit while she was seven months pregnant with our son. It cemented the truth that this woman who had borne three children and was in her last trimester with her fourth, only cared about herself. Not once had she ever put them first.

Hands shaking, I try to swallow the lump that blocks my throat when the memory of that late afternoon comes flooding back, slapping me in the chest with the weight of the most torrential tidal wave. I struggle to breath.

Chapter 11

Vlad

"I was raging with the thought that she was putting our unborn child in danger and when Pete let me know that she seemed to be on her way back home, I jumped in my car to meet her there. I was at the other side of town and knew I would have to tackle the busy traffic. I prayed that this was her first relapse while she was carrying Lucas and if I could get home quick, I might be in time to stop her from taking it." I glance at Holly and I can see she's fighting back the tears that want to flow. No matter how fucked up this situation is, she cares. Cares for my boys, feels for the hurt they had endured through no fault of their own.

"When I arrived home, she wasn't there. My mother was with the boys, so I asked her to take them out into the back garden while I waited for Natalia. I paced the floor like a fucking mad man, it had taken me thirty-five minutes to get to my house and from what Pete had said she had been only fifteen minutes away. I called and called him, but he didn't answer, so I called Natalia, she didn't answer either. Twenty minutes later Pete called me back. Natalia's car had gone through a red light and she had been hit side on by a van. He had waited around for the emergency services, the firemen had to cut the car open to get her out. But she was alive and on her way to the hospital.

Sasha met me at the hospital, and we were told to wait as the doctors were with her. We waited three hours then when the doctor came to speak to me, I was informed that they had been some complications due to the crash they had had to deliver Lucas through caesarean section. They had taken him to the neo-natal unit and the next few days would be crucial to him surviving..." Holly takes my hand as I choke out the last word. The warmth that always surrounds her travels through me. That, and knowing my son survived gives me the strength to carry on.

"He asked me what I knew about my wife's drug taking. I told him what I knew and that I thought she had been clean while she was carrying Lucas and only suspected in the last few days that something was wrong. Only I was wrong because my little boy was addicted to them too and he was fighting for his life. I broke down there in front of Sasha and the doctor. This huge mob boss' son, covered in tattoos and scars. Reminders of how many men I had killed. Reminders of how many times I had been foolish enough to listen to him and her and fall for their lies and manipulating ways. Reminders how I had rose from a scared young teenager and grown into a ruthless killer that would not bow down to anyone except him. Because I knew he would rope my boys into the same world if I didn't fight to bring him down. Well in that moment I was no stronger than my baby and I cried like one too and I didn't fucking care who was there. My father; the devil himself could have walked through the door and I wouldn't have cared in fact I would have probably killed him with my bare hands.

Eventually, I pulled myself together and a nurse escorted me to see my son. Sasha waited outside the ward while I went in. The room was dark with just a few nurses and one doctor working in there. I was led to a glass incubator where Lucas' premature body was lying. There was so much machinery and wires trying to keep him alive. Tubes running in and out of his tiny body, I was sure he wouldn't survive the night. The noise of the machines, beeping and pumping will stay with me forever. The nurse brought me a chair which I was glad of because my legs felt as if they couldn't carry my weight. It felt as if I had sat watching his still body for hours, but I don't think it was. Tears flowed freely as I prayed for forgiveness for the ugly crimes I had committed. It was never my choice to take the lives I did, and this was my penance, to watch my son die. I prayed to god to let him live; that this little man was innocent in the world of violence and drugs.

I would have given my life then and there for his survival, knowing Sasha would fight for what I wanted if I wasn't around and take care of my sons.

I wanted to cradle him in my arms, hold him and tell him how much he was loved. There were two tiny holes in the incubator, there was no way my large hands would fit in without causing some damage, so I put my fingers in. His little hands were curled into fists and I was able to reach them with my finger. I stoked his knuckles and spoke to him. I described his three brothers to him, Sebastian the big brother who would protect him. Nicholas the comedian who would have him laughing until his sides split and Daniel the little hugger, he would always make him feel loved.

I told him he had to fight because I couldn't go home and tell them their little brother wasn't coming home." Holly sniffles, stopping me from going on. I feel as if I've been reliving this nightmare all evening, I need a rest from it and from the tears that fill Holly's eyes, I think she does too. Standing from the cold marble floor, I put my hand out for Holly to take, she doesn't delay in getting to her feet.

"I'll make a coffee while you freshen up," she nods her head and blows her nose on the tissue she has just picked up. Before I turn to walk out of the bathroom door, she places her hand on my chest. "Whatever you have done…" she breathes through her nose and swallows trying to combat her emotions. "You are a loving, caring father and have a good heart," putting my hand on hers, I pull hers to my lips and brush them across her knuckles then I head out of the bathroom, needing a stiff drink.

When I've made Holly a coffee, I pour myself a large brandy and a small one. I'm sure it will help her with the strain that this night as put on us both.

Holly chooses to sit opposite me when she comes in the living room from the bathroom, she looks anything but freshened up. Her eyes are bloodshot and still watery, her lips pressed together. When she thanks me for her drink it's a choked-out whisper.

She downs the brandy in one, shivering as the liquid hits the spot then she picks up her coffee.

The pain in me for this whole fucked up situation has left me with a dull ache in my chest. Seeing Holly hurting for my crimes and reliving the years I would sooner forget has left its mark. However, I must carry on for Holly and for my sons. I want to take her in my arms and hold her tight; letting her know that we will be ok, but I don't think we will be. She'll forgive me for my outburst last month, I know that. She'd already told me that but unfolding the dark life I had come from will stop her from wanting to be with me. Consequently, this will leave us to hurt for the rest of our lives because she has shown time after time that her love for me is as strong as mine is for her.

I play with the empty glass and let out a heartfelt sigh as I shift forward in my seat, resting my elbows on my knees. Holly lifts her eyes to me waiting for me to continue.

"I'd been there for quite a while when a nurse advised me to go stretch my legs and get a drink. Not wanting to leave my little boy on his own, I asked her if she would stay with him until I got back. She nodded, squeezing my shoulder and her warm smile told me she would. I stroked Lucas' knuckles again while I spoke softly to him, letting him know I wouldn't be long and in that moment, I knew God had listened to me. I watched my baby's finger move. It was slight, but it was there. I watched his chest rise and fall with the help of the respiratory machine. Then a flicker of his eyelid and I knew he would fight to live. With the help of doctors and nurses he would survive.

I strode out of the ward, heading for the carpark where Sasha was having a cigar. My heart had swelled with the hope that my boy was strong enough, so I joined Sasha in celebrating Lucas' birth by indulging in one of his cigars. Although I didn't want to, Sasha persuaded me to visit Natalia to see how she was doing. According to the doctors she was doing much better than our son," my tone bitter. Holly worries her bottom lip between her thumb and finger, the frown on her beautiful face and the shake of her head lets me know she too is disgusted with the way Natalia behaved.

"Deep in thought with what I would say to her, I bumped into a man as I was entering the lift to her floor; he was just exiting it. I thought I recognised him, but I didn't pay it any attention. Wanting to let her know that I was divorcing her and that she was on her own from that moment on had me ignoring anything around me. Once I had said what I wanted to say, I would make my way back to Lucas.

Arriving at her room door, I placed my hand on the handle and took a few calming breaths; not wanting to go in all guns blazing. I would tell her calmly then just leave. But I never entered the room.

I happened to glance in the small window on the door just to make sure I had the right room, that's when I saw Natalia with a syringe in her hand." Rubbing my hands up and down my face, I stand and walk to the window, trying to calm the blood in me that wants to erupt with rage. "She had just caused a crash, causing her to go into early labour with our child because of her drug addiction…" I spit out, pausing for a minute to get my breathing in order then I sit back down and watch Holly who is still pulling at her bottom lip.

"She knew our baby was fighting for his life, but she still chose that shit over him." I shake my head at the thought. "I let go of the door handle and walked away. There was a coffee machine halfway down the corridor, so I stopped to get a drink. Just as I finished putting in the last coin, alarms sounded around me. I retrieved my drink and within seconds the hallway was overrun with nurses and doctors. I watched them enter my wife's room with the crash machine and I never felt a thing." Holly just stares at me. There's no shock on her face at what I've just told her, she just stares at me.

"I sat on the chair at the side of the machine while the medical team did their thing and I sipped my tea. After about half an hour one of the doctors approached me, to let me know they couldn't save her that she had died.

I felt nothing. It was like he had just told me that a total stranger had died. Someone I didn't know. And… in all fairness, I don't think I did really know her, so I shook his hand and walked away back to my son." I glance at Holly and she still hasn't moved or said anything. She sits there as if she's been struck dumb and I'm starting to worry about her. "Holly." She doesn't answer. Slowly, I get up and go to her.

Crouching down in front of her, I put my hand on the settee at the side of her. "Holly say something." My voice is a whisper, but she still doesn't speak or move.

"Holly, sweetheart. Are you ok?" I ask placing my hand on hers.

She flinches at my touch and I watch her pale face turn an angry red as her nostrils flare at me.

"Am I ok?" her eyes glare at me, then she's up out of her seat. "Do I look bloody ok?" she seethes, pointing at her chest. I know what I have divulged tonight is a lot to comprehend and understand, half the time I can't believe my boys and I lived through it. Revealing my darkest secrets to Holly has caused me distress, so I understand what she must be feeling.

"How dare you?" Whack!

She slogs me one right across the face. I deserve it, so I don't stop her.

Slap!

"You bastard!" she screeches at me when she slaps me again. "How dare you compare me to her!" Slap! This time it's a little harder and has me rocking back from my crouching position. I manage to scramble to my feet but I'm not quick enough to move out of her way. "All I've ever done..." Slap! "Is love you and your sons since the first night I met you..." Slap! Her slaps are coming thick and fast and I understand why she wants to get out this frustration she has because I did insult her when I compared her to Natalia. My angel is nothing like her and I could kick myself for saying it. But, if I don't stop her, she will end up hurting her hands. I let her get one more in at me then I envelope her in my arms, cradling her into my chest. "I loved you and you brought me into this cruel world you came from. How could you?" she cries, sobbing into my chest.

"I'm sorry, Holly," I breath into her hair, but she tries to wiggle out of my hold. "Holly stop this you will hurt yourself," I pull her closer, but she manages to pull one arm free and socks me in the nose. "Fuck," I curse because it fucking hurt. For a small woman she's got one hell of a punch. I also witnessed Holly grimace and shake her fist, so I know she is hurt.

Taking her hand in mine I examine it. One of her knuckles is red and swollen and will probably be sore for a few days.

She's still fighting my hold when I try and walk us both to the icemaker, so I pick her up gently and carry her to it. She slaps my chest with her free hand when I go to wipe the fluid that is running down my nose. Yes, it's bleeding. "Holly you can hit me all day long and I won't feel it, but you will," I say as I sit her on the worktop. "Now stay put while I get some ice for your hand," my tone firm, challenging her not to defy me on this. To my surprise she stays there while I pick up some tissue for the blood trickling down my nose and wrap some ice in a hand towel for her knuckle.

"I'm sorry Holly, you know that," I tell her as I place the towel on her hand. "I know I shouldn't have said it. I know now how you must feel after hearing all I have had to say, so I will say it again, I should have never compared you to her. You are caring and loving. Beautiful inside as well as on the outside." I want to touch her, but I dare not chance riling her up again. "I am lucky to have had you in my life and so are my sons." Her head is hung down and I chance her wrath by lifting her chin, wanting to see her eyes. "Please forgive me Holly for my hurtful words, I will always hate myself for them."

Moving away from Holly to give her a bit of space, I stride into the bedroom and out onto the balcony. The nights are becoming cooler now and I welcome the temperature change. Trying to clear my head of the hurt and anger I just witnessed from the woman who means the world to me. After a few deep breaths, I make my way back inside, finding Holly sat on the settee. The towel still wrapped around her hand and a glass of wine in her other, she takes a large mouthful as I sit opposite her.

We don't speak for what seems like a lifetime, but I don't push it. I will wait until she is ready to listen to the rest of my story. Sitting back against the settee, I'm almost astonished that she wants to sit in the same room. I'd have bet my life that she would have asked me to drop her off home or even phoned one of her friends to come and get her. Finishing her drink, she places the empty glass on the table. Chewing on her fingernail, her rimmed red eyes close then flicker open. She lets out a soft sigh as she lays her head back on the soft cushion of the settee. She's exhausted. Convinced she's nodded off, I'm just about to stand with the thought of either carrying her to bed or covering her up when she lifts her head and rubs her temples. Remembering she suffers with bouts of migraines, I curse, hoping I haven't caused the start of one. "Do you need a painkiller?" I ask, concerned.

"No," she murmurs, shaking her head. "Just tired," her yawn verifies this. She picks up one of the cushions and holds it against her, for comfort, I think. Again, I curse because it's me she would normally hold close against her.

"Do you want to leave it until tomorrow, Holly? You look shattered."

She shakes her head again, "No, let's get it over and done with tonight."

"Holly it's turned two o'clock in the morning, you're drained. Have some sleep and we can carry on in the morning," I plead.

"I'm fine. Just continue; that's what we came here for." She waves her arm around the room, the hurt in her voice apparent. I understand why. I had booked this same suite for a romantic weekend over a month ago. Some time alone just Holly and I sharing a four-poster bed, sinking into the steaming bubble bath after we had made love for hours. Laying in until midday without being disturbed except for room service. Wandering round the grounds hand in hand like two love-struck teenagers and delighting in the amenities this place has to offer. Unfortunately, we never made it here due to my stupidity.

I take my seat, wanting to get this torture over and done with. The quicker I get the rest out the better, then we can move on. Where that will be who knows. She knows the worst now and I'm sure she will have more questions to ask, that's if she doesn't decide to leave.

"The next three or four weeks were rough. Explaining to my boys that their mother had died and that their baby brother might not make it through the next couple of days, almost broke me. However, Sebastian and Nicholas took the news better than I thought they would and Daniel… He was quiet as if he had not understood what I had told him, and he probably didn't he was only nine.

After her funeral we had lengthy talks about our lives. I had promised them that I would not work for my father again and fingers crossed once Lucas was able to leave the hospital we would travel for a little while.

Anyway, like I said the first three or four weeks were hard, but we coped. I hadn't seen anything of my father; not that I wanted to, but I knew it wouldn't be long before he reared his ugly head. He wasn't aware I would not be returning to his firm; I think he assumed I was just taking some time off with my sons.

Most of the time we would be at the hospital. The boys had taken some time off from school, I didn't think it would do them any harm even though Natalia was never a mother to them they still needed some time to grieve.

Lucas was becoming stronger week by week and we found ourselves not wanting to leave him alone. He had more teddy bears around his cot that the boys had bought him, it was a struggle to get near him. One morning, Daniel woke up with a stomach ache which meant he would not be able to come to the hospital. I telephoned my mother to come and sit with him; he got upset because he didn't want to be left behind. My mother couldn't make it until dinnertime, so Sebastian and Nicholas offered to stay at home with him until their grandmother arrived. I was happy with this because they would only be alone for an hour. I arranged to call back and collect them later in the afternoon and they were happy with that. I asked Sebastian to keep his phone on, so I could check in with them and I went off to the hospital. I left at eleven and returned home at one thirty. I hadn't been able to call Sebastian as the doctors were going through Lucas' progress with me and what their next steps would be. When I returned home my mother wasn't there and Sebastian and Nicholas were sitting in the kitchen, their expressions worried." My head falls into my hands, remembering how I thought they would be ok without me. Safe at home with their grandmother for a couple of hours. We hadn't been separated for nearly four weeks; this being the first and that's when he made his move.

"My mother didn't come to my home to sit with them, my father did," my tone angry. I try to rein it in a bit knowing it will upset Holly even more. "He had persuaded her to stay at home and he would visit his grandsons as he hadn't seen them since before Natalia's funeral.

Sebastian was reluctant to tell me what was bothering him and became very distressed when I continued to ask him. Once they had told me about my father visiting, I knew he had done or said something to upset him. Although Sebastian didn't want to say, Nicholas was only too willing.

I had to hold myself back from storming out of the house, finding my father and killing him with my bare hands for his comments to Sebastian." I blow out a breath as Holly cringes at my words. She rubs the middle of her forehead with her fingers and I'm sure she's had enough of this night, so I decide not to prolong this any longer.

"According to Nicholas, their grandfather turned up not long after I left to visit Lucas. He chatted with them for a little while then asked Nicholas to check on Daniel who was in his bedroom. With him out of the way, he told Sebastian he was growing into a fine young man and would be an excellent addition to his firm. Once Nicholas had started telling me, Sebastian chose to join in. He knew what my reaction would be that's why he was averse to telling me.

I found out from them that he wanted both Sebastian and Nicholas to join him and had even brought out a gun in front of them. He told them he would show them how to use it to a standard that would make everyone else envious of them. He made it out that it was a great life that would make them rich and be able to have many men working for them. Oh, and I would never have to know. The man was deranged and was attempting to recruit my sons into the world I had tried so hard to keep them from. I was never able to hide certain things from them, they weren't stupid, but they would never have to do what I had done.

Finding out what he had tried to do left me in no doubt what I had to do. When my boys had refused him, he told them they were weak, like me. I don't think they realised just how strong they were by refusing his offer and I was so proud of them. My sons were his heir and he wanted them with him but if they stood together then they were stronger than they knew. He had trapped Sasha to carry on working for him by threating to kill our mother and he trapped me as soon as he introduced Natalia to me. He walked away from them telling them that one day they would be living with him then they wouldn't have a choice. That threat said it all. He wanted my sons and the only way he could get them under his roof was if I was out of the way." Holly lets out a yelp as if she's in pain, she's just realised what my father's intentions were.

"To say I was angry was an understatement, but I could not let my boys see what I was going through. Once they had settled down, we ate and got ready for our late afternoon visit to the hospital. Daniel felt much better, so the four of us went together. Before we set off, I had telephoned Sasha, so he was aware of my father's intentions and to let him know I would meet the devil head on. He pleaded with me to wait and not do anything stupid, my words had him cursing before I put the phone down. My only choice was to end him that night. I had tried bringing down his empire but struggled over the years, now he had made it more personal. He'd done the one thing I always knew he would, and I couldn't allow that. Trying to recruit my sons cut deeper than a knife and I would make sure that he would be last life my knife took.

When we arrived on the ward where Lucas was, I spun my sons a lie and told them the doctor needed to speak with me on how their brother was doing. They knew to be quiet and if they were hungry or needed a drink, they were able to visit the family room which had a drinks machine, and a machine where they could grab a snack. The TV wasn't up to much but at least there was one in there.

No sooner had I got in my car, I drove like the wind to my father's home, catching the attention of a couple of guards as my car screeched to a holt in the grounds of what I once called home. My father, always one step ahead, knew I would find out what he had said and that I would turn up. The guards must have been ordered not to stop me from entering the house because they let me storm in without a question. His plan to get me there had worked.

I didn't sneak round corners to his office, I was on a mission and nothing or no one was going to stop me. Sergei and some other bodyguard were stood chatting outside the office door when I approached it. Without a care I took out my gun, hitting the big guy straight between the eyes, he went down like a ton of bricks and while the new guy struggled with Sergei's weight on his feet he fumbled with his gun. In a heartbeat he was lying next him. Did I feel anything for killing a man I'd known most of my life? No." I shake my head and watch Holly cover her mouth with her hands as a lone tear slips down her face. I don't go to her because I can't. I don't think she wants my comfort anyway. How could she? A man who has taken many lives, no matter what the reason, I had no right. I need to finish what I have to say then let her go.

"My father's office door flew open before I had chance to put my hand on the handle and there stood the man who had damaged so many lives. He grinned at me with such arrogance, my reaction to wipe that smug look off his face was swift. I had disarmed him of his weapon and had him shoved back into his office before he had time to call out for any of his staff. For the first time in my life I witnessed fear in his cold eyes. He had no protection and he knew he would not be quick enough to get to his phone to call for help. He was getting older and his game was up. He knew it and so did I.

But..." I sigh and blow out a breath, remembering how he still taunted me. Wanting to catch me off guard. "He spat words at me telling me I was weak. How I had made my brother Sasha weak by being born. How he was destined to set up a firm in America and run things from there but because of me Sasha wouldn't leave. I was so angry. I knew his words were lies, but I still let them seep into me. Choking me like a coiled snake around my neck. Guilt pulling tighter and tighter, strangling me with the thought that I had held Sasha back. With one powerful kick, I had sent my father flying over his desk. Picking him up and throwing him in his chair I punched him in the face, just once, the blood from his lip trickled into his mouth.

He laughed and laughed, spitting the blood at me when I leaned over him. I actually think he either wanted me to kill him or to see if I had it in me to try because his next words should have had him dying by my hands."

"You didn't kill him?" Holly asks, her soft voice stopping me. My hands are held tightly together, and my focus is on them, but I raise my head to see Holly hanging on to my every word.

"No," I shake my head. "He told me I should have never been born. That fathering a son who trembled when he held a gun at thirteen, who should have had his first kill then but embarrassed him by crying like a baby, disgusted him. He cursed at me. Angry with me for not wanting to be part of his organisation. Then his next words shocked me to my core. He laughed when he told me about the night I was conceived. How my mother screamed at him to stop. How he took what he wanted without one ounce of guilt. How she learnt quickly her place in his home. I... staggered back from him not wanting to believe my father had raped my mother and I was the product." I wipe the wetness from my eyes not one bit embarrassed that Holly is watching me.

"I'm sorry," I feel her gentle hand on mine and feel her warmth as she sits at the side of me.

"Don't be," I give her a warm smile. "It happened a long time ago."

"How did he die?"

"When I staggered back, I toppled over one of the chairs behind me. My father saw his chance and tried to get to his gun. He wouldn't have had time to reach it but that didn't stop him from trying. Suddenly, I was aware there was more than me and him in the room. Sasha kicked his gun out of the way and directed him to sit in his chair. Calmly, he poured three drinks from my father's decanter. He offered one to me then passed one to our father and had the other himself. I downed mine in one while my father sipped at his.

He finished it, put his glass on his desk then minutes later his head fell onto the desk and he was dead. Sasha had dissolved something into his drink and to this day I still don't know what it was. According to Sasha, it brought on a heart attack without being traced."

"Wow," Holly says while still holding my hand. I'm not sure what she is thinking, her expression gives nothing away, so I don't speak. I wait to see if she as any questions and when she stands, I'm surprised when she walks over to the table and pours two large brandies. She finishes hers quickly, shuddering when she does then she turns to me. "I'm going to bed, please don't follow me."

Chapter 12

Holly

Smudged mascara and bloodshot eyes never look good on a woman, and I'm sure that's what I will see in the bathroom mirror as soon as I get up. Well that's if I can prise them open. They seem to be stuck together and I'm having to rub at them to rid the sticky substance that I know is due to all the crying I have done and the lack of sleep.

Eventually, when I came to bed, exhausted with what I had learnt about Vlad's life, I couldn't sleep. As much as I tried, I could not stop his words from popping in and out of my head. A few hours later and still awake, I heard him come into the bedroom, so I faked I was asleep. Who knew it would be so hard, trying to lie there still while peeking out of one eye to see what he was doing?

I watched him step out onto the balcony with a drink in his hand then half an hour later he came back in. He stripped down to his boxers, retrieved a throw over from the other room and got himself comfy on the bedroom chair. I felt guilty that his large frame was sleeping on a chair, thinking he would ache in the morning. Out of all the nights I had slept alone, last night was the one night I needed him to comfort me. Hold me in his strong arms, pulling me into his chest where I felt safe. Telling me everything would be ok, and we would get through this together.

I'm not naïve enough not to know what drugs can do to people, or how greedy and violent people can become when they want something. But what I became aware of last night, the world Vlad came from and what he had to do to survive, confirms I'm out of my league with this.

Anyone in their right mind would have left last night and not looked back, maybe would have not given him another second of their time when he erupted in the club that night. Staying away from him and his family would have been the right thing to do. Letting my aching heart heal over time.

I knew the night I met him that he held a darkness in those eyes of his. Something so overpowering I was helpless under his stare. Amongst the dark intensity was a vulnerability that no one else saw. Someone lonely with lots of love to give and a side of fun. A warning if I took what he was offering it was for keeps. I held his heart. And, he held mine. Only I don't think he expected his past, the ruthlessness of his father and the games his wife played, to bring out a side to him he had not seen before.

Jealousy can be a vile thing and cause a man or woman to become someone they don't recognise. Envy and hate for anyone or anything that causes them to think someone they love will be taken from them. The hurt and rage that is felt can become so uncontrollable that they react without thought. In Vlad's case it was brought on by the need to protect me and never share. The merry dance and hurt his wife and father had put him through had left its mark.

Unable to trust fully. I was his and no man had the right to touch. Even though I showered him with love and proved how much his family meant, he always believed someone would try and take me away from him and I would leave him. My heart aches for this larger than life man who has been through so much; no matter what he has done, to protect his family. Keeping his heart closed off from the love of a good woman for so long then when he does open it, it causes so much pain and hurt.

I hear him enter the room from the balcony. I don't know how long he has been out there; I don't even know what time it is. I try not to move, pretending to still be asleep. With one eye closed and the other slightly covered with the bed sheets, I can make him out. He's freshly showered and shirtless. He's wearing a well fitted pair of jeans, feet bare and he looks yummy. Even with the tattoos that show his past he's still one hell of a man. The muscles in his back swell when he reaches to pick up his bag and his powerful arms have me letting out a little sigh. Yes. Even with his history out in the open he still affects me. As if he's heard me, he turns to look at me. Quickly, I close my eyes, not ready to discuss what happens next. I feel the bed dip, so I know he's sat on it then I feel his hand on my covered hip. He doesn't linger long before he gets up and I hear him leave the room.

Needing to pee, I make a quick dash for the bathroom. Once I've finished, I jump in the shower with thoughts of Vlad circling like sharks around my head. My heart and my head are at war and have been since last night. I still love him; that's for sure. My heart can't shut him out that quickly, if ever, but my brain tells me to leave. The sensible person in me, the Christian girl that was brought up to know right from wrong and always abide by the law, knows what he has done is so wrong and to get myself out of here now. Only, I was brought up to forgive and to remember people can change. Knowing why he killed those men has confused me because I'm sure most people would kill for their children's safety. Like I said at war.

When I'm back in the bedroom, I notice the balcony door open. I hear movement and know Vlad is out there. The sky is bright, and it looks like it will be a sunny day. I dress with speed then make my way out onto the balcony.

There's a pot of coffee and a continental breakfast on the table and my stomach rumbles on cue. Taking a seat, Vlad turns from looking out over the hotel grounds. "Morning," the low rumble of his voice calls to me.

"Morning," I greet, not sure of what else to say.

"I ordered coffee and a light breakfast, I wasn't sure how hungry you would be," always so caring towards me.

I pour myself coffee and offer him a refill. He accepts then I pick up a croissant. I pick at it as Vlad turns to watch the activities in the grounds. "I'll drop you off home once you have eaten or I can ring Sebastian to collect you, if you prefer," his words sound pained as if he doesn't want to let me go. He probably thinks that once I leave, he will never see me again.

I don't answer him. I'm thinking about home. Home; what is

there for me? Just rooms with no love in them. A few months ago, my tiny apartment was my home then I met the man standing in front of me. Now he's my home. Him and his family.

"It's a beautiful view," I break our silence.

"Yes, it is," he turns to me, taking a seat on the opposite chair. "Am I phoning Sebastian?" he asks as he picks up a strawberry and pops it in his mouth. I'm drawn to his kissable lips and how they make me feel. "If you want him to take you home, we need to give him time to get here," his dark blue eyes capture me, trapping me in the love that oozes from them.

I don't want to go home, leave without him. Not today anyway. I want to stay, exploring all that this magnificent place has to offer with my magnificent man. It sounds stupid, I know, but my man has a huge heart with a lot of love to give. I've seen it on many occasions. With his family, nothing comes close to the love he has for them except our love. He shows me time after time that I hold his heart in my hands and that he would do anything for me. And I him. That's why I've decided to stay.

Today we will be the couple that has come here for a romantic evening. Taking in the grounds and history of this place through the day, then, eat in one of its exquisite restaurants. We will sip cocktails in the lounge while listening to the piano player. As the darkness descends, we will venture outside to watch the walls light up. Lastly, we will retire to our room where Vlad will make love to me in that four-poster bed. "Holly," Vlad says, bringing me out of my thoughts. "Are you ok?"

Aw don't ask me that because really, I'm not, but for today I will be. I'll put aside everything I have learnt about him and cope. I nod my head, "I don't want to go home," I murmur.

"What?" he shifts his chair closer to me. Shock covering his face. I put my half-eaten croissant on the plate then take his hand that nervously plays with his coffee cup.

"I said, I don't want to go home. Not today anyway."

"You don't?"

"No," I shake my head. He looks down at our hands that are now joined together, and he gives me that cheeky smirk that often has me throwing myself at him.

"We can stay. I booked this suite until tomorrow. So, if that's what you want. I… assume you mean both of us?" he questions, feeling a little unsure, he raises an eyebrow and tilts his head.

"Yes, I would like that," I tell him. He nods his head and I can see the cog wheel going around, him thinking of what we could do first. I know he will be chewing at the bit to hold me in his arms and breath in my scent, so I put him out of his misery. Standing, I walk round to where he is sat, placing myself on his lap.

My arms wrap around him as I bury my head into his chest. His lips attach themselves to the back of my neck and he inhales deeply and that's how we stay for a good few minutes. When we unwrap from each other, I place my hands on his cheeks and gaze into his eyes. "Vlad, I want to remember today because I'm not sure what tomorrow will bring." I wait for him to catch on with what I mean. It doesn't take long. He nods with the acknowledgement of what I mean then takes my breath away with a kiss so profound, I almost pass out with the intensity. When we break apart, there's that familiar spark in his eyes that has been missing since we arrived in this room last night and the cheeky grin on his face lets me know I will remember today for a long time to come.

It's one thirty by the time we make it to the gardens and the sun is burning hot. Taking my hand, Vlad leads us to the maze passing a couple of sculptures of old kings and queens that visited here centuries ago. There's a group of people listening to a guide educating them on the history of this famous castle as they move along, we decide to join them on their tour.

We learn about the family who owned it for centuries and that it was mentioned in the Doomsday book. Ron the guide informs us that in the thirteenth century it was largely damaged due to a fire after being attacked but re-built some years later. Many battles were fought here and the surrounding areas along with visits and stop overs by Monarchy. Vlad soaks up all the information as we both act like Japanese tourists. I can't help but chuckle at the amount of questions he asks poor old Ron, who looks old enough to have been around during one of the battles.

Eventually, we detach ourselves from the group and opt to walk one of the trails that run through the beautiful countryside. We're not dressed for a long hike, so only venture halfway then make our way back to take in the rest of the grounds.

The afternoon has whizzed by when we realise we haven't eaten since the light breakfast earlier in the day. We glance at some of the artwork and tapestries that speak of life and death of the families that once called this place home as we make our way to grab a sandwich and coffee.

Throughout the day, Vlad's attentiveness has held no bounds. A perfect gentleman with a side ordering of flirty fun sums him up and I love it. He's opened doors, pulled out chairs and always given me the choice of where in the hotel we would visit. I have had his mischievous smile when he's stole sly kisses whenever I have sat down, he would press his lips on the top of my head or the side of my neck. Every time I stepped through a door before him, his hand would either be on my lower back or slip down until it settled perfectly on my bottom. When I tried to give him the slip while we were strolling around the maze, I was growled at then thrown over his shoulder. His hand landed lightly across my bottom which caused an elderly lady to tut at us when I let out a little squeal. Her husband had the cheek to laugh and nod his head with approval at Vlad.

Giving him a questioning eye to some of his flirtish ways would have him throwing that naughty wink at me. He knows what he is doing and so do I. One of his hands has never left my person since I told him we would stay another night and he's making every minute count.

Vlad is more than aware what his feather-like touches do to me and those fingers are working their magic of igniting the flame within. The low tone and Russian seductive words that he thinks I don't know the meaning of have now set the flame alight.

The restaurant we chose to eat in was The Guardsman, it serves Italian cuisine which we both enjoy. After devouring the special, brown shrimp and artichoke tagliatelle followed by vanilla panna cotta served with raspberry sauce, we make our way to the cocktail lounge.

Sipping our cocktails and listening to the soft melody of the piano, I try to bat tomorrow out of my mind and focus on the rest of the evening.

Couples hold each other on the small dance floor, swaying in time to the music while others chat and laugh as they taste each other's florescent drinks. All the while Vlad keeps my hand in his, stroking his thumb over my knuckles. When he stands, he never lets go of me and I find myself standing with him. He leads me on to a small area of the dance floor where he takes me in his arms.

He holds me like his life depends on it and I clutch him tight to me so there's not an inch of room between us. There's no gyrating of hips or hands touching and feeling their way around our bodies like usual when we dance. It's just him and me breathing in the scent of each other, keeping the hurt at bay. Because when we hurt the emotions we feel can become too deep to comprehend that we find that the one who caused the pain is the only one who can take it away.

The music ends but we don't make our way back to our table. No.

Desire sweeps through like a thief in the night not caring what or who it harms and within minutes we're breaking through our suite door. I don't have time to kick off my shoes before Vlad has me in his arms devouring my mouth, backing me up until we're stood in the bedroom. Once he's kissed the hell out of me, leaving me dizzy and dazed, his dark eyes roam up and down my body. "Strip for me, angel," there's no argument from me, this dominant side of him drives me wild and I do as he commands.

Stepping back slowly from him, my eyes never leaving his, I leisurely untie the wrap round dress I'm wearing. I don't have much to take off before I'm naked, so I play it out wanting to bring out the animal in this beast of a man. I let the ties drop to the sides, the dress opens revealing me stood in my knickers and bra. He swallows as his eyes darken and swiftly, I turn so my back is facing him. Looking over my shoulder, I watch him loosen his tie and kick off his shoes as I lower my dress exposing my shoulders. The dress slips slowly down my body, my skin igniting with the touch as it pools at my feet.

I unclasp my bra and that too follows my dress. Left with just my lacy red knickers and shoes I step away from my clothes on the floor and sashay towards Vlad who has a sexy glint in his eyes.

He runs his finger around my lips and on to my chin. They follow a path down my neck and along my collar bone. Once they reach my breastbone, he changes direction swirling round each nipple until they stand out like two clothes hooks. A growl escapes from his throat and every nerve ending I have is electrified. My knees become week as his fingers trail down my stomach taking a dip in my belly button and reach the rim of my knickers. As I wait for him to rip them from my body, a routine I've gotten used to, he lowers his mouth to my ear. "Take them off slowly, sweetheart."

I do as he wants; my hand landing on his chest for support and I can feel his heart pumping hard. As seductively as I can I peel them down my legs then bend to remove them from my feet. I lose the shoes as well.

Naked before him, I don't feel shy wanting to cover parts of myself with my arms. Before him, with that hooded look he is giving me I feel sexy and alive.

"Remove my shirt, Holly," and again I do as he says. Starting with the tie he's already loosened, I untie it, pulling it from his collar slowly then drop it on the floor. One button at a time I unfasten his shirt, baring his broad chest and firm stomach. Starting from his stomach, I run my hands up feeling the heat from his body. He sucks in a breath through his teeth as my fingers travel onto his chest pinching his erect nipples. They carry on until their slipping the material over his solid shoulders and just because I can I kiss one of them baring my teeth as I do. Again, he sucks in a breath and I can feel his erection on my stomach.

When his shirt lands on the floor he kicks it out of the way then takes a step back, observing me unwrapped just for him. Dark desire fills his eyes, never leaving the gift he's been given as he circles me, taking in all my naked form. A pleased look on his face.

The heat from his chest against my back seeps through my skin and as he gently twines my hair around his fist, he tilts my head back to gain access to my neck. His breath a whisper across my skin, sending a shiver down my spine, "Lay on the bed, Holly, with your arms above your head. Close your eyes and don't speak," he releases my hair as his command penetrates deep into a part of me where there's no room for anything beyond him and me. This carnal desire for the man that I had no other choice than to fall madly in love with, heats me to the core and has me following his request.

I walk with a little sway in my hips, and as I lay down on the fore-poster bed, I stare at the man who will just for tonight remove any pain I am feeling. For tonight he will take me higher than ever before, where we sore amongst the stars like two rockets that will burst into millions of shinning sparks. Sparks that only he can ignite. Eradicating the darkness that had brought us to this point and replacing it with a passion that burns so bright it will light up the skies above.

He turns towards the large floor standing blue marble vase with an assortment of peacock feathers and removes one. He strokes the feather over his hand then turns back to me, the want in his eyes leave me weak and when he throws in that sexy wink along with mischievous grin, I know I'm all his. To do whatever the hell he wants with. There stands a man that has me wanting things I would never have dreamed of. Leaving him is not an option, not tonight anyway.

"Sweetheart, do I need to tie you up and blindfold you or are you going to do as you are told?" he strokes his fingers down one of my thighs, his words and touch doing things to cause a stirring low down. He swings his tie from his other hand and quickly I do as he asked.

With my eyes closed and my hands holding on to the wooden frame above my head, I give over my trust. There's a tremble in my arms and the first thing I feel are his soft lips on mine. "Relax Holly, there's just you and me," he speaks when his lips lift from mine, I do relax. I know he would never hurt me physically. All he's ever shown me from day one is love and kindness with that in mind I sink into the mattress and let him lead me into a night of passion.

Feeling the bed dip at either side of my hips, I know he his straddling me. He kisses me hard and when he pulls away, I'm breathless. Tender kisses trail down my neck as feathery strokes trace a path up my thighs. His touch soft and gentle which ups my already heated body and as the talent of his mouth continues its assault on my skin, I ache to hold him. I can already feel the tell-tale signs of an almighty climax creeping close. I moan, and with a mind of their own, my hands move straight to his hair.

I'm left wanting when he stops his exploration and I let out a groan in protest. My eyes still closed, I feel him move then his teeth gently nip my ear, "Lift your arms, Holly, wrists together," his voice is controlled as he follows his order with fervent sucking and nipping at my neck.

I feel the silky caress wrap around my wrist, nervously I open one eye to get a look at what he is using to bind my hands. The tie back lacy curtain that's attached to the bed is now being used to strap my wrists together. It's not tight but secure enough to keep them in place.

"You ok sweetheart?" He places a finger on top of my lips, reminding me not to speak, so I nod my head to answer him. "You are so beautiful, Holly," he whispers against my lips then steels a kiss before I hear him taking a step back. Suddenly, I feel cold not having him as close to me as I want. I'm not left wanting for long when I feel a soft feathery touch run up my shin and when his mouth lands on my heated area, my legs fall apart giving him the access he wants.

He keeps me on edge as his lips and his touch play me like a fine-tuned piano. Vlad is so in tune with my body he knows where to kiss, suck, bite and lick to get the maximum effect. And right now, his mouth covers mine as I explode into a thousand pieces; my toes curling while he greedily consumes the moans that emit from me.

I need my arms to hold him and as he senses my need, he unties me. Bundling me against his chest as he sits me on his knee, "Are you ok, Holly?" he asks, as I play with the hairs on his muscular thighs. I didn't even realise he had stripped out of his trousers.

"Yeah," I reply dreamily, as my hand now runs up said thigh. He chuckles into my hair knowing that I'm still high from his touch.

Turning in his arms so I'm straddling him, both my hands run up his thighs as I lean in to kiss him. His lips are warm and inviting, with all the passion I have come to love so much. When we part, his large hands roam up my back then settle back down on my hips. Our eyes lock together as I take his hardness in my hands, stroking him slowly, I see the love, the desire and the need he holds for me all at once. I move in closer, hovering over him and in one swift movement I sink down until he is buried deep within me. His eyes close, a moan escaping him as the sensation of our attachment overtakes him and he bucks his hips. I slowly move up and down and every now and again twirl my hips and run my hands over his solid chest; this adds to his pleasure. If I thought I had any control over this man, then I was wrong. As we lavish in our love-making both his hands move from gripping my hips and without losing contact, he turns us over so I'm under him.

He picks up the speed and I can feel the animal in him breaking free as he growls into my neck. I hold onto him tight as I feel another orgasm approaching and as soon as he rears up, supporting his weight on his arms at either side of me, I know he's close. The sight of his beautiful toned sexy body spurs me on and has me screaming his name as he pounds on until we're both soaring higher than ever before. My legs wrap around tighter and tighter not ever wanting to let this man go but knowing I must. I sink my teeth into his shoulder as he collapses and buries his face into mine. Water seeps into my eyes and I'm sure I feel wetness on my neck from Vlad. Overcome with emotions we lay there longer than normal and when eventually he moves, I miss the intimacy, the weight of him.

He snuggles me into his chest, his arm around me. His finger drawing circles on my back as I sprawl across him. I think back to the things I've done with him, that I've let him do to me that no man has done before. I think about how easily I let him bind my wrists and followed his orders while he made me feel desired, sexy and wanted. I wonder if he has ever done that before. Made a woman feel the way he makes me feel. "What are you thinking about, Holly?" he asks, his voice low and husky. His always knows when I'm deep in thought.

"I'm just wondering if you've ever done that before," he chuckles, a low rumble in his chest vibrates in my ear.

"Done what sweetheart?"

And I should be embarrassed. The old Holly would have been speaking about sex, but this Holly the one lying in his arms is a far cry from the old one. "Tied someone up."

"No." His fingers stop circling my back and play with my hair. "I never cared enough about another woman to want her to give me all of her," he kisses my head and settles further into the mattress. "I love you, Holly, and no matter what happens tomorrow I will never stop."

I play with the hairs on his chest as I take in the words he says, "I love you too." I whisper into his chest. Neither one of us moves to go clean up nor do we say anything else. I think we both said and heard enough over the weekend.

Chapter 13
Vlad

Hearing the soft click of the door awakens me from the deep sleep I'd been in. I don't bother jumping out of bed to chase or call after her, there's no point. I know she's left me without even looking around the rooms to see if there's any sign of her things still here at the chance she's just popped out for a walk or to use the gym. No point at all.

As I breathe in the scent of her that she's left behind on her pillow, on my skin and in the air, I understand why she needed yesterday together after hearing all about my sordid life the night before. And I understand why she has left this morning without a goodbye. Hurt. She's hurting and doesn't know how to deal with it. How could she? She's pure and beautiful and couldn't comprehend the type of life I grew up in. It's easy for me to defend my actions, the things I had to do to protect my sons. And I would do it all again to have them in my life. I would go through the deceit, torment, and sorrow my wife put me through and the immorality my father bestowed on me just to keep them safe. What I can't go through with though, is the rest of my life without Holly. Maybe a few months ago I was happy with just my family, no permanent woman in my life. But now I've tasted true happiness with a woman. True love. I can't give her up. But, I'm not sure how to win her back.

Once I'm showered and dressed, I make my way to the reception to pay the bill then I make the half hour drive home. Arriving home, the house is eerily quiet which is unusual, but this morning I appreciate the peace and quiet. It's Sunday and I'm normally at work by now, so I gather the things I need ready to leave. The peace and quiet that surrounded me doesn't last long because just as I'm finishing my coffee the front door opens.

Lucas wraps his arms around me with his head on my chest, "We'll get her back dad," he mumbles. My head shoots up, giving Sebastian a questioning look as I take him in my arms and place my hand on the back of his head. Sebastian mimes putting the telephone to his ear then points at Lucas and mouths Holly. I get the gist that Lucas has spoken with Holly. I'm not sure what was said but I'm sure I'll find out. "Together we will bring her home," my youngest says as he pulls out of my arms then turns to walk out of the kitchen. Before he makes it to the bedroom stairs he turns and stares at me, "I love you, dad," then he dashes up the steps with my words following behind him.

"Love you too, Lucas," I listen until I hear his bedroom door close then I turn to Sebastian. "What was all that about?" I query. My eldest takes a seat at the breakfast bar and pours himself a coffee. Just as he's taking a drink, Nicholas and Daniel arrive.

"Holly called him an hour ago," he tells me. "From what I can gather she was careful not to upset him. She told him she wouldn't be coming over here for a while and invited him to call around to hers whenever he wanted if it was okay with you. She also said that if he needed her for anything just to ring her." If I felt overwhelmed at all in this fucked up situation then I do now. Just knowing Holly thought about Lucas makes me love her more.

I nod at him, holding back any emotions I am feeling. Nicholas stands at the side of me, eyeing me with amusement edged around face. "Can't have been all bad," he says as he points at my uncovered neck. "Looks like you had a lot of fun old man."

"What can I say, I'm a passionate man," I smirk at him and bat his hand away from my neck.

"Too much information, paps," Daniel joins in with. "What's with the mark on your nose," he taps his nose, reminding me of the light bruise I have there after taking a punch from my little woman.

"It's nothing," I tell them.

"You did the dastardly deed then?" Sebastian asks as his mouth turns down in a look of concern.

"Yes," I nod at him, picking up my coffee and taking a drink, to hide any emotions that might show them I'm upset.

"Fuck," I hear Nicholas curse. I turn to look at him, "Sorry, paps," he grabs me in one of his man hugs and Daniel joins him.

"Sorry, dad," Daniel says, squeezing my shoulder. "I take it didn't go that well then," Daniel stays by my side with his brother. I blow out a breath, feeling overwhelmed with the love my sons hold for me.

"It went better than I thought it would," I tell them, and it did. I half expected Holly to run out of the door and never look back, not want to stay an extra day.

"But she left you this morning," Sebastian says.

"Yes. Yes, she did." I bite my lip to stop the tremble. Fuck, what has she done to me? I keep on biting, almost drawing blood because I'm sure my sons don't want to see their old man blubbering like a teenage girl. They all stay quiet not knowing what to say to me. They're probably hoping and praying that I don't revert to the bottle and become the bastard I was a few weeks ago. That's not going to happen. I'm determined I will get Holly back and I don't care how long it takes, she will become part of this family.

"Have you told him about Lucas?" Nicholas asks Sebastian. My eldest pales and I can see in his eyes there's something he's hiding and by the way he suddenly looks sick with worry, it must be something important. He shakes his head at his brother and closes his eyes.

"I've just got here. How have I had time?" he states to his brother.

"What is it Sebastian? What's wrong?" I ask him calmly. I know something is bothering him and I know it has to do with Lucas. I take a seat at the breakfast bar, trying to look less intimidating, although my build, scars and tattoos have never bothered my sons, I always sit when we have something to discuss. I know their grown men now, but it's something I've done ever since they were small boys. I always crouched or sat on the floor with them or sat around the dining table if they had something to say.

"While you were telling Holly all about your past, I told Lucas," I'm not sure I've heard him right. He did not just tell me that he told my twelve-year-old son about what I did for a living in Russia.

"You did what?" I'm calmer than I should be as my eyes narrow on my eldest son wondering what the hell gave him the right to take it upon himself to tell Lucas anything that happened back in Russia.

"Dad don't freak out just listen," nervously he gets up from his seat and sits next to me. "I didn't intend to tell him,"

"Then why did you, Sebastian? It is not your place… He's twelve years old. I'm his father not you!" My elbows rest on the breakfast bar and I bury my face in my hands. I can't deal with this. He's going to fucking hate me and I've just shouted at Sebastian, I'm not used to raising my voice at them, arguing with them. We've always talked about any important matters, and any disagreements we've had we've always been able to hash out without falling out.

"He could never understand what I had to do, Sebastian, he's going to hate me," I inhale deeply trying to combat all the emotions consuming me. Eating away at me.

"He doesn't hate you," he puts his hand on my arm. "Did he look like he hated you when he came home?"

I turn and look at my eldest, his face full of remorse but he's right. Lucas said we would get her back together, meaning Holly and that he loved me. I shake my head at Sebastian in answer to his question, but I need to make him understand that whatever was said should have come from me and not him. "You still shouldn't have told him, Sebastian…"

"I know, I know, but he was asking questions and you weren't here to answer them," he cuts in with. "I'm sorry ok. I'll consider myself told and in future if he wants to know anything, I'll tell him to come to you," he holds his hands up to me and backs off. Now I feel like shit, looking at him out of his depth. Why is it always me that ends up feeling like the bad guy?

"Come here," the firmness of my voice leaves no room for arguing, even if it is directed at a twenty-eight-year-old man. I stand from my seat, holding out my hand. He takes it and I pull my eldest into me for a hug. I can't stay angry with him; he's always been my strength.

From the day he was born, he's always been the reason I had to stay strong and not give in. He's always been the sensible one and looked out for his brothers, helping me keep them on the straight and narrow path of life. Then meeting Izzy, he rose to the challenge of becoming a father to some other man's child. I should be grateful that he's grown into a man any parent could be proud of and I should be thankful to him for probably doing a better job than me at answering Lucas' questions

"Thank you," I say as I hold the side of his head in my hand. He stares at me for a while confused then like a light switching on it registers to why I'm thanking him. He nods his head at me then sits back down.

"No need to thank me, just looking out for my family," he says as he picks up his coffee. His brothers haven't said a word and I didn't expect them to. Not when it comes to Sebastian and me. They know out of anyone he's the only one that would get away with interfering in my life and the only one that will get away with confronting me. Although I'm sure they would get away with putting me in my place if they were in the right.

"So, tell me what he asked and what did you tell him?" I direct my questions to Sebastian, but I'm sure his brothers have had their part in it. I've been gone since Friday which gives them plenty of time to rally round, if Sebastian had needed them for support.

"He was asking questions about his grandfather and grandmother. He said he'd overheard us talking once," Sebastian points between himself and me. I rack my brain trying to come up with a time we would have been discussing my father and I can't. "He said it was a few years ago and that he didn't understand then what we were talking about but now with things coming out about his mother he remembered the conversation."

"Did he say what he had heard?" I ask, still no wiser to what it could be.

"It was on my twenty-fifth birthday. When we had all been out drinking and Mrs White was babysitting here for the kids." Sebastian stands, tucking his hands in the pocket of his jeans as I try to recollect to that night just a few years ago, but to be truthful I can't remember a thing, too many vodka shots.

I shake my head. Our past is not usually up for discussion so, maybe I had had a few too many.

"Listen, Paps. Don't worry, I don't remember either but from what he said he had heard enough to know that your father put a gun in your hand at thirteen and ordered you to shoot a man."

Fuck, I could kick myself for my drunken ramble that I have no recollection of, and the fact that the past I had tried to keep there has come back, hurting the people I love the most. I run my hands over my face, rubbing at the stubble on my chin. Shaving has been the last thing on my mind over the last couple of days but if I'm to show Holly and Lucas that I'm not going to fuck up again, I need to keep my appearance in check.

I nod my head at Sebastian acknowledging what he told me, I also pick up on how he said my father and not his grandfather. He also referred to Natalia as Lucas' mother and not their mother something he has done for so long now.

"Anything else?" He nods his head at me as he sits back down.

"Does it matter?" Nicholas asks. "He knows enough to know all wasn't sweetness and light back in Russia and that you did what you had to do to keep us safe." He blows out a breath and places his hands on the breakfast bar. "Paps, you have no need to worry and you don't need to explain anything to him. For some reason he gets it. He understands…"

His words drift off as Lucas makes an appearance, holding a rolled-up piece of art paper. "We need a plan," he states as he sits down with his brothers and me, nudging me with his elbow. I look down at him, he's a lot smaller than his brothers were at his age but he's a lot more grown up than they were.

"And what is that, little brother?" Daniel asks as he rustles his hair. Lucas slaps his hand away, placing the paper on the breakfast bar. "We need to get Dad and Holly back together," I bite my lip trying not laugh because this is so unreal that my nearly teenage son thinks he can help with my love life. I can't help it when I let out a little snort of laughter, but it is soon followed by a scowl from Lucas which has me biting my lip even harder trying to stop the laughter. This is so fucked up. If this was any other woman, I would not be sat here contemplating making plans with my sons on winning her back because I wouldn't give a flying fuck but it's not any other woman. It's Holly. And I need her back and so does my family.

"What do you have in mind?" I ask my youngest, as I lean on the worktop so I'm at his height. I know I should be sitting him down and explaining what happened before we came to live in England and how Holly is feeling because I told her all about it. It would be the right thing to do, but right now he's happy to help work out a plan to bring Holly back.

"Errr, I thought between us," he points around at his big brothers who all have an amused look on their faces, I know why and I'm sure before Lucas has finished with his plan, they will have all had a dig at me. "We could work together to show her how much she is loved and needed," his face turns a darker shade of pink and he lowers his eyes to the rolled-up paper he had placed in front of him.

"Ow look at you being all grown up," Nicholas says. He's up out of his seat, wrapping his arm around his neck while rubbing at his hair with his knuckles. Lucas can hold his own with his brother and knows just how to get back at them when they take the piss out of him.

As Nicholas releases him from his hold, Lucas dips his fingers in my coffee and flicks it, so it splatters across his brother's Ralph Lauren camouflage rugby shirt. Nicholas looks down at the dark wet patches, his dark eyes wide, "You little shit," he grunts at him. "I've only just fucking bought this," his hands shake the bottom of his shirt. What for? I don't know.

Nicholas' hand moves to touch Lucas' hair again but he's too fast. He dips out of his way, rounding the other side of me ducking under my arm for protection.

As Nicholas reaches to grab him, I slap his arm out of the way cuddling my youngest into my chest. "Leave him alone and let him finish what he was saying."

Lucas chuckles, knowing he has the upper hand while he's got me for protection.

"You can't hide under his wing all day little one," Nicholas points at him, sniggering.

"Come on stop acting like a big kid, Nicholas," Sebastian speaks. "I've got my wife and kids to get back home to. By the way we're making a roast dinner if you all want to come. It will be ready about three," he tells us.

"Count me in," Daniel says.

"And me," Nicholas answers as he sits back down, screwing his face up at Lucas. He really needs to start acting his age.

"I need to call into work, but I'll come over once I get finished," I tell him. "Is Lucas coming with you?" I ask as I pick up the rolled-up art paper, unravelling it and laying it out on the worktop.

"Wow," Daniel says as Sebastian lets out a low whistle.

"What's this? Have you drawn this?" my eyes take in the sketch in front of me from the bottom upwards.

Bare feet pointed, ankles together. Legs stretched out angled to one side, knees also together as the white feathers of a wing spans out covering the most intimate parts of the nude body from thigh to breast. The tip of the plumage hiding half the mischievous smile of the angel. Sapphire eyes hold a radiant stare as highlighted hair gathers over one shoulder. The apex of the other wing pointing up behind her head. The detail of the wing is complexed with every feather standing out with the vanes and barb drawn in them the whole thing shaded white. The body of the angel is outlined in blue and equally detailed with the eyes standing out like gems.

"Do you like it?" Nervously my boy looks up at me.

"Yes. It's…" I try to find the words to describe his work. For such a young boy he has a very special gift and I'm privileged to have him as my son. "It's amazing," I tell him, and it is.

How he has caught the features of the innocent angel with a touch of naughtiness. My angel.

"Why?" I glance down at him, wanting the reason behind his drawing.

"Hmmm," he takes the drawing from me. "I thought it would cover the tattoo on your back. I'm working on one for your chest but I'm still deciding what might cover it," he's deadly serious. There's not one hint of awkwardness coming from his body language as you normally detect when he suggests something he's not so sure about.

"Why? How long have you been working on this, Lucas?" I ask.

"About a month," he answers one of my questions.

"But why?" I ask again.

"Because I've seen the way Holly looks at your tattoos, she doesn't like them," he tells me. "So, I started playing around with an idea then it became a drawing. I've been emailing a tattooist who specializes in cover ups. I sent him a picture of your back from an old photo and sent him this." He points to his sketch. "He thinks he will be able to copy my sketch but he will need to size it which means he needs you to call in at his shop," I nod my head at him understanding his need to rid the disturbing art work that spans out from the nape of my neck, across my shoulder blades and fades off half way down.

"I was going to wait and show it to Holly but with everything that's happened I didn't want her upsetting any more than she already is. But now I think the time is right for you to cover it up at least then she can see your trying to put the past behind you."

"It's a good idea. Will it cover what's on his back?" Nicholas asks, discussing me has if I'm not here.

Lucas nods his head, "Yeah. Spike the tattooist said he might need to thicken the ink on the feathers but it's doable."

"What about the dagger handle, will it cover?" Sebastian asks. That's the only part of the tattoo that has colour. The rest is blue and black, sculls all twisted together and if you look close enough, which I don't think anyone has, you can see parts of a gun hiding between the crevices.

With a close look you can make out the muzzle of the gun behind one of the eye sockets. The trigger secreted in the nasal socket and the handle and magazine buried between the varies sculls. None of them seen clearly without knowledge or close scrutinization.

Holly been the only one ever close enough to see it. The nights she'd trail her finger round the ink without questioning what she was seeing but I doubt for one minute that she would have noticed the makings of the handgun.

"Yeah," Lucas answers Sebastian. "The point of the wing

there…" he points to the tip of the wing behind the angel's head. "Will travel up his neck, and hopefully cover it."

"When did you become so smart?" Daniel asks him as he gets up from his seat. He stands at the side of Lucas, putting his arm across his shoulders.

"I just thought if we can show Holly that we want her in our lives," he points to his brothers. "And dad keeps away for a while."

"What?"

"Listen," my young son says, pleading in his eyes. "I don't know, I just thought… If you sent little text messages and flowers letting her know your still here and we visit her… Once she's got over the shock, she might come back," he shrugs his shoulders as if it's as easy as that.

Maybe he's right. Maybe if I stay in the background and not pester her, give her time to come to terms with it all. Let my sons keep her busy, having them around her she's not going to forget me in a hurry. Izzy and my grandchildren surrounding her with their love. My family that she cares so much about could be my ammunition. Maybe it will work.

I nod my head in agreement while I trace a finger around the face of the angel.

"I tried to get Holly's smile and the shape of her eyes," Lucas says quietly. "If I practice a bit more, I might get it right."

"It's perfect," I respond to him. "Are you ok with all this Lucas?" I ask. He's only young and has just found things out about his father, I'm sure he must have questions. "We'll talk tonight," I tell him as I give him a hug.

"You've done a good job, Lucas," Nicholas says. "You've created the perfect cover up, I can't wait to see what you design for his chest," he gets up and pats me on it. "And on your own you've come up with a plan which we will all help with."

"Ok. Do what you have to do," I tell them. "But don't go upsetting her any more than she already is. I will keep out of the way, but I won't sit on the side lines for long, I'm not that patient when it comes to Holly."

"Paps if you want her back then you need to be patient; it could take a while for her to get over what you've told her. There's always the chance that she might not, and you will just have to live with that," Sebastian says as he stares at me with that look that tells me we must be realistic about this. Only I don't even want to think about Holly not coming back.

"Right I need to call into work, I will see you later for dinner. Lucas get me the man's number for the tattoo, and I will give him a ring," I pick up my car keys then rinse out my cup.

"He can fit you in a week on Friday, I've already made you an appointment and I can come with you because I break up from school on Wednesday," he tells me, his eyes lighting up because the summer holidays are on their way.

"Ok, make sure you all clear your cups away before you leave. I don't want to come home to a mess later." I know I sound bossy, but my mood changed as soon as Sebastian mentioned Holly not coming back. I need to calm myself down, it's unfair on them.

"Dad," Daniel calls me.

"Yes," I blow out a breath.

"We're in this together, we care too."

"I know… I'll catch you all later, I need to leave."

With that I leave my sons in the kitchen hatching a plan to bring my woman home. I'm happy that they care enough to get involved and I will be patient for a while. But not for long.

Chapter 14

Holly

"You can't tell anyone Olivia," I stare at my closest friend in her frozen state and I don't know whether to laugh or cry. Laugh because it's the first time I've seen her speechless. Cry because I've just revealed Vlad's darkest secrets and if it didn't seem real before it certainly does now. Retelling his story of his life in Russia, his cruel, heartless father, the things he had to do because of him and his wife. Well I don't know if I have any words to describe a woman who could put her sons through the torment she did even if her father was as bad as Vlad's. You would think she would have wanted to keep her family safe and away from any evil in the world.

"Bloody hell," Olivia finally speaks after taking a very large gulp of her wine. She places her glass back on the table, rubs her hands down her arms then sits forward in her seat.

When I sneaked out of the hotel suite early this morning, I came home, showered and was going to have a workout at the gym. Deciding I didn't want to talk to anyone, I opted for a run instead to try and clear my head. I ran and ran, replaying everything Vlad had told me. Trying to fathom out the wrongs and rights of his actions and how he justified what he did left me even more troubled than I was before I went out on my run. I showered again and when I thought about his sons, I broke down and cried for the small boys who had no mother to care for them. For Lucas, how he had to fight to survive as soon as he came into this world. They had all suffered in some way but had got through it together with the love of their father.

"Holly," Olivia says, she still looks in a state of shock. "I thought the big man would have a past; you get that with just one look but what you've just told me... My god it's what films are made from." Her voice is a little higher than normal, shaking her head she picks up her glass again, "I can't believe you stayed an extra day after he told you everything. Did you sleep with him?"

I nod my head just as she's taking a drink, "Yes." She spits the wine everywhere choking on my answer. She quickly wipes herself down and once she's stopped coughing, she starts laughing.

"I can't believe you, Holly. My shy little friend who wouldn't say boo to goose has fallen in love with some ex-mafia man and after finding out all his deepest darkest secrets still sleeps with him."

"Olivia, I fell in love with him before I knew any of that stuff..."

"Yeah, but you still stayed and still had sex with him afterwards," she's still laughing at me.

"I can't just turn off my feelings for him. I just needed to spend another day with him. Just him and me. I know it sounds bad but no matter what he has done or how he chooses to justify them, he still treats me like I'm the most precious thing in the world. In his world. And I know he would never hurt me..." There's a tremble in my voice, stopping me from continuing because physically he wouldn't hurt me but in other ways, he's ripped my heart to shreds. I take a sip of my wine to try and stop my emotions from getting the better of me. I've cried enough today; they will be none of them tonight.

"Yes, you're right. I understand," she says. "So, you left this morning while he was still sleeping."

"Yes, I couldn't go through the whole goodbye thing, it would have been too hard for both of us. He might look intimidating, but he has a heart of gold and I didn't want to see the hurt in his eyes when I told him I was leaving." I blow out a breath knowing I couldn't have done it anyway, just one look from him and he has me bending to his will.

"Probably for the best," she says. We sit there silent for a little while; I know Olivia will have a lot more to say but for now I think she's trying to keep her opinions to herself.

"Has he not been in touch since you left this morning?"

"No," I shake my head. I didn't expect him to. I think he knew last night that that would be our last night together. "I spoke to Lucas and Sebastian this morning." Olivia lifts one of her eyebrows at me in questioning. "I didn't say anything to either of them, but I got the feeling Sebastian knew what his father was going to tell me. He's old enough to know and remember everything that went on."

"Do you think Nicholas and Daniel know?"

"Nicholas yes, but I'm not too sure about Daniel. Maybe." I rub at my knuckle, that's still a bit sore from when I punched Vlad in the nose. I can't believe I hit him that hard.

"What did you say to Lucas?" Olivia asks.

"I told him that I wouldn't be around for a while but if he needed me to come over or call. He seemed a little upset, so I went into how adults can act like children and hurt each other but don't mean it. I didn't really know what else to say other than that I'd always be here for him and that we could meet up in a couple of days." Olivia eyes fill with tears and as she gets out of her seat and cuddles me, I realise mine are too. So much for not crying.

"Ow Holly, I'm sorry," she soothes as she rubs my back. "I know you love that boy like your own."

"Do you think I've done the right thing?"

"What do you mean?" she sits back down in the seat next to me.

"Telling Lucas, he can come over or call me… I mean, what if Vlad doesn't want him to? What if it's too hard for me to see him without thinking about his father? I'm never going to get over him…" I sniffle.

"Stop, Holly," she takes my hand. "Listen to me," she says as she wipes a tear from my face. Olivia and I have been friends for years; along with her husband Jack, his brother Nick and his wife Sarah but out of all of them Olivia is the one that I can tell anything to without judgment. She's always been caring in nature even when I was a shy little teenager, she'd look out for me and has done ever since. She shows me the love that a big sister would to her younger sibling, and I love her for that. Both of us being only children, I think we connected on some level that was stronger than the friendship between Sarah and two of us.

"Holly from day one of meeting Vlad you changed. That night in Eruption you showed a side to you that no one had ever seen before and that was due to him. And I know from speaking with his family that you changed him. The change was for the better. It was like you both looked at each other and bam. There was no one else in the room. You lit up like a thousand-watt light bulb and only he had the switch that could turn it off. Even now knowing what you know, the tears, you're still glowing. You're feeling, Holly." I look at her thinking she's lost her bloody mind or is it me who's lost mine. Maybe it is.

"A lot of the time we go about our business, it's routine. We think we know love, that we've been in love. We think we've had our hearts broken until something happens or someone happens to change that and prove us wrong. Throughout your life you've seen hurt and felt it. Tell me which one of them hurt the most, your mum, your adopted parents, Rob or the feeling of losing Vlad and his family?" She pats my hand as she gets up then after pouring us both a glass of wine, she takes a seat next to me.

"Holly you don't have to answer my question because I already know the answer. What you do need to answer is, do you really want your relationship with Vlad to be over?"

No, I don't. It hurts like hell. I can't even think of all the ways I'll miss him without my heart aching. I shake my head at her. "But I can't stay with him knowing what he's done." As if my mind and body has just connected the dots and mapped out the magnitude of Vlad's confession, I start to shake. I'm up out of my seat flying through the bathroom door, unable to stop the few glasses of wine I'd consumed from hitting the toilet bowl.

I don't think I fully understood until now, how him telling me he had taken the law into his own hands and killed someone, more than one, would affect our lives. Saying it out loud, telling Olivia what he had done to try and put a stop to the organised crime his family ran. Years of striving to bring down his father's illegal activities and evil ways that put more than one person on the other end of his gun or knife. Starting with the first when he was in his late teens to protect his mother. Then many more as he worked tirelessly to protect his sons from the clutches of the vile man they called their grandfather and his criminal underworld.

My first fears of Vlad's insecurities that brought out his jealous rage runs deeper than a scorned husband due to an unfaithful wife. It runs deeper than a man who has lost in love and had to fight to keep his family. Vlad's life runs deep into a world where men sell their daughters for greed and power, determined to climb higher in the hierarchy of men whose hearts are as black as hell. Where women lure men in, offering wild nights and pleasure. Trapping, to gain the same as the men who offered them their services for money.

Drugs, violence, guns and murder; easily bought and sold on the dark streets. Seeping into the innocent and stealing their light, covering them with something so sinister it snakes around them, tightening its grip until any hope for them is diminished.

Although I know deep in my heart that Vlad was put into circumstances where he had no choice than to protect his family any way he could, I cannot condone it.

My breathing comes in short fast blasts as I sink to the floor, my mind racing like two one-hundred-meter sprinters competing for gold. Olivia shoves a paper bag into my hand, "Breath into this, Holly," her concern is apparent as she rubs my back and strokes my hair.

My unexpected panic attack keeps us sat on the bathroom floor for the next thirty minutes and has me remembering Friday night when I sat on the bathroom floor in the hotel suite while Vlad's life unfolded. I was sick then too, but it was anger that consumed me most of the evening.

"How are you feeling?" Olivia asks, bringing me back to the present. I stand on shaky legs and swill my face, Olivia hands me a towel once I've finished swilling my mouth with mouthwash.

"I don't know," I answer her, making my way back into the kitchen. I switch on the kettle to make a cup of tea. "Am I supposed to be angry, heartbroken, confused...?" I turn to my friend for the answers I know she doesn't have. She takes over making the tea and directs me to take a seat. "My head hurts with it all," I tell her, rubbing at my temples. "My stomach feels if it as had a kicking and my chest feel as if it's been squeezed in a press."

"I'm sorry, Holly. I know it must hurt, but I don't think he divulged his past to hurt you," I give her a sideways glance and nod my head. This I know but it doesn't stop the feeling in my chest.

"I think he struggled with his love for you and from what you've told me about his wife, his struggle manifested itself when he felt you could be taken away from him…" She pauses as she passes me a cup of tea then pulls out one of the stools and takes a seat. "He was with that women a long time, putting up with her games as well as having to work for his father. She'd fucked with his head that much that he probably should have had some form of therapy for putting up with her," I sit there silently listening to my friend who is trying to make sense of Vlad's actions.

Taking a drink of my tea, I'm at a loss as to why he could think that I was anything like her.

"Holly think about it. He came here over twelve years ago for a new life and for that twelve years he kept his heart closed to any woman then you come into his life.

Both of you never stood a chance. I've known you a long time, Holly…" She puts her hand on mine. "And in that time, I've never seen you glow as much as when you're with him." She takes a sip of her tea and pulls a face. "Bloody hell I can't believe I'm drinking tea when we're having this conversation," she chuckles. "We should be on the good stuff for conversations this deep."

"There's another bottle in the fridge if you want a glass," I tell her. She shakes her head at me, taking another drink.

"It's fine, I'll stick with this. If I have too many, I might end up bawling with you."

"Thanks," I joke.

"Anyway, as I was saying, you came into his life with all your beautifulness," she chuckles again trying to lighten my mood. I laugh at her this time. "What's not to love, Holly? You have it all and Vlad saw that first hand. How you loved and cared for him. The way you were with his sons and grandchildren, how you connected with them. You were his angel. His light and he was not going to let anyone take that away from him. He'd waited all his life for you and you him. Unfortunately, all it took was for a man to go near you and that loving family man who worships you, changed into that intimidating man he looks like." I let out a sigh, seeing first-hand how he can change from the man I know into one I don't recognise.

"Sometimes men and women see what they want to see and that night in the club, he saw you flirting, laughing and dancing with another man."

"What?" I question my friends turn of events.

"I know that's not what happened, Holly, and you know," she stresses, squeezing my hand to reassure me. "But like I said he saw what he wanted to see and that was his wife playing her games." I understand what she's trying to say. He'd kept away from getting close to women because of her, not wanting to trust or love any woman. That's why he played the field, never taking a woman home or introducing anyone he met to his family. He used them for one thing and one thing only, sex; as did they.

"He's broken, Holly."

"He's not the only one," I whisper. She hears me and nods her head.

"I think he's fixable as are you with time and some sort of counselling, but as for the other thing..." She blows out a long breath. "His father." She chews on her bottom lip, shaking her head. "That is so out of our league, I don't want to touch it with a ten-foot barge pole. The only thing I will say Holly is that there's gangs and underworld in every country. Killings and murders over drugs and weapons. Do you think Vlad would have chosen that life if it wasn't for his father throwing a woman at his feet when he was sixteen then her falling pregnant? I know it takes two to tango, but he was so young with ambitions that were robbed from him. He embraced fatherhood and did what he had to do to support his family..." Olivia's phone chimes with a text message. She reads her text then puts her phone back in her bag.

"That was Jack, he's on his way to pick me up," she says as she lifts her head to look at me. "I've told him I'll meet him downstairs; I didn't think you would want him coming up tonight," she gives me a tight smile as she takes a drink of her tea. "I know the twat can be a bit overprotective and if he sees you've been crying, I'm sure he won't stop until he's nagged the truth out of you."

"You can't tell Jack," I say in a panic. I don't want anyone knowing. I've only told Olivia because I needed to speak to somebody before my mind exploded. I'm so confused with my emotional state and the conflicting feelings I have. I'm at a loss.

"I won't say a thing, but you need to pull yourself together Holly or at least try and hide the hurt you're going through. Jack, his mum and dad as well as Sarah and Nick know you, they will pick up that you're hurting and won't stop prying until they get the truth," she states, getting up off her seat and picking up her bag. I know she's right but it's going to be hard to stop the pain I'm feeling.

"I'll keep out of the way for a while until I can be trusted not to break down in company," I tell her, I try to smile at my comment, but it's a struggle.

"I don't bloody think so lady." She slams her bag on the breakfast bar, giving a stare that says, I'll drag you out by the hair of your head if that's what it takes. "You hid away enough when you were getting over that dick of an ex of yours. Then buggered off to the coast for over a week on your own when the big man had his melt down. You are not..." she almost stamps her foot with her little rant. "Hiding away." She stands with her hands on her hips, daring me to challenge her. I'm not going to. I know she's right.

This time I will try. I know it's going to be hard to be around Vlad's family without him but it's something I'm going to have to do. I don't like to let people down, especially people I care about. I've told Lucas I'll be there for him and I've still got to help Izzy with the club. It's going to be difficult, but once the bands are up and running, I can take a step back...

"Holly," Olivia says at the same time my phone dings. And there it is. The first text from Vlad. I don't need to look to know it's him; I have our song as his ring tone and my text alert. Olivia knows it's him too and lifts my phone to read the message. I know it's invasive, but I don't stop her, she'll vet the message before she shows me it. A smile crosses her face as she passes me the phone.

Vlad: Night angel. Sleep well. I love you xxx

It's short but it tells me everything. He's not going to let me go easily. I really do need to be strong.

"I know I have to pull myself together and I will," I reassure her that I won't slip into the way I was over Rob. He betrayed me and embarrassed me. I wasn't heartbroken and wasn't bothered that he didn't want a second chance even if I'd have wanted to give him one.

"I need to go but before I do," she takes my hands in hers. "I know I sound as if I'm defending the big bastard," she chuckles. "But I would do anything to protect my children, Holly. Anything," she articulates the last word, her smile gone. "If you asked any decent man what they would do to protect their mother, I'm sure they would do anything and their children... well I know what Jack would do." She doesn't say what he would do, and she doesn't have to because I know most parents would take the law into their own hands to keep their children safe; that I can understand. He did what he had to do.

"Think about it, Holly," with that we hug and say our goodbyes.

An hour later, I'm in bed twirling my phone between my finger and thumb and all I've done is think. I've thought about what he had to do, and I've concluded that he didn't have a choice. A whole different world to what I know. It's not him or his fault, I get that but what I can't get is me being with him knowing what he's done. Talk about confused and conflicted.

Chapter 15

Holly

My feet hit the pavement hard as I round the corner onto the familiar street that I'd long forgotten. The slate grey building stands frozen in time as I reach the stone brick wall, staring up at the steeple that seemed to reach out and touch the sky when I was a child. It's been nearly twenty years since I stood here wanting answers and here I am nearly twenty years later seeking the same.

The rays of colour from the stained-glass windows float through the warm air as the hot sun beams down onto them. The gnarled old oak tree stretches out in vain trying to grab at the rainbow affect.

Out of breath, I glance around the kept grounds where I ran between the long-forgotten headstones as I waited for my adopted parents to finish chatting with fellow worshippers after mass.

Taking off my backpack, I check the flowers inside to make sure they're still intact, sitting on the wall as I do. A few petals have fallen from the bouquet of the red and pink roses Vlad had sent me, the fifth bunch in the last seven days.

In the last week, I've received a text every morning with the same message. *Morning Holly have a good day. I love you xxx* and every evening before bed. *Good night angel sleep well. I love you xxx* I haven't replied to any of them. My fingers had twitched to send one back telling him I love him but conflicted with what I should be feeling, stopped me.

When the flowers started arriving, I had to go out and buy some new vases as each bunch were that large, they filled two of them.

Sebastian and Izzy came to visit Monday after they had picked the kids up from school, Lucas came with them and they stayed to have tea with me. It was great to have the kids over; it had seemed ages since I had last seen them. We chatted about the club and the fact that it would only be four weeks before the new themed nights would be starting. I felt bad for coming up with the suggestions in the first place then over the last month not putting as much time an effort into it as I would have liked. Izzy was sympathetic as to why and told me not to be so hard on myself. Between Daniel, Izzy and me, we had selected the bands that would perform and picked out the dancers that still worked at the club to which bands they would perform with. The bar staff and security had all been put onto the rota so with all this already in place I'd needn't worry. I promised both Sebastian and Izzy that I would be in the following day, they were still a lot to do and check before the opening night, plus I needed the distraction.

Throughout the week, I'd met them most days at ten and stayed until we were satisfied that we were happy with the progress. The building work was finished early which meant the dancers could now practice their routines with the bands. This was all new to both parties as the bands had never had dancers accompany them and the dancers were used to choosing their own music. There was also the opening night where four of the bands would share the stage. These consisted of Motown, Seventies Disco, Eighties, and Soft Rock which would all have a spot each to showcase the upcoming artists that would play at the club each week for the next three months. There was also a couple more bands that would be playing there but not as often as they had other commitments.

Lucas visited every day and is now on holiday from school, he told me it was ok with his dad because he had a lot of work on with the buildings he had bought. I had wondered why I had not seen him around the club and a little disappointed when he wasn't there even though I knew it was for the best.

It was fun having him and his brothers around, Nicholas and Daniel joined him on a couple of occasions. It wasn't as difficult as I first thought it would be having them around without their father. Their presence was comforting and reassuring that I wasn't slipping back into old ways when I got divorced.

We visited the Art Gallery at Lucas' request. Went bowling with Olivia, Jack and their family along with Sarah, Nick and theirs, and spent a few evenings just catching up. I was coping just fine. Wasn't I?

My 'I'm ok' pretence didn't wash with my close friends; even Vlad's sons could see through my whole charade that I was fine not having their father around. Maybe it was in my eyes every time they mentioned him; they could see I missed him. It could have been that they were used to seeing their father and me together, happy and in love.

As the week went on and I spent more time with Vlad's family, my understanding of what he had done and why got easier to deal with. Seeing his sons and how they were there for each other. How much they showed their love and that they were not prepared to let me go without a fight. I knew why he had no other choice than to protect his flesh and blood even if it meant shedding someone's in return. Every time I looked at one of them, I saw him, and I saw the torment he must have gone through trying to keep them from having to grow up in such a cruel environment that his own father had created for them. The strain to cope with a wife who couldn't mother such beautiful boys. A woman who enjoyed making his life a living hell. My heart bleeds.

Even though I came to realise that he had no choice than to fight, I was in a fight of my own. More than one. First, if Vlad was unable to control the rage that overtook him each time he thought any man was coming on to me then I would not be able to take him back. He needed to realise I would never hurt him in that way. Second, was my deep-rooted beliefs that what Vlad had been mixed up in was against the law. All the illegal activities that had made him the man he is, the dealing in drugs, weapons and killings no matter the reasons why, still disturbed me.

Was I capable of loving a man who had committed such criminal acts without always feeling whether his actions were right or wrong?

Opening the large wooden door to the church that I had spent so much time at when I was a child, I glance towards the small area of land behind the old headstones where my parents were buried. Guilt washes over me for not visiting as much as I should and a tear leaks from my eye. I wipe it away and sniff the sweet smell of the flowers I'd brought with me curtesy of Vlad.

Nothing's changed since I was last here. The décor is still cream, the brightness the large oval leaded windows let in and the smell of lilies and candle wax still floats around the air. I wonder if Father Martin is still here or whether the old priest has been shipped off to somewhere resembling the Father Ted show on Craggy Island. I'm sure he would be knocking up seventy now.

Placing my backpack and flowers on one of the pews, I make my way over to the south corner and light a candle. On my way back, I see movement in the small kitchen through the window of the door at the back of the church. I pay them no more attention, knowing whoever it is won't bother me as I kneel to say a prayer.

My knees are aching when I eventually get up and take a seat, I prayed for everyone and their dog and asked for answers to questions that I'm sure will not come. They didn't twenty years ago. Why should they now? After sitting there for half an hour, I decide that its time I visited my parents grave.

Passing the door to the kitchen I notice a white-haired man hobbling around. When he turns, the twenty years have taken their toll, but I still recognise the wise old man that tried to make sense of why my parents were taken from me. I offer him a little wave and open the door to say hello. His eyebrows raise, and a familiar smile greets me. "Holly?" he questions is it really me.

"Yes," I answer, returning a smile as I walk towards him.

"My goodness, it's been years. How are you my dear?"

"I'm well. And you? I can't believe you're still here," I say. He takes my hand, looking at me. Scrutinizing me. He always knew when something was bothering me.

"Sit," he gestures. Pulling out one of the chairs. "I'll put the kettle on. You've time for a cup of tea?"

"Of course. Let me help you."

"I leave here in three months," his hand waves around us. "I'm so glad you called in before then. I saw you walk in, but my eyes aren't so good these days. I couldn't tell it was you."

"It's been a long time Father, I'm sure I've changed a little since you last saw me," I finish making our tea and we both sit around one of the tables, I spent a lot of time colouring and reading.

"I hear you got married, Holly," he smiles, but I can see in his eyes that he's a bit put out that I didn't get married in his church. I didn't get married in any church.

"Yes, I did, but I'm divorced now," I wave my left hand to show no ring. "Sorry," I say. "He wasn't religious. We married in a hotel with a registrar." My eyes lower to my tea as I take a sip.

"Not to worry, so what have you been up to? And what brings you here today?" he asks.

We chat idly about my divorce, how I felt let down and betrayed and refused to socialise except with my close friends. He told me about parishioners that had moved on or died and some new ones that had moved into the area. I found myself telling him on how I met Vlad, leaving out some parts and how him and his family became my world.

"Where is he now?" he questions, lifting one old grey eyebrow. He knows why I am here. That all is not well, and I need to find answers. This old man has always been good at reading people and he's always tried to answer questions honestly according to his beliefs even if the answers were not what you wanted to hear.

Blowing out a long breath, knowing this will be the second person I will have told Vlad's secrets to, but in all fairness one of them is my closest friend who will not speak a word of it. And Father Martin, I'm sure, is obligated to keep what people say in confession to himself but then again, I'm not altogether sure if someone breaks the law and they are told by someone else what he would do with the information.

Over the next half hour, I cram in as much information as I possibly can without breaking down in tears. Revealing Vlad's past. All his sins and the reasons why. Making sure I add in what a great father he is. How he's made a life for them here in England and gives generously to relevant charities. When I finish speaking, I hold my breath not sure what I expect him to say. I fidget nervously and play with my fingers while I wait for a response.

I'm surprised when he finally speaks, "I think your friend needs to take a trip to the confessional box, Holly," his tone friendly. He lifts his cup of tea and takes a sip when he puts it down, he takes my hand in his. "I can't condone what he did, Holly, but…" he lets go of my hand and sits up straight. "I can understand why. It is not our place to judge, he will be judged by God when the time is right. Saying that, I can see he didn't have a choice and has made amends for his crimes whether they were forced upon him or not." He stands to remove the cups and I follow him, hanging on to his every word.

"And what about his jealousy and anger? He can't seem to get passed that every woman will betray him just as his dead wife did," I say as I take the cups and wash them out. I'd told Father Martin what kind of man Vlad was before he met me and that I was the first he had introduced to his family.

"If he loves you and he wants to save your relationship, then he will do whatever it takes. Counselling would be good," he bends to place the cups in the cupboard, and I can hear his old bones crying out in pain. I take the cups from him and help him up, scanning the cupboards for one that's empty so there's no bending or reaching. Once I've found one, I transfer the cups from one cupboard to another, listening to the words of an old man that cares and wondering if it's that easy.

"You make it sound so easy to put the past behind."

"It's not your past, Holly, it's Vlad's," he tells me shaking his head. "And that's what he needs to do to move on with you."

"And what do I need to do to combat the conflicting feelings I have of right and wrong?" I ask, still as confused as I was when I first walked in here.

"Give him a second chance, Holly," he shrugs his shoulders at me as if it's that simple. Could it be that simple? "Holly, you're a smart woman. I'm sure you are aware what your life would have been like if you had stayed with your birth mother and all the men that came and went as well as the drugs, wouldn't you have wanted forgiveness if the boot had been on the other foot. That's what your parents brought you up to do. To forgive."

I think about my life for a few moments. I was given the chance to be brought up in a stable home with loving caring parents even if it was only a short time. Then taken in by Mr and Mrs Anderson who were hard working, loving and kind in every way again I was given the chance to live amongst good people. Vlad never had that chance growing up.

"You're right," I tell him. "I think I need a little time to get over the shock and hopefully while I'm doing that, I can get Vlad to go to some form of therapy," I say, smiling. My heart feels a little lighter now, hoping and praying we can move on from this.

"Good luck with that," he lets out a little chuckle. "In my experience men are not very good with baring their souls and he's done it once when he let you in, so be patient." Father Martin walks with me as I make my way to collect my flowers and bag. He blesses me, and we say our goodbyes with me promising to come by before he leaves to join the older members of the clergy in the bishop's office.

I sit on the ground, chatting away to my dead parent's grave, hoping wherever they are they can hear me. An overwhelming feeling of calmness washes over me as I lay the flowers on the ground and start to place them in the holes of the flower bowl. Footsteps approach from behind me and as I turn thinking Father Martin has decided to join me, I'm shocked to see the man I've just been discussing stood there looking as handsome as ever.

His warm smile wraps around me like an electric blanket and I let out a chuckle when I think of the saying. *Speak of the devil and he shall appear* which gets me a raised eyebrow from Vlad as he lowers himself to the ground, so he is sat facing me. I can't believe he's sitting on the ground in an Armani dark blue suit, a crisp white shirt with light blue stripes and shiny black shoes. We might have had a lot of sun lately, but the ground is dusty with cut grass everywhere and nowhere for such an attire. He must have been in a meeting but what I'm curious about is how he knew I was here.

"Are you stalking me, Mr Petrov?" I raise one eyebrow at him as he picks up a rose and inhales its perfume.

"What? No." He shakes his head then places the rose in the rose gold bowl. "I was passing and saw you enter the church," he nods towards the building to his right.

He picks up another rose, putting it in another hole, "I was just on my way to the restaurant, I've been in a meeting all morning," *Thought so.*

"Oh," I say as I try to force one of the roses into the hole, but it gets jammed because of a thorn. As I try to snap the thorn off, it pricks me, and I let out an "ouch." Sucking on the end of my finger because it's sore and bleeding, Vlad moves so he is crouching in front of me.

"Here let me see," he takes my hand, brushing his thumb over the tiny pin prick. The familiar touch sends shock waves through my system and has me trembling with the need to be held in his arms. Quickly, I take my hand back.

"It's fine," I tell him, sucking on the end of my finger again to try and numb the sting.

"You're bleeding, Holly. Here," he takes a tissue from his pocket and wraps it around my finger. "I have a plaster in the car," he moves to stand, giving me a caring smile. I place my hand on his arm to stop him.

"It's ok, Vlad. The tissue will do the trick."

"Are you sure?"

"Yes, I'm not going to bleed to death," I joke. He sits back down placing his elbows on his bent knees.

He picks up a flower and so do I, both of us placing them in the bowl at the same time.

"So, you were in there for some time," he nods his head towards the church. "Were you confessing your sins, Holly?" I can see the amusement dancing in his eyes as he gives me that flirty smirk.

"No," I tell him, shaking my head. "I was confessing yours," giving him a little smirk of my own while I gather up the wrapping from the flowers and the leaves that have fallen off.

He stares at me for a moment, probably contemplating whether I'm having him on or not. Then he blows out a long breath.

"Wow. Well, all the windows are still intact, and the building hasn't burst into flames..." His head turns towards the church and he chuckles, "Maybe I've been absolved of all my sins?" As his dark blue eyes flick across to me, I can see there was a question in his last statement and he's searching my face for any sign that perhaps I might show some compassion to the battle he engaged in.

I'm still coming to terms with the things he told me and need more time before I can discuss it with him. But I don't want him thinking I'm without any sympathy. So, as I reach into my backpack for the bottle of water and cloth that I'd brought with me, a whisper slips from my lips, "Maybe."

He hears me and as I stand to dust down the headstone he stands too, offering his hand to help me up. He opens the bottle of water and pours some over the flowers while I clean off the dry grass and dust from the headstone when I finish, I find him watching me. His eyes rake over me lovingly, but I see the anguish in them. It's the same thing that I see in my own when I look in the mirror. Suffering. Missing the person that makes the heart beat faster. The person that can shatter it into pieces or keep it whole and alive. Each other.

"Where's your car, angel?" he asks, calling me by the name he bestowed on me the night we met. I look down at my running gear and brush the muck from my knees.

"I ran here, my car's at home."

"What's wrong with the gym?" He gathers the rubbish, bottle and cloth and strolls over to the bin to dispose of them. I watch him. No matter where he is, he never loses that sexy walk. That tall, straight up posture, broad shoulders, long strides and an arse you want to sink your teeth into. Only today the broad shoulders have taken on a slouch, carrying the weight of the world and the eyes that always look ahead and beyond search the floor as he returns with his hands shoved in his pockets.

"Nothing's wrong with the gym," I answer his question. "I wanted to come here, and I needed to clear my head," I say, releasing the hair bobble from my hair and running my fingers through it then I gather it back into a ponytail and replace the bobble.

"And did you… clear your head?" he picks up my bag watching me, waiting for my answer.

"It's clearer," I try to take my bag from him, but he keeps his hold on it and directs his eyes to his car.

"I'll drop you off home." Before I can say I planned on a brisk walk back, he has his hand on the small of my back, moving me forward, slinging my bag over his shoulder. It's warm and sends the heat spiralling throughout my body. Every part me crying out for him to wrap me in his arms and do his usual thing of breathing me in just so I can get my fix of his scent on me. It's just one of the things I miss about him. I miss him.

When we reach the car, he opens the door for me. Throwing my bag on the back seat, he crouches down at the side of me, holding the car door open. "There's a small café half a mile down the road. Would you join me for a coffee, Holly?" His eyes wander to my lips and I can see that longing to taste them battling within him. He closes his eyes for a split second, gathering himself then leans over me to fasten my seat belt. This time it's me who is left battling when I breathe in his masculine scent because he's that close.

"Yes," I let out in a whimper. The flutter in the bottom of my stomach that he is causing by leaning over me has got me not wanting to let him go yet.

He steps back, giving me that cheeky smile; he is more than aware of what he's just done to me and I know he leant in on purpose and maybe I should make him drop me straight off home. It would be safer, but the wink as just made an appearance, leaving me without the power to say no to him.

Chapter 16

Vlad

As I pull into the garage and turn off the car ignition, I drop my head back on to the headrest, blowing out a breath. It's been three days since I saw Holly at her parent's grave and three days since I last got to speak with her. And here she is at my home, her car parked in my drive. I have no idea why she's here, but it could have something to do with one of my sons or all of them. My money's on Lucas. He's become a sneaky little shit as he hatches his plans to bring Holly back.

I'm lost without her and as soon as I turned the corner on to the road where the church her family attended when she was a young girl stands, I knew it was her entering through the door. I waited almost an hour for her to come out and even contemplated going in to check she was okay.

When she came out, she didn't see me leant up against the car. While she made her way to her parent's graveside, I followed at a distance then stood against an old tree, giving her time alone with them.

She was shocked when she turned and saw me stood behind her, but she certainly wasn't upset with me. Her eyes danced with humour when she asked me if I was stalking her and when she told me she had been confessing my sins, her mischievous grin lit up her face. *It would have taken her a lot longer than an hour to profess my sins.*

I could tell she was affected by my touch just as much as I was, a breath catching in her throat and the flush on her cheeks when I leant over her to fasten her seat belt. I watched her eyes rake over me, undressing me and when we went for coffee, she seemed to enjoy being together. I know she misses me and what we had but her ethical ways are fighting with my demons.

Our conversation was kept to discussions about my sons and the club. Once she had finished her coffee, I sensed she wanted to leave, so I did the decent thing and dropped her off. Not once did either of us mention our relationship or the lack of it. Neither did we mention where we went from here.

Climbing out of the car, I shake off the nerves of knowing she's in my home. It's been weeks since she was here in my house, in my bed and I'm not sure how much longer I can retain this bravado that I'm okay with this. I'm weakening with each day that I'm sure I'll fuck up any plans my sons have set up, either by falling to my knees and begging her to take me back or throwing her over my shoulder and locking her away in my room until she comes to her senses.

I take off my shoes as I make my way into the utility room from the garage and straight away the aroma of herbs, spices and garlic fill my nostrils. I can also see a considerable amount of foil trays, scattered about the work tops. *So that's what my youngest was up to this morning when I caught him with his feet dangling from the chest freezer in the garage as he was looking through it.*

If I'm not mistaken, he has asked Holly to help him whip up a few dishes on the pretence that the freezer we use in the utility room is empty, only he's moved it all into the one in the garage. What's the betting he's told Holly that Mrs White is unwell and got Holly to make a batch of meals, so we can just pop them in the oven. He also asked me to be home for five o'clock. Looking at my watch, I'm five minutes early but I make my way quietly into the kitchen. Lucas is nowhere to be seen but Holly is bent down with her head in the oven. A smile graces my lips and that familiar feeling of happiness, fulfilment and love that only this woman; the woman I can't live without, can evoke, overpowers me. My heartbeat races and I find I need to lean against the door frame to steady myself.

"Wow! Whatever you're cooking smells delicious, sweetheart," I say once I've got my heart rate settled. Holly turns quickly as she closes the oven door, the low tone of my voice shocking her.

"Vlad… What are you doing here?" she asks, a startled look on her face. Her cheeks heat up a little and I don't think it's because of the heat from the cooker. She picks up a towel and wipes her hands on it as she shakes her head and bites her lip. The flush on her cheeks deepen as if she's just realised what she has just asked me.

"Last time I checked, I lived here." There's humour in my voice as I close the distance between us picking up the spoon to taste whatever's in the pan. Inhaling it, my lip curls up, "This smells good, Holly," I say as I dip the spoon in then place it in my mouth. The food is red hot and I find I need to play with it in my mouth before I can swallow it. "Hmmm, lamb madras. My favourite." I throw her a wink and try to get another spoonful. I'm unsuccessful though because she slaps me with the towel causing me to drop the spoon.

"Aw, sweetheart I'm starving I haven't eaten all day," I'm not lying, I missed lunch today. It's not the first time. I find I need to keep myself busy throughout the day to distract me from either texting Holly or phoning her. I then forget to eat.

"It's not ready yet and why are you here?" she asks again.

"I've told you angel," I move a little closer to her causing her to back up against the worktop, "I live here."

"I'm not stupid, Vlad, I know you live here but Lucas said you wouldn't be home until eight."

Ah, Lucas the devious little shit has set this up. Who am I to complain? He's done what he set out to do and got Holly here. Now all I need to do is tread carefully so she stays.

"Where is Lucas?" I ask.

"Errr," she looks around. "He was here a few minutes ago… I'm not sure where he has gone." She tilts her head as her gaze worriedly looks me up and down. "Why did you miss lunch?" Her stare holds mine. I'm not going to tell her the truth that half the time I can't be bothered, too churned up inside with the thought of losing her or that I make sure I'm that busy, so I don't think about her that I forget.

I smile and shrug my shoulders, "Busy day."

"You're losing weight," she scolds me, but I see the concern in her eyes. "Go freshen up and call Lucas while I set the table for you both then I'll leave you to it." She nods her head towards the food then bends down, taking out of the oven whatever is in there. "This is for now," her head nods towards the pan on top of the cooker. "And these are for the freezer," she points at the trays and moves to grab some plates from the cupboard.

"Holly," she ignores me.

"You'll need to leave them a few hours to cool but the ones in the utility room will be ok to put in the freezer." I move to the side of her, taking the plates from her hands and placing them on the worktop. Then placing my hands on her shoulders, I feel a shiver run through her. I turn her to face me.

"Holly stay and eat with us," my hands run down her arms until they meet hers and I take hold of them. "You have cooked all this," my head nods to the vast amount that she has made for my sons and me, "Please stay," I plead and if I need to, I will beg. I run my thumb over her knuckles and wait for her response.

"Ok," she nods, her sapphire eyes holding so much emotion then she takes her hands back and starts to stir the rice in the pan. "Go freshen up while I set the table and call Lucas, he must be in his room," she says as she takes another plate from the cupboard and walks over to the dining table.

"Are you sure you'll be still here when I come back, or will you have bolted out of the door as soon as my back is turned?" I'm thinking about when she left me at the hotel without a word that she was going. I know I shouldn't have said it as soon as it came out of my mouth, but she looks nervous. Nervous of me and I don't want her to be, I want her to relax around me. The other day she seemed to be fine then I noticed she couldn't look at me when she was speaking, and she's just done the same thing.

"Sorry," I say as I step towards her.

"It's fine, Vlad." She meets my stare this time. "I'll still be here don't worry I won't be bolting anywhere." She moves past me as she makes her way back into the kitchen area and reaches up into one of the cupboards to get the serving dishes. My hand shoots up to help her and my other seeks a place on her lower back. It's nothing unusual, there's many of times we would cook together and reach for the same thing or if she was struggling to reach something, I would come up behind her and help just like I'm doing now.

"Thanks," she says as I step back, placing the dishes on the counter. I decide I will shower later; I'd much prefer to spend my time here helping Holly just like we used to.

"Let me help, Holly."

"There's not much to do, it just needs serving up," she says. "I thought you were going to get changed," she looks me up and down then takes out the cutlery from the drawer and sets off towards the table. She seems to be comfortable with us been in the same room now which I'm grateful for, so I'm going to make the most of having her here. I'll get changed when she has gone. I say gone, but who knows the gods might be on my side and she might end up staying over.

"Nah, I'll wait until later," I smile while grabbing a couple of wine glasses and a juice glass for Lucas who has miraculously disappeared. She nods at me as we both continue to set the table.

"Hi dad," the sneaky little devil says as he wanders into the kitchen. "I didn't know you were home." *No course you didn't, fibber.* "I thought you said you wouldn't be home until eight," he eyes me wearily. *Of course, you did, Pinocchio.*

"No, can't remember saying that," I say as I pull playfully at his nose, grinning at him.

"Must be your age," he comments as he takes his glass from me and fills it with apple juice from the fridge. Taking a drink, I can see the laughter in his eyes as they watch me over the rim of his glass.

"Yeah, must be," I say as I pass by him on my way to the utility room to retrieve a bottle of wine.

Having Holly here with Lucas and me should feel normal and to Lucas it probably does. He will see the two people he loves together in the same room, eating, chatting and hopefully laughing and think everything's the way it should be. That he has helped to bring those two people together even if it is just for that evening will give him a sense of achievement.

Only it's not the same as it was and that's on me and as much as I love having the backing of my sons and their help to try and win her back, I'm the one that needs to show her I'm still the same man she fell for. Even though I looked intimidating, she still fell in love with me and craved me just as much as I craved her when we were not together. It's me who needs to prove to her that I'm sorry for what I did and said in the club that night. It's me who needs to reassure her that the man I was, that I needed to be to protect my family at that time in my life is not the same one who adores and worships her. And it's me who needs to get her to relax around me, so I can prove that I am the man she still needs and loves even if she is trying to fight it.

"Oh, this is hot," Lucas says as he holds his mouth open, wafting his hand in front of it. His cheeks heat up and his eyes water as he swallows the mouthful of curry.

"I thought you had an asbestos mouth like your dad," Holly chuckles at Lucas as he downs a glass of water.

"He normally does. Can't hack it today, son," I comment while pouring him another glass of water.

"I think I went over the top with the chilies," his face scrunches up as he places his fork at the side of his plate. Holly gets up and wanders into the kitchen, coming back with a tub of cream.

"Here let me add a bit of this," she mixes a couple of teaspoons of the cream into Lucas' food then offers him to taste it. She waits patiently for him to swallow it, "Better?" she asks, smiling.

"Yeah," he nods. "Lots," he says as he shovels another forkful into his mouth. "Thanks, Holly," he says once he has finished swallowing his mouthful.

Conversation flows easily between the three of us as we indulge in the rather hot dish that Holly and Lucas had whipped up. Lucas adding too many chilies but although hot it is very tasty. I've just finished my second helping and I'm full to bursting.

Lucas excuses himself once we have finished eating and cleared the table, leaving Holly and I alone, finishing a glass of wine. She reluctantly accepted a small glass because she's driving home and as she sits there sipping it, I load the dish washer.

Watching her sitting at the table with her feet up on the chair next to her, she's relaxed. She takes another sip of the wine, closing her eyes as she does. Savouring the fruity taste. Holly's legs stretch out and her head leans back on to the chair as she places the glass on the table. I watch her hand come up to the top of her head where she releases her wavy golden hair from the bobble, shaking it and running her hand through her soft locks.

She sits up, still with her feet on the other chair and wiggles her toes as she examines the red polish on her toenails. When she picks up her glass again and finishes off the wine, I know it won't be long before she wants to leave, and I don't want her to leave just yet. If ever.

Picking up my briefcase that I'd left in the kitchen, I make my way over to Holly. As I take out the catalogues of kitchens units, sinks, tiles and splash backs, Holly straightens in her seat glancing at the magazines. I remove colour charts and a small catalogue which contains various types of flooring.

"Can you help me with something, Holly?" I ask, turning to see her tapping her teeth with her fingernail as she scans all the booklets that I have thrown on the table.

"Yeah. Sure, if I can." She gets up and stands at the side of me. Her arm brushes past mine as she picks up one of the catalogues. "Are these for the apartments?" she asks, flipping the pages. I can't answer her right away because that one little delicate touch, along with the smell of her hair that wafted by as she moved close to me has heightened my senses. Bringing out the usual urge whenever she is near. It was kept at bay when I first came home and saw her in my kitchen, I was just happy to have her here. But now that's changed. Carnal desire runs through my veins. Wanting to feel her beneath me riving and biting at my skin. My lips trailing over hers as I nip and kiss my way around her beautiful body. Both of us chasing the same thing.

"Vlad," I shake my head, bringing me out of my sensual yearning when I hear her voice.

"Sorry," I say. "Just thinking." She raises an eyebrow at me, questioning my silence. I'm sure she can see the lust in my dark eyes and the pulse beating out of my neck. I take in a deep breath and answer her earlier question.

"Yes, they're for the apartments. I need to choose the kitchen and colours as well as the flooring. I thought maybe you could help me."

"Of course. Let me have a look." She moves in closer, stepping in front of me, so her back is almost touching my chest. And all I want to do is wrap my arms around her and nuzzle my nose into her hair then make my way into the crook of her neck. I don't.

Leaning over her I pick up the kitchen catalogue and point out the three that I can't decide which one of them I prefer. Straight away her enthusiasm comes to the fore. I know she's passionate when it comes to picking out any home improvements and if the excitement of when she first saw my kitchen is anything to go on, I know she will pick the perfect one.

"Wooh, look at this one," she gushes as she runs her fingers over the pages of the high white gloss cupboard doors. "This one would look good with black and white tiles. Or if you wanted to add a bit of colour for warmth, you could have the tiles or splash back in a claret colour."

She glances up at me to get my take on her idea but I'm too busy thinking about how natural this is. Us together. Me leaning over her with my hand on her hip and my chest pressed up against her back. Yes, in the few minutes it has taken her to pick out one of the kitchens we have stepped into our normal. *That close a breath of fresh air couldn't pass between us.*

I don't move my hand that is resting on her hip nor do I make a big deal about it. Without breaking contact, I lean in a bit further pointing to a few other colours that we could use so that the block of apartments doesn't have all the same. Holly agrees.

As we pick out the kitchens, tiles or splash back, we also choose a few accessories from one of the other brochures. All the kitchens have a built-in cooker and hob along with a fridge freezer and as Holly picks up the next brochure to look at the flooring, she angles her head up to speak, "Do you want tiled flooring, laminate or vinyl?" She asks, meeting my gaze. Our mouths are so close it wouldn't take much for me to connect them together and from the look in her eyes, I think she sees what I am thinking. "Vlad," her soft voice calls to me but I'm so lost in her. The innocence in her sapphire blue eyes. The way her cheekbones become like tiny little red apples when she laughs and how her plump bottom lip is calling for me to nip at it. All I want to do is cover her mouth with mine and hold her tight in my arms for the rest of our lives.

The wanting is all-consuming as we stand there spellbound, struck with the love we hold for each other, but neither of us daring to move first.

"Wow, this smells good," and that there breaks the spell as we both turn our heads to see Nicholas spooning a mouthful of the lamb madras into his mouth.

"Here plate it up," Daniel says, passing him a couple of plates. They don't notice Holly and I stood by the table, my hand on her hip and hers on my chest. I felt the warmth as soon as she laid it there.

We continue to watch my two sons as they fill their plates with enough food to feed an army then sit at the breakfast bar to fill their faces. Daniel gets back up to retrieve a bottle of becks from the fridge, passing one to his brother as he sits back down. They eat with speed as if they haven't eaten all day and unaware that we are watching them. I feel Holly shaking and when I look down, she is struggling to contain her laughter. Daniel looks up as if he's heard something, it's then his eyes land on Holly and me.

"Oh, sorry. Didn't see you there," he smirks as he shovels another forkful of food into his mouth. Nicholas quickly spins round and chuckles. "Love this, Holly," he points the fork at his food while chewing the mouthful that he has. His head tilts down towards his plate again as he continues to eat like an animal. My sons have no table manners, well these two don't.

It's then Holly breaks our hold when she erupts into a fit of giggles. She covers her mouth with her hand. "Sorry," she splutters out, tears pooling in her eyes and I can't help but laugh myself.

She breaks our contact and strolls over to the two idiots that I could quite easy strangle.

"It's like watching two bloody horses at feeding time. Next time I'll just pop it into a bag, strap it to your head so you can nuzzle into it." She chuckles.

"Aw, don't be mean. You know we can't resist a home cooked meal, especially when it's you or Mrs White who's done the cooking," Daniel says as he finishes his meal in record time. He gets up to put his plate in the dish washer and Nicholas turns to me.

"What's up, Paps?

"Nothing," I tell him as I pick up the empty wine glasses. It's a lie. I'm pissed that my sons couldn't make themselves scarce for one evening, but I'm not sure if they knew Lucas had planned for Holly to be here. So, I can't stay mad at them even if they do have an apartment of their own to go to which they don't only when they have some woman to warm their bed.

"Right, I'm off," Holly announces just as Lucas makes an appearance. He lays his elbows on the worktop and cups his chin in his hands.

"Are you leaving?" he looks put out and I can understand why. He set this all up and his older brothers have just fucked it up.

"Yes, kiddo." She grabs him in a hug and kisses the top of his head. "I had a nice time today," she tells him. "Let me know next time Mrs White isn't feeling well and I'll come over and help you cook," he looks at her sheepishly, knowing he's told a little white lie. Holly knows it too as she throws him a wink and ruffles his hair.

My other two sons give her one of their bear hugs and kiss her on the cheek as they say their goodbyes.

"I'll walk you out," I say as I pick up her bag. She grabs her keys and I follow her out of the front door to her car. I open her door slightly then close it again, refusing to let her go without her acknowledging what just nearly happened between us. "Holly," I take her hand in mine and she lifts her head to look up at me. Her watery eyes and the tremble in her lip sends a pain to my heart. I can see this whole turmoil is getting to her and I'm at a loss with how to put this right. "Please, tell me what I need to do, Holly… I don't know what to do to make this right…" I'm stopped when she places her finger on my lip and I can see she is fighting with her emotions. We both are. We need to talk. We need to stop this charade that we're both okay when we certainly are not. She needs to tell me what she is thinking and what she wants before we both go out of our minds. I know the time she has spent with my family has helped her, kept her spirits up but it's time for her to talk to me. I've kept my distance, given her time to comprehend what I had told her. She needs to tell me one way or another whether we are over.

"I can't do this now, Vlad," there's a plea in her voice, "but we'll talk soon." With that she opens her car door, gets in and drives away.

Leaving me standing there watching the back of her car disappear out of my drive.

"You idiots," I here Lucas say, and I know he is speaking to Nicholas and Daniel. When I walk into the kitchen, my sons are putting away the dinners that Holly and Lucas had made.

"Sorry," both my sons say at the same time. I hold my hand up to them.

"It's fine."

"No, it's not," Lucas says. "I had to lie to get Holly here and these two screwed it up." They both look at Lucas, not knowing what to say to him as he stands there worrying his bottom lip. "Hey there," I take him into my arms. I know we treat him like he's a baby sometimes but with nearly losing him once when he was a baby, also his brothers do have some years on him, he is the baby of the family. "You did good today," I tell him. "We talked and laughed, and we did spend a few hours together instead of twenty minutes over a cup of coffee," I explain. He nods his head, wiping at his eyes. He's such an emotional boy, I hate to see him upset. "Plus, you did manage to persuade Holly to come here without any help. You should be pleased and I'm sure being here with you and me will have shown her just what she's is missing," I knock him under his chin, and he gives me a shy smile.

"They still cocked up," he points at his brothers who I'm sure feel bad for coming home at the wrong time.

"We know," Daniel walks over to Lucas and gives him a hug. "Sorry. We'll come up with something to get her back here." His eyes look over at me, "Sorry, dad."

"Yeah, sorry," Nicholas says. "We didn't think."

"It's fine," I wave my hand at them. "For what it's worth, I don't think she is quite ready yet. She may need a little more time."

Chapter 17

Holly

Vlad's hands on me, his breath on my skin. The low tone of his husky voice and the way his masculine smell ignites a fire within has consumed my thoughts and plagued my dreams since I left his home the day before yesterday. The passion in his eyes, the wink, the cheeky smirk that makes him look younger are all the things that have kept me awake and even the few hours I have slept he's taken over those too. Not that he had ever been far away from either.

No sooner did I hear him speak while my head was in the oven, he had me. When I turned and saw the love and want in his body language, I wanted him too. The happiness and playfulness on his face; I'd missed the fun side of him that's only seen by the people he loves. Oh, I tried to stay strong, pretending I could leave but as soon as I heard the plea in his voice, I couldn't do it and I didn't really want to.

I wanted to be there with him and with Lucas doing our norm. Eating, chatting, laughing together, being a family. It's so natural for the three of us to spend the evening together eating, watching a film then Vlad and myself being left alone while Lucas gets on with his homework or plays on one of his games. So, when Lucas disappeared it wasn't unusual. When Vlad stood so close that the heat from his body warmed me to the core, I welcomed it. The touch when he placed his hand on my hip, I craved it. Rather than stepping out of his way, I relished his touch, his smell, his voice. I wanted to be wrapped in his arms. I wanted his lips on mine and when we were so close, eyes locked together, lips so close I wanted to taste him. I would have given anything for him just to take charge and claim me, but we were both scared. Him scared of me rejecting him, I could see it in his eyes and me scared by my morals.

Being interrupted by the chuckle brothers brought me back to my senses. Brought us both from the spell we had been caught in and it was probably for the best, only I felt bad for Lucas. He had fabricated a little white lie to get me there, I knew he had, and he did a good job of it. But his brothers put a stop to it.

Leaving Vlad's gave me time to think. As if I hadn't done enough thinking. But now I know what I want. I want us back together. However, we need to talk. Vlad needs to prove to me that he will never become that violent man again, the one I saw in the club.

How he's going to do it? I haven't got a clue or how to approach him on the matter. How does one tell someone like him, a man who has done the things he has done? Been through the things he has been through and come out of it still with his sanity. Someone who has brought four boys up on his own and kept his heart closed to anyone but his family, until me.

I know what he has done and the reasons behind them. Although these still worry me, I know the man I love would not have done them without good cause. The safety of his family being the reason and they are the ones I need to speak to before I challenge their father.

I've been around them over the last few weeks since Vlad unloaded his past and they have never mentioned anything about it. I'm sure they know and I'm sure they're aware that I know. It's something we need to discuss. I want their feelings on it. I want to know how they dealt with the life that they were born into and how they live with the knowledge of the crimes their father has committed. We spend so much time together, I think I'm owed the truth from them.

*

"Will you sit down woman, you're making me fucking dizzy,"

Nicholas chuckles as he watches me prepare lunch. I'm on a mission, wanting to surprise Vlad at his office which I haven't been in since he berated me. I need to talk to him, and I need to do it today before I have a nervous breakdown. So, I decided to make him lunch because I know fine well he has been missing too many meals. "and put the knife down before you lose a finger." He takes the knife from my hand that I had been using to slice tomatoes and directs me to the sofa. Daniel and Sebastian follow us, both biting into a tomato that they whipped from the kitchen.

I had text the three of them to come over urgently, wanting to speak to them before I speak with their father but now that I have the three of them here, I don't know how to approach the subject.

"Holly, what was so urgent?" Sebastian asks, sitting down next to me, concern edged on his face. Looking at his two brothers, I can see they're all waiting eagerly for me to give them the reason why I needed to see them all together. "Holly, you look nervous and have no reason to be. Whatever's wrong you can talk to us about it." Sebastian is so much like his father when it comes to people he cares about, always trying to put them at ease.

"As long as it has nothing to do with lady's things then I'm all ears," Nicholas chuckles as he leans back on the settee, crossing his legs at the ankles. Sebastian rolls his eyes at him and shakes his head; Daniel lets out a chuckle of his own.

"Too early in the day for that kind of talk Holly," Daniel sucks in a breath. "In fact, it's not a good topic at any time of day." I laugh with them this time because their just what I need, alleviating the tension is one thing they're good at.

"Will you two grow up. Holly hasn't asked us here to talk about girlie shit," Sebastian tells his brothers. Then turns to me, "You haven't? Have you?" he looks panicked.

"What? No." I shake my head at him. He puts his hand on mine.

"I mean if there's a problem then.... You're not pregnant, are you? It's fine if you are but this conversation should be for the old man not us," there's a touch of humour on his face.

"Sebastian, I'm not pregnant and it's not about girlie shit. But thank you for your concern." I cover his hand with mine this time.

"Ok. But just so you know if you were pregnant, we would be fine with that." His dark eyes shift to his brothers and they both nod their heads in agreement. Pregnant, I haven't thought about having children since I was married and then I gave up on the idea towards the end of our relationship. I doubt for one minute Vlad would want another child, his youngest is almost a teenager. His eldest in his late twenties, he has two grandchildren and one on the way. Plus, he's no spring chicken even if he does look and act as if he's around the same age has his sons. I push that one right from my mind.

"Thank you," I tell them. "It's good to know you're on my side."

"What is it then?" Daniel speaks up.

"It's..." I struggle to get it out. "I don't know where to start," I tell them.

"The beginning is always good," Sebastian suggests.

"Yes, it is," I agree. "Hmmm, your father has told me all about your mother and your grandfather..." I leave it open for them to ask me what he has told me, but they just nod at me.

"We know," Sebastian is the first to speak. His tone is laid back as if he's just heard something as natural as the sky is blue. "What is it Holly? There's nothing we can tell you that our father hasn't already."

"I know," I say as I stand, feeling more comfortable now that I don't look as small sat amongst these large men. They're not intimidating like their father; I know that they are good men and think the world of me. But this discussion is making me nervous, I need the space. "I wouldn't expect you to tell me anything without consulting with your father first and I didn't invite you here to..."

"Then what did you want, Holly?" Daniel asks, interrupting me. Standing, he puts his arm around my shoulder. "Sit down and talk to us," his tone is caring. I sit down, and he joins me as Nicholas moves from his seat, sitting on my other side.

They both turn sideways to look at me and as I take them in along with Sebastian, I know I can speak to them about anything, so I just dive right in. "How did you cope with knowing that your father had killed people?" I watch all three mouths fall open and three pairs of eyes widen as the three men stare at me. Oh shit. Maybe they didn't know as much as I thought they did, and I've just opened a whole new can of worms. Before I have chance to explain my question Nicholas speaks.

"Fucking hell, Holly, say it as it is why don't you. Straight for the jugular." He gets up, rubbing the back of his neck as his dark blue eyes meet Daniel's.

"Don't fucking look at me," he puts his hands up. "I was only nine when we came here and yes, I had heard and seen things when we lived in Russia," he blows out a breath. "Things I didn't understand but after a while I figured it out. Pieced two and two together… And with the help of these two and my father, I coped with it." I watch him shift in his seat, pulling at his shirt collar. He's nervous, uncomfortable discussing this with me. "Why wouldn't I?" His eyes meet mine. "Holly, I don't ever remember a time in my life when my father wasn't there for me, for us," he twirls his finger around, letting me know he means all of them. "He might have done some things that's hard to take in, that would shock the average person, but he did them for us…" He swallows down his emotions, Sebastian handing him a glass of water. "While I remember my father being this big strong man who would always put us to bed, read stories to us and be there in the morning at breakfast time. A father who wanted to spend quality time with his sons, crawling around the floor with the three of us swinging from him then him tickling the life out of us. Playing football in the back garden and making dens, I can't say the same thing about our mother." He doesn't go on and he doesn't need to, I know enough about Natalia to know she wasn't a good mum.

Daniel stands and rubs his hands up and down his face, emotions getting the better of him. I feel bad for bringing this up, having him and his brothers reliving things they would sooner forget but I needed to know how they felt about it.

I do the only thing I can and take Daniel into my arms, comforting him. His arms wrap around me tight like a son who wants a hug from his mum. We stand like that for a few moments and as we pull apart, I see how much not having a loving mother in his life has affected him, even if Vlad thinks it hasn't. "He's a good man, Holly. Give him a chance to prove that to you, you won't regret it," Daniel says then leaves me standing there as he makes his way to the bathroom.

"Such an emotional boy," Nickolas jokes, as Sebastian shakes his head and throws his eyes up at him. "But he is right. He was young and didn't see, hear or understand some of the things that went on. Whereas me and big brother here," he slaps Sebastian on the back. "Were privy to the good the bad and the fucking ugly." Again, there's humour in his voice, but I'm not stupid. I know that what I am witnessing is his way of covering up the years he endured of being neglected from his mother as well as the danger that surrounded them because of their grandad.

And I know I would be right in thinking that each one of Vlad's sons have their own way of dealing with the hurt that surrounded them.

Sebastian; keeping himself busy, protecting his brothers. Helping to keep them on the straight and narrow. Nurturing them to be the good people they are. Then meeting Izzy and throwing all the love his father had showed him into his relationship with her and becoming a father who will love and protect fiercely. Nicholas; the life and soul of the party. He too, the protective brother and loving son who will play the fool, have his brothers in fits of laughter no matter what the situation. Take the piss out of his dad to lighten the mood, so he didn't have to see them upset and hurt. Masking his own hurt with his high spirits.

Daniel; ploughing his time into his music. His guitar his solace. Pouring out his hurt in song even if it's not noticeable to the crowd and his band members. Now I know their story it's more than noticeable to me and I'm sure his father and older brothers are more than aware too. Then there's Lucas, the youngest of them who grew up in England but born in Russia, fighting for his life. Spending his first two months in an incubator. No early bonding even though he was loved and cherished daily by his brothers and father. Growing up the youngest in a family where all the men are larger than life while he struggles with being small for his age. Sketching being his comfort when he needed someone or something other than male members of his family. Not missing the love of a caring mother because he had never had it but wanting and needing it without knowing.

Daniel walks back into the room and Sebastian jumps up from his seat. "You ok?" His concern for his brother's emotional state is there for us all to see.

"Yes, I'm good," he answers with a tight smile.

"I'm sorry, Daniel." I tell him. "I didn't want to upset anybody when I asked you here, I just needed to know how you dealt with it all."

"I know you didn't, Holly. The past doesn't hurt anymore but can't you see it's the relationship you have with our father that's hurting us all now? We've all been affected by what's going on with you two. In one way or another." He shrugs his shoulders and sits down.

"He's right, Holly," Sebastian says, shifting forward in his seat and resting his elbows on his knees. "We had put that life behind us long ago, but it all came flooding back like a bad fucking dream when you two met." He blows out a breath and has me wondering what the hell he means.

"What? Why would you say that, I thought you approved of our relationship?"

"I do… and I didn't mean that to sound the way it did." I stare at him waiting for him to explain.

"Holly sit down please, let me explain." I do as he asks, sitting on the opposite settee to him.

"I'm not going to go into details about how SHE led him on a merry dance," he refers to his mother as she and the way he rubs at his temples with his fingers tells me he struggles when referring to her. "I know you know all about her and how she trapped my father and neglected her sons." I can hear the hurt in his voice and wonder just how much he struggles with being the pawn in her game.

"Sebastian, I know your father would go through it all again for you all. He loves you all dearly and whatever Natalia did or didn't do, trapping him gave him you and your brothers. He would never want to be without you, it would kill him," I know I sound overly dramatic, but he lives and breathes for his boys. He's proved what he can do and will do to keep them safe.

"I know. What I'm trying to get at is that he's never been in love. He didn't love her and any women in between her comings and goings were just… Well you know what there were. When we came to live here, he never went out for over a year; not to socialise anyway. It was work, work, work and us. Lots of trips to the hospital with Lucas, nights of helping with our homework and trips to the coast in the holidays. Then when he met Mark and Dave he started to go out, let his hair down a bit but never once did he bring a woman home or stay out the whole night." I know this already, it's one of the things that became clear the morning after our first night together.

"Our father has never been in a proper relationship. He didn't marry for love and has never been in love until he met you."

"Dancing on a table, dragging you off the dance floor with such urgency, we thought he had gone mad and grinning like a Cheshire cat after you had been texting back and forth proved to us you were something special," Nicholas beams as he knocks me with his shoulder.

"Here, here," Daniel agrees, a wide grin on his face. Mine is as big because no one's ever told me I was special before. Being among Vlad's family over the last few months has brought us close, close enough that his sons will speak freely and openly to me about anything and everything. Including my relationship with their father.

"Thank you," I tell them.

"Holly," Sebastian gets my attention. "What I was getting at with what I said," he's referring to the comment about a bad dream. "The incident in the club and how he behaved afterwards, wasn't the man we know. The things he said and did, how irrational he was and the heavy drinking, shocked all of us. And I hate myself for saying it but there were times I wished he had never met you." I think he's just shocked his brothers with his comment as they both narrow their eyes at him. I'm just sorry that he was made to feel that way, but I don't think his father's behaviour was my fault.

"Seb?" Nicholas questions.

"Let me finish." We all sit waiting for him to get to the point.

"Will you say what you mean because you're fucking annoying me now," Nicholas rubs his chin and moves to the edge of his seat.

"Sorry," Sebastian says. "He grew up in a violent world. One where his wife would fuck anything that moved, was higher than kite most days and never once showed any love towards her sons. His father who was supposed to love and protect him made his life a living hell, took all his dreams from him and replaced them with nightmares. The things he had to do because of her and him aren't something you would wish on your worst enemy, but he survived it.

You know, the number of women that threw themselves at him in Russia and here in England, you would have thought he would have fallen for one of them, but he didn't. He closed himself off for years then you came along, and he fell hard. He couldn't cope. He didn't know that his feelings would spiral into something he couldn't comprehend. He knew… He fucking knew you were nothing like her but every day he tormented himself with the thought that you would leave him for another man. He struggled with hiding his past, he wanted to tell you. He hated it when you asked questions and he was unable to tell you the truth. 'Oh, I was in the Russian Mafia. My father and my wife fucked me over for fifteen years.' Not the conversation you want to have. Again, he knew if he did then you would leave him," he sighs and it's heartfelt. When he stands, one hand rubs at his face and the other goes into his trouser pocket. Daniel and Nicholas stare at him. This is their older brother, the one they look up to, another father figure even if the difference in ages are small, they still respect him.

He walks over to where I am sat and crouches in front of me, taking my hands in his. "Holly." He closes his eyes and shakes his head as if he's trying to rid the memories. "My father has always been a good man. Circumstances caused him to do things he would sooner forget and coming here was supposed to be a fresh start for us all. And I know that for us it was. However, our father will never forget… He can put it to the back of his mind, hide it away. Pretend it's forgotten but I see the regret. The pain he conceals, the guilt and whether that's for his father's actions, his own or Natalia's who knows. But what I do know," he lets go of my hands, sitting next to me on the settee and blowing out a long breath. "He's paid tenfold for it." I pat his leg, understanding that the love they hold for their father could never be matched, it holds no bounds. And the love he holds for them is without condition. To his sons, he's the hero every child wants in a father, with the added unconditional love of a mother.

"All the suffering and anguish he went through within those years," Sebastian continues, "Leaving all that behind and coming here to live, he's worked hard. Don't think for one minute that everything he has is paid for out of dirty money because it isn't. He paid for the restaurant with the money he had inherited from his great aunt. The house was paid for out of his own bank account. Yes, the money was from what he had earned while working for his father but that's all he took from it. Then over the years, besides raising money for the hospital, he donated from the revenue of the restaurant the same amount he paid for the house to various charities. All the charities either here in England or in Russia were to help families who had problems with drugs or shelters who supported them. The hospital where Lucas was born and treated were sent a rather large donation from his father's estate, my father not wanting a penny from it. The rest was split between other drug charities." He tilts his head to look at me, his eyes filled with tears. "I'm sorry, Holly. After the incident in the club and you going away, he couldn't handle it. What he had done and said, how he had behaved towards you. When you wouldn't return his calls or let him show you how sorry he was, he flipped. We didn't recognise him. He wasn't the man we knew and loved and to be truthful he made it quite clear he didn't want us around. So yes, there were times I wished he hadn't met you but that was just me wanting my father back. Wanting the man I knew who was strong and determined, who never let anyone in but us. It was selfish of me and I'm sorry." His hand covers his mouth as he sits forward in his seat. I can only imagine what these men were feeling while their father was on a drunken binge, one that I may have been able to stop if I had stuck around but it's not like Vlad gave me an alternative when he behaved as he did, I was hurting too.

"You have no reason to be sorry, Sebastian," I lay my hand on his arm. "I understand how hard it must have been for you all, seeing your father in such a state and I'm sorry that you had to feel that way." He nods his head at me then stands, walking over to the window.

"Holly, you wanted to know how we dealt with what our father had to do. Well, dealing with it wasn't hard at all because we have always seen the good in him. The man underneath; the one he had to become to survive a world where if you were weak then..." he blows out a breath. "You didn't survive." I understand what he means about the good in him, I have seen it in bundles many times and I understand that protecting his family whether it was from his father and the life he wanted for them. Or whether it was from their mother, he would do whatever it took.

"Give him a chance, Holly. You won't ever see that side of him again, he knows he fucked up and that you're nothing like her. He won't make that mistake again; you just need to give him a chance to prove himself." This time it's me nodding my head because how could I not want to give Vlad another chance to show me the man I know he is. The one who loves with passion and protects with the heart of a lion.

"How can I not?" I murmur through the tears that stream down my face. Nicholas is up out of his seat, wrapping me in his arms. Soothing me.

"Hey, stop the tears," he comforts. "The old man will have our heads if he knows we've had you in tears," he chuckles into my hair. I sniffle and laugh with him, wiping at my wet eyes. "Come on, let's have a coffee and finish that lunch you were making." He squeezes my shoulder. I excuse myself, needing the bathroom. I just need a breather for a moment. When I return, Sebastian, Nicholas and Daniel are filling my kitchen drinking coffee and finishing up the lunch I had started to prepare for their father.

"Wow, that's one big lunch," I chuckle.

"Well we thought he might get his appetite back when he sees you," Daniel tells me, grinning.

"Talking of appetites," Nicholas slides up to the side of me putting his arm around my shoulder.

"You know it won't only be his appetite for food that will come back when he sees you," he wiggles his eyebrows at me. I slap his arm knowing fine well what he's implying.

"Nicholas," I chastise. His brothers both shake their head at him but grin at his comment.

"What?" his eyes wide. "You could put him on rations…"

"What planet are you on?" Sebastian asks. "Wait until you have a woman you can't live without, we'll tell her that," he chuckles. Nicholas shakes his head at his brother, dismissing what he just said. Daniel stands there smirking at them both and I'm at a loss not knowing what to say as they casually discuss their father and my sex life.

"If Holly suggests laying off sex until he proves himself to her, it will give him a challenge and you know how he loves a challenge," he looks at his brothers. "He will do anything to prove that he is the man you need. Plus let him wine and dine you, spoil you with presents."

"He knows I don't need gifts."

"But you could let him spoil you," Sebastian suggests, siding with Nicholas while he puts the lids on the tubs that they have packed enough meat and cheese into to feed them all. Nicholas opens the fridge, taking two bottles of water out and a bottle of prosecco. Daniel holds open the cool bag as they fill it.

"Is this everything?" Nicholas asks while he collects the coffee cups they had used, still with that mischievous twinkle in his eyes.

"Yes," I nod my head at him.

"Grab your bag then we will drop you off, hopefully you'll be able to put a smile on his face."

"Oh, okay. Thank you." I was going to drive myself, but a lift would be great, I'd struggle with getting a parking spot at this time of day anyway.

Daniel carries my bags that have the lunch prepared in them while Sebastian collects his car keys from the living room table. "Oh, Holly," Nicholas says, opening the door smirking. I tilt my head at him waiting for what he is going to say next. "Think about my suggestion," he lifts one eyebrow. "Even if it's just for a few weeks, it won't hurt him, but it will give us a bloody good laugh."

"You are evil, Nicholas Petrov," I shake my head at him. "But I'll think about it."

Chapter 18

Vlad

I ignore the timid knock that threatens to disturb me while I'm working. I've been trying to write this email for the last hour but I'm having trouble focusing and it needs sending to the council before the end of the day.

Izzy, my daughter in law, brought me a digital photo frame. It switches from picture to picture and holds god knows how many. What I do know is that in most photos Holly is present, with my grandchildren, sons, on her own or with me. Every one of them showing off her perfect smile, her angelic features; it captures her beauty perfectly and I can't take my eyes off it. Hence the reason I haven't written my email and now someone wants to disturb me.

The knock sounds again and this time it's grown a backbone as the bang on the door sounds urgent. I know it's not one of my sons as they wouldn't dream of knocking, they don't even knock on my bedroom door so why would they on my office door. Frank would knock while he was walking in. My restaurant manager would do the same which leads me to believe it's one of any number of employees I have working here, and they can wait.

I set about typing up the email again, ignoring whoever is there and hoping they piss off and leave me alone. No such look as the knock becomes anxious and has me deleting the email and sitting up in my chair "Come in!" I growl, not having the patience to deal with any trivial matters now.

"Hello," comes the sweet voice of the woman that has had me daydreaming all morning and suddenly my solemn mood as lifted. "You sound grouchy," she says as she steps further into my office, arms full of bags and what looks like a cool bag. "Need feeding?" she questions with her hand on her hip and an eyebrow raised, bags now placed on the floor. "Have you missed lunch again?" she scolds, looking at her watch. I love how even though we're not technically together she still cares, but her unexpected presence has got me all disorientated.

"What? Yes. No. Sorry." I fumble with my words and struggle to string a sentence together as I round my desk to meet her in the middle of my office.

"Huh, which one is it?" she laughs at me, leaning down to pick up one of the bags.

"Sorry," I excuse myself. "No, I haven't had lunch," I look at my watch. "But it's not quite lunch time yet. Yes, I was grouchy," I roll my eyes at her, making her chuckle again. "But I've suddenly got over it. This is a welcomed surprise. What brings you here?" I ask, lifting her bags and placing them on the table next to the settee. "Sit down," I point to the settee. "I'll get you a coffee." I don't wait for her to say she doesn't want one and in seconds I'm back with a latte for both of us. I silently thank my sons for upgrading the coffee machine in the office.

"I brought you lunch, and I thought we could talk. That is if you're not too busy." Now she sounds nervous.

"No, I'm not busy," fuck the email, I'll do it later. I wasn't getting anywhere with it anyway. "Anything particular you want to discuss, sweetheart?" She sits on the floor on her knees and starts to unpack the food she has brought, so I take a seat at the side of her. Holly unloads a couple of plates and two glasses then quickly turns to me.

"Us," she points between us and I can see the tremble in her hand as she sits back against the cushion I have put at the back of her. She's nervous and I don't want her nervous around me.

"Good, we do need to talk, Holly," I too sit back against the settee. "Let's eat first then talk," maybe she'll be less edgy once we've eaten and she's been here awhile. I move forward and help with unpacking the mountains of food she has brought. "Are my sons joining us?" I lift my eyebrow at her. There's enough to feed them and then some, she chuckles as I open tubs with rolled up slices of ham and turkey. Various types of cheese, tomatoes and pickles. Crackers, bruschetta and crusty bread as well as fruit. More than enough of everything for two. Holly laughs at my comment as she brings out two bottles of water and a bottle of Prosecco.

"Yeah, I got a bit carried away with the meat and cheese. What we don't eat we can put in the fridge for tomorrow," she blushes. I take the bottle from her and pop the cork then pour out two glasses offering Holly one. She takes a sip then places it on the table. We both load our plates with the buffet, Holly sitting back against the cushion as she pops a piece of bruschetta with feta cheese into her mouth. I tuck into mine not realising how hungry I really was.

"I thought maybe you could get some sort of counselling," she doesn't look at me while saying it. She just murmurs it as she pops a tomato into her mouth, but I hear it clearly. I cough into my hand to give me a minute before I speak, a little shocked to say the least.

"And why would I need therapy?" I ask, not looking at my angel who sits there staring ahead into the empty space of my office, legs stretched out under the table while she eats her lunch. I find myself doing the same, sat at the side of her with my back leant against the settee.

"I just thought it might help you with what… with what your dead wife put you through." She puts her plate down and turns to face me, as she chews on the inside of her cheek.

"Holly," I sit up straight. "If this is about what happened in the club, I can promise you…" She puts a finger on my lip to silence me, I should be annoyed at her for stopping me from having my say but I'm not. I'm relieved she wants to talk about it and move on.

"Don't promise me, Vlad." Her eyes beseech me. "Just prove it to me," her voice is tender and welcoming but how can I prove it? I'm always going to want to rip someone's head off if they look at her the wrong way or touch her. Again, I'm fucked if I do and fucked if I don't. But I need to try for us.

"Holly," I put my plate down and take her hand in mine. "I'm not going to lie to you, it's going to be hard for me…" I rub at my jaw. "I know that the man you saw me become won't ever appear again but it won't stop me from not being the man I am. I will always want you as mine and only mine."

"I know, and I can accept that you're going to grunt and growl like a cave man and come and defend me if needed but I'm not that woman." She shakes her head. "The woman who would hurt you in the way your wife hurt you."

"And what about the other Holly," I search her eyes for any signs that she might struggle with what she knows about me. "Can you cope with knowing what I have done in the past? Can you lay in bed with me in the dead of night knowing what my life was like and what I had to do?" I place my hand on her cheek. "Can you let these hands touch you knowing what they have done?" My thumb strokes over her cheekbone as I watch for any signs that this would be too much for her. Her eyes close and she leans into my hand, relishing the feel on her skin. When her eyes open, I can see any trepidation she had when we've been near each other has gone and the longing to be with me is as strong as ever.

"Yes," she nods her head. "It's your past, Vlad, and it's you who needs to put it behind you, so we can move on." She manoeuvres herself so she is sat up straight then reaches over to pick up her drink. "I think…" she stops and holds her hand up while she takes a sip of her prosecco, "I think that for the last twelve years you thought you had put it all behind you…" I go to speak to let her know that the life I had in Russia is well and truly buried in the past, but again she places her finger on my lips to stop me, "but you hadn't."

"I hadn't?" I'm shocked by her comment and question her to why she thinks it. "Why would you think that, Holly? When I've done everything I possibly could to bring my boys up to respect the law and work hard for what they want out of life."

"You misunderstand me, Vlad. I know you have, and your sons are a credit to you. What I mean is that you still let Natalia and your father interfere even though they are dead, by not trusting people. I would never hurt you the way she did, but you didn't trust me enough to speak to me… You just assumed I was like her and resorted back to the old Vlad with violence… Which is what you grew to know because of your father."

I don't answer her because I can't. Maybe she is right and the demons I thought I buried a long time ago are still with me. Fuck. There's no maybe about it, I know that she is right, and I just didn't want to admit it. I blow out a breath and pick up a bottle of water, my throat suddenly becoming too dry.

"You're right," I say once I've had a drink. "But what can I do…? What do you want me to do, Holly, to prove that I can be the man you need in your life?" How the hell do I prove to her that I will never be that man she saw in the club that night? The brutality she witnessed when I attacked the idiot who thought he stood a chance with my woman and the way my venomous words were spat at her, I hurt her so much. Then divulging my past, I understand why she needs reassurance.

"We'll take it slowly, one day at a time." She takes my hand and I thread our fingers together. "I know there are things you cannot tell a therapist, but there are some things you can which could help. You need to prove to me that you trust me and that no matter what, I will never cheat on you." She pouts her lips, wiggling them a little then chews on the inside of her cheek while she thinks.

"Okay," I agree. "How slow are we taking this? And how will I know when I have proved myself to you?" I question. "I'm out of my depth here, Holly, you need to explain how we go about this then we can fix this together."

"Well, I thought if we take it slow. You know? Proper dates and going home to our own homes just until we're sure…"

"What?" I break her off, not quite sure at what she is getting at. "What do you mean?"

"I mean," she takes a deep breath then blows it out. "We went full on into our relationship without really getting to know each other, it was all sex, sex, sex and more sex. Which was fantastic by the way," she puts her hand on mine, giving me that mischievous grin of hers.

"It was never going to be anything but, Holly," I wink at her "But, I'm still not sure where you're going with this."

"Oh shit, I'm no good at this," Holly puts her hand on her forehead then runs it down her face.

"Holly," I take her hand in mine. "Take it slow and just tell me what you're getting at."

"Right." She nods her head and finishes her drink. "Don't speak until I finish, Vlad, otherwise I'll never get to the point."

"Ok. My lips are sealed," I mimic zipping up my lips and throwing the key away. She rolls her eyes at me and shakes her head.

"What you told me was huge, Vlad, gigantic, and threw me into a whole new world. I knew what I was feeling but was having difficulty in what I should be feeling. I've done nothing but think and think of what you told me and whether I should or should not be with you. I spoke to Olivia and the priest at my old church…" She stops to let what she has just told me sink in. I close my eyes and nod my head knowing what I had confessed to her was a lot to take in and I can understand that she needed to speak to someone. Olivia is her best friend and the closest person she has to family, I'm sure my secret is safe with her. As for the priest, I already knew she had spoken with him. She told me in the church grounds and although she made a joke of it, I could see she was telling the truth. When I open my eyes, she continues.

"They helped me understand, Vlad, that the things you did and the life you grew up in was not of your own doing. You did what you had to do, I get that, and I can deal with it. However, I can't deal with you going all Mr Psycho when we're out. I know some women love that Macho bullshit, but I don't." I'm dying here, wanting to take her in my arms and hold her tight. I will never forgive myself for behaving the way I did, I'm more than aware of how she hates violence. I lift her hand and place a gentle kiss on her knuckles then hold her hand tightly in mine.

"So, getting to the point. I thought that maybe if we want to move on from this, that if we refrain from sex…" Holly stops and glares at me when I let out a little chuckle and like a naughty schoolboy, I bite my lip to help me hold back the laughter I know will erupt. Who is she trying to kid? Refrain from sex, she can no more resist me than I can her.

"Vlad, if we do this and stick to it, it will give you even more reason to prove you can overcome that hostile man that lurks within you." I know she's serious and wants to do whatever it takes to get our relationship back together and on the mend. I know she wants to be able to go out without the fear of me torturing myself with the thought of her behaving as my wife did. And I know I shouldn't have those thoughts. I know she is true to me and would never become that woman. I didn't just shock Holly when I attacked that man and his mates, I shocked my boys and myself. I had built up this notion that as beautiful and caring as Holly is that she would still leave me probably for another man. How stupid and immature of me. I'm a forty-five-year-old man, with adult sons and grandchildren but can still behave like a fucking teenager.

Even now my immaturity wins because I should be focusing on what Holly is saying but I know I'm not. I can see that glare when she thinks someone is laughing at her and the hand on the hip is a big give away that she is displeased with me. She has every reason because I've all but chewed the inside of my lip trying to hold back my laughter, tears are flowing freely from my eyes and now I've just mimicked unzipping my lips.

The laughter I had tried to keep submerged bellows around my office, bouncing off the walls. Why? Because she thinks that we can keep our hands off each other and not indulge in sex. She's priceless.

"Don't laugh at me, Vlad," she slaps my arm and throws a tomato at me while she narrows her eyes at me.

"I'm not, angel," I choke out. Taking her arm and pulling her gently so she is sat on my lap.

"Yes, you are."

"Holly," I calm myself down and try to be serious. "I'm not laughing at you. I just find it amusing that you think you can resist this," I smugly run my hand down my fine physique. "And I know for fucking certain I would rather cut off my left arm than not have you in my bed," I wink at my angel then go all in. "Or over my desk, up against the wall," I run my finger down her thigh and she lets out low moan. "In the shower," my mouth nips her ear, "On the rug in my living room," my lips kiss down the column of her neck.

"Vlad," she whispers.

"Hmmm," is all I manage. I'm enjoying myself too much and could quite easily flip her on her back and take her on my office floor.

"You need to stop."

"Are you not enjoying my touch, sweetheart?"

"Yes, but we need to stop." She pulls out of my arms and sits up straight. "You need to help me out, Vlad. It can't be all about sex."

"Try telling him that," I readjust myself and groan because I'm as hard as rock.

"Grow up," she tells me.

"I can't around you. You know this. We have discussed it before, I'm like a randy teenager."

"Well, you could try," she's serious and she's right.

"Ok," I agree. "I will do whatever it takes."

"Ok. Whatever it takes?" she questions my agreement.

"Yes."

"Good. So, no sex and no stopping over at each other's house," I groan and nod my head.

"Yes," I tell her.

"And you'll talk to someone?"

"I'll look into it." I'm not happy about sharing my married life with anyone. I think letting it all out to Holly has helped me. I'm also aware that if I fuck up like that again then it's the end of us. She's put up with a lot from me and still stuck around and now she wants to give us a real chance, knowing everything about me. I should be kissing the ground she walks on and agreeing to anything she says but I'm not sure I would be comfortable speaking with a stranger about my past. "I'd rather speak with you… If something is bothering me," I swallow hard, hoping she'll understand how hard this is for me. I can see the softness in her eyes as she nods her head.

"That's a start." She leans her back against my chest as we sit silently. She holds my arms around her waist, playing with the short hairs on them while sat between my legs. It's soothing to feel her body pressed against mine and I hope she is ok with this.

"Is this allowed?" I chuckle because I don't think I've ever had to ask such a question.

"Is what allowed?" Holly turns in my arms to look at me.

"You, sat on my knee." Her fingers run up my chest in a teasing way as she smirks at me.

"It's welcomed. Often." My hands move so they hold the sides of her face as she answers me, and I inch closer, my lips gently stroking over hers.

"And this?" I whisper into them.

"It's required. Always," she breathes, and quicker than the countdown clock my mouth covers hers. My hands stay in place, thumbs stroking over Holly's cheekbones while her hands hold on to my shoulders. Our kiss is everything we are and everything we represent. The need to be together. Happy that what we feel is mutual. Delighting that we are where we want to be, wrapped in each other's arms, our mouths sealing the deal. This time I know I will not fuck this up, I will not let my insecurities beat us. What we have together, our love will fight to keep us growing stronger.

Our moment is broken with the sound of my phone vibrating on my desk. "Shouldn't you answer that?" Holly asks as our heads rest together, our breathing fast and my tongue wanting to continue exploring her mouth.

"No," I answer. "It'll wait."

"It might be important."

"Then they will call back," I say into Holly's lips as my phone rings off. I take her mouth again, but within seconds our kiss is stopped when Holly's mobile rings.

"I should get that," Holly says as she moves back from our embrace. I nod my head, giving in to whoever wants to disturb our intermate moment. Holly reaches into her bag, lifting out her phone and showing it to me.

"Lucas," she grins at me. The little shit, maybe I should give him a hard time like he did his brothers. "Hi sweetie," she answers. "What? I'm with your dad," I watch as Holly listens, her hand going to her chest and her mouth turning down, concern written all over her face. "Ok, Lucas we're on our way," she stands as she continues to speak. "Have you phoned an ambulance?" I don't hear anything else as I'm up from the floor, grabbing Holly's hand, my phone and keys off my desk and hurrying us both out of the door.

Holly relays back to me that Izzy has fallen down the stairs and hurt her back and is complaining of stomach pains. Lucas, Joe and Rebecca are at home with her, Lucas has tried to contact Sebastian but he's not answering his phone and Rebecca and Joe are becoming upset due to their mum being in pain. Lucas has telephoned an ambulance and made Izzy as comfortable as possible while trying to calm his niece and nephew's anxiety.

We race to the car, my heart pounding in my chest, worried for my daughter-in-law and the baby. She's just over eight months pregnant and although her and the baby have both been healthy through her last trimester, she has had problems in the past. My grandchildren will need their father to lessen their worry and even though Lucas is an intelligent boy who acts above his years, he will be out of his depth with this.

As we make our way towards my son's house, I try his number on the car's hands-free phone; after three rings he answers. I don't give him time to speak.

"I hope you have a good reason for not answering Lucas's call?" my tone leaving no room for arguments.

"Huh," he grunts. "I've just finished training with Nicholas and Daniel, I didn't even know he'd called. What's wrong?"

"Izzy has had a fall..." I don't even get chance to finish what I was saying.

"Fuck. I'm on my way."

"Sebastian!" I shout before he puts the phone down and hits the road like a bat out of hell.

"Yes?" he answers. I can hear him ranting at his brothers as he struggles with the thought of his wife and unborn child being hurt.

"Let Nicholas drive. There's an ambulance on the way. I don't want you driving like an idiot, son," he hears my concern for him. I don't want him and his brothers getting in an accident because he can't concentrate on the roads. Hearing him telling Nicholas to drive calms my overprotectiveness and I hang up.

Holly is still chatting with Lucas when we hit a tailback of traffic. "Fuck," my hand hits the steering wheel, frustrated that I'm stuck ten miles away from my family when they need me.

"Vlad," Holly takes my hand in hers, placing it on her knee. "Calm down. Getting upset isn't going to help," her voice soothes me like nothing else. I pick up her hand, kissing her knuckles and place it on my thigh with mine on top. "What's that noise, Lucas?" She has him on loudspeaker, so I can hear him clearly.

"It's the ambulance."

"Good," she says as she turns to give me a reassuring smile. "Listen, Lucas. Sebastian should be there any minute, he's coming from your house. Nicholas and Daniel are with him, ok?"

"Ok."

"Take your next left, Vlad. They'll probably take her to the hospital, it might be easier to go straight there," Holly points at the junction coming up. She's right. By the time we get through this traffic, Izzy will have been admitted into hospital.

"Sebastian has arrived," Lucas speaks through the loudspeaker of Holly's phone.

"Ok, Lucas. Tell him we will meet him at the hospital. Is Nicholas and Daniel with him?"

"Yes."

"Tell them to take you, Joe and Rebecca to the hospital and we'll pick you up from there."

"Ok. See you soon."

"See you soon, sweetheart," Holly says, and I tell him the same. Holly squeezes my hand in comfort. She's more than aware of how much I worry about my family. Besides Izzy being hurt and heavily pregnant, there's also Lucas and my grandchildren who will have been distressed.

*

The traffic around the one-way system moves at a snail's pace and by the time we arrive at the hospital, Izzy has been taken into a room and is being assessed by a doctor.

Rebecca, my granddaughter, squeals with delight when she notices Holly and I walking through the corridor and wriggles out of Daniel's arms. All heads turn our way as she sets off racing towards us. I bend down to her level, letting her launch herself into my arms, straight away she snuggles her face under my chin while wrapping her chubby little arms around my neck. She might love her three uncles to death, enjoying endless hours of play time with them, but when she's upset it's her grandad she wants.

While Joe wraps his arms around one of my legs, Lucas snuggles up to Holly, laying his head on her shoulder. It's been a distressing time for the three of them and they need lots of reassurance and comfort. I pick up Joe so I've got him snuggled into the other side of me, telling them Mummy and the baby will be ok.

"What have the doctors said?" I ask, directing my question at both my older sons.

"Nothing yet," Nicholas says, getting up from the chair he was sat on. "Sebastian said he will come out once they have scanned to check that everything is ok with the baby. She started with contractions in the ambulance. As far as we know, she hurt her back and bumped the back of her head on the stairs when she slipped." Daniel steps in front of Lucas, knocking him playfully under the chin.

"This one stayed calm and followed Izzy's advice to telephone an ambulance while assuring these two that mummy was ok, and daddy was on his way." Holly cuddles him tighter and presses a motherly kiss on the top of his head. He doesn't blush with the affection Holly shows him or show that he is uncomfortable with it. My heart swells with how much she has taken to him and treats him like he is her own son, never letting him shy away from her affection and love. This has brought out a new side to Lucas, a more confident and happy side to him which shows how much he needed a mother figure in his life where his three older brothers didn't. Saying that the two daft ones enjoy her company and love to tease her, calling her mother.

"Maybe we should see if there's a canteen open, so we can get the kids some lunch," I know Izzy is in good hands, hanging around a busy hospital is not something she would want for her children and neither do I.

"We've already eaten," Rebecca mumbles into my chest. "Mummy made cheese and ham wraps and carrot sticks and ice cream and wafer with marshmallows and sauce," she lets out in one breath, lifting her head while she pokes me in the cheek.

"Did she now?" I grab her finger between my lips and pretend to bite it then blow a raspberry on her cheek. This has my cheeky cherub chuckling which is good to see. It pains me to see them upset or hurt and has me wondering how any parent could hurt a child.

"I'm hungry," Daniel announces. "I haven't eaten since breakfast."

"Yeah, me too. I…" Nicholas is stopped from finishing what he was going to say when Sebastian and the doctor step out of Izzy's room.

"Daddy," Joe tears himself from me, clambering down my legs and wrapping himself around Sebastian.

"Hey little man, you okay?" Joe nods his head as Sebastian bends down, giving him a fatherly hug. He turns to the doctor as he crouches next to his son, comforting him. "Thank you," he says as he shakes his hand, not letting go of Joe. The doctor nods his head, giving a reassuring smile then moves on to the next room.

"How is she?" Holly asks, her caring nature always at the forefront.

"She's good, all things considering. Her back is sore. The doctor thinks she has a bruised Coccyx and mild concussion from bumping her head," he bites his lip, controlling the emotions that has built within him. He idolizes Izzy. The love he holds for his wife and her him would stand the test of time. They both struggled for the first six months of their relationship. Izzy having her secrets and trust issues and Sebastian unable to deal with Izzy not trusting him enough to reveal that she had a three-year-old son as well as the problems she was having with her ex.

"And the baby? Everything ok?"

"Yes. She's had a few contractions, but they're not strong enough for them to be worried plus she's had a scan and the baby's heartbeat is strong," he smiles, ever the proud father.

"Are they letting her home?" Nicholas asks as Sebastian puts his arm around Joe's shoulder then moves towards Lucas. "No," he shakes his head. "They want to keep an eye on her, so she needs to stop in." He reaches out and ruffles Lucas' hair. "Thanks mate." Lucas doesn't flinch when Sebastian messes with his hair. "You did well, taking care of them for me." Lucas has a lot of Sebastian's temperaments, taking care of his niece and nephew would have been paramount to him. He hates to see them upset or hurt. As for Izzy, he did the right thing phoning the ambulance before he contacted anyone else and making her comfortable, even though his worst fear is for Izzy to go into labour while she's taking care of him.

"I didn't do much," he shrugs his shoulders, Holly letting go of him, so his brother can give him a hug.

Rebecca wants down and as I place her on the floor, she slips her tiny hand in Holly's. Sebastian blows a raspberry on her cheek and she giggles at him just as the door opens to Izzy's room and two nurses step out. One of them approaches Sebastian, "You can go back in now, Mr Petrov, but not for long. We'll be moving your wife onto one of the maternity wards in the next hour…"

"I want mummy," Rebecca moans as a tear slips down her cheek. I think she's just realized that her mum won't be coming home today.

"It's ok pumpkin, you can go in and see mummy," Sebastian bends down and lifts his daughter up into his arms. Her head snuggling straight into his chest as her arms wrap around his neck.

The nurse looks around at my sons, Holly and grandchildren. "Can you take it in turns to go in? We don't normally allow more than three in at once," her tone suggests she is not to be messed with.

"Of course, not a problem and thank you for taking care of my daughter-in-law," I say, smiling at her as Rebecca leans over to me, tugging at my rolled-up shirt sleeve. The middle-aged nurse runs her greedy eyes up my body until they land on my face. Her smile is over the top and when she places her hand on my bicep, my little minx who is stood at my side lets out a cheeky chuckle.

"No thanks needed. It's my job, but you're more than welcome," she purrs at me, blatantly flirting with me as she rubs at the muscle under my shirt. I'm shocked that this professional woman would give me the come on in her place of work and in front of Holly and my family. Granted she doesn't know who Holly is and the need in her chocolate eyes shows that she doesn't give a flying fuck. I don't want to be rude to the woman; even before I met Holly, if a woman came on to me and I wasn't sexually attracted to her, I would have bought her a drink then walked away. However, I'm not in a club and I'm not on the market. The only woman I want, and need, stands to the left of me and as I side a glance at her, I can see she is nearly sucking in her cheeks to stop her laughter from bubbling over. Oh, she's overly amused that I'm uncomfortable with the situation and is doing nothing to let this woman know that I'm hers.

I let my hand cover hers for a moment, patting it gently, "My family and I are still grateful," I tell her then I search for Holly's hand. When I find it, I lift it to my lips and softly kiss her knuckles. The nurse glances at Holly and her face turns a nice shade of embarrassment mixed with a touch of envy in her eyes. Said eyes shift to her watch as she moves her hand from my arm, "Well like I said, no more than three at a time and we will be moving Mrs Petrov within the hour." With the firmness back in her voice, she turns and heads down the corridor.

Sebastian grins at me as he leads his children into their mother's room while Nicholas' amused expression indicates I'm about to bear the brunt of his teasing.

"What an old flirt," he smirks at me while he taps me on the cheek.

"I did not flirt," I fire back, keeping a tight hold of Holly's hand. Chancing a quick glance at Holly, in fear that I might have come across too friendly with the needy nurse but in my defence, I was only being polite. Her sapphire eyes sparkle, entertained with my son and his absurd accusations.

"Oh, come on. The way you said thank you and smiled at her was enough. I'm surprised she didn't drag you into one of the empty rooms and offer you a bed bath," he wiggles his eyebrows at me and stalks off towards Izzy's room.

"Don't be stupid and where are you going?" I ask. He nods his head at the door as he puts his hand on the handle.

"I'm going to see Izzy," giving me that look to say fuck the rules, only three in at once I'm going in. I look at Holly who is still smiling at Nicholas' comments. I shake my head at her because she can't help but play their stupid games with them. Daniel's next to put his spoke in.

"Really, father, you need to stop with that seductive charm of yours. It gets a little embarrassing when every woman your father looks at wants to drop their knickers for him." He rolls his eyes at me, smirking, then saunters off, following his brother.

"Fuck off," I spit at him, not one bit amused at either of them or their comments. When in this lifetime would I give any woman the come on when I have my family with me and Holly at my side, there's not one that could hold a candle to her. Every ounce of me belongs to her and nothing will ever change that. My eyes seek hers and I can see she is still smiling at the two fucking idiots.

"Don't laugh at them, Holly, they are not funny."

"No, but the expression on your face is," she chuckles.

"I did not flirt with her, Holly, and no disrespect to the woman but even if I was pissed, I would not entertain her," I try to explain myself, not wanting Holly thinking bad of me.

"I know, love. You don't know you're doing it most of the time," she pats my chest, smiling as she passes by me to get to Izzy's room.

"Wooh there," I grab her hand and bring her firmly into my chest. "What do you mean? I don't know I'm doing it?" I enunciate the last part, speaking into her lips that I want to taste. She laughs at me then steps back a little.

"Vlad, you have this presence that the average man would give anything to have just a tiny fragment of." She holds her thumb and finger up, indicating a little bit. "Women watch with want. Hoping and wishing they can get your attention." She strokes her finger down my nose and onto my lips which I kiss lightly, watching the fire that burns brightly in her eyes for me. God I'm one lucky bastard.

"Your dark dangerous eyes captivate them; snaring them in while your soft lips promise so much pleasure," her breathing faulters. My little minx aroused by her own words of me. Hospital or not, I place my hand on her hip and pull her closer. "The low erotic tone of your voice dominates their whole being, surrendering themselves to you is not an option. It's inevitable. Then your touch goes in for the kill," she breathes in deeply through her nose, her eyes closing slowly. When they open, I see the lust in her eyes bubbling over. She swallows, collecting herself before she continues. "Once they feel the heat from your fingertips... your body... your mouth," her fingers run over my bottom lip as her tongue runs over hers. "It ends up being a craving. They need it like they need to breathe."

"Wow," I say, smirking. "I'm a catch then?" I wiggle my eyebrows at her.

"Oh yeah. You're definitely a catch."

"And is that how you see me?" I speak into her lips.

Mischievousness flickers across Holly's face and she bites at my lip. "Yeah, I'm the lucky one who gets all this," her hand waves around my body. "I'm also the lucky one who gets to see what's in here." She pats my chest where my heart is. "And I'm the lucky one who gets to feel these on her," she runs her finger over my lips. "And these, I get these," she threads her fingers with mine, "to caress my skin and make me feel…" I know how they make her feel. I swallow hard when I think of how my fingertips work her body and have her screaming my name. Her hooded eyelids show me she's thinking about it too. She moves her mouth to my ear and in that soft tone of hers she whispers. "And I'm the one who gets to listen to that sexy voice of yours that could melt a woman's knickers off with just one word." I'm left there speechless as she steps back from me. "Yes, I see you as a catch but so much more as well." I know what she means, our relationship is more than just physical. But at this moment I'm all about the physical.

She winks at me while patting my chest and I don't give her time to walk away. With a quick glance around, making sure we are not being watched, I grab her and kiss the hell out of her. God only knows how I'm going to make it through this no sex thing because I could pin her up against the wall and show her how much I need her. We're both breathless when we part, "Are you sure I can't tempt you to a quickie on the staircase?" my need to have her wrapped around me apparent with my erection bulging into her lower stomach.

"Not a cat in hells chance," she chuckles, turning on her heals and stalking into the room leaving me alone, adjusting my need.

"Can you have the kids, dad?" Sebastian asks when I eventually make my way into Izzy's room. Apparently, we're all breaking the hospital rules today.

"Of course. How are you?" I walk over to Izzy, leaning down to place a kiss on her forehead.

"I'm good thanks," she says, trying to sit up from laying on her side. I help her up and adjust her pillows then stand at the side of Holly, taking her hand in mine.

"Are they okay to stay overnight? I want to call home to collect a few things for Izzy then I'll spend most of the evening here."

"Not a problem. They can stay as long as you need them to." Rebecca squeals as she jumps off the bed, running into my legs. I pick her up and she beams at me.

"Are we having a sleepover, grandad?" she's suddenly all excited with the fact she will get to stay up late at my house. She doesn't realise that when she stops at my house it's normally the weekend or school holidays, so there's no reason for her to go to bed as early.

"Will you have a sleepover with us, Holly?" she asks. Now it's my turn to chew on my lip to stop the laughter from erupting because Holly had only just mentioned she would not be staying over at mine when we had our little talk. All eyes move to Holly as we wait for her to answer. I can see the questioning looks on Izzy's face. To them it looks as if we are back together, but they are not privy to the understanding we have come to. Nicholas and Daniel are sat there smirking at me and as I narrow my eyes at them, I wonder what they know.

"Pleeease," and without warning Rebecca launches herself from my hold into Holly's arms. Holly lets out a squeal of her own, laughing when Rebecca lands a sloppy wet kiss on her cheek.

"Okay, sweetheart, we'll have a pyjama party," she smiles, the warmness oozing from her. I stop laughing at how she's having to give in and stay at my home. I know how much she wants us to work and with that comes the promise I made to her that I would do anything to make it work. No sex. With her staying tonight, that will be a challenge. But she's willing to put aside what we had discussed for now to make my granddaughter happy.

"Thank you," I whisper into her ear when Rebecca climbs down and snuggles onto her daddy's lap.

"Will you look after mummy while we're at grandads?" she points between herself and Joe who is laid out on the bed, cuddled up to his mum.

"Don't I always?" he questions his daughter as he playfully pulls at her nose.

"Yes, but you have to give her lots of hugs and kisses because I'm not there to give them." She taps his nose. Izzy lets out a chuckle as does Holly at her sweetness.

"Not a problem, I love kissing your mum," he winks at his wife.

"Urrrrrrrr," both Joe and Rebecca say in unison, giggling. My son is not one to keep his hands off his wife, showing his affection to the love of his life and Izzy is always eager to except it. As he leans into Izzy to show nothing will keep him from his wife's lips, the door opens. In walks a porter and luckily for me not the same nurse. Her eyes scan the room, taking in how many of us are in here, four larger than life men, three children and my Holly.

"Oh, my goodness. Don't let nurse Ratchet see you all in here, she'll burst a blood vessel." Our laughter echoes around the room, leaving her looking confused.

As the children hug their mother and father and we say our goodbyes, I notice Holly smirking at me. That look in her eye tells me she's in a playful mood and because I can't resist riling her up, I lean into her, whispering in her ear. "How's that not staying over at mine working out for you?" I wink at her, smirking.

"Shut up," she elbows me in the ribs, giving me that cheeky grin of hers while she rounds up the children and makes her way out of the room.

"What's all that about?" Sebastian queries, smirking at me.

"You don't want to know," I tell him, shaking my head, chuckling.

Chapter 19

Holly

"Where is everyone?" Olivia's head turns towards the living room then back again as she waits for my reply.

"I have no idea," I answer, as I am unaware as to where Vlad rushed off to this morning. Lucas adamant he was going with him and Joe wanting to tag along too, leaving me with Rebecca.

"I know Sebastian will be at the hospital; as for Vlad and the boys, I don't know. He got a text about nine o'clock this morning and said he needed to go out."

"Didn't he say where he was going?"

"No," I shake my head. "He just said he would be a few hours and asked if I minded taking care of Rebecca. Hence the reason I have invited you to bring Megan over to play."

"Sounds like a certain someone might be getting a present," she sings, her eyes growing wide.

"Huh. How do you know that?"

"I don't really," she says. "When the kids were small, Jack would often take them with him when he wanted to pick out a gift for me. Unless it was sexy underwear then he'd go on his own," she adds with a smirk on her face.

"That's sweet, but he has no reason to go out and buy me anything." I like pressies as much as the next person when it's my birthday or Christmas, but I'm not one of those women that expects her man to lavish her in gifts.

"Maybe he thinks he does…" The screech of the two girls racing down the stairs, closely followed by Sarah and Lucy, halts Olivia from finishing what she was saying.

"Stop running on the stairs," I say firmly, getting up out of my seat to meet them, worrying about them falling. They both come to a stop in front of me, big eyes full of mischief.

"Sorry, Holly," they say together then rush off towards the living room.

They had been happily watching Little Mermaid before Sarah asked Rebecca to show her her room. Both girls happy enough to take Sarah and Lucy to Rebecca's room not knowing Sarah just wanted to snoop around. She's been here before when Nicholas and Daniel were barbecuing in the hot weather but didn't get the chance to look around.

Within half an hour of coming through the door this morning, she couldn't help having a sneaky peek at the gym, guest room that Sebastian and Izzy use when they stay over, the huge utility room and garage. She didn't try to snoop in Vlad's office, I think she thought that would be overstepping the mark. I'm almost certain he locks it when he goes out anyway.

"Wow!" she says once the children take the TV off pause and continue to watch their film.

"It's bloody huge up there," her finger pointing towards the ceiling.

"You are one nosey cow," Olivia says, chuckling.

"Do you know there's seven bedrooms up there with an extremely large bathroom?" She looks at me, the shock on her face has me laughing.

"Of course, I know. I do sleep here."

Lucy sniggers and bites her lip. I know they have been snooping around up there, I can tell by her face. I raise my eyebrow at them, "What have you been doing up there?"

"Nothing," Sarah insists, but I can see she's holding back and so can Olivia.

"Have you been rummaging in Holly's drawers?" Olivia questions. I laugh at this because they are not my drawers. It's Vlad's home even if I do have a lot of my clothes here.

"No, I'll leave that to Vlad," she wiggles her eyebrows at me. They can't help but lower the tone, they're worse than a couple of men. "But Rebecca did want to show us where Holly and her grandad sleeps." She glances at Lucy for support that it wasn't her who asked Rebecca to show them his room.

"You're a bloody liar," Olivia states. "I can tell by her face," she points at Lucy. "You asked Rebecca to show you Vlad's room, didn't you?" Her eyes narrow on Sarah, challenging her not to lie.

"Ok. Yes. But she did want to show us the bathroom in his room. And oh boy, I could fucking live in there. You need to have a look at Vlad's bedroom before he comes home Olivia. Holly was right when she said his wardrobe was bigger than the bedroom in her apartment and the bathroom," she gushes. "It's all marble tiled and the sunken bath, I swear to god I could picture Holly as Cleopatra and Vlad as Mark Antony dressed in a toga, tending to her needs," she fans herself, letting out a puff of air. I let out a squeal at the same time as Lucy; as for Olivia, she sits there impassive for a few seconds as if she hasn't heard what our close friend has said. I shouldn't be surprised because Sarah and Nick have been known to enjoy a little role play in the bedroom department from time to time.

Olivia shakes her head and in no time at all, laughter dances in her eyes and her mouth turns up into a wicked smirk. "Does your husband know your visualizing another man in a toga?" She slaps Sarah's arm.

"No. It's not like I'm picturing Vlad with me is it," she declares.

"I'm not sure which is worse," Olivia says rolling her eyes. "Anyway, I'll let Holly show me round before we leave. You didn't happen to see any handcuffs in the drawers while you were rummaging around?" she asks, biting her lip.

"Olivia!" I choke out, shocked. Again, I don't know why because it's a tossup who is worse out of these two.

"What?" Her face lights up. "Nothing wrong with a little play between two consenting adults."

She places her hand on top of mine, patting it.

"Mother," Lucy's face reddens. "I really don't need to know what you and dad get up to," covering her eyes with her hand, she shakes her head. "Too late I have a visual now," she moans, grimacing dramatically.

"I didn't see any," Sarah answers Olivia's question then looks down her nose at me as if I'm letting the side down. My mind wonders back to the last time we were together sexually in the hotel where I trusted him enough to let him tie me to the bed. Even though he didn't blindfold me, I kept my eyes closed; knowing what ever he did he would be gentle with me and have only my pleasure in mind.

"Holly?" Olivia questions my silence.

"Hmmm," I answer.

"Where did you go then?"

"Nowhere, I was just thinking."

"I bet you were," she chuckles.

"Our sex life was off the scale without implementing any gadgets into the bedroom thank you very much," I tell them, not giving them any details of what I was thinking about. "Although I'm sure if we wanted to explore that avenue then I know he would be up for it and would make it fun," I shrug my shoulders, looking down at the kitchen worktop, embarrassed that I'm even discussing this.

"Well you better get out there and buy yourself a gadget or something because this no sex until he's proved himself is going to be a struggle if that look on your face is anything to go by. I'm surprised you've kept your hands off each other staying under the same roof. We've all been privy to the chemistry between the two of you," she says, her eyes twinkling at me. "You might just have to eat your words love," Olivia states, tapping her finger on her bottom lip.

Where she's aware of the whole story behind Vlad's life, Sarah and Lucy are not. They know about him kicking off in the club and know that his wife led him a merry dance which led to the situation in the club. They are also aware of the no sex rule until he proves himself, which they all found hilarious. And even though it sounds silly every time I think about it, I think the idea of refraining from sex until we can move on from his insecurities will help.

He knows he needs to talk to me about the things that worry him instead of brooding and becoming angry. He says it will never happen again. That being without me hurt too much to put us through that again. Telling me all about his past has lessened the load and he might be right. But it's not just him that needs to get over his past, I need to understand him more. Understanding that his teenage years were taken from him by his evil father and vile wife. Their plans stopping him from wanting to travel and follow his dreams. Needing to protect his sons, no matter what the cost, changed and affected him in such a way that twelve years on from leaving his home in Russia, he is still struggling with the hurt and deceit that transformed his life.

Maybe putting something in place, like no sex, might not be the right thing to do, but it will give us time to talk more instead of ripping each other's clothes off every chance we get.

Only now I think she might be right, and it will be a struggle. Especially if last night is anything to go by.

When we left the hospital, we took the kids to the park and after spending a couple of hours there we decided to eat out. The children had opted for pizza and Nicholas and Daniel met us there. Once we arrived home, we checked in with Sebastian to see how Izzy was. He informed us that she had had a few more contractions since we had left but wasn't expected to have the baby that night. Her back was still sore, but her headache had worn off. He spoke to his children over the phone and so did Izzy once they had finished, we bathed Rebecca and got her ready for bed as she was sleepy. Joseph played on his DS along with Lucas but by eight thirty his eyes were closing so we put him to bed too. Nicholas left not long after to meet up with a friend and Daniel took himself off to the club. While Lucas continued to play on his game, Vlad went into his office to send a couple of emails and I chose to go have a bath; in his room.

I'd already decided to sleep in the spare room but when I came out of the bathroom wearing my pyjamas and saw Vlad sprawled out on his bed, I could see he had other plans.

Within seconds of me informing him that I would sleep in the spare room, he had me thrown over his shoulder then pinned beneath his large muscular body on his bed. Determination and longing set firmly on his face. He didn't waste any time taking my breath away with one of his passionate kisses, leaving me panting and wanting more. Letting me know that even though we had come to an agreement that we wouldn't stay at each other's homes, but because of circumstances beyond our control, here I was, I would still be sleeping in his bed. Again, the determination and authoritative tone in his voice left no room for argument, so I didn't.

I let him hold me tight while his soft lips left tender kisses on my neck, shoulders and jaw; as his fingers stroked lovingly up my back, all the while whispering across my skin how he can't wait for the day that we share the same bed every night. And neither can I, but we have a little way to go yet.

I drifted off to sleep in his arms and when I woke an hour later, he was gone. I took it that he had gone to sleep in the spare room once he had been content that I would be staying put.

"Holly why would you suggest such a thing knowing you will both struggle to keep your hands off each other?" Sarah asks. None of them know it was Nicholas who suggested it just to wind-up his father and to throw a challenge at him. Nevertheless, I jumped at the idea even if now I'm not so sure I can keep up with it while I'm sleeping under the same roof. Hopefully, Izzy will be home soon, and I can go back home. "I can't believe you slept in separate beds last night," she adds.

I don't tell them how much I wanted him to stay with me once he had me in his arms and was disappointed when I woke, and he had gone. I'm also not telling them whose suggestion it was but the look on Lucy's face tells me that her and Nicholas have been on the telephone again and the topic of conversation was Vlad and me.

"It was hard, but we coped. Plus, Izzy will be home soon, so I will be going home which will make it easier until the time is right when we can resume normal services," I laugh.

"That's going to be some thorough servicing, Holly. You better send Lucas over to my house for a few days while Vlad's lubricating your valves because I think once he's got your engine running, he's going to keep retuning that engine until it's purring like a pedigree Persian."

"Mother, my god you sound more like my dad every day," Lucy chastises but chuckles at her mother's inuendo anyway.

"We're hungry," the girls call from the living room, stopping our conversation immediately which I'm grateful for. "Can we go on a picnic to the park?" Megan asks as she comes skipping into the kitchen. Rebecca is by my side asking the same. "Pleeeease mummy," Megan tugs at Lucy's arm.

"I don't know love," Lucy looks around at us all. "We didn't bring anything with us to have a picnic with," she tells Megan as she tugs on her ponytail.

"Don't worry we'll just raid Vlad's fridge, it's always packed full of goodies," I tell them as I start taking out cheese and meat for sandwiches and bottles of juice for them to drink.

Arriving at the park, we manage to get set up at one of the picnic tables. It's cooled down a few degrees since our little heat wave a couple of weeks ago, today being warm but cloudy and not a lot of people here. Rebecca and Megan are happy playing in the park and keep running back to pick at their food and have a drink. Lucy is telling us about a few jobs she has applied for and an interview next week she is preparing for. My phone is on the table and lights up with Izzy's name displayed.

"Hi Izzy," I answer with. "How are you feeling, love?"

"Not too bad, apart from the contractions," she pants.

"Are you in labour?" This gets the attention of my friends.

"Yes," her voice a bit breathless. "How's Joe and Rebecca?"

"They're fine," I reassure her. Letting her know that Joe is with Vlad and Lucas and Rebecca's happily playing in the park with Megan.

"Good," she breathes.

"Izzy maybe you should get off the phone and focus on your breathing," I tell her.

"Yeah, I'll put Seb on we have something to ask you."

"Okay."

"Holly," Sebastian says as I put him on loudspeaker.

"Hi Seb. I hope you're rubbing your wife's back and making her comfortable," I tell him.

"I'm trying," he chuckles. "She keeps hitting me telling me it's my fault she's in pain." We all laugh at him as we hear Izzy telling him to ask me.

"Holly, it's Rebecca's birthday next week and we were supposed to be having a party for her. There's only ten children from her class that she wants to invite, and we were going to take them to that children's play centre that's just opened, they cater for birthday parties. Izzy was supposed to book it a few weeks ago but forgot and yesterday when she remembered, she ended up in here. So, we thought about just having a party for her at my father's. He can fit a bouncy castle in his garden and other activities for them to do but we could do with your help with the invitations and arrangements. That's if you don't mind."

"Leave it with me, Seb. I'll speak to your dad and we'll get something sorted out for her."

"Thank you, Holly," he says. "I'll text Nicholas to pick the telephone numbers and the addresses of her school friends from our house and drop them off to you."

"What date is her birthday?" I ask, needing to know the date to put on the invites.

"August 9th. Next Thursday, but we'll have the party on Saturday, 11th."

"Ok, like I said Sebastian leave it with me, you take care of Izzy."

"Thanks, Holly. We're really grateful for everything you're doing for us," his voice is soft, and I can hear the honesty as he speaks. I'm sure their appreciation extends to the help I am giving taking care of their children.

"No thanks needed, Seb. I'll get back to you tonight, sounds like the little one might be here by then, so I'll see you at visiting time." He says goodbye and I press call end on my phone.

"Looks like the baby will be arriving sooner than they thought," I tell Olivia and Sarah while popping my phone into my bag. "That fall yesterday must have sent her into early labour."

"That and the fact it's her third," Olivia adds. "Babies do tend to arrive quicker and earlier the more you have."

"You know Holly? If you need a hand with organising Rebecca's party, we'd love to help," Sarah says, stopping Olivia from going into details about how long she was in labour with the twins and how her other two children were half the time. In fact, Nathan, her forth, came so quickly that she gave birth to him in the ambulance on the way to the hospital.

"How hard can it be to organise a little girl's birthday party?" I ask. I'd put my phone on loudspeaker, so they're both aware of why Izzy and Sebastian were calling.

"Well these days it's not the little girl whose party it is that's the problem," Sarah says as she gets out her mobile phone.

"It isn't?" I ask, not understanding why she is showing me her social media site. I take her phone and scroll through some of the messages that were left about a young girl's birthday party.

"No," she says. "It's the bigger girls that the little girls call mother who are the problem." She shakes her head, lifting her eyebrows at me. "Bitches." That one word tells me everything as well as a message I am reading on her phone. Some mothers being catty about some kid's party.

"Holly, some of the mothers at Megan and Rebecca's school are stuck up cows. You've seen them, all false tits and bleached teeth. They wouldn't dream of dropping their child at school without a stylist and beautician giving them a make-over first," Olivia states.

"Shit," I comment because I've just realised that their school is only five minutes walking distance from Vlad's home where it's ten minutes' drive from Olivia's. If most of the children live near the school, then they live in homes that cost either around a million pounds or over. "Shit!" I say again this time with a bit more grit.

"Don't worry, I'm on it," Sarah says, standing with her phone to her ear. "Valerie, darling, how are you…?" she says as she wanders off, so we can't hear what she is saying.

When she comes back, she relays that Valerie is the owner of the ballerina school that her daughter Emilia attended for four years.

Apparently, they now cater for children's birthday parties and are very sought after. Valerie and three of her top students supply an hour's lesson, providing leotards, tutu and tights. After the lesson the children put on a show for the parents. She also says that they can't be any more than ten and the age range is between four and seven. It's not cheap but to be fair they do supply the outfit which the children get to keep.

"I think it's a great idea," Olivia states. "Plus, Vlad's home is more than big enough for them to rehearse and if the parents want to stay and watch the show his patio will accommodate it."

I think about it for a moment. Will he want strangers in his home? Not sure but it is for Rebecca, so I don't think there will be a problem.

"Book it," I say to Sarah just as my phone alerts me to a text message.

"Already booked. Valarie owes me a favour, so I just cashed it in." She takes a seat on the bench with a satisfied look on her face.

"Thank you."

"No problem. They will be at Vlad's next Saturday at noon and if all goes to plan the children will put a show on at one fifteen. Then afterwards they can play a few games, dance and eat cake, it should be over by three."

"Sounds good," I say as I read the message on my phone.

Izzy: I wanted to ask but had to wait until Sebastian left the room. He's just left to get me a bottle of water, so I'll need to be quick. It was his birthday last month while you were away at the cottage. He didn't want to celebrate it with the way things were with his dad, so I thought we could kill two birds with one stone. Once we've got rid of the kids if the weathers good, we could have a get together at Vlad's. x

Poor Sebastian. I know it won't have bothered him but still he deserves a party with what he does for his family and how much he cares for them. Quickly, I text her back.

Me: Leave it with me. x

I don't get another text; I assume Sebastian is back with her not wanting to leave her for too long with the baby due anytime.

I inform Olivia, Sarah and Lucy that we need to organise a party for Seb, they agree and tell me that they are willing to help with anything I need.

Megan and Rebecca come back to the table for a drink, and we decide to make our way home.

We're not back long when Rebecca falls off to sleep while snuggled on the sofa watching Frozen and it's been a whirlwind of text messages, phone calls and Nicholas flying through the door to drop off the names and addresses of Rebecca's school friends.

The first message came from Sebastian, letting me know that they were now proud parents of a healthy seven-pound-five-ounce baby boy. He sent a selfie of the three of them cuddled together, both Izzy and Sebastian looking shattered but overjoyed. Baby Petrov, of which they are calling him now because they can't agree on a name, is beautiful. Chubby red cheeks and a tuft of fair hair. His eyes were closed and I'm not sure who he looks like, but I don't think you can tell when they're only a few minutes old. I sent them one back saying how gorgeous he is and will see them all at visiting time.

Then I've had text after text from my two friends with ideas for the party: food, banners, balloons and who to invite to Seb's. I'm sure Izzy will only want family and close friends; probably a barbecue and a few drinks. Sarah offered to bake the cake for both Rebecca and Sebastian which I know will be something special and delicious. I've also had Valerie from the ballet school on the phone. She phoned wanting to know the age of the children and how many, so she can sort out their outfits. She also suggested that the children perform their show after the party which I agreed with, that way once it's over with their parents can take them home.

Nicholas called in looking flustered, he couldn't stop because he needed to get back to Daniel who was having a meltdown due to one of the bands unable to play at the club. According to Nicholas, both singers and guitarist had been in a car crash. Although it wasn't serious, between them they had broken ribs, cuts and bruises so they had cancelled the dates they were expected to play at the club. I'm not sure which band it was, he didn't say just passed me the list of names for the invites and shot out of the door.

When I tried to telephone Daniel, his phone kept going to voice mail, so I sent him a text letting him know that if he needed a hand to search for another band to call me back. He did text me back saying he had it in hand. He knows lots of upcoming singers so I'm not worried, I'm sure he will fill their spot.

With the phone calls stopped, and Rebecca asleep, this gave me time to design an invitation for her party on my phone. Happy with my design: pink and white paper with a glittery gold edge. A lone gold ballerina at the bottom of the page and matching slippers in each corner at the top. 'You are invited to Rebecca's 5th Birthday' written in cursive writing along with the usual who to, where and when written on it, I was impatient to get them printed.

With no word from Vlad all day, I decided to ring him. When it went straight to voice mail, I sent him a message asking if it was okay to use his office to print off the invites. I know there must be a spare key somewhere in the house, I just don't know where. Half an hour later I still haven't had a reply and with wanting to get the invites printed off before Rebecca woke, I decide to check the office to see if it's unlocked.

Surprisingly, it was.

Chapter 20

Vlad

It's been a long day with so much happening all at once and I feel as guilty as hell for leaving Holly alone all day looking after Rebecca.

When I got a text message this morning from the tattooist reminding me I had an appointment at ten o'clock, I had no other choice than to ask Holly to take care of my granddaughter. I knew Lucas wanted to come along, therefore Joseph would come along too. Luckily for the boys and myself, Spike the tattooist had two arcade games in his shop which kept them both entertained for the five hours we were there. He sent out for burgers, so yes, my son and grandson were more than happy. Me not so much.

The cover up that Lucas had designed hurt more than having salt rubbed into an open wound. Who knew having my angel on my back would be as painful? And take so long and it's not finished yet. I need to go back in a couple of weeks to have some of the colouring on the wings filled in and the blue on the angel's eyes.

During my time at the tattooist, I had a strange call from Daniel. He seemed a little edgy but said they had been a problem with one of the bands that were booked to play at the club. He didn't give me any other details other than he needed to speak to Holly and me together and would come over as soon as I got home.

Not long after that my phone went flat, so when a text came in from Sebastian informing me I had another grandson, I didn't get it until Lucas checked his phone and had the same message and photo that he had sent everyone. To say I'm prouder than a strutting peacock in full bloom is an understatement. I was also aware that I hadn't spoken to Holly all day. Although I could have used Lucas' phone, I didn't want her to hear the buzzing of the tattooist gun and start asking questions. It's supposed to be a surprise.

Glad to be home stood in my kitchen, I switch on the kettle and put my phone on charge. Rebecca has just been woken up by the noise coming from the boys and I'm assuming Holly is upstairs. As soon as there's a bit of life in my phone, I congratulate my eldest letting him know I had no charge on my phone earlier. He was also aware as to where I was going this morning, so I don't think he was that bothered when I didn't get back to him straight away. Then I send Daniel a text to tell him I'm home and that's when I notice a missed call from Holly and a missed text message. Inquisitive, I ask Lucas to keep an eye on his nephew and niece, reminding him not to let slip to Rebecca that she has a baby brother, Sebastian and Izzy want to surprise her when we get to the hospital. Then I set off in search of Holly.

Standing in the doorway of my office, I can see Holly rummaging around in one of the drawers of my desk. Normally, they would all be locked along with the office door, but I was in a rush this morning and assumed no one would come in here.

"Is there something I can help you with?" I ask, as I move closer to my desk, crossing my arms over my chest.

"Shit," I hear Holly curse when my voice startles her, causing her to bump her head on the underside of the desk. Leaning over from the other side I watch as she slowly rises from her crouching position. Her hands hold onto the top of the desk as she lifts her head to look up at me. I chuckle inside because she looks as guilty as hell. There's a blush to her cheeks and she chews on the inside of her lip.

"Why do you look as if you've stolen the crown jewels, Holly?" I lift one of my hands to cover my mouth so she can't see the smirk on my face. My woman is as honest as the day is long. I know this and so does everyone who knows her but being caught in my office drawer has made her feel guilty. She has no need to be I have nothing to hide anymore from her and she's free to roam around my home whenever she wants.

She gets up then plonks herself down in my chair, letting out a long breath. "I only wanted to use your printer but couldn't connect my phone, so I set about looking for your laptop. Only, I can't find it, and I wanted these invites printed off before Rebecca woke," she shows me her phone as she gets more flustered and I take it from her. While she rambles on about a party for Rebecca and Olivia, Sarah, Lucy and Megan visiting this morning. Then something about Sarah and Lucy nosing around my home. She also rambles on about the children's parents coming here to watch them put on a show. I dial the code into Holly's phone to connect it to my Wi-Fi then press print. Before she's finished with, "I'm sorry, Vlad, I know I should have waited for you to get home before I gave them permission to book the party and shouldn't have allowed Sarah and Lucy upstairs." I've printed off the invitations and put them on the desk in front of her. Then I lean down and shut her up with a long hard kiss which is just what the doctor ordered because she now looks relaxed.

"Hmmm," she breaths as we pull apart. I sit back on my desk and watch her eyes flutter open.

"Feel better, sweetheart?"

"Yes, thank you." She reaches forward, picking up the invites. "You don't mind that I came in here?" Holly's eyes search mine while she worries her bottom lip between the fingers of her other hand.

"No," I take the sheets of paper from her and take the hand that's pulling at her plump lip and bring it to my lips. Turning it over I place a soft kiss on her wrist then gaze at her. "I've said many times, Holly, treat my home as your own." Kissing her wrist again, I stand pulling her up from my chair. "I don't say things I don't mean, angel. My office is included in that."

"I still feel guilty that I didn't stop my friends from snooping around," Holly's hands rest on my chest and mine hold her hips.

"It's fine," I chuckle. "It's not your fault you have nosey friends." I rub our noses together then steal a kiss.

"What about the party?"

"Holly it's for my granddaughter. I'm not going to be annoyed about that," she's worried over nothing. Holly always puts others first and while I've been out leaving her here with Rebecca that's what she has done. Organising a party at short notice for my granddaughter has my heart swelling even more for this woman.

"I know. But they will be strangers coming into your home, I didn't think when Sarah mentioned having a ballerina theme…" I put my finger to her lips to quieten her and pull her in to me. My nose buries into her hair, inhaling her sent, I move my lips to her ear giving it a little nip with my teeth.

"Ouch," she slaps my chest with a chuckle. I kiss the sting away then take her hands in mine. Her head lifts so her sparkling gems are gazing into mine. She lights up my world with her beauty. My home she fills with love and kindness, not just for me but for my family as well. Do I care if she's about to invite a bunch of strangers into my home? In answer to my question, no.

"You need to stop fretting about it, Holly. I don't care if you invite the world and his wife. As long as you are happy then I am." This time it's Holly that pulls me down, assaulting my mouth with such an attack, I fall back against the desk taking her with me. Laughing, she doesn't let me up until she's shown me how happy she is.

It's becoming a habit now, my two middle sons' spoiling the intimate moments that Holly and I share and that's what has me cursing when I hear Daniel clearing his throat and Nicholas asking, "Do I need to throw a bucket of water over them?"

"Fucking irritating twats," I curse. I don't mean it or maybe I do, they do pick their moments. Holly slaps my chest while she laughs at the pair of idiots then sits back in my chair. Nicholas gets comfy in the chair on the opposite side of my desk and Daniel stands at the back of him scrolling through his phone.

"What's wrong?" I ask them both, I can see that there is something bothering Daniel. I wore that same look too many times when I was his age.

"We have a problem," he says looking at me then at Holly. Holly sits up straight, all ears. Ready as ever to help.

"What is it?" I take a seat on the edge of my desk, hoping it's something that can be sorted quickly. Normally I would tell my sons that they need to come to me with solutions to solve any problems that occur and normally they do. Which has me wondering what has them looking so nervous.

"I got a call this morning," Daniel says as he pulls up a chair and sits down next to Nicholas.

"And?"

"And one of the bands had to cancel the three gigs they were due to play at the club."

"Which band?" I ask. I know they all think that I'm not interested in what happens at Aphrodite or that I don't know who will be playing there over the next three months. Well they'd be wrong. It's not just Sebastian and Izzy that's been working tirelessly. Holly's had a huge input and so has Daniel. So, yes, I've looked them up. Read the reviews about them, watched their YouTube videos and know exactly which bands are playing and on what night.

"Fake It," he says.

"Aw, I was looking forward to seeing them," Holly says, screwing up her nose.

"I know, they have a big following," Nicholas states. I know this too. It's a brother and sister who lead the vocals of a six-piece band that sing a variety of songs. Where the male singer has a big following so does his sister as she leaves nothing to the imagination. From her next-to-nothing attire and her erotic dancing, she would fit in well at Aphrodite.

"Can't you get another band to cover them or pay back the money to fans that have bought tickets?"

"No," Daniel shakes his head. "It's a full house on all three nights and a lot of the tickets were bought on the door at Eruption. The one's who paid through the internet we could reimburse, but that's only half of the sales."

"Have you spoken with anyone from the band about placing an advert on their site, letting people know that they have had to cancel their shows?"

"We've spoken but we've been trying to find a band that can put on a show like theirs and who have time to practice over the next few weeks with the dancers from the club. Then they would put it on their website about the crash and that they are unable to perform. But have a replacement who can fill their place."

"And have you found one?"

"We think so," he says quietly. "Well we hope so."

"So, what's the problem then? Offer them more money if needed." Nicholas snorts out a laugh and shakes his head. I glare at him annoyed that they have brought this to me. My sons are not stupid in business when it comes to making decisions. Nicholas has been doing this since he was nineteen and Daniel is following very well in his brother's footsteps. With this he has the upper hand because he knows lots of singers and bands.

"Who are they? Do you want me to speak with them?" Again, Nicholas chuckles, earning himself a dig in the ribs from Daniel's elbow.

"Will you stop that?" I chastise. "Your brother is trying to fix this."

"Oh, I know he is, and he has my full support and the support of Fake It if he can pull it off but I'm a little unsure he'll get yours," I frown at my son not knowing what the hell he is talking about. I've always supported my sons. Sometimes I don't agree with them, but I let them try new things and stand by them with the decisions they make.

"Will one of you tell me what he means," getting up from where I was sat on the corner of my desk, I move to stand at the side of Holly. She sits there quiet. I know she's probably as confused as me and wants to know what the problem is.

"Paps sit down," Daniel gets up from his chair and directs me to it.

"I don't need to sit I am fine."

"Ok," he gives up and sits back down. "I've had lengthy conversations with Sam and Jenny, the lead singers of the band," Daniel moves forward, resting his elbows on the desk. "Between them and me we think I would be able to cover Sam's songs and throw in a few of my own. In fact, we don't just think it we know it and their band are eager and excited to start practicing." He sits back in his seat and I nod my head at him. I know he's more than capable; I've heard him play and sing and I've watched Fake It perform on their social media site. However, that leaves them a singer short a female singer. And just as I think it, there it comes.

"But..."

"Over my dead body, Daniel," my tone firm and not to be challenged.

"That's a bit dramatic, Vlad. You haven't even heard what he was going to say," Holly looks up at me, shaking her head.

"Oh, I know exactly what he is going to say," I tell her then look at my son, tilting my head at him.

"Tell her," I state, folding my arms across my chest.

He shakes his head at me, as Nicholas narrows his eyes on me. "We thought, Holly, that you would be more than capable of filling in for Jenny," Daniel sits back in his chair, giving her his megawatt smile while his brother sits there nodding his head in agreement.

"Me?" Holly squeals, covering her mouth with her hands. Her eyes showing the excitement of a small child on Christmas Day.

"Yes," he says. "I've spoken with Sebastian and he agrees. You would be perfect." They're right, she would be perfect, more than. She can sing. She can dance. She's sexy and she has the power to command any room. So, why am I against this? I know why, I'm fucked up.

Walking over to the office door, I close it gently. I do not want my grandchildren hearing me if I can't contain my anger. Then I walk back to my desk, all eyes on me.

"This is not happening," I keep my voice low, but they know I'm in no mood to be challenged.

"Why?" Nicholas does it anyway.

"Because I am not having Holly ogled by a club full of men." I know how I sound but I don't give a shit. I've seen what this Jenny wears on stage and how she gets the crowd worked up. No, not happening.

"It's not like that," Nicholas says.

"Shut up!" I growl, pointing my finger at him. Both my sons sit there frozen, eyes wide and mouths open. Yeah, I've shocked them; I don't speak to them in that way, but they need to keep out of it. I can see Holly is on their side and it's going to be a struggle for me to get her to see it from my point of view.

"Vlad, it's just singing and dancing. No big deal," Holly soothes, smiling at me.

"Holly, no," I shake my head at her.

"You can't stop her," Daniel says.

"I've told you two to be quiet, I am not allowing Holly to get on that stage," and I know I've just fucked up big time with what's just spilled from my lips as I watch my angel rise from her chair, placing her hands firmly on the desk and scowl at me.

Her sapphire eyes glare at me as she leans over the desk until she's close enough to jab me in the chest with her finger. "You cannot stop me," she pronounces each word as she jabs me four times in the chest. From my peripheral vision, I see both my sons rise from their sitting position and watch as Holly and I go head to head over this.

"Oh, I think I can," I glare back at her and even add a sarcastic smirk, daring her to continue. What the fuck am I doing? Why have I let this get to this stage? I should have just suggested that Daniel ask the girl who was playing the drums the night we went to watch him play. He told me she was a singer in a band and was just helping him out. She would have been perfect and, to be truthful, so would Holly. But I'm being selfish again. I don't want her wearing next to nothing and everyone seeing her. She's mine. I also don't want the male dancers putting their hands on her which they would, it's part of the act. I also know I'm treading on a fine line here and that Holly might just walk out of that door. I try to rein it in.

"Holly listen…."

"No. You listen. If I want to do this you can't stop me," she points at me this time. Focusing on my angel, I lean further over the desk, she does too. Our heads nearly touching.

"Oh, I think you're forgetting one thing, sweetheart," I have a cockiness to my tone which causes Holly's glare to harden but at this moment in time, I don't give a shit. "I own the damn fucking club and I will shut it down before I see you strutting around that stage." I stab my finger on the desk then turn to walk out of the door, ignoring Nicholas' comment about me overreacting and Daniel's sharp intake of breath.

I hear Holly calling me to get back here and my sons telling her to leave me be. And that's what I want; to be left alone while I get my head together. I know one of two things are going to happen. Either Holly will walk out the door because of I've just shown her that I'm not attempting to change. Or she'll join Daniel and the band and go against my wishes anyway.

I know she should, and I should support her and my son. And I will, I just need to get my head around it. Having this just thrust upon me, not having time to see reason has now caused a setback between Holly and me. Just when we were getting back on track. Just as she was beginning to see the good in me and we had come to an understanding, I let her down again.

Chapter 21

Holly

"What the hell just happened?"

"Holly leave him. He'll come around, he just needs time," Nicholas suggests. Leave him? That's what I should do! He's pig-headed, arrogant and has my blood boiling. Who does he think he is?

"Maybe it was a bad idea. We knew there was a chance he would flip, but we thought he'd give in for the sake of you and your relationship," Daniel states, sitting down in his chair looking defeated. Well I'm not going to let that happen. If Daniel has his heart set on playing at the club then that's what's going to happen.

"Daniel do you want to do this?" I ask, both Daniel and Nicholas as they stare at me.

"Yes, but if it's going to cause a rift between the two of you then no." Bless him, he looks adorable when he speaks about the people he loves. Nicholas has that cunning look on his face, he's more than aware that I'm going to fight this.

"Holly what have you got planned?" he chuckles at me.

"Nothing yet, but before I go to war with your father, I need to know that Daniel really wants this."

"I do. I just don't want the big man having a fucking coronary over it," he says. We laugh at him just as Lucas walks in the office.

"Where's dad?" he asks as he stands at the side of Nicholas.

"He's gone to get changed," I lie. Lucas doesn't need upsetting, he's better off not knowing.

"I'm coming to make you something to eat before I get changed then we can all go to the hospital, ok?"

"Ok," he says. "Have me and Joe got time to play another game before tea?"

"Yes. What's Rebecca doing?"

"Annoying us," he smirks, letting us know he needs a hand with her.

"Okay, I'm coming," he leaves the office and I know what I need to do. There's no chance I'm going to challenge my man while he's still acting like a spoilt boy. However, once I've fed his brood and give him time to see sense then I will be kicking his arse. Intimidating, not to me.

"What are you going to do, Holly?" Daniel asks once Lucas is out of the way. I rub at my temples, hoping I can bring him round.

"We are going to make something to eat," I answer, pointing at them both. "Then I'm going to butt heads with the awkward one," Nicholas chuckles.

"Good luck with that. I wish I was a fly on the wall when you lay into him." I'm not going to lay into him. Arguing with him will only make it worse. I know deep down he's a good man he just has issues that we need to address together, and him coming to terms with Daniel and me playing at the club will be just the thing to prove to us both that we can move on from his past.

"Thank you, Holly," Daniel says as we make our way out of the office, him holding open the door for me. Raising my eyebrows at him, I tap his cheek and give him a small smile.

"Don't thank me yet. Winning him round might be harder than we think."

The children, Daniel and Nicholas are all sat eating when I make my way up the stairs to see Vlad. Since storming out of the office an hour ago, he hasn't shown his face, so I'm sure he's still brooding over our argument.

Knocking lightly on the door as I enter, I'm surprised when I spot Vlad laid out on the bed. He's stretched out on his stomach with his bare back showing and it's that that has me creeping quietly towards him. If he's asleep, I don't want to wake him, but I do want to get a good look at whatever that piece of cellophane is covering. Vlad went out this morning with his usual disturbing colours covering his skin and from the looks of it he's had it covered with something beautiful and heavenly.

Sitting on the bed at the side of him, my fingers delicately trace around the edges of the angel. He shivers slightly at my touch but doesn't stop me. "What do you think?" his low voice asks, muffled by his pillow.

"I think it's beautiful," my fingers continue to trail around the eyes, nose and mouth. "Who did this?" It really is a surprise. I can't believe Vlad has had someone draw such a magnificent piece capturing my features. I can't believe he's had his past covered, he's done this for us, and it brings a tear to my eye.

I know we both want the same thing. To be able to move on, so we can live our lives and look forward to the future together. I just wish he would stop thinking the worst and understand that I want to do this for us.

He turns and sits up, eyes full of remorse, I can see he is struggling, so I shift closer hoping he will see I'm here for him. "Lucas sketched it and a tattooist copied it then covered the shit that was on my back."

"Wow. He's very talented."

"That he is. He thought it would help," Vlad takes my hand bringing it up to his lips. "I shouldn't have sounded off like that, Holly, I'm sorry." I nod my head at him. Looks like we're moving on from discussing the tattoo. "I know you want to join Daniel and you should. Ignore me, I'm an overbearing idiot."

"No, you're not," I stop him from continuing with beating himself up. "I get it Vlad, I really do. I understand why this is hard for you, but we've discussed this…" I climb onto the bed, getting comfy on his knee and without delay he wraps his arms around me. "This could be one of those times where you prove you're a bigger person."

"I know and I'm going to try. But I've watched this Jenny woman perform on stage, she's very enticing and leaves nothing to the imagination when she practically fornicates on stage with some of the band members." I let out a chuckle at the word fornicate because I haven't heard it in such a long time and watching Vlad's face: his eyes close, the shake of his head and the way he says it, anybody would think he was Mr Innocent. He's anything but. I also think he's been watching her old videos because she doesn't incorporate that act into her shows anymore because it's her brother's band now.

"Vlad, I think you've been watching her old videos," I tell him, placing one hand on his cheek while I straddle his lap. His eyes widen as he puts one arm around my waist helping me to get comfortable.

"I have? What do you mean?"

"Technically, she isn't in the band anymore, it's her brother's band and he invites her to come up and perform a few songs. Her followers know this, so they tend to get a mixture of fans, the ones that follow the band now and the ones that followed it when she was the lead singer."

"I didn't know that."

"Obviously," I laugh. "Do you think I would behave that way?" I chuckle at him when he opens his mouth and closes it again. "Your sons know this too; they wouldn't have asked me otherwise."

"Thank God," he nuzzles into my neck then leaves featherlight kisses all the way up to my ear. After he nibbles at the lobe, he brings his kissable lips to mine. "What about the random man in the audience? She practically gives him a lap dance." I sense there's still a bit of stress in him, so pecking at his lips, I hope I can alleviate that with what I'm about to tell him.

"That man is her husband," I feel the weight of his stress leave his body with what I just told him.

"I didn't know that either," and the smile that's been missing from him, returns.

"I gathered. He's her biggest fan and has never missed a show."

"I don't blame him," Vlad sighs then blows out a long breath. "Okay, let's do this. So, there's three shows?"

"Yes," I answer, nodding my head, excited that he's had a big turn around since leaving the office and is willing to support me. "But in the first show they only perform once because there's four bands on that night, all of them only have one spot each. I think her brother has asked her to sing three songs."

"And the other nights?"

"They are full nights with three spots per night and she's down for singing one song per spot."

"Okay. And if you cover for her, you'll keep it tame?" His thumb strokes over my cheekbone and his dark blue eyes investigate mine while he waits for my confirmation.

"Vlad, I would have toned it down anyway. I'm not about making a spectacle of myself; you know this. Or have you raging like a bull." He winces, closing his eyes, remembering his outburst in the club and the aftermath it had on not just our relationship but the one he has with his sons. When he opens his eyes, mine search his hoping he sees that now I know what he struggles with, I would never put him in a predicament where he would fly off the handle again. I love him too much to see that amount of anger and pain he was wrapped up in overwhelm him again.

Wrapping his arms tighter around me, he rests his head on my shoulder, leaving it there while he gets his emotions in check. When he lifts it up, I can see the trepidation has slighted a little and undying love oozes from him. "Holly, I love you and my sons with all my heart. You could ask me for the world, and I would try my fucking hardest to get it for you. I hate that I feel this way and act like a fucking immature fool, but I'm getting there. You make me see sense. You challenge me and won't let my insecurities win and I love you even more for that. And even though you know all my darkest secrets you're still here fighting for me, for us. And I sure as hell know that I'm not going to fuck up what we have again." Tears stream down my face for this larger than life man who fights with his demons every day. Knowing that his strong love for me brought on his extreme behaviour and now he's fighting every day to combat that.

"Please don't cry sweetheart. We'll get through this. When you talk to me it soothes me, I rationalize and see things clearer," he wipes the tears from my eyes and leans his forehead on mine. "Holly

I will struggle sometimes with our relationship but that's not because I don't love you or that I don't think you love me, it's because it's the way I am. But I will change..."

"I don't want you to change, Vlad," I cut in. "I love you the way you are." I run my hands up his chest. "And yes, I know the worst about you, and I can live with that. What I can't live with is you wanting to beat any man to a pulp because you think he wants to steal me away," I chuckle and so does he. "Sounds silly doesn't it?" And it does. He's forty-five and I'm thirty-seven; we shouldn't be having this conversation.

"Yes. When you say it out loud, it does."

Vlad scoops me up and sits me on the bed, "I need to pee." He gives me a soft kiss then strides off to the bathroom, leaving me to think about what I can do to help him stop getting so worked up. When he returns, I'm sprawled out on my stomach. He lays next to me on his side, leaning up on his elbow.

"Ask me to do something that you know I will find hard to do," I say as I turn on my side so I'm facing him.

"What?" he asks, his eyes smiling at me. "What do you mean?" I sit up and hug my knees.

"You know I love you, right?"

"Yes. But feel free to tell me repeatedly, I'll never tire of hearing you say it," he smiles and throws me that cheeky wink.

"Well, I love you and I know that you will struggle with what I want to do. Even though I have your support and that you'll be there centre stage all three evenings, I still know it's hard for you. So, I thought maybe, I should do something that I find hard and you can name it," I tap his nose. He laughs at me and shakes his head, taking hold of my finger.

"You're serious, aren't you?"

"Yes. I've never been more serious. You're going along with this even though you're not totally happy with it and because we're in this together then I will do anything you ask me to do."

"Holly, now I know you're not going to be half naked, I feel I could cope as long as the male dancers keep their hands off you then there shouldn't be a problem," I feel the growl vibrating from his chest as he says it. He's fooling himself if he thinks he can cope with this.

"Right, Vlad." I sit up hastily, knocking him slightly off balance and he collapses on his back, wincing when his back, that I'm sure is sore, hits the mattress. "Are you okay?" I ask, placing my hand on his broad chest. He pulls me down to him so that I'm sprawled across him.

"Of course, it's just a bit tender in places," he moans while he wraps his arms around me, spreading his warm hands across my bottom, giving it a squeeze. He throws me off balance and I forget why I was jumping up and what I wanted to say to him when his gifted fingers do their usual trick of setting me alight. This not having sex must be one of the most ludicrous suggestions I have come up with and it wasn't even my idea. Vlad's fingers increase their dance and when his hips buck underneath me, he lowers his mouth to my ear, "You wanted to do something hard, sweetheart?" he chuckles, and I whimper into his shoulder. The warm air from his breath sends a shiver down my spine and the seductive tone of his husky voice nearly has me ripping at his clothes and showing him just how much I want him.

I give myself a swift kick up the arse and remind myself why we are here but just because I want to repay him for getting me hot and bothered, I bite down on his bare shoulder, leaving a delicate kiss then jump up quickly before he can take this any further. He lets out a groan and adjusts his crutch, "Come back, Holly, I'll behave," he puts out his hand for me to take. I reach for it and sit back down on the bed, trusting that he won't try to seduce me. It doesn't take much, he only needs to speak and I turn into mush.

"We are not having sex," I tell him, trying to keep my tone firm and a straight face but it's hard to do while he's nibbling on his lower lip, holding back his laughter and his usual dark blue eyes gleam with excitement.

"I know. I thought you wanted to talk. You said something about me asking you to do something that you would find difficult."

"Yes, I did," I move further on to the bed. "I meant it too."

"You mean, like tit for tat?"

"No. I'm not playing games, Vlad. I'm serious."

"So am I, Holly." He takes my hands in his, raising them up to his lips, his eyes never leaving mine. There's nothing I wouldn't do for him, even knowing what I know about him and the way he can behave. It doesn't stop me from loving him. He wants to try. Refraining from sex, going ahead with my plans to sing at the club, these things are all trying to him.

"Ask me then," I say to him, kneeling up on the bed. He runs his hand over his face then pulls at his bottom lip before he joins me kneeling up, taking my hands in his and placing them on his chest.

"Move in with me?" I cough, hoping it hides my shock. I did not expect that. He places his hands on top of mine that have never left his chest. I think I need him for support because the rapid beat of his heart, the shake in his hands and that twitchy smile tells me he's nervous which means he's deadly serious and scared I'm going to reject him.

"Vlad," I move one of my hands and run it down his cheek. "That's a big step from where we are…"

"But it's the next step in our relationship. Isn't it?" He moves closer, so our noses are almost touching. He is serious, he wouldn't ask if he wasn't and I'm not sure if I'm ready for such a big leap. But then I think about it. The times I had stayed here, the times we were together before his past started to creep into our lives, before he erupted in the club and then the revelation into his life in Russia, I was happy. Never felt more wanted and loved. Even knowing all I know about this man when I'm with him, I feel cherished. His love is beyond anything I've ever known before. Yes, he has issues, don't we all, but he's not beyond mending. Between us, together our love will grow stronger and with that strength any hurt that has caused this intimidating man who loves fiercely and fights just as fierce will fade until it's dead and buried. And the love that holds us together will flourish and bloom, brightening both what was once sorrowful lives.

"Holly?" His fingers come up and tuck a loose piece of hair behind my ear. He's waiting for my answer and as much as I want to answer yes. With all my heart, I want to say yes but there are a few questions I need answers to.

"Vlad," I see him deflate, his head hanging low when I don't answer him with a straight yes or no. Taking his hand, I lead him to sit down on the bed with me. "I'm not saying no," I give him that just to ease his anxiety. He nods his head and keeps hold of my hand. "I just want to know when you want me to move in. I mean were not even sleeping together…"

"We could rectify that now," he grins and throws that sexy wink at me. I swoon as usual but smack his shoulder playfully reminding him of our agreement that we only made yesterday, god it's been a long twenty-four hours. "Holly I could have you under me," he flips me on to my back, laid out on the bed with him hovering over me in one swift movement. "Or over me," and just as quick, he's on his back and I'm plastered across his chest. His back's not so sore now.

"Vlad, stop. You're making me dizzy," I slap his chest and get a pout for my assault. He smooths his large hands up my thighs and rests them at the top, his thumbs circling a little too close to an area that's getting a little too hot and bothered. Placing my hand on top of his, I halt his attempt of pulling me into his sexual lair. He lifts from the bed, his stomach muscles rolling as he sits up and presses his hard chest against mine. "Sorry," he kisses my nose.

"No, you're not," I chuckle. He just shrugs his meaty shoulders at me. "Vlad, I want what you want but we only came to an understanding yesterday, we haven't been together since…" he places a finger on my lip to silence me and shuffles me further against his body, leaving his hands on my hips.

"Holly we've never really been apart except for the couple of weeks that you went away. Before then we were with each other every day. Then when you came back, we spent a lot of time together and slept together. It wasn't until after the weekend at the hotel that we didn't see each other," he shakes his head not liking that we have spent far too much time apart. "As I was saying before I made you dizzy, if I wanted you in my bed it wouldn't take much persuading. Would it?" His fingers stroke down my cheek and my neck then his thumb comes up to stroke my bottom lip.

He's right though, it wouldn't take much, he knows this and so do I. But that self-assured cockiness on his face needs wiping off, so I'm not about to feed his ego.

"Oh, you underestimate me, Vlad," his eyes widen when I run my fingers up his bare chest then tap it a couple of time. "I'm more than capable of keeping my libido under control when you are around." He smirks at me, bending his head down and placing a kiss on my hand when he lifts it, he throws a cheeky wink at me.

"You keep telling yourself that sweetheart, but I'm not going to push it because I think we've gone off track with what we were discussing." He gets off the bed, walks into his over the top wardrobe then comes back out minutes later wearing a pair of blue jeans and buttoning up a dark blue shirt. "I'm not going to push you, Holly, into what I want, it's your decision. I want you here with me and my family living under my roof," I'm stood up from the bed now and he comes and stands in front of me. "And I will do anything to get what I want," it almost sounds like a threat, but I know it's not it's just his accent that make the words sound harsh, I already know he will do anything to get his way.

"I think going along with yours and Daniel's plan to play at the club should be enough proof to show you that I'm trying, so I don't see any reason why you shouldn't move in. We know that's where we are headed. Why delay the inevitable?" He brushes a chaste kiss across my cheek then grabs my hand. "Come, we need to leave," he taps his watch. "Visiting time at the hospital." The size of his smile, knowing he's going to see his new grandson, melts my heart, why wouldn't I want to see that morning and night, but is it too soon?

He leads me out of his bedroom door and down the stairs, "We'll finish this conversation when we get home, Holly," he says as we step into the kitchen, his arms coming around my waist while his chest presses firmly against my back. Nicholas and Daniel watch our interaction with humour in their eyes and smirks on their faces. They know I've managed to get him to agree with our plan to sing at the club. Now can he persuade me to agree to his request. Do I really need persuading? Or am I as ready as he is?

Chapter 22

Vlad

Placing my empty glass on the table, I look up to the clear night sky; the wispy white clouds drift by while the branches of the magnificent tall trees whisper in the silence of the night.

It's been a bizarre couple of days, I muse as a smile graces my lips. I say bizarre because after my little angel stepped into my office yesterday lunch time, it's been one thing after another.

I must be getting soft in my old age because agreeing to Holly's request that I seek therapy for my anger issues and that we refrain from sex until I can show Holly that I'm not going to throttle any man that looks at her with lust-filled eyes is nothing but crazy. But then I'm crazy for her, so I will agree to anything.

Then Izzy having a fall and going into labour had me at my wits end. Having to leave early this morning and sit through covering up the past I so want to forget, took longer than I thought it would which kept me away from Holly and the birth of my grandson. Coming home to find Holly in a fluster over Rebecca's birthday party, only increased my aching to be at home with her, so I could have lessened the burden of her anxiety with setting it all up. Finding out through Holly that I'd missed Sebastian's birthday when I was selfishly trying to ease the pain I had caused by getting out of my head on cheap whiskey, ripped into my heart. I've never once missed one of my son's birthdays and I'm adamant I will make it up to him.

Nicholas and Daniel, my middle two sons, are enough to give me a stomach ulcer on the best of days but having their idea of Holly and Daniel covering Fake It's performances at the club nearly gave me heart failure. I know their intentions were good and that having them duet would be spectacular, they're both outstanding singers. However, knowing Holly would be not just singing but would also be dancing in a way that should be kept to the bedroom and for my eyes only, threw me and had me arguing with Holly to the point I became unreasonable. Holly showed me just how strong her love for me and my family is by not giving in. Nope, my little minx challenged me, made me see sense and had me falling further in love with her than I already am. I'm not sure if that's even possible.

This got me thinking that I need her here in my home night and day and the only thing to do was to have her move in with me. To say she was a little shocked when I asked her was an understatement, but in all fairness, she did want me to ask her to do something that would test her. Well I wasn't going to let the chance pass me by, so I jumped in with both feet and to my shock she said yes. Not straight away though, she questioned our relationship and what we have together.

Once we got home from the hospital and settled the kids down, I gave my two middle sons the job of babysitting their niece and nephew; Lucas can take care of himself, so they only had to put Rebecca and Joe to bed without disturbing Holly and me. This gave us time to talk. It did take longer than I thought it would because I couldn't get her to stop cooing at the photos on my phone of Benjamin: our new addition to the family.

We'd stayed longer at the hospital than we were allowed, all wanting to hold and cuddle the little bundle of joy, me being the devoted grandparent was the worst instigator. I couldn't get enough of him. He's so much like Sebastian was when he was born, with his wispy fair hair. When his eyes opened the darkness of the blue and his chubby flushed cheeks were identical to my eldest. Even his smell took me back to when I first held him in my arms.

After Holly had finished flicking through my phone, we settled down for a very in-depth discussion. We concurred that living together was what we both wanted. It surprised me somewhat as when I had first asked Holly, she didn't seem as keen as I was. Where I would have had Holly moving in tonight, my angel had other ideas. Still wanting confirmation that I'm a changed man, she put in a few clauses. One, we still refrain from sex until she moves in. Two, instead of me going to therapy and divulging my past, I could open up more to Holly, discuss issues that could jeopardize our relationship, besides what she already knows about me she wants to know other things. Three, she will be going along with Daniel's plan to perform at the club and while they are rehearsing, I will keep out of the way. Four, Izzy and the baby will be going home tomorrow from the hospital which means Joseph and Rebecca will be going home too, this means Holly will be going back to her apartment. I wasn't happy. Even though we're not sharing the same bed, knowing she's under my roof calms me. But I gave in, throwing in a little clause of my own. And finally, if I attended all three nights that they were playing at the club and behaved myself then Holly would move in the following day.

Five weeks isn't a long time; surely, I can keep it together until then. We'll both be kept busy this week organising Rebecca and Sebastian's party. Still lots of quality time together.

Then the two weeks rehearsing that lead up to the first night they play, Holly has agreed to join me for lunch and make time for us both in the evenings. That's my little clause. Which leaves me with the three nights that she will be performing. These are spread over ten nights and then she'll be here in my bed every evening, every morning and anytime in between. Yes, I can keep it together. For us I can.

"What are you thinking about?" comes the soft voice of the women that keeps me on my toes and has me wanting to pick her up, throw her over my shoulder, lay her down on my bed and bury myself in her. After our little chat, Holly went for a shower and I came out here to reflect on my day. Now she's standing before me wearing one of my T-shirts that stops at her thighs and clings to her damp skin outlining her breasts and a towel wrapped around her hair exposing her delectable neck that I love to kiss and suck on so much. Adjusting myself, I stand, offering her a drink. She chuckles and shakes her head at my discomfort but doesn't offer to help me out.

"I hope you're wearing knickers under my T-shirt," I say as she takes the glass from my hand. She gazes at me with those mischievous eyes over the rim of her glass and shakes her head. Fucking hell, I adjust myself again, struggling to keep myself from pinning her against the wall and devouring her. "Holly, five weeks," I remind her, taking the glass from her hand and finishing it off. "You need to play fair, sweetheart, or I'm not going to be held accountable for my actions." I tug at the bottom of the T-shirt and then run my fingers up her smooth thighs. Her eyes light up and she chuckles as she steps back from me. She lifts the T-shirt and laughs.

"Shorts," she says, still laughing at me. I can't help but laugh along with her as we walk back into the bedroom, my hand slapping her arse for tormenting me. She turns and as quick as a flash I pull her into me. We might not be having sex but that doesn't mean I can't have a quick feel while I'm kissing the hell out of her. My hands run amuck while I continue my attack on her mouth, my tongue acting out what another part of my anatomy wants to do. When we pull apart, we're both panting and the glow on Holly's skin tells me she's as affected as me.

"I… I need to dry my hair," she stutters out, swallowing hard as she breaks our embrace.

"You do that," I tell her. "I'm off for a shower. A very cold one." I kiss her cheek then walk away, leaving her in a fluster as I strip of my shirt and trousers showing her just what she is missing. Hearing her moan as I close the bathroom door has me laughing. I don't know why because the next five weeks are going to be painful to say the least. Maybe I'm laughing at the fact that it's not just me who will be struggling.

When I come out of the bathroom a good while later, let's just say a man's got to do what a man's got to do, the bedroom light is out, and Holly is snuggled up in my bed. Quietly, I make my way over to her, kiss the top of her head then head out of the door towards the spare room. Hoping and praying that I can keep up with our agreement.

Chapter 23

Holly

"What's that?" I point at the clear liquid that Nicholas is pouring into six shot glasses. Olivia, Sarah, Lucy, Daniel and Sebastian take a small glass each, down it in one, shiver then lick something off their hand.

"Tequila, baby," Sebastian says on a slur as he puts his arm around my shoulder, pulling me into him. He kisses the top of my head, "Thank you, Holly. You are truly an angel," he slurs again. "And thank you two, three," he says, squinting and pointing at my friends.

"You are welcome," Olivia says, patting his cheek.

"Rebecca was ecstatic when she realised she was having a ballerina themed party; you made her day and this." He points around at friends and family that have gathered to give Sebastian a belated birthday party, his dark eyes widening with a broad grin on his face.

He knew we were putting on a party for his daughter, but we kept it under wraps that we were having one for him as well. It wasn't that hard to keep it from him and everyone mucked in making it larger than first planned.

Once I'd given out the invitations for Rebecca's party, I got eight confirmations back straight away. The other two children couldn't make it as they were going away on holiday. The stuck-up parents that weren't that stuck up or vindictive were only too happy to drop their children at the ballerina school then attend the show the children were putting on later in the afternoon.

As you can imagine eight little girls together, there were lots of screaming and squealing but to be fair they were very well behaved. During the lesson they listened to Valerie and the other two girls that were helping her and took everything in. They practiced for the routine that they would be performing and once they were told they could keep the leotards, tutu and tights their toothy grins and sparkling eyes lit up the room.

Back at the house they played on the bouncy castle, danced to the music and took part in musical statues and chairs then sat around the table to eat the party food. Rebecca's face never letting go of how excited and happy she was.

Vlad stayed in the background during the party, taking care of his new grandson as the noise the girls were making kept waking him up. This meant that Izzy and Sebastian were able to enjoy the party with their daughter. When the parents turned up to watch the performances, Vlad came out to join us, wrapping his arms around my waist and dropping his chin on my shoulder. Izzy and the girl's mums watched in amazement as the children skipped out to perform.

The girls settled on the floor in a tuck position, like little flower buds, while Rebecca spun and twirled around, sprinkling glitter dust on them (sunshine). Gracefully, she moved until she had showered her friends with sunshine then the buds that they had formed started to grow, swaying their arms until they became a flower in full bloom.

They went on to perform a short routine which they did with grace, swirling and trying to get up on their tiptoes. One trying a pirouette. Glancing at Izzy, Lucy and the other mums as they held their hands to their chests, eyes watery and nothing but love in their hearts, I sigh and let a tear of my own fall. I might not have been privileged to have children of my own but it's times like this that I'm thankful that I have my friends. They have made me part of their family, giving me the chance to experience times like this and now I have the added advantage of being part of Vlad's loving family too.

As the song came to an end, they all dropped to the floor, some in the splits and some crouched in tiny balls. "Why are you crying?" Vlad's concerned voice asked me.

"I don't know," I mumbled. "Maybe because I'm happy." And I am. Suddenly, I was whisked away quickly, led into the kitchen and down the corridor to Vlad's office. Once we were in there, he shut the door and moved to his desk. He opened one of the drawers and brought out a wrapped gift box.

"I bought this for you," a nervous smile appearing on his face, he knows I don't need gifts.

"What is it?"

"Open it," which I did, carefully. The pink wrapping paper was too beautiful just to tear apart, so I took my time. When I got to the gift box, I nearly dropped it on the floor, the quality telling me I was going to find something exquisite. Vlad took my hands and helped me to open it. My hand covering my mouth when I saw what was inside. "It was supposed to be a thank you gift, but I needed to let you know how much I love you," he said, his eyes never leaving mine. He took out the yellow and white-gold infinity bracelet, each link wrapped together with tiny crosses, it's more than beautiful and the most precious gift I had ever been given. Even more so because I know the man who bought it has a meaning behind it. His love for me is forever...

When he fastened it around my wrist, I lifted on to my tiptoes and placed a gentle kiss on his lips, "Thank you," I whispered. "But you didn't need to, I know how much you love me, and I love you just as much." He leant down and pecked at my lips, his hand holding mine while his thumb rubbed over the gift, he'd just given me.

"I know," he utters against my lips then moved away with that smug look on his face. He's such a cocky git. "I'm one lucky bastard," he announced as he led us both out of his office and back to the party. And so am I, I thought to myself.

Once all Rebecca's friends had gone, Vlad asked Sebastian to run him to the club office so he could pick something up. His car was blocked in which was his excuse to get Sebastian out of the way. During that time, friends and family started to arrive and the bar and barbecue was set up. And before long Sebastian's party was in full swing.

"Try one," I hear Nicholas say as he thrusts a shot glass towards me. I don't take it from him, it's a drink I've never tried before. In fact, I haven't tried a lot of drinks, I usually miss out on the shots and just go for the wine. I say usually but the last few times I have been out either with the girls or with Vlad I have tried something different, so maybe I'll give it a go. He places it on the bar in front of me and I place my hand round the glass. 'Holly, Holly, Holly' is chanted from Vlad's sons and my friends. Quickly I pick up the glass and down it in one, screwing up my face in disgust when I finish it. Not a drink I care for, but my friends like it and they all follow suit with finishing off another glass.

Nicholas pours another round and I shake my head at him, telling him not for me just as two strong arms wrap around me. "Don't be getting sick, angel," Vlad whispers into my ear, he knows I'm a lightweight, so do Olivia and Sarah but that doesn't stop them from tempting me. Vlad picks up three of the glasses, kisses my cheek then strides back to Jack and Nick who he's been sat with playing cards. I watch his fine arse, wondering what he would do if I ran over and sunk my teeth it to it. Wow, I've only had one glass of wine and that shot of tequila and I'm feeling frisky. When he sits down his eyes catch mine ogling him, he grins and winks at me and I can't help reaching out grabbing the shot glass in front of me as I dissolve like an ice cube on a hot summer's day.

The clear liquid doesn't touch the sides and as I hear the laughter around me, I tell Nicholas to top me up. I'd struggled all week to keep my hands off Vlad and I know tonight will just be the same. "You still not getting any?" Sarah brings me out of my daze.

"Shush," Nicholas says as Mary and Ivy come around with a bin liner collecting empty bottles and paper plates. Nicholas' eyes search mine as he raises his eyebrows at me, questioning.

"Yes, they know," I whisper to him. He shakes his head at me. I don't mention that they're not aware that it was his idea to put the no sex until Vlad proves himself in force.

"Well from the way he's been smiling all evening he looks as if he's getting plenty," Olivia says, throwing her head towards my man who is sat laughing at something Jack is saying.

"Yeah, I agree," Sarah states, putting her glass down. "Every time I've seen him this week, he seems different. Not as intense. More approachable with a softness to his features," she scrunches up her lips, tilting her head to one side as she studies Vlad. "Hmmm, can't put my finger on what it is."

I can. Since I told him I would move in with him, he's been more relaxed and very attentive, but then he usually is with me and his family. He's a big softy really and very lovable.

"He is a softy and very approachable," I pout, defending him, placing my elbows on the bar and fiddling with the shot glass. Six pairs of raised eyebrows stare at me as if I've gone mad and Sebastian bends over, holding his knees, unable to contain his laughter. Then the rest follow suit. "Top me up barman," I chuckle, knowing the man sat across the garden, with his eyes narrowed on these giggling idiots, looks anything but approachable.

"Only the woman who loves him would say that about our father," Nicholas announces, once he's stopped laughing. Then he pours another round of tequila.

"Agreed," they all shout, downing the clear liquid and slamming the glasses on the bar. I'm a little slower than they are and just as the tequila starts to warm my throat, I realise I'm on my third. Oh, what the hell, it's a party.

Chapter 24

Vlad

With legs like Bambi, Holly struggles to keep her balance, her legs giving way causing her to fall back on to the sofa that she has just tried to get up from. "Wooh there," I hear her chuckle out. Turning from the patio doors that I've just locked; I can't help but wonder if she's going to have her head down the toilet. She's had one tequila too many and has that same look in her eyes that she had on our first official date. It doesn't take much for my angel to get all wobbly legged and from the way she's squinting at me it looks like her focus isn't too good.

"Come on, sweetheart, let's get you to bed," her arms shoot out for me to pick her up which I do, welcoming the feeling of having her wrapped around me.

I should have kept a closer eye on her when I saw that Nicholas had got out the tequila, but the way her face scrunched up after she drank her first one, I didn't think she would want anymore, so I continued with the game of poker I'd been playing with Jack and Nick.

The children were all taken care of with my grandchildren and Megan, who was sleeping over, all tucked up in bed by eight. It had been a long day for them, so it wasn't hard for Izzy to get them to bed. She too had an early night and was only too happy to leave her husband with his brothers to enjoy the rest of his party giving him a warning to share Daniel or Nicholas' room because she didn't want him waking the baby when he came to bed. Jack and Nick's kids were staying at their grandparents who took them home around ten when my sons started on the tequila along with Olivia, Sarah and Lucy.

Which brings me back to the bundle I have attached to my chest, legs wrapped around my waist, arms around my neck while she giggles into my neck as I climb the bedroom steps.

"Where are you taking me?" she slurs, still giggling.

"To bed," I say, placing my hand under her arse and hitching her up a bit.

"Oooh," my little minx giggles again. "Are we having sex?" she pulls at the bottom of my T-shirt and runs her hand up my back, delicately scoring her nails into my flesh. I might be a little inebriated myself but I'm not about to take advantage of Holly. Not that I don't want to, it's been too fucking long since we slept together and I would love nothing more than to strip her naked and feast on her until I have her writhing around my bed, screaming my name. But…

"No, sweetheart, we're not doing that," I tell her, gritting my teeth, trying to combat the stirring in my boxers. I shift her to my side as I open the bedroom door then stride over to the bed and lay her down, adjusting myself.

"Ow, you're no fun," she pouts, and I could bloody swear. She made the fucking rule and now she wants to break it when she's fucking drunk. I ignore her, helping to get her undressed, my body heating to the core when her breasts are thrust into my face. She didn't mean to do it, just as I was taking off her shirt she sat up to help me and there they were. I swallow hard as I help her out of her skinny jeans and she wiggles, lifting her bottom to help. Once they're off, her hands dart out for my shirt and as she tugs at it, trying to rip it from my body, I take hold of her wrists.

"Holly," I warn. I'm trying so fucking hard to follow her rules but she's making it difficult for me. The day Izzy came home from hospital with the baby, Holly went back to her apartment. Although it's not what I wanted, she could have stayed here; I've gotten used to sleeping in the spare bedroom but it's what she wanted so I went along with it. Every day since, we've spent time together and every evening, I've made sure she went home. I didn't leave straight away.

In fact, I didn't leave her until I'd tucked her into her own bed, making sure I'd kissed the hell out of her then I would leave and lock the door behind me. We both struggled with it, but we had both agreed, me reluctantly, that we would refrain from sex and that Holly would stay at her home until the day after she finishes at the club. With that in mind, that I get her here in my home every day and every night, I've managed, but here... now... knowing she wants me as much as I want her... I'm struggling but she's drunk and I will not take advantage of her.

"Holly, you're playing with fire, you need to go to sleep, angel," I run my fingers through her hair, and she lets go of my shirt, sitting back on her haunches. She looks fucking beautiful, pissed but still beautiful.

"I just wanted to see you," she whispers, her hand waving around my chest. "I miss seeing you... you're beautiful." And I blush at her words. I fucking blush. I know over the years women have thrown themselves at me and wanted to see me naked, but I refused to bare all to them. Holly my angel, the one I normally call beautiful, sees me. She sees behind the ray of colours swirled around my body, the darkness and all the ugliness that has scared me. She sees me. And with that I slowly remove my shirt giving her what she wants. How could I not?

She kneels on the bed, reaching until her soft delicate touch ignites my skin. Her fingers follow a trail around the patterns on my biceps while mine stay pinned to my side not trusting at this moment that I could only touch. When she's finished with my arms, they carry on their trail along my skin on to my chest which she runs her hands over then lowers to my stomach. All the while her eyes stay focused on what her hands are doing and the tattoos that her fingers stroke gently over. I don't move, I let her finish exploring and when she does, she flops backwards on the bed, I can't help letting out a little chuckle. One minute she has me immersed in deep thought, the next I'm laughing at her while she looks as drunk as a Lord. "Feel better?" I ask smiling.

She climbs under the sheets, tucking them under her chin and closes her eyes. "No," she huffs out. "This no sex rule stinks," she moans, covering her mouth with the sheet.

"Well you made the stupid rule, sweetheart," I sit on the side of the bed, my hand resting on her hip, gazing at my intoxicated woman who is mumbling away to herself. Carefully, I tug at the sheet, so I can hear her. "Can't hear you, sweetheart," I tell her while her tired eyes flicker open then close again. Repeating herself with a whisper, I catch what she says.

"It wasn't my idea," she lays there, eyes closed and without moving while I sit here not understanding what she is telling me.

"Holly," I move further up the bed. "What do you mean it wasn't your idea?" And as I repeat her words, I'm confused to whose idea it was because it certainly was not mine. Sheepishly, one of Holly's eyelids lift while she covers her mouth again with the sheet. She's hiding something. "What did you mean, sweetheart?" I ask, pulling at the sheet again so I can see her face. If she is hiding something from me, her face will give her away.

"Nothing," she whispers, quickly covering her mouth again as her tired eyes close just as quick and I know for definite she is hiding something from me.

Moving off the bed, I crouch in front of her; watching her, listening to the gentle puff of air she blows out. I don't think I'm going to get any sense out of her tonight, that soft snore telling me she's fallen asleep. I get up from my crouching position, making my way into the bathroom wondering about Holly's slip of the tongue. While I'm there, it hits me like a bolt of lightning that this has my son's names written all over it. She didn't mean to let it out that it wasn't her idea, I knew that as soon as she said it and the way she covered up her face to hide her guilty look, sealed it. Nicholas would be the one to come up with a plan so he could laugh at my discomfort and his brothers would back him up for the fun of it. If not all three of them then definitely Nicholas has coaxed Holly into this, well we will see who has the last laugh. With that thought, I strip out of my clothes and instead of making my way to the spare room, I climb in at the side of Holly, snuggling my chest into her back and wrapping my arms around her.

*

Holly lets out a puff of air and wiggles her nose to get rid of what it is that's tickling it. Her eyes are closed but flicker when she wiggles her nose again. I can't help but chuckle at her face and the fact that

I'm nestled snugly between her legs, resting on my elbows while I tickle her nose with a lock of her hair, her sleepy face looks adorable. Knowing it won't be long before I have her full attention, I roll my hips, adding a little thrust which gets me a soft moan for my action and her body moulds into mine.

Trailing my lips down her neck while my fingers run up her thighs, I feel her body shudder. Yes, I've got the affect I wanted. Now to enhance her arousal. My fingers continue to stroke her inner thigh as my lips continue to kiss and suck on to her collarbone. There's another shudder and a moan then her hands move to my hair where she gives a little tug. I might be as hard as rock, but I'm determined to put my little minx through the same turmoil she has had me in. To get her attention and bring her out of that, oh, so lovely dream she is having, I rub my hardness against her heat again and her legs involuntary wrap around me. My body knows that this is its favourite place in the world, and I would normally be in heaven when her legs are wrapped around me but today it's all about payback.

One more motion of my hips and a delicate kiss on the swell of her breasts has Holly moaning again. Within seconds her eyes flick open and the blush on her neck creeps on to her shocked face. She really does look in a fluster, all wide eyed and breathless.

"Vlad, what are you doing?" She sits up quickly, resting on her elbows while I land one last kiss on her stomach before I sit back, kneeling up in front of her. Her hair is in disarray and that beautiful look of arousal is donned perfectly on her face.

"Just waking you up, sweetheart," I answer her while I place my hands back on her thighs. She swallows and shakes her head and I can't help but lay my body over her and kiss her passionately. Her legs wrap around me again and her fingers run through my hair. I know I've got her, and she will give in to me when I feel her hips gyrate, wanting to quench her thirst, it's tempting but I'm not going to let it happen. With all the will in the world, I pull myself from Holly, leaving her with a delicate kiss on her cheek.

"What…? Why…?" she stutters out, running her fingers through her hair and sitting up straight, a look of perplexity on her face. Sitting on the bed at her side, I take her hand in mine, running my thumbs over her knuckles.

"Holly, I was just waking you up," I bite my lip to stifle a chuckle when I look into Holly's lustful eyes.

"But…"

"No buts. This was your rule," I say, standing as I see the longing in her eyes. I've probably got the same in mine, but Holly went along with my son's games who just wanted to have a laugh at my expense. Well, we'll see who has the last laugh. "Oh, and my son's," I add on while lifting one eyebrow at her.

"What…? How…? How did you know?" She sits up straighter now, eyes wide, waiting on my answer.

"Oh, angel," I say, sitting back down on the bed while I run a finger over her bottom lip. Her tongue comes out to wet it when my finger moves and then her teeth scrape over. "Too much tequila and you can't help but let out your secrets," I tell her tapping her nose. Smiling, "Who knew it was a truth serum?" I say.

"Yeah, who knew?" she says as she grins then takes my hand in hers. "Please don't say anything to Nicholas. It was just a bit of fun and I thought that it might help." I know why he suggested it and I know why Holly went along with it, but I think it's my turn to have a bit of fun.

"Sweetheart, I know," I say, "but it's my turn to have some fun." With that I lean down, placing my lips by her ear so I know she hears me clearly. "Four weeks, Holly. Be prepared to be tormented the whole time then after your last show, I will be locking you in this bedroom where I will torment you some more. You will be begging for me to give you release." I give a little tug on her ear, throw her a wink and saunter out of the bedroom. I snigger when I hear her call out, "Well that's a little over-dramatic, Vlad." And it might be because I can't torment Holly without causing myself the same amount of torture. Adjusting myself, I make my way downstairs to make breakfast and hatch a plan to get back at Nicholas without him knowing that I knew it was his idea.

Chapter 25

Holly

Fully dressed and feeling a lot better than I did when I was awakened earlier by a man who had a very naughty streak about him, I make my way into the kitchen. Vlad sits innocently at the breakfast table reading a newspaper, shirtless, looking his usual handsome self while Sebastian and Nicholas are laid out on the sofa groaning. Looks like I'm not the only one to have woken with a bad head.

The house is unbelievably quiet considering how many slept here last night. Apart from the noise coming from the two across the room, you wouldn't have thought that this house was full of children yesterday afternoon, then had a party which went on until late.

As I switch the kettle on, the man who promised to torture me for the next four weeks lifts his head. He folds the paper, dropping it on the table then sits back in his chair while folding his arms over his muscular chest. His eyes study me for a moment then he stands, striding purposely towards me. Without a word his lips cover mine tenderly.

"Sit," he says when we pull apart, "I'll make you a coffee." I do as he says and watch his back as he goes about filling the cups. My eyes travel to his bottom that I contemplated biting last night then the over events of the evening come to mind. One too many tequilas, me asking if we were having sex and Vlad sticking to our agreement and telling me no. That's when I pouted and moaned that it wasn't fair and let it slip whose idea it was. Therefore, giving Vlad a reason to torment me for the next three to four weeks. Oh boy I'm in trouble.

"Make me one, paps," Sebastian yawns, strolling into the kitchen, his eyes all red and puffy. Slapping his hand on his dad's shoulder, "Please," he adds.

"You look like shit," Vlad turns to him, placing another cup at the side of mine.

"I feel like shit," he groans, taking out a couple of painkillers from the top cupboard and popping them in his mouth. "But these and a nice greasy breakfast should do the trick," he says when he's swallowed them. "Want one, Holly?" he asks as he places the pan on the hob then turns to the fridge to gather the bacon and eggs.

"No, thanks. I'll just have toast," I answer as my stomach flips on the thought of a greasy fry up. I get up to make my toast, but Vlad takes over the duty telling me he had prepared breakfast for me earlier but when he realised I'd gone back to sleep, he let Daniel eat it.

Nicholas makes an appearance, scratching his stomach and yawning. Wearing just a pair of boxers he gets an eye roll from Vlad and a shake of his head when he sits on the stool next to me.

There's an unusual smirk on Vlad's face when he places the toast in front of me along with my coffee which has me wondering what he is up to.

He made it quite clear this morning that I wouldn't be getting away with agreeing with Nicholas, so I'm sure he'll have something up his sleeve for his son. I'm just glad he doesn't know that Sebastian and Daniel knew about it too.

Nicholas gets up wondering around the kitchen, rubbing his hand over his morning stubble as he looks for something just as Daniel appears from the gym. Looking like he's had quite the workout. Beads of sweat drip down his face and his damp skin glistens. He uses a towel to wipe it dry, then slings it over his shoulder. "I'm going for a shower. What time do you want to start rehearsing, Holly?" he calls over his shoulder as he makes his way towards the bedroom stairs.

"She's not," Vlad answers for me. Before I have time to tell him off, he's by my side. His arm around my waist and chin resting on my shoulder. Not that I can be bothered practicing today, I can't. I'm tired and just want to relax all day, tomorrow would be fine with me. "We're going out, Holly." He kisses my cheek.

I open my mouth to ask him why he hasn't bothered to ask me when he puts a finger on my lip. "Holly you're going to be busy for the next few weeks. You've been busy taking care of Rebecca and Sebastian's party as well as watching the kids, you need to relax today and let me spoil you." He kisses my cheek again. "Jack came over early with Lucy to collect Megan and they have taken Rebecca, Joe and Lucas with them. Lucas is having a sleepover at theirs tonight. Izzy has gone home with Ben and these three will be pissing off soon, so it's just you and me, sweetheart."

This time he plants a soft kiss on my lips. "And I've booked a table at Marcos." He throws that wink at me and how can I resist. How can I not when he looks at me with those eyes that are usually dark and intense but today have a playfulness about them? And when that cheeky grin makes an appearance, I melt.

"Well I'm not even going to try and compete with that," Daniel shouts from the staircase.

"No neither would I," Sebastian chuckles.

"I'll rearrange our first rehearsal for tomorrow. Ten o'clock, leave the big guy at home," I hear Daniel call as I look forward to having a restful day just me and my man and our romantic evening for two.

"Has anyone seen my phone?" Nicholas asks while Sebastian plates up their breakfast. Vlad lifts his head and I catch an amused expression on his face as he watches his son scouting around the living room, lifting the cushions as he searches in vain. Vlad returns to his seat and takes my hand in his.

"Did you find it?" Seb mumbles as he tucks into his fry up. Again, I watch Vlad, his eyes glinting with mischief.

"No."

"What are you looking for?" Vlad asks, taking a drink of his tea. He places the cup back on the island and looks up at his son. His face now showing no sign of amusement.

"My phone, I…"

"Oh, it's in the drawer," Vlad points at the set of drawers next to the fridge and takes another sip of his tea.

"Why is it in there?"

"It wouldn't shut up ringing and when I answered it, it was some woman. Vanessa, I think she said her name was."

"Isn't that the woman you were seeing last Christmas?" Sebastian questions as he stands, grabbing a carton of milk from the fridge. "Didn't she tell her friends that you had asked her to marry you and wore her mum's engagement ring, pretending it was the one you had bought her?" Sebastian chuckles as he slaps his brother on the back. "I wonder what she wants."

"I don't know," Nicholas shrugs his shoulders. "I haven't heard or seen anything of her for nearly nine months."

"She said she has a surprise for you. She's calling over at eleven…"

"What?" Both Nicholas and Sebastian turn and look at the clock then snap their necks back to their father. Sebastian drops the milk onto the work top and Nicholas starts scrolling through his phone.

"There's no number… What surprise?" The poor man looks pale and sick with worry as he stares at his father.

"No, it came up as a private number," Vlad tells him while he continues to drink his tea, "and she didn't say what it was."

"Paps, why would you allow her to come here? She's poison," Sebastian retrieves a glass from the cupboard and pours out his milk while his brother paces the floor like an expectant father. "She stalked him at the club for four weeks after he broke it off with her then sent her two brothers to have a quiet word with him. If Daniel and I hadn't have been leaving the club with him that night who knows what might have happened."

"I wasn't aware of this," Vlad stands, taking my plate and putting it in the dishwasher then he turns his attention to Nicholas. "What surprise could she have for you, if you haven't seen her for nearly nine months?" While Nicholas shrugs his shoulders, Sebastian eyes widen, and he blows out a long breath.

"Nearly nine months. Surprise, you do the maths," his brow furrows.

"Oh, fuck!" Nicholas curses loud enough to make me jump, it's then when I put two and two together and come up with Nicholas has got some woman pregnant. Bloody hell, his dad will kill him. He said she was coming at eleven and it's ten thirty now.

"Nicholas," I say calmly. "Don't stress. You don't know why she's coming over, don't go jumping to conclusions."

"Conclusions about what?" Daniel asks, making his way into the kitchen. He sits at the breakfast island freshly showered; Sebastian passes him his breakfast that he's kept warm for him. "Vanessa has a surprise for Nicholas, she's on her way over." Daniel's fork stops mid-air, his mouth wide open then he places his fork back on his plate.

"You're joking."

"Nope. Apparently, she's phoned this morning, said she had a surprise for him…"

"What surprise?" Daniel asks, his head tilts to one side as he looks at his older brother. Seb shrugs his shoulders while Nicholas has his elbows resting on the island with his face in his hands. He's very quiet.

"Not sure but it's nine months since he last saw her," Daniel eyes flick from Seb to Nicholas then to his dad and me. His eyes are narrow then as the sudden impact of realisation hits him his eyes widen.

"Fucking hell, no."

"No," Nicholas stands up straight. "She's playing with me, I always used protection, she can't be. What time is she coming?" He looks at Vlad.

"In fifteen minutes…" Nicholas flies out of the kitchen like he's just caught fire, calling over his shoulder that he's going to get dressed.

I watch Sebastian as he sits, rubbing at his morning stubble. A frown deeply rooted in his forehead. Daniel eats his breakfast slowly, struggling to get it down. The ramification of this woman and the phone call has certainly got them stressed.

Vlad squeezes my hand and when I turn to look at him, his lip rises at one side which has me narrowing my eyes at him. Why's he smiling? His son thinks he's got some woman from his past pregnant and will probably turn up carrying a new-born or ready to give birth. And this woman, from what his sons have said, isn't one that can be trusted. Surely, Vlad can sympathise with that.

He throws me a wink and I know he's up to something.

He wouldn't? Would he?

Just as Nicholas wanders back into the kitchen, a buzzer sounds and Vlad's up off his stool. "Come in," his firm voice commands. I've never heard the gate buzzer sound, everyone including me have a fob.

"What are you doing?" Nicholas leaps into the air and runs into the hallway, his father follows behind him chuckling. "Why have you let her in? I'll never get rid of her." He puts on his trainers, all red faced, shaking his head. "And I don't know why you find this amusing. You out of all people should understand what I'm going through." He points his finger at his father and I've just become aware that the rest of us have followed them into the hallway.

"I'm not laughing at you, Nicholas," Vlad bites his lip and it's obvious he is finding his son's predicament funny. Why? I have no clue. His son's face has taken on an all new shade of colour, the greenish tint looks as if he could throw up, or pass out, "but you cannot discuss personal issues at the gate."

The bell rings on the door, and there's also a rattle on the letter box. "I'll get it?" Sebastian says. Nicholas stops him, shaking his head. Blowing out a breath, he rubs his hands down his jeans then hesitates. With his hand on Sebastian's shoulder he takes in a deep breath then blows it out slowly.

"Fuck it. Let's get this over and done with." Sebastian, Daniel and I stand near the staircase and Vlad hovers near the entrance to the kitchen, his arms are crossed over his broad chest and he's wearing that unusual smirk again.

Nicholas' hand lingers on the door handle for a moment and when the letterbox rattles again, he yanks the door open.

His head tilts to one side and his eyebrows lower in question. "Mrs White what are you doing here?" He steps to one side as Mary marches through carrying a small card in her hand.

She passes the card to Nicholas who takes it with a bemused look on his face.

"What is this?" He shakes it in the air then starts to tear at the envelope.

"I don't know, Nicholas, your father asked me to give it to you."

There's an almighty roar of laughter and when we all turn Vlad is doubled over, his shoulders shaking violently. Sebastian and Daniels puzzled faces turn to one of amusement when Nicholas bellows out, "YOU BASTARD!"

He shoves the card from the envelope into my hand as he strides towards his dad. Reading it, I now know why Vlad has been wearing a strange smirk all morning. "GOT YA!" it says with an emoji, laughing with tears in its eyes.

"Why the fuck would you do this to me?" he shouts but you can see that cheeky smirk, lighting up his face with relief that it was his father having him on.

"Because," he says as he wipes the tears of laughter from his eyes then puts Nicholas in a head lock, rubbing his knuckles on his head, "you think it's funny to mess with my sex life."

He lets go of him and Nicholas' eyes find mine "You told him?" Oh, shit. I shake my head trying to come up with an excuse but fail miserably and end up laughing along with Vlad and his sons.

"No, she didn't. Getting her drunk on tequila," he points at the three of his sons, "did."

"You lot need to grow up," Mrs White huffs as she makes her way into the kitchen, "And it's about time someone played a trick on you, Nicholas. God knows you've played enough on the lot of us over the years."

"Yeah, but that's just cruel," he whines to nobody as we all sit down at the breakfast bar, leaving him stood in the kitchen entrance.

"That was priceless, paps," Sebastian slaps his father on his shoulder. "You even had me believing it."

"Yeah, well I know you two will have known about the little agreement between these two," he nods his head at both Nicholas and I, "so count yourselves lucky that I haven't got anything planned for the both of you. Yet."

"Please, don't," Daniel says. "I'm too busy to play silly games." He picks up his car keys and asks Sebastian if he's ready to go home. Sebastian jumps up, still amused at his father and kisses my cheek.

"No doubt you'll get your punishment, Holly," he chuckles again, and I lower my head on to the work top groaning, remembering Vlad's words from early this morning.

Chapter 26

Vlad

"Vlad, I'm fine it's just nerves," my little minx shouts from her tiny bathroom that she's just disappeared into to have a shower, leaving me stood in her kitchen contemplating whether to lock her in there, so she misses tonight's show. I chuckle to myself because she'd fucking kill me. She's worked so hard getting to this point and wanting to give her all, she's even practiced while being unwell. She says she's fine now, but she is kidding herself thinking that.

After Rebecca and Sebastian's party and finding out my son had been collaborating with Holly, I took my revenge on him. Playing him at his own game highly amused me and he took it all in good fun when he realised that he'd been had.

Holly and I spent the whole day on our own which was a first in a long while. I kept to my word, tormenting her the whole day. Not once did I relent on showing her what she was missing and the way she moaned and flushed told me I was accomplishing my goal. I carried on with my flirting, getting her all worked up then leaving her all needy and frustrated for a full week while she rehearsed late into the evening with Daniel and the band Fake It. I also kept to my word that I would make sure she slept in her own bed at night and I would sleep in mine. It was hard to leave her not only because I knew she wanted me to stay, I wanted to be with her too. While I enjoyed watching the lust in her sapphire eyes, the sexy blush creep up her skin and the way her chest rose and fell, it had its side effects. Me taking cold showers daily.

Every evening, I picked her up from the club, we ate at my restaurant then I'd drive her home. Once she was tucked up in bed, I would claim her mouth, satisfied for the evening I would then leave, locking the door on my way out.

On the second week, rehearsals came to a stop. Well it did for Holly. Coming down with a virus knocked her on her arse. For five days she was either throwing up or feeling nauseous. It left her weak, dizzy and unable to stomach the smallest amount of food. According to her she'd had something similar a few years ago and could only drink fluids for a week.

Over the weekend she dragged herself back to rehearsals, drinking plenty of water and eating small amounts. I wasn't happy that she wanted to go back while she still had the virus in her, she'd already learnt the dance routines and the songs she didn't already know but my woman has a stubborn streak. So, on the promise that she would only stay for a few hours and would keep on with eating small amounts often, I didn't kick up a fuss.

Seeing her just now has me wondering whether tonight might be a bad idea. I've been at work all morning and suggested to Holly that before we go to the club this evening, we call to the restaurant for something to eat.

It's going to be a long evening with Holly, her friends and my sons wanting to watch the other bands play before their performance at ten o'clock then stay on to watch the last band.

Our table has been reserved at the restaurant and at the club and with Mr and Mrs White staying over at Sebastian and Izzy's to take care of Lucas, Joe, Rebecca and Ben, they are meeting us there. Nicholas is joining us and so are Jack, Olivia, Nick, Sarah and Lucy as Jack's parents are taking care of all their kids. I know it will be a good evening, but I'm concerned that Holly will make herself worse. She says it's just nerves now and maybe it is. I know I get overprotective and I know she's a grown woman and can make up her own mind but with the virus and her nerves getting the better of her, I worry.

She steps into the kitchen, towel drying her hair and another one wrapped around her beautiful body that looks as if it's lost a few pounds. Although her eyes are dark and heavy, she looks brighter than she did last week.

Getting up from my stool, I take her in my arms, "You don't need to perform tonight, Holly. Daniel and the band will cover for you. You still look tired, sweetheart," I say into her hair. I inhale her smell then pull myself away so I can see her eyes.

She looks at me as if I've just spoken a foreign language then smiles and shakes her head. "I've told you I'm fine. I'm over the virus and just a little nervous. That's all." She kisses my cheek, and pecks my nose, "Thank you for caring, Vlad," then she turns and vanishes into the bedroom to finish getting ready.

I follow her into the small room that I know in just ten days we will be packing up, ready for her to move into my home. Well, our home.

I'm pleased with myself that I haven't fucked up yet but then again, I was never going to let it happen. Holly has shown me what true love is and I will show her for the rest of my life how much I love her and what she means to me.

She finishes drying her hair, fastening it into a bun on the top of her head then sits at her dressing table to apply a light covering of make-up. She never plasters it on, it's always light and carefully applied.

Tonight, at the club, Sarah's sister will call over to top up her make up and do whatever she wants to do with her hair, and I know she has an outfit to change into once it's time for her to perform. I've also had a room chosen for Holly, so she doesn't have to share with the female dancers or anyone from the band. Many of the dancers don't mind using the unisex changing room and that's fine but my Holly will not be. She knows I've had a changing room set up just for her and she's ok with this. I half expected her to challenge me on it, but to my surprise she didn't. I think she's a little shy and I'm fucking grateful of that because I would have had a hard time if she had told me she was changing with the rest of the band and dancers.

"Nearly ready," she smiles, grabbing my attention from my thoughts. As she stands there, slipping her beautifully toned arms through a silky black dress, I'm so grateful that she gave me a second chance and I can't wait for the next ten days to be over. I can take my time slipping off anything she is wearing and slowly take my time getting reacquainted with every curve on her body, the softness of her skin and the sounds she makes when she falls apart in my arms.

"What's wrong?" Holly asks, as she turns her back for me to fasten the clasp at the back of her neck.

"Nothing," I reply, adjusting myself then take a little nibble of that delectable neck that is calling to me. She turns in my arms once I've managed to attach the tiny loop to the button, with the size of my fingers it's a struggle, then she pats my chest.

"How do I look? Any better?"

"Stunning."

"What, even with the dark circles under my eyes?" she giggles.

"They aren't that bad, Holly," I kiss her soft lips. "You know I overreact when it comes to you and my family." Her head tilts to one side, her sapphire eyes sparkling, and that angel smile appears on her face. She stands on her tiptoes and kisses me tenderly.

"We are very lucky to have you," she whispers into my lips.

"You'll always have me, sweetheart," I whisper back and before I get ahead of myself, I step back and take her hand. "Come on, I'm starving and if we don't move now, you'll be on the menu." I get the usual slap on the arm for my comments and as we make our way through Holly's apartment, she collects her shoes and bag and I collect my keys.

We arrive at the restaurant, our rowdy friends and family already seated and ordering their meal. Jack orders a few bottles of champagne, to toast Holly and Daniel's big night and I decide just to have one glass. My intentions were not to have any alcohol tonight, just because I know Holly won't be drinking. However, I want to raise a toast and show my talented son and my beautiful equally talented Holly how proud I am of them both. Holly declines the glass of fizz, like I knew she would and chooses a glass of sparkling water, getting her a moan and screwed up noses from her two close friends.

I watch Holly pick at her lasagne, chasing it around the plate rather than putting it on her fork and into her mouth. Olivia sees it too and assures me it's just her nerves which I can understand, I would be nervous if it was me performing to hundreds of people.

As we finish our meal, I stand to wish them the best of look and give a long-winded speech of how honoured I am to be Daniel's father and how I'm the luckiest man alive to have Holly by my side. Everyone agrees, clinking their glasses and whistling while Holly squeezes my hand as she stands on her tiptoes to kiss me. She places a soft kiss at the side of my mouth and whispers, "I love you." Which I reciprocate with another soft kiss.

After our meal, we make our way next door to Aphrodite, everyone eager to get in and settled into their seats before the first band starts off the evening.

Chapter 27

Holly

I can still hear the audience applauding as I grip hold of the dressing table to steady myself. Kicking off my three-inch heels, I sink into the chair letting go of the white oak dresser, my overheated skin delighting in the air-conditioner that has just switched on.

My head spins as bile continues to climb, burning my throat. The virus that I'd had last week still lingers and my nerves have the better of me making me feel like crap.

Tonight's performance went better than we could have ever imagined. Starting off with Daniel leading the band into a couple of songs that had been written by Sam, the lead singer of Fake It, he then went on to sing a few of his favourite numbers and even sung a song he had written himself. He introduced me near the end of their set where we sang our version of Promises by Calvin Harris and Sam Smith and the dancers performed a routine which didn't involve me. Once the song had ended the band broke into a seventies number, Hot Stuff, this was my turn to show Jenny's fans that I had what it takes to replace her as it was one of the songs that she had performed repeatedly with a very racy dance routine.

Singing and dancing at the same time takes a lot out of you and by the time we had got to the end of a well-choreographed routine, I was glad I only had one song left. My third song was Titanium, acoustic style which slowed things down a bit. I had heard it played a few times this way and when Daniel suggested it, I jumped at the chance to give it a go.

The audience have quietened down now and low music echoes around the room that I am in at the back of the stage. There are various changing rooms for the staff, but I have one of my own, which has its advantages, only now I could do with someone here to untie the lace on the back of this damn corset I've been wearing. It's threatening to cut of my oxygen supply and as my skin starts to overheat again, so does the light-headiness.

"Holly you were fantastic!" My two friends screech as they burst into my changing room. I'm so grateful for them and stand up too quickly, wobbling when I do.

"Quick unfasten this for me will you, before I pass out."

"Bloody hell, Holly, be careful," Olivia grabs my arm to steady me. "Are you ok?" she questions as she pulls at the ties on my back.

"I will be when I get out of this." I pull at the corset and unfasten the side button and zip to the skinny leather trousers that have become my second skin. Taking in a large breath and letting it out slowly, I whip off the restriction covering my boobs with one arm as I reach for the over-sized T shirt that's thrown over the back of the chair.

"Where's Vlad?" I ask, pulling it on over my head. I know if he sees that I'm still feeling unwell, he'll be dragging me off home, no questions asked.

"He was on his way but got stopped by Frank and a few others. Good thing we got here first because you look as if you were about to pass out, Holly."

"I'm fine, honestly. I just got overly warm and these bloody clothes were too tight," I point down at the corset, then sit down and wiggle my legs for Sarah to help me out of my pants.

"Thanks," I say as she tugs them off my legs. Olivia passes me a bottle of water which I drink while fanning myself with a leaflet from off the dresser.

"Are you sure?" Sarah narrows her eyes at me, tilting her head to the side.

"Yes," I answer, putting down my makeshift fan and taking another drink of the water.

"Your colour is coming back," Olivia states, resting the palm of her hand on my forehead. "You do feel a bit clammy though," she stands back from me, picking up my make-up bag. "Go give your face a swill then we'll top up your make-up before the big guy comes in," she raises an eyebrow at me and nods her head towards the door, "and my dear, I would go get a check-up at the doctors because I think you're a little run down after that virus."

Within a few minutes I've had a quick wash, topped up my makeup and changed into a loose-fitting short dress that I had brought and left here during the week. Vlad enters and takes me straight into his arms, none the wiser to my little wobble.

"Sorry," he whispers into my hair as I watch my too friends leave the room smiling. "I couldn't get a few feet without being stopped by someone." He stands back from me, so he can see me and has the most gorgeous smile on his face. "You were amazing, Holly." He presses his lips softly against mine.

"It was a joint effort," I say against his lips while my hands run up from his chest into his hair.

"I know. I've spoken with Daniel and congratulated him and everyone else on my way to get you," he chuckles, "I couldn't get away from them."

"Good," at least it gave me time to get myself together before he saw that I was still a little under the weather.

"Shall we get a drink and join everyone else or do you want to go home?" I'm tempted to say take me home and put me to bed but that would only give him a cause for concern. His reaction earlier when he came to pick me up and he saw how tired I looked, he wanted me to stay at home.

"Let's get a drink and stay for an hour then we'll go." He nods his head, letting go of me so he can grab my bag. "I'll just have iced water, no alcohol for me."

"No problem," he says, kissing my head and slinging his arm around my shoulder as he leads us out of the dressing room.

"Thank you," he stops suddenly.

"What for?"

"For this," his hand waves in the air. "Tonight, has been a great success, Holly. All the bands have been fantastic and I'm sure the bands that are due to play here over the coming months will do just as well. The club is packed, and tickets are selling well…"

"Vlad, I was only too happy to help out. I've enjoyed it," I cut him off.

"I know," he pulls me into him, kissing the side of my head. "You and Daniel were a big hit with the crowd. I think your performance wasn't just favoured by me." He knocks my shoulder with his, making me chuckle then we make our way to join friends and family.

Making our way to the table, I'm stopped and hugged by all our friends and family; every one of them happy with tonight's performance. Vlad pulls out a chair for me to sit down then sits himself down at the side of me, his arm wrapping around my waist. As the waiter places our drinks on the table, I spot Daniel at the side of the dance floor being mobbed by a group of young women. Vlad shakes his head as he watches his son lap up the attention from the barely dressed women that have draped themselves around him as if he's some rock legend.

The last band of the evening are kicking up a storm with their mixture of rock and country rock from the seventies and eighties and as the lead singer belts out Fleetwood Mac's "Go Your Own Way" the dance floor fills to the max. All in all, it's been an amazing evening even if I haven't felt well. Each band along with the dancers have surpassed themselves, egged on by the enthusiasm from the mass of people here tonight.

"Want to dance?" Vlad whispers in my ear as the song changes, then stands holding his hand out for me. I'm feeling a little more myself, so I stand and let him lead me on to the dance floor. His strong arms wrap around me, enveloping me into his solid chest and this is where I belong. Where I am at my happiest. Where I feel cherished, desired and safe. With my head on Vlad's chest, my hands travel up and over his muscular shoulders and wrap around his neck as I relish in being at home. At home in his arms.

Swaying and humming to the Eagles hit "Desperado" we lose ourselves in the haunting melody of the piano and guitar. The crowd join in as the husky voice of the singer echoes around the club.

"Are you ready to go home, Holly?" Vlad's hushed voice says into my hair as the song comes to an end.

"Hmmm," I'm sleepy and comfortable and don't want to move from his warm embrace. "You're my home," I murmur into his chest. He hears me and chuckles as he separates our bodies and we head back to our table, to wish everyone a goodnight. Vlad's happy to leave his sons taking care of things, along with the security staff and bar manager the place is in good hands. Olivia and Sarah tell me they will be heading off home as soon as the band finishes.

Outside the cool air causes me to shiver. I haven't brought a jacket, so I cuddle into Vlad's side. We don't need to wait for a taxi with only having one alcoholic drink earlier in the evening Vlad's able to drive us home.

Heading out of the carpark, my sleepy head rests on the back of the seat and my right hand lies on top of Vlad's meaty thigh. He places his hand on top of mine and gives it a little squeeze. "Tired?" he says, quickly taking his eyes off the road then averts them back onto the road ahead.

"Hmmm," I turn in my seat, so I'm sat sideways looking at him. "Shattered. I just want to snuggle up in bed and sleep until dinner time tomorrow then have a day doing nothing."

"Sounds good," he says, adding that cheeky grin. "You want someone to snuggle up to angel?" this time I get the cheeky grin and the wink. I know he's playing with me and as much as I do want to snuggle up with him, I know he won't.

He's adamant that he's sticking to our arrangement, that we don't sleep together until he's proved himself. Even though he knows it was Nicholas' idea of a joke that I stupidly went along with, he's keeping to his word. Looks like he's also back to tormenting me about it too, like he promised he would.

"Just take me home, Vlad, and stop being mean," I moan at him, not wanting to entertain his games tonight. Turning back in my seat I lay my head back, letting out a sigh. He glances my way, sensing that I'm too exhausted for his games, a look of concern on his face.

"Have I upset you, Holly?" The unease in his voice tells me he's worried with the way I've just spoken to him. I don't normally ignore his flirting; in fact, I find it quite amusing and entertaining but not tonight. Tonight, I want to be with him, wrapped in his arms in his bed. Listening to his heartbeat as my head lays across his chest, lulling me into a deep restful sleep.

I shake my head to answer him because he hasn't done anything wrong to upset me, he's just sticking to our agreement. He glances sideways again to look at me. Not happy with the shake of my head, he pulls the car over to the side of the road, switching off the engine then turns in his seat, so he is facing me.

"Holly, what's wrong?" The low tone of his caring voice strokes over my skin, and has me wanting to go to him. Unhooking my seat belt, I climb over onto his knee. He doesn't delay in swaddling me in his arms and placing his face in my hair. "Sweetheart, talk to me." At that moment I can't. I don't know why I feel so emotional. Tears well in my eyes and there's a lump in my throat. Maybe it's because I've been unwell and felt a bit low. Maybe it's something to do with tonight's performance and how nervous I felt. Or maybe it's just because I don't want to be alone tonight and need the one person in the world that shows me how much he cares.

His hand lifts my chin and concerned eyes search mine. "There's nothing wrong, Vlad," I say, wiping at my eyes. "I'm just feeling a little overwhelmed with everything that's going on, that's all."

Our heads rest together, and Vlad kisses my lips lightly. "You're coming home with me, Holly," he speaks into them. He won't get an argument from me if he's expecting one. I nod my head confirming that it's what I want then I kiss his cheek for always understanding what I need.

I climb off his knee and fasten my seat belt as Vlad starts the car again. It doesn't take long for us to reach his home which will be my home too in less than two weeks. I may have been a little apprehensive about it when he first asked me to move in with him, but now I'm all in and counting down the days.

When we pull up in his drive Vlad exits the car and in no time he rounds my side, opening the door. He helps me out then lifts me into his arms, carrying me to the front door. Once inside, he locks the door then strides up the staircase as if I weighed nothing but a feather. I chuckle into his chest when he struggles to open the bedroom door, using his elbow and almost stumbles through it when he pushes at it too hard.

"Feeling better, angel?" he asks with a raised eyebrow and yes, I do. Funny how I always feel better wrapped in his arms. I nod my head at him and run the hand I have round the back of his neck through his soft hair.

"Yes," I tell him as he places me on my feet.

"Good," he says, smiling, then helps me out of my dress. I unfasten his shirt, slipping it off his mountainous shoulders then unfasten his trousers, leaving him just in his boxers. Our clothes are left on the bedroom floor as we both make our way into the bathroom. Once we have finished in there we climb into the middle of the bed where I sprawl myself across Vlad's chest. Best place in the world. One of my legs spread over his muscular thighs as his arms wrap around me tightly. Looks like I'm not the only one who needed to snuggle. My head rests on his chest which I angle, kissing his chin. "I love you so much," I whisper. I feel him inhale deeply through his nose then he manoeuvres himself, brushing his lips across mine.

"I love you too, Holly, so fucking much."

Chapter 28

Holly

My small changing room is full to the rafters with hot sweaty bodies, most of them male. Daniel has invaded my space bringing with him Amy, Emma, Callum and Josh, the four dancers that have been performing with us this evening and the lads from the band who are carrying with them bottles and bottles of champagne.

"To a fantastic fucking night!" Noah the drummer bellows around the room as he shakes the bottle of fizz then pops the cork. His thumb is placed over the neck of the bottle while he continues to shake it, letting it spay everywhere. Two of the other band members open theirs and follow suit with the spraying then place the bottles to their mouths. God only knows why they have gathered in here, but they need to leave soon before Vlad arrives.

The bottles are past about, everyone drinking from the neck; all ecstatic and in high spirits with tonight's performance. Amy passes the bottle to me and I decline. It's never been my thing to drink alcohol from the bottle and I would never drink out of the same bottle that someone else has been drinking from. "Come on, Holly, have a drink with us, it's a celebration," Amy says, her smile big and wide with excitement. Daniel, who is stood at the side of her, takes the bottle from her hand, passes it to Emma then picks up an unopened bottle. His eyes scan the room then, when he spots the glass tumbler, he opens the bottle and pours a small amount into it.

I'm not as giddy as the rest of them and maybe that's the age difference between us. Having between ten and fifteen years on some of them, I'm a little less crazy and animated with my delight of being able to put on a show that was given a standing ovation.

"Here, Holly, just have a small one," Daniel's eyes plead with me to join them, he tilts his head at me giving me that cute smile of his and I take the glass from him.

"Okay," I tell him, rolling my eyes at his cuteness. I take a sip and shout cheers with everyone else as they raise the bottles in the air. Amy and Emma cuddle Daniel and the rest of the men in the room and I sit down at the dressing table, placing my glass on it.

"You all need to leave now so I can get changed," I tell them. "Your dad will be here shortly, and he'll never fit in here with you lot in," I say to Daniel.

"Ow, he's scary," Amy says, blushing when she realises that she's said it out loud. Her hand shoots to her mouth, covering it and her brown eyes widen as they shift between Daniel and me. "Sorry." Her nervous giggle causes me to feel sorry for her and I shake my head.

"It's fine," I put my hand up, smiling. "But he's not that scary when you get to know him, he's a big softy really." Everyone laughs at my comment, shaking their heads. Obviously, they don't see the same man that Daniel and I see daily.

"He really is," Daniel agrees with me, slinging his arm around Amy's shoulders. "But we do need to leave because he will growl like a fucking grizzly if he can't get Holly alone."

"Yeah, I agree. He's not that bad," Callum says. "I had a long conversation with him the other day. First one ever…" he stops, lowering his eyebrows for a moment, chewing on his lip. His hand rubs over his chin then he shakes his head, smiling.

"What's wrong?" I ask.

"I think in our little conversation he may have mentioned not to get too close to you in our dance routine," he shakes his head again. "He said it smiling so I took it as a joke. I mean we're dancers right… We can't help but put our hands on each other if it's in the routine…" He looks a tad worried now while everyone else chuckles at his swift turnaround of my complexed man.

"Don't worry, Callum, you'll be fine," I get up and go to him, putting my hand on his shoulder, to reassure him.

"That's easy for you to say. He's the boss... the big boss... I don't want to lose my job, I..." Daniel steps in, stopping Callum from getting worked up.

"Mate don't worry. You see that woman there?" he points at me while wrapping his arm around his shoulder. "My father will do anything for her, and I mean anything." The serenity in his voice makes me smile. He knows I'm capable of calming the beast within him, soothing him and making him see sense. "Which means he won't do anything or say anything to you, knowing it will upset Holly."

Daniel moves away from him and Callum nods his head, understanding what he is trying to say. "What did he actually say to you?" I ask, because I want to know what Vlad said to have this young man thinking he may lose his job or worse. Vlad is a professional man, a businessman and this is his business. I know he doesn't always think rationally when it involves me or a man being near me, but Callum can't be any older than twenty-three, so I don't think he would threaten him.

"Err, we were just chatting about the club and all the different bands that are playing here. He asked if we were all comfortable with the changes." He points between himself and the dancers.

"He said to let him know if there was anything any of the staff weren't happy with or needed.... He mentioned something about Sebastian and Izzy being busy with the baby, so to go to him if there was anything. Then as he was walking away, he turned and said, be careful where I put my hands when I'm dancing with you..."

"Oh, you're fine," I chuckle. "Believe me, you won't have upset him." The dance routine was tastefully put together even if Callum had to put his hands on my hips as well as stand behind me running his fingers down both of my arms lovingly while claiming my hips again. It's nothing he won't get over. He nods his head at me, the uneasiness now gone, and I sit back down at the dressing table, pushing the glass of champagne to one side.

"Well, I'm going to get changed if we're all going clubbing," Emma states. "Are you coming, Holly?"

"No, I'll give it a miss. Thanks for the invite though." They'd all decided earlier that they would nip over to Eruption to celebrate after tonight's show. This place will be closing now, and they want to party. Again, the age difference showing. It's turned midnight and I'm shattered; I know I ended up being involved in a few more songs than we originally planned but this lot have been on all night and still have the energy to party.

"Come on everyone, let's leave Holly to get changed." Daniel gathers everyone together, the lads from the band happy just chatting amongst themselves. They take the champagne bottles with them arranging to meet at the main entrance in half an hour and all shout goodnight to me.

Stretching and letting out a yawn, I glance in the mirror. Deciding to get rid of the false eyelashes and take off my make-up, I pick up the cleansing wipes then tug at one of the lengthy lashes that Olivia had attached earlier in the evening. Just as I've got one off and tugging at the next one there's a knock at the door. Well I know it's not Vlad or Olivia, they wouldn't knock. Sarah's not here, she stayed at home tonight taking care of Nick, her husband, who isn't well which as me thinking it's one of the dancers or lads from the band coming back for something they've forgotten. Standing, I make my way to the door, opening it as I finish pulling at the false eyelash. I take a step back, keeping hold of the door handle as I do.

"What are you doing here?" My voice is firm and in control even though I'm shocked to see Rob, my ex-husband, standing there. "You shouldn't be here… How did you even get back here?" I question, knowing Vlad has that much security staff you would think it was some big A-lister playing here tonight, and not some band that gets its fan base through playing in clubs and pubs around the country.

"Holly let me explain." His hand shoots out as if he wants to stop the door shutting in his face which I want to do but there's a plea in his voice, stopping me. The thing is, I don't want to hear why he's here, why he thinks he has the right to sneak backstage to say it and I do not want Vlad to find him here. That would set him back months. I know he had stewed over Rob's behaviour in the pub the night we went to watch Daniel and his band play and throughout the week leading up to that terrifying night in the club. We really don't need a repeat performance.

"You need to leave, Rob. Now," I say firmly, the conviction in my voice shocks me. As I try to shut the door on him, this time determined to get rid of him before Vlad turns up, Rob puts his hand up again to stop it from closing.

"Please, Holly. I haven't come here to cause trouble… I didn't even know you were singing here." I'm confused as I stand steadfast in the doorway, adamant I'm not letting him in this room. Confused as to why if he didn't know I was singing here then what brought him here because I know for sure he's not in to live bands?

Looking at him I can see he's not here to cause trouble. That cocky look he wore a few months ago has gone, he's not drunk and the conceited man who always thought he was above me and my friends, lacks confidence. I step back, holding the door open for him and he steps in.

"Thank you, Holly," he nods his head at me, giving me a tight smile, then lowers it, looking at the ground. He can't look at me and I don't need to ask why. Guilt, probably, and he has a lot to feel guilty about. I gave him my all in the years we were together. Putting him and his career first. Making a home where he could invite his colleagues and business associates over, to help push him up the ladder. All the while he wanted someone else. Then getting himself drunk and behaving like a complete idiot out to cause trouble. Yeah, I'd say he is feeling a little ashamed of himself.

"What are you doing here, Rob?"

"I want to apologise… My behaviour the other month was… Inexcusable. I don't know why I behaved that way, but I am truly sorry." I move further into the room and he follows me, rubbing at his chin, waiting for my acceptance. I still don't understand how he knew I was here or why he's waited until now.

"Rob, how did you know I was here?"

"I didn't. We came to watch the band…"

"We?" I question, as I sit down.

"Rachel and me. She loves Fake It, so I bought the tickets a while ago We haven't been out together since the baby was born…" he stops, knowing how much I wanted a baby with him, and he was always against it. Well, I'm over that now. Whatever I felt for him and wanted with him is all in the past. Vlad and his family are all I care about now.

"Carry on, Rob, it's fine."

"Like I said, it was hard the first couple of months, so I thought I'd surprise her with a night out to see one of her favourite bands."

"You didn't know about the car accident that the lead singer was in with his sister?"

"No. Didn't get the memo," he tilts his head and chuckles.

"Bit of a shock then when you saw me up there," and I can't help but chuckle this time because I would have loved to have seen their faces.

"You could say that, yes. But it was a good shock, Holly. You and your fellow's son were fantastic, Rachel and I loved it."

"Good, I'm glad you both enjoyed it," and to be truthful I am. I'm not a spiteful bitch, like some women would be.

"Rachel knows all about how I was a twat to you, Holly. When I woke the following morning and saw the messages on my phone from the lads I was out with, I was mortified with my behaviour." I nod my head at him because he should be ashamed of himself. "I told Rachel and she was disgusted with me too. I really did want to go to Olivia's to find you, but I thought it wouldn't go down well. Anyway, when we saw you here tonight, I just had to come and say how sorry I am for my behaviour." I can tell he means it. He struggles to apologise to anyone, so I know this must be hard for him. Maybe Rachel has brought out a decent side to him.

"Okay," I say, standing from the chair. "I accept your apology, Rob." I look at my watch and wonder why Vlad hasn't come to see me yet. If it's like last time he got stopped on his way here and I'm hoping that's the case tonight at least it will give me time to get rid of Rob.

"I need to get changed now…" I nod my head towards the door, letting him know his time is up.

"Of course, sorry. I need to get back to Rachel, she's waiting at the main entrance for me." He turns to walk towards the door, and I follow behind him then he turns back. "Thanks again, Holly…" He tries to put his hand on my shoulder, but I step back, not wanting his touch.

"No. You don't get to touch her." It's a warning that surrounds the room, commanding attention, and has Rob turning quickly. I freeze, not wanting to envisage what will happen next.

Vlad strides into the room, taking his place by my side. "I asked you to wait until Holly came out on to the floor." He points his finger at Rob, the authority in his voice tells me he's unhappy with his orders not been followed. Rob just stands there, his eyes narrowed on Vlad and I'm gobsmacked with the understanding that they had spoken in the club before Rob came to see me.

Vlad's body tenses at the side of me, as Rob continues with his staring game and my hands start to tremble as my lungs struggle to take in air, "Vlad, I don't want any trouble in here tonight…" My eyes take a sideways glance, apprehension seeping through me at the thought of a violent eruption taking place in this small room that's growing smaller with every second that passes. I feel him take my hand, connecting our fingers together and his warmth spreads through me like wildfire. Then he moves closer to me, his dark blue eyes shifting from my ex, revealing the love he holds for me and that puts me at ease. His warm smile lights up his face and I know he will not revert to the man he once was.

Over the last month, he's become more laid back. Less hostile. Relaxed. The nod of the head and one-word greetings towards people who are not family or friends have converted into light conversations. His gorgeous smile, brightening up the darkness that had been embedded on his handsome face for so long, causes the female staff to giggle as they crush on him. The male members of staff now find him approachable….

"You've apologized, it's been excepted," Vlad's new calm approach brings me out of my thoughts, "There's nothing more to say." His towering body moves towards the door, holding it open for Rob to exit, and just before he does, he speaks, directing his words at Vlad.

"As I told Holly, I didn't come here to cause trouble and I couldn't wait any longer for you to come from your office before I spoke to her. Rachel's in a hurry to get home to our daughter, that's why I came to find Holly…" Vlad nods his head at him, accepting his explanation but doesn't encourage the conversation to continue.

"Your wife is waiting in the main entrance; I suggest you go to her and not keep her waiting any longer." And just like that, my ex is dismissed by a man who doesn't suffer fools gladly. He's also just shown me he can deal with things rationally instead of using his hands. It's a small step but it's one of many that has accumulated over the last month which tells me I'm making the right decision.

The door clicks shut as Rob makes his way back to Rachel and I let out a long breath that I didn't know I'd been holding. "Are you ok?" Vlad's deep voice asks. I nod my head, letting him know I'm fine. Still wanting to know what was said between the two of them while they were on the club floor and how Rob remembered what Vlad looked like. I have a feeling that he may have questioned one of the many employees that are working here tonight. Then again, Vlad's the type of man that once seen is not forgotten.

"Come here," his arms pull me into him, wrapping around me as my head lays on his chest. When his large hands run gently up and down my back, I welcome his soothing touch.

"What about you? Are you ok?" I question as I lift my head, my eyes meeting his.

"Yes." Vlad's lips brush against mine as his hand comes up, and his thumb strokes over my cheek.

"Thank you, Vlad," I say as I return his kiss with a light brush of my lips. "Wasn't sure how that was going to play out for a moment there," I let out a nervous laugh, not wanting to imagine separating two men from ripping each other apart or should I say one of them.

Vlad takes my hand and leads us to the dressing table where he perches himself on the corner then takes both of my hands in his.

"Holly, believe me when I say, I will do anything for you." His hand comes up, fingers stroking over my chin. "I am not going to jeopardize our life together," he pulls me further into him, so I'm nestled between his legs. "I love you so much and I'm lucky that you're giving me a second chance to prove that to you, so I'm not about to let some jumped up…" his grin lights up his face, meeting his dark eyes and I can't help but reach up and run my fingers over the creases that gather at the edge of them. Vlad turns his head and kisses the palm of my hand then takes it in his. "In the words of my sons, he is a jumped up tosser who didn't deserve you. Fuck, I don't deserve you, but I'll spend the rest of my life trying, proving myself to you. Hoping one day that you will see how much you mean to me and hope that I mean the same to you. So, you see Holly I won't let him or anybody else ruin that for us. I won't take that away from us." My lips crash against his and I knock him slightly off balance, and as he rights himself, wrapping me in his arms and holding me between his thighs, I know what he is trying to say.

He understands what I need. I don't need reminders of the man who lived in Russia or what he did and why. And I don't need any repeat performances of the man he became that night in the club. I just need him and his love.

I pull away from him, chuckling. "Wow, I've really built up some brownie points over the last few weeks," he grins at me wiggling his eyebrows. "But tonight, I've even surprised myself. What with having to deal with Callum putting his hands all over you," he shakes his head, tutting then lifts off the dressing table standing in front of me. "If that wasn't enough, I had your ex approach me as I was coming out of the gents…"

"What did he say?" I ask, grimacing, wrapping my arms around his waist as Vlad wraps his around mine.

"Nothing much. Just that he wanted to say he was sorry to both of us. I accepted his apology but told him he would need to wait until you had got changed and came out of the changing room before he could speak to you." He shakes his head, knowing Rob didn't wait. "Frank called me to the office, and I asked him to wait at his table until I came back. It took me longer than I thought to get back to him, and you know the rest…" He shrugs his shoulders, smiling, delighted with himself for holding it together. I'm also delighted with him and bloody thankful that I wasn't in the middle of two brawling men.

"Which means angel, you owe me…" he throws me a cheeky wink and that devilish grin appears as he slaps my backside. I giggle like a love-struck teenager then roll my eyes at him. He puts his lips to mine, "And I will be taking what is owed to me in five days' time," he says against them. I nod at him, loving his threat and how he makes me feel when this flirty side comes out to play. Just a few minutes ago he was all serious with wanting to prove and show me he's the man I need and now he's the fun-loving man that I need as well. There's also that little reminder that I will be performing my last night here in five days and our agreement was that I would move in with him afterwards.

He is trying. Since our little chat on the day that Daniel and Nicholas had asked me to sing at the club, Vlad has been showing me he's slowly getting over his past life and the torment it brought him. He freely answers any questions I ask, even the ones about his father and Natalia which he does without reluctance. Oh, I don't go in all guns blazing. I'm diplomatic with my interrogation and take it at his pace without pushing too hard for information. I know all I need to know about his adult years, becoming a father and husband at such a young age and then what came with those years and I know the man he is now. What I want to know is what he was like as a child, his school life. His favourite subject, what sports he liked and his friends. He knows everything about me. He understands the life I was born into and what I went through in my younger years just as I understand now the life he was born in to.

"Holly, sweetheart?"

"Hmmm," I lift my head off his chest to look up at him, realising I've been hugging him while lost in my own little world.

"If you squeeze me any tighter angel, I'm likely to pass out," he laughs lightly and caresses my cheek. "You okay?" Yes, I am. I'm better than ok. I'm happy and in love with a man that loves fiercely and doesn't mind showing it. One who wants nothing to come between us moving forward in our relationship and isn't scared of whatever that brings with it.

"Yes," I answer. "I've never been happier." This time he takes my mouth, pouring so much love into our kiss that my heart gallops, my stomach flutters and my legs go weak with its intensity.

"Aw, come on you two. Can't you leave one another alone for two bloody minutes?" Nicholas' laughter pulls us apart.

"Every fucking time," Vlad moans, shaking his head, then turns towards the door where Nicholas and Daniel stand, filling it with their arms folded across their chest and a broad grin on their faces.

"Impeccable timing as usual, boys. What's the problem?" I let out a chuckle because the two of them constantly walk in on Vlad and me, disturbing our moments together and it doesn't embarrass them in the slightest nor does it me.

"Nothing's wrong. We just came to let you know we're going over to Eruption and not to wait up," Daniel says, wiggling his eyebrows.

"Okay. Who's going?" Vlad asks, tucking in the back of his shirt that I had pulled out while we were kissing. Daniel informs his father that the dancers and the lads from the band are all going, and Nicholas tells us he's going along with Lucy.

"Nicholas, you make sure you get that young lady home safely and I mean her home," Vlad's tone is not to be challenged. He knows his sons have been around a lot of women without ever having a serious relationship. He's also aware that Lucy is my god-daughter and the daughter of my closest friends. She's also the mother of his granddaughter's best friend, so he won't want his son playing his usual games and neither do I. Saying that, Lucy and Nicholas have become very good friends and he's always the perfect gentleman around her and Megan.

"Err don't I always," he says as he ventures from the doorway and stands at the side of me. "Want to come with us Holly? Leave the old man here…" he steps quickly out of Vlad's reach, chuckling as his hand attempts to slap him on the back of the neck.

"Cheeky little bastard," he gripes at him. I link Vlad's arm, smiling and tell Nicholas that I'm too tired tonight but reinforce Vlad's warning to Nicholas about getting Lucy home safely. Both Nicholas and Daniel promise that they will then say goodnight.

"He'll look after her, Holly." I'm not worried, I know Nicolas and Daniel like to have a bit of fun with the ladies, but I see the respect Nicholas has for Lucy. I also see something else when they look at each other.

"I know. He's a good man," I pat his chest, smiling. "I'm going to get changed then go see Olivia and Jack before they leave." He nods his head and sits down, waiting for me.

"I'm surprised Jack isn't kicking up a fuss. I'm not sure I'd want any daughter of mine clubbing with a bunch of guys from a band as well as my two whoring sons."

"Vlad," I scold, while pulling on a pair of jeans. "Those guys from the band are decent lads and I hope you're joking about your sons because they are good men and I trust them to take care of her. Plus, Lucy isn't stupid, she knows how to take care of herself."

"I know she does, but they're all young and in full party mode…" I walk over to him, understanding that he's worried Nicholas and Lucy's friendship will turn into something more that might end up with one of them being hurt.

"Vlad they're both old enough to do what they want without their fathers getting their knickers in a twist and they are very good friends. I don't think they want to ruin that by getting into something that might," I tap his nose and continue to get dressed. Knowing what I see in their eyes is want. I think he sees it too.

"Yeah, you're right. Come on let's have a quick drink before I take you home." He checks his watch, getting to his feet. He knows the bar will be closed but it won't stop him rounding the bar and helping himself. Well he is the boss.

I nod at him. "Just a soft drink for me thanks." I run the brush through my hair and apply a coat of lip gloss. Then he takes my hand as we head out of the door. I nudge him to get his attention. He gives me a sideways glance. "Just so you know, I always repay my debts…" He tilts his head in a questioning look then realisation hits him as to what I mean.

"Good to know," he winks, and I chuckle, wanting the next five days to hurry up.

Chapter 29

Vlad

Standing with the rest of the club, my hands clapping loudly at Daniel's performance. The women scream and yell out his name as he falls to his knees, ripping open his white shirt as he lowers his head. He's just sung Queen's "Somebody to Love" and I must say between him and the band they've raised the roof on this place. If I thought that my son's last performance couldn't be topped, then I'd be wrong because Daniel on that stage just now expressed himself in a whole new light. He poured out his heart into that song, owning it. The band worked the stage with him, their instruments becoming their lovers, playing them hard enough you almost saw the sparks.

As Daniel stands, the shirt he had ripped open drops from his broad shoulders, and he tosses it into the audience. The women scream and scuffle between them to reach it. With his body hot and sweaty, my son saunters back from the catwalk-style stage and joins the band, he picks up a towel and wipes the back of his neck then grabs a T-shirt from the stand next to his guitar. The crowd calm down as the lights go out, leaving us all in darkness. I know Holly's got one more song to sing before she finishes for the evening, so maybe this will be her spot while Daniel gets his breath back.

With the room still in darkness, and the thought of Holly singing her last song, I smile broadly. After tonight, Holly will be moving in with me and I can't fucking wait. We've kept it quiet from my sons and her friends, not for any reason other than it's our business and nobody else's. However, I think tomorrow we'll have no other choice than to tell them when we start to move in Holly's personal things from her apartment.

The flashing lights bring me from my musing and I'm in awe of how much work has gone into the pyrotechnics for tonight's performances. I'm also wondering why one of the party tables has been moved from the side of our table. When this room was revamped, they extended the stage, so it had a catwalk and at either side of the stage they raised the flooring and cornered the area off. It's a large area which can comfortably fit five extra-large tables at each side and, because they are so close to the performers, the customers pay more. This area stands out in the club due to the platform it's risen on which the public love, they also enjoy having the waiter service that is thrown in with the price of the tickets.

With the club lights still out, the flashing lights shoot around in various directions; the brilliance of the display is outstanding. The smoke machine kicks in filling the stage, the music starts, and the crowds of people cheer in appreciation.

I know the music to Rihanna's "Don't stop the music." What I didn't know is that Holly had it in her list of songs that she'd being preparing for tonight's show.

I hear her voice without seeing her, but I know she's close.

"Please don't stop the music," is repeated four times, encircling the club and with the streams of light that are darting in different directions along with swirls of smoke, I'm really struggling to pinpoint where Holly is.

In the darkness, I hear her sing the lyrics but still I can't see her.

"It's getting late, I'm making my way over to my favourite place.

I gotta' get my body moving, shake the stress away."

A Spotlight lands on our table and the crowd roar out their approval when she appears standing on the far end of our table. She's a vision, lighting up my darkness. Her golden hair is pulled back loosely tied, her feet are bare and as she sings the lyrics, she moves towards me, slowly taking her sweet time.

"I wasn't looking for nobody when you looked my way.

Possible candidate

Yeah...

Who knew that you'd be here looking like you do?

You make my stay over here impossible

Baby I must say your aura is incredible."

She gracefully lands in front of me, tapping my chest with her toes. Our table are all up on their feet, me included, taking her all in.

She's wearing white shorts, showing off her fine lightly tanned toned legs. The boob tube that covers her breasts is also white, enhancing her flat stomach and the curve of her hips.

While she continues to sing the next few lines of the song, two male dancers lift her off the table, so we are stood together closely. She carries on with song, swaying those hips of hers as she strokes her fingers over my chest, onto my throat and then around the back of my neck...

"Your hands around my waist

Just let the music play

We're hand in hand

Chest to chest

Now we're face to face"

Holly stands in front of me, a mischievous twinkle in her eye and when she raises her hands above her head while she continues to sing, I take hold of her hips. The female dancers join the two men in the area next to our table and perform a very erotic dance while we perform one of our own. Throughout the song, Holly moves seductively, her hands and fingers dancing around my upper body. When she turns and leans her back into my chest, she raises her hands above head again and I can't help but place a soft kiss on the side of her neck.

As the song comes to an end the lights go out again, she turns in my arms, brushing her soft lips across my cheek and then she's gone.

This is Holly's toned-down version of the lap dance that Jenny, the female singer of the band, would perform during her show, so the people here tonight wouldn't have been shocked to see Holly up on the table giving a tame sexy performance to a man in the audience. They're used to a lot more but enjoyed it none the less. It's so gratifying that Holly listened to my plea and didn't stoop to that level. A lap dance from Holly would be the biggest turn on and should be kept between the two of us and not shared with a club full of people. What she's just performed was no different to the night in the pub when she sung and got me up to dance with her during it.

The clapping and cheering slow as the stage lights up, everyone waiting for the last song of the night which will be performed by Daniel.

This is the last night for him too and the band Fake It, though I'm sure if they wanted to come back and play it wouldn't be a problem. All in all, they have been amazing with lots of fantastic comments on their social media site referring to the nights that they have played here.

I don't move from the table to go see Holly as I have done the last couple of times, she knows I planned on staying to watch the end of the show. I need a moment anyway to calm my racing heart. If I followed after her, I would have her pinned up against the dressing room door in no time at all.

*

It's been hectic since the band finished; people slow to vacate the club with a few arguments breaking out in various areas. Even though the security team that I have working here tonight were quick to respond, I stuck around to make sure they were no repercussions outside. With Aphrodite recently opening back up, I don't want it getting a bad name. Both of my clubs have always been given outstanding reviews and while I still have my name to them both that's how it will stay.

Making my way to the stage area, the club is quiet now, apart from a few patrons left and the staff who are clearing up. The band are putting away their instruments when Frank, the head of security, stops me wanting to discuss Daniel's outstanding performance. He's known my son since he was in high school and was stunned with the way he worked the crowd and how they were all screaming his name. Listening to Frank chuckle when he refers to Holly, I laugh with him. His comment about how she can get me doing things I wouldn't normally do has me agreeing with him and has me wondering how I got so lucky. Meeting someone as beautiful, honest and caring as my angel, gives me a whole new lease of life and yes, I will do anything for her.

"She's special, Vlad. Don't fuck up again," it's a warning which I'm all too aware of and which I plan not to do. I put my hand out to shake Franks which he takes, and I thank him for his support and friendship.

"Dad!" Hearing Daniel's panicked voice startles me and as I turn swiftly in his direction, I can see his rigid frame beckoning to where he is stood. The concern on his face stops my chat with Frank and has me hurrying towards him. I watch him fly through Holly's changing room door, calling for me to hurry up.

In no time at all, I'm behind him practically falling over my own feet, causing my head of security to slam into the back of me. Daniel fills the room and when he steps out of the way, Olivia and Sarah do too and I see my Holly sat on the floor, looking as pale as a ghost. I'm on my knees before I have time to think, placing my hands on her cheeks.

"Sweetheart, what's wrong?" my eyes scanning her quickly to see if she's hurt anywhere.

"Vlad, she's fine. She just needs a bit of air," Olivia tries to reassure me, but I'm having none of it.

"She doesn't look fine," I snap as Holly pulls my hands from her face, taking one of them in hers and gives it a tender squeeze.

"Honestly, Vlad I'm ok..." she sniffles. Her eyes look tired and her tiny hand trembles in mine. "I just got overly warm and felt dizzy which caused me to wobble and I fell over." She squeezes my hand again, trying to calm my worry, only I do worry about her.

It's only a few weeks ago since she was poorly but she seemed to be over it in the last week or so I thought.

"Holly you look very pale, sweetheart, and you don't have dizzy spells for nothing. I think we need to get you checked out at the hospital." I smooth my hand over her hair then place it on her forehead, she feels clammy.

"I'm not going to the hospital, Vlad. I'll be ok. If it comes back again, I'll make an appointment to see the doctor…"

"Holly," Olivia says, crouching down at the side of us. "I think you need to listen to Vlad's advice and get booked in anyway. I've told you you're probably run down after the virus you had. They can stay in your system for some time, love." She's worried too. I know how much Holly means to her friends; they've always been there for her when she hasn't had anybody to take care of her. Well she has me now and I'll carry her to the doctors tomorrow if she tries to fob me off.

Sarah passes Holly her bottle of water which she takes a sip from then places it on the floor at the side of her. I move to the other side, sitting down then lift her onto my knee. She snuggles into my chest and I ask everyone to leave us for a moment. Daniel and Frank leave straight after they've placed a soft kiss on Holly's head.

"We'll give you a moment but we're not leaving until we know she's ok," Sarah warns as she bends down, kissing Holly's cheek then plants one on mine. Holly chuckles when she sees me shake my head then chuckles again when Olivia does the same. I'm still getting used to the women in Holly's life that are now in mine and who think nothing about invading my personal space. I nod my head at them knowing no matter what I say they'll be back in no time at all.

Once they're gone, I lift Holly's chin from my chest to get a good look at her. She has a bit of colour back and her sapphire blue eyes gleam up at me. "You look a little better, sweetheart," I run my finger down her cheek. "Do you still feel dizzy?"

"No. I'm fine now but I always am when I'm snuggled into you," she grins as she kisses my chest where my heart is.

"Good to know because you're coming home with me and that's where you're staying." I wink at her, but my voice is firm. I'm not letting anyone else take care of her if she's unwell, that's my job now and she needs to realise that. I know if it was me that was feeling a little under the weather, she would do the same.

"Ok," Holly says as she holds onto my thighs to support herself when she stands. I help her up, noticing she does have some colour back now, but I think she still needs to get checked out by the doctor.

"We'll phone the doctor in the morning, Holly, see if we can get you booked in for a check-up then, if you're up to it," I take hold of her hands, hoping she hasn't changed her mind about moving in with me, "We can go to your apartment and pack up a few boxes."

"I don't think I'll get an appointment tomorrow, but I'll phone and take whatever they have available." She picks up her bottle of water and her bag, not mentioning anything about packing up her things.

"Holly do you still want to move in with me?" I sit on her dressing table, hoping and praying she still does. The door opens before she answers me, and Olivia and Sarah stick their heads in.

"How are you feeling, love?" Olivia asks as she steps into the room, Sarah following.

"A lot better, thanks, but I am tired, so I think we'll just go home and not bother with a drink," she tells them then comes and stands by my side linking my arm. Originally, our plan was for everyone to stay behind so we could have a drink together, however, with what has happened with Holly, plans have changed.

"Not a problem," Sarah says. "I'm ready for home too and Nick and Jack have an early start in the morning…"

"Yeah, I'm ready for home, we'll leave the younger ones to it," Olivia suggest, smiling.

We make our way out of the dressing room and I take Holly's hand in mine, still aware that she hasn't answered my question yet. Before we reach our table, she stops me and reaches up placing a kiss on my cheek, her delicate hand lays on my chest then she whispers "Yes," in my ear. I can't help but smile knowing what she means and waste no time in saying our goodbyes and taking my angel home.

Chapter 30

Holly

I'm rewarded with one of Vlad's soft kisses to my cheek as my eyes flicker open after having one of the most peaceful night's sleep that I've had in a long while. His bed has got to be the comfiest bed ever and with his loving arms wrapped around me all night, I was as snug as a bug in a rug. Feeling well rested, I sit up and steal a kiss from his kissable lips which has him chuckling against mine.

"Wow, you must be feeling better," he says when he breaks our kiss, sitting up straight he takes my hand in his.

"Much," I tell him, nodding my head. "Where are you going?" I ask, noticing he's wearing a pair of suit trousers with a well-pressed shirt unbuttoned. Last night he was all for whipping me off to the doctors first thing this morning then he wanted to box up some of my things to bring over here.

"I forgot I've got a meeting this morning. I know we had made plans, and I was going to cancel it, but Olivia and Sarah telephoned to say they were on their way over…" He shakes his head and smiles. He knows how protective they are and how much they worry about me, it's a tossup who's the worst: them or him. "I was all for cancelling it. However, with your friends being here I thought I might as well get it out of the way, I'll only be a couple of hours," he tells me while buttoning up his shirt.

"Ok. What time are they coming over?"

"They are here now. So, you better get dressed sleepy head because they're invading my kitchen as we speak." He playfully slaps my backside then stands to tuck his shirt in.

"What…? What time is it?" I ask. I know Olivia was dropping Megan off at school this morning. The kids went back to school a couple of weeks ago and although Lucy has finished university and is back home, Olivia still likes to drop her granddaughter off a couple of mornings a week. Friday mornings being one of them which means it must be after nine o'clock.

"It's nine forty-five…"

"Wow, I've slept well," I'm surprised, I don't normally sleep past eight o'clock except when I've been out and had a drink. We might have got home late from the club, but I didn't touch a drop last night and we went straight to bed when we got home.

"Yeah, you must have needed it." Vlad takes my hand as I throw back the sheets and climb out of bed.

"Are you sure you're ok?" His eyes roam over me while his hands rub at my shoulders.

"Yes," I feel great, better than I have in a long while.

"And you don't mind pushing our plans back until this afternoon?" Vlad's arms come around my waist and he pulls me into him, he buries his face into my hair that I'm sure looks like a scarecrow that's been blown about in a gale force wind.

"No, not at all." There's no need to ring the doctors now and we can sort out what I'm bringing here another time, there's no rush. "I'm going to get dressed and go see what those two are up to," I tell him as I stand on my tiptoes and place a kiss on his lips. He obliges by bending down so I can reach.

"They were making a cup of tea and some toast when I came up here." He raises his eyebrows at their cheek. "I was ordered to come and get you up. You women can be very bossy," he shakes his head and steals a kiss before he turns and picks up his tie from the bedside table. Oh, I know Olivia and Sarah can be interfering, but they do it for the right reasons. Plus, Vlad seems to be getting used to their ways.

"Thank you," I kiss his cheek then make my way into the bathroom, leaving him looking puzzled as to why I am thanking him. He'll get it one day that him liking my friends means everything to me because Rob never made them feel welcome when they came to visit and never really liked to go out with them.

When I'm dressed, I make my way downstairs where I find my two friends and my man sat drinking tea and eating toast at the breakfast table, laughing. Vlad turns when he hears me and pulls out a chair for me to sit down. There's tea and toast ready for me and no sooner do I sit down and say morning to my friends, Olivia is on me.

"Eat up, Holly, you need to build yourself up otherwise you'll never get that virus out of your system." Sarah agrees and I catch the look of concern they throw at each other. Vlad takes my hand while he pushes the plate of toast closer to me. I don't normally eat when I first get up, it's usually an hour or so before I start to feel hungry, but I pick up a piece just to pacify them.

Pleased with themselves that they've accomplished what they came to do, they chat with Vlad about Megan and Rebecca. Never one to pass up on discussing his grandchildren, Vlad relishes in conversation about how well both girls have settled into their new class in year one. He continues chatting with them about Joe, Lucas and the baby while Olivia and Sarah moan about some of the new school rules that have come into the high school that Nathan, James, Emilia and Lucas attend.

After I have forced my toast down, Vlad stands to collect the empty plates and takes them to the dishwasher. He returns moments later with a bowl of chopped up fruit.

"I chopped it before these two arrived…" he raises his eyebrows at me knowing I enjoy fruit for breakfast. I pick up the chopped-up melon and place it in my mouth as Vlad retrieves his jacket. Once I've finished chewing, he bends down and kisses my lips. "Phone the doctors and make an appointment and don't worry about any boxes for the move, I have plenty in the garage."

As he steps to one side, I watch Olivia and Sarah's eyes widen and as they both smirk at Vlad's slip of the tongue. Not that either one of us are bothered about our friends and family knowing we're moving in together, we're not. We would have been telling them this weekend anyway. Saying that, I'm sure they will both be giving me a telling off for not informing them before now.

"Right ladies, I'm off," he places a kiss on my head this time, and I feel his smile. He knows he's just dropped me in it and he's not one bit bothered. "Enjoy your morning," he adds, as he saunters off towards the utility room to get to the garage.

"You sneaky mare," Olivia grins as she reaches across the table, tapping it. "Come on, fill us in."

She sits back up straight in her seat and turns to Sarah, "Can you believe this…?"

"Did he mean what we think he meant, Holly?" Sarah asks, and I nod my head slowly at them.

"When did you decide this? We thought you weren't sleeping together. Are you sleeping together? Course you are, otherwise, you wouldn't be moving in with him." She throws question after question answering the last one herself.

"So, when did you decide this?" Olivia asks, getting up from her seat and coming to sit at the side of me.

"About five weeks ago…" Olivia's head tilts to one side and she chews on one of her nails as she thinks about what was happening five weeks ago. I don't let her ponder for long as I explain to them both what Vlad and I had discussed and agreed in his bedroom the day Nicholas and Daniel had asked me to sing at the club. I remind them it was the same day they had come over with Megan and Lucy when we went to the park and that it was the same day that Sebastian and Izzy had Benjamin. They sit and listen without making judgement or comment on Vlad's reaction that day and when I inform them that although we have shared the same bed on numerous occasions, we still haven't had sex since the night in the hotel; they just nod their heads.

"Well you do make a beautiful couple, Holly, and it's obvious how much you care and love each other. So, yeah, I can see why you're taking the next step," Olivia says. Sarah agrees as she gets up from her seat. She says she won't be a moment and heads towards the hallway. I hear the front door open and then close before she's back with us.

"Right, he's gone." She takes a seat at the other side of me and then they both pick up their bags off the floor and place them on the table. I look at them both perplexed. Olivia seems to be in the know as to what Sarah is up to and why she's just stuck her head out of the front door.

"Who do you mean? Vlad? He'll be long gone by now," I tell her. "Why do you need him gone anyway?"

"Because…" they both glance at each other as they reach into their bags. At the same time my two friends produce a box each and place them on the table, pushing them towards me. "We didn't want him here when we gave you these," Olivia says all wide eyed and an even wider grin on her face. I look down at the boxes they have shoved in front of me and read the box. My nervous laugh erupts, and I think the two of them have gone completely bonkers.

"Are you kidding me?" I pick up one of the boxes. "You brought these for me…? Why would you think that I am pregnant?" And as I say the last word my heart starts to pound in my chest, and I lose my breath. How could I have been so stupid? My hand covers my mouth when I can't remember the last time I had my period, then my other hand takes on a life of its own and covers my stomach when I remember the last time I had taken my contraceptive pill.

When I shot off to the Northumberland Coast, I forgot to take them with me. Understandable. When I came back and found Lucas in my home and why he was there then dealing with his father, my mind was on other things. Again, another reason to forget certain things. Then the weeks that followed, wanting Vlad to talk to me and let me in to his world, not knowing what was going to happen, threw me, I was hurting. I never gave it a thought the evening of the barbecue when I seduced him. Stupid of me. After hearing all about his past, what he had done. I still wanted him and never batted an eyelid when I slept with him the night after. Protection should have been one of the first things on our minds only it wasn't even the last. It never got a thought.

"Holly, don't stress, love," I hear Olivia say through the thick haze that's clogging my brain, but I don't answer her.

I always wanted a child of my own. My ex not wanting one put paid to that. Now I might be, and I should be happy, over the moon.

I am happy. Ecstatic. Only my happiness has taken a downward turn when I think of Vlad.

Oh, he's a great father. A protector and provider. With enough love for his sons that they didn't need their mother. He says he loves me, and I know he does. He wants us to live together and be a family, but I don't think adding another addition was on his list.

"Holly, love," Olivia squeezes my hand and I look up at her through my blurred vision that my tears have created. Created. That word causes me to rub at my stomach again. I have created a life. We have created a life. Me and Vlad, and my heart swells as I turn up a smile, but I don't think my man will be as pleased as me.

"Go pee on the bloody stick," Sarah says as she tears open both boxes and puts the plastic sticks in my hand.

"Both of them?"

"Yes," Olivia tells me as she gets up from her seat. I take them both and get up from mine. "Just to be sure, Holly," she pats my hand, comforting me.

I make my way to the downstairs bathroom, closely followed by my two friends who know me so much better than I know myself. All this time I thought I'd had a virus, throwing up. Dizzy spells and the feeling that I wanted to be sick, I thought were after effects lingering as well as being nervous about singing at the club and here they are thinking I'm pregnant. They could be wrong. "Pee on them both then come straight out, and we'll be with you when you find out," Sarah reassures me, rubbing my back.

I'm out in minutes, my hands shaking as I hold onto two white plastic sticks that will tell me whether I'm going to be a mother or not. As we sit at the table, I'm unable to look at them, too nervous to know the outcome. Olivia and Sarah hold my shaky hands in theirs and rub at my shoulders. "You know, Holly? The nausea and dizzy spells as well as the lack of appetite should have sent alarm bells before now, but it didn't cross our minds until we left you last night." Sarah points between her and Olivia which she nods her head at. I know they're right. I should have realised myself, I'm very rarely poorly except for the odd migraine.

"How long does it take?" I nod my head at the sticks.

"Anytime now…" Olivia says as all three of us stare at them intensely. One by one on the little transparent screen the word Positive pops up.

"OH MY GOD!" Sarah pronounces each word and a tear trickles down my cheek. Olivia's fingers wipe it away as her arms come around me.

"Congratulations," she whispers into my hair and I sob lightly.

"I hope they're happy tears," she says, and I nod my head. I am happy. Shocked but happy about it, I just hope Vlad will feel the same way.

"You know, Holly? He loves you," she can read my mind. "He'll be ok with this." I wish I knew that for sure and I know I need to think about how I'm going to break the news to him that at forty-five with four sons and three grandchildren, he's going to be a father again.

Olivia and Sarah stay another hour, encouraging me to tell Vlad as soon as he gets home. Their comforting words calm me a little and when they leave, I make my way up the stairs to the one place where Vlad goes to think. The only place he gets any privacy and the place that hopefully will help me think of how to break the news to him.

Chapter 31

Vlad

I watch Holly through the window that separates our bedroom from the balcony, and I know she's upset, I can see her wipe at her eyes and nose using the tissue she is holding. Maybe she's upset with me for leaving her this morning, we had made plans and if she thinks she can't rely on me for the simplest of things then maybe she's rethinking about moving in with me.

I shouldn't have left her to go to a meeting that had been set up for the last couple of weeks, but with her looking and feeling better as well as her friends being here, I thought she would be okay about it. I could have rearranged signing the paperwork for the second building I have purchased but the sooner it was done the better. Once both projects are finished, it will make me and my boys a lot of money, not that we don't have enough already but I have plans which include Holly.

I've never really travelled. No fancy holidays or sunny beaches, not even when I lived in Russia. Since coming to England, my boys and I have been happy just taking in the English coastline and all the history that comes with this country. Now I want more. I want to see the wonders of the world. Sit drinking cocktails side by side with Holly on white sandy beaches. Stay in five-star hotels with room service. I know I still have Lucas at home who I know won't mind coming with us but in five years' time he'll be off to university, doing his own thing which will just leave me and my angel.

I don't spend much, I leave that to my sons. Yeah, I have nice cars, a huge house and wear designer suits but I don't spend unnecessarily. Like I said, I have my sons to do that. They'll realise one day and maybe become less extravagant.

I look at Holly again and decide I need to grow a pair. If she doesn't want to move in with me then I must except that, maybe she thinks we have a little way to go yet and she wants to get to know me better. She knows everything about me, the good and the bad, there's not much left to know.

Slowly, I push the door open and Holly's eyes meet mine. Although she's been crying, she doesn't look sad so maybe I've got the whole situation wrong. We hold each other's stare for a moment, her knowing she has something she wants to get off her chest and me hoping it's not something I don't want to here. Holly's aware I come out here for peace and quiet, she's also aware I come here to think. When I'm troubled or need to put things into perspective and I presume that's why she is out here.

"Can I join you?" I ask cautiously. She doesn't speak but just nods her head, patting the seat next to her as she licks her dry lips. When I sit, I sit forward resting my elbow on my knees waiting for Holly to speak. My heart starts to pound hard in my chest when she stays quiet but quickly returns to its normal rhythm when she places her hand on my back and gently rubs it. Shifting my body so that I'm facing her, I take her hand in mine.

"What is wrong, Holly? Why were you crying?" I hear my voice and it doesn't sound like me. I'm scared of what she is going to say to me. I don't want to be without her. She moves from her seat and crouches on the floor in front of me and I catch the tender smile she gives me as she places her hand on my cheek then runs her finger over my bottom lip before she gets settled between my legs. Her hands take hold of mine and she takes in a deep breath through her nose, gathering strength to say whatever it is.

"Do you love me, Vlad?" Holly gazes into my eyes, searching for the truth as to whether I do or not. Do I love her? Yes, I do with all my heart, she knows this. Doesn't she? I tell her often enough or maybe I don't. I show her all the time. I don't understand.

"You know I love you, sweetheart. Why do you feel the need to ask?" My hand runs down her cheek this time then I take her hands in mine, feeling a slight tremble.

"When I was a little girl, I thought my mum loved me… but she didn't." She blows out a breath and I lean down, kissing her forehead.

"I know," I murmur. "I'm sorry she wasn't there for you." She shakes her head as if to say it's not your fault and continues. "I thought God loved all his children but found myself questioning his love when he took my adopted parents from me." She swallows, trying to suppress the hurt. "Then I met Rob. Again, I thought he loved me, and he probably did in his own way. But I wasn't enough. So, I was hurt again. All three times it hurt in different ways but was still painful."

My mouth covers her, stopping the torture she's putting on herself. Pouring everything I have into that kiss, showing her how much I love her and what we have. I won't let her past hurt her anymore and I won't let mine. We have a future together. A fantastic future full of love, fun and surprises.

"Holly," I'm breathless when we pull apart and need a moment to catch my breath then I put my hands on her cheeks. "Sweetheart don't ever question if I love you. You, Holly Spencer, are the only woman that I have ever loved and the only one that I ever will." She closes her eyes and leans into my hand, leaving a gentle kiss when her eyes open, I carry on.

"They say there's a reason for everything that happens in the world and I now know why my mother had to lose her family, leave her home here in England and live in Russia. She had to meet my father to have me. I knew there was another reason why I always wanted to come to England, and it wasn't just because my mother came from here or to get away from my father… It was because you were here waiting for me. Holly we've both gone through so much hurt in our lives and I know I'm not innocent in causing some of that hurt, but we had to go through it to find each other." She tilts her head and I see that beautiful smile on her angelic face, and I can't help but smile with her. She does this to me all the time. When she hurts, I do. When she's happy and smiling, I am.

I sit down, taking her with me and get her comfy, straddling my knees. Smoothing her hair back around her ears, I get lost in her sapphire eyes, the ones that see me. The real me. "Holly, if you had still been with Rob then I doubt very much you would have been out with the girls in my club and we would have never met…" I shake my head, not wanting to think about never meeting her. "Do you see? We were meant to find each other, Holly, we just had to go through a lot of hurt before we did. Now I've found you I'm never letting you go," my lips touch hers, "I love you so much, Holly Spencer," I whisper against them.

Her head falls onto my shoulder as she wraps her arms around my neck, and I hold her tight while she sobs hard against it. I have no clue why's she's feeling emotional or what could have brought it on. I thought it was because I had left this morning but now, I feel it's much more.

When she lifts her head, she's stopped crying and there's a glint in her eyes. "I love you too, Vladimir Petrov, with all my heart," she tells me and with that smile she holds for me, I know she's telling the truth.

"Good, now we have that cleared up. You love me and I love you. Can you tell me what brought all that on?" I raise an eyebrow at her while I wait for her answer and she reaches down to the floor, picking up her bag. She places it between us then reaches inside it, bringing out two white and blue plastic sticks. And I now have my reason why.

It's not the first time I've seen a pregnancy testing kit. Sebastian was only too happy to thrust Izzy's in my face when they found out they were having Rebecca. I just never gave it a thought that it's something Holly and I would be sharing. I'm forty-five with four sons and three grandchildren. Am I shocked, surprised? Yes, I am but that doesn't mean I don't want this baby, quite the opposite really.

"Vlad are you ok?" I hear Holly's question and I look up at her. I must have been staring at the pregnancy kit for far too long. "Are you ok?" she says again, and I can see the apprehension on her face.

"Yes," I answer then look down at what I'm holding in my hands again, two of them both reading positive. A chuckle escapes from me. I don't know if it's the shock, nerves or excitement but then I find myself laughing louder than I have in a very long time. That puts paid to us sinking our toes into white sandy beaches while we sip cocktails or taking in the sights of the capital cities of the world. We could always use one of those contraptions that you put the child in and strap it around your body, she'd be fine in one of those. She. Oh God please let it be a girl. I have four sons a daughter would just be perfect. I hear a giggle then a screech which brings me out of my over-excited musing, and I find Holly and I are now in the bedroom. I have Holly laid on the bed and I'm straddling her hips, careful not putting my weight on her. The two pregnancy sticks are laid at the side of us.

"You needed two, Holly?" I nod my head toward the sticks. She chuckles and lifts herself up on her elbows.

"Olivia and Sarah brought them over. It was them that realised what was wrong with me, I didn't have a clue."

"There's nothing wrong with you, Holly. You are perfect and she will be too," I lean down placing soft kisses around Holly's stomach, then it's my turn to shed a tear as I feel my eyes welling up.

"She?" Holly questions, widening her eyes at me, smirking. I make my way to the top of the bed, laying us both down on our sides so we're facing each other while I wipe the wetness from my eyes. Fucking emotions.

"Four boys, Holly," I hold up four fingers. "There's got to be a girl in there somewhere," I chuckle as I grab my crotch. Holly laughs along with me then cups my face.

"Are you ok with this, Vlad? I mean are you happy?"

"Yes," I answer without hesitation. "Having another child wasn't something I had ever thought about... But then I never thought I was going to fall in love and to be truthful I didn't want to. However, you came along, and I never stood a chance," Holly giggles when I roll my eyes at her and kisses my lips.

"Neither did I," she whispers against them then pinches my nipple when I get cocky.

"I'm hard to resist sweetheart," I hold my nipple that she's just tweaked, feigning that she's hurt me, and she lowers her head to place a soft kiss there. Something comes to mind and I know I need to ask and get it out of the way.

"Holly I thought you were on the contraceptive pill?" I know she was on it; I've seen her take the tiny tablet. She blows out a breath and sits up against the headboard.

"I am, I mean I was…" Holly stops and pulls at her bottom lip. I sit up too, waiting for her to continue. Taking her hand in mine, I raise it to my lips, kissing it softly. Letting her know I don't really care how this has happened. It takes two to tango and all that.

"When I went off to the coast…" she stops, and I nod my head understanding. "I forgot to take them with me. Then when I came back…" she shrugs her shoulders. Holly doesn't need to explain anymore. The last couple of months have been chaotic. She's been there for my sons and grandchildren as well as dealing with my past and trying to get her head around it. Then the club, I'm surprised she knows her own name.

"I'm sorry, Vlad, I forgot."

"Please don't apologise, Holly. This is as much my doing as yours. We were both there…" I raise my eyebrows and chuckle. She slaps my hand, laughing with me.

Holly lays on her back staring at the ceiling, both her hands laying on her stomach and a contended smile on her face. I move down the bed, resting my chin on her hip, watching her flat stomach rise and fall. You wouldn't know she was carrying a baby in there. My baby. Our baby. Kissing her hip, she lifts on her elbows and looks down at me. "Do you think the baby was conceived in the hotel room?" I ask.

"Yes, I think so," she nods her head. "Or…" I know what she's thinking about. It could have been the evening when my boys were barbecuing, and I was trying to hide away in my office until Holly appeared and seduced me. There's a mischievous grin on her face which I know oh too well. She wants to play.

"Spit it out, Holly," I tell her as I climb up her body, covering hers with mine. "Do you mean the evening you threw yourself at me?" I bite her lip and get a moan from her.

"I did not throw myself at you," her tongue runs over her bottom lip. "I just gave you the nudge you needed," this time she bites mine and the electricity surges straight to my groin which I thrust into her. Holly chuckles at my predicament as she runs her hands up my arms that are taking my weight. "You know I am feeling a lot better," she flirts while running her fingers to the back of my neck then she pulls me down to her.

She takes my mouth, her tongue sliding in, her taste is addictive. Our kiss turns wild and passionate and before I know what I'm doing, I've rid her of her top and my lips are doing their usual rounds of her neck, collarbone and boobs. With her hands in my hair, she moans when I twirl my tongue around one of her hard nipples, my other hand running up her thigh. She moans again and I'm so fucking hard, I could pop like a balloon. I stop myself from going any further, I need to know that she is genuinely ok, I don't want to hurt her.

"Holly..."

"I'm ok, Vlad. Honestly. Plus, I owe you," she winks at me and wiggles her hips. The little minx is taunting me. I know I threatened to keep her tied to my bed all weekend and that she owed me for...

"Vlad stop overthinking things and show me how much you love me," she says while she unfastens her jeans and pushes them off her hips. I oblige her by ridding them completely then rip her silky knickers from her in one swift movement. She wants me to show her I love her; I can do that all day. Every day for eternity.

Standing from the bed, I strip down to my boxers and glance at my bedside clock, it's one thirty which means we have a couple of hours before Lucas arrives home from school. We also need to get Holly booked in at with the doctor.

When I turn to the naked angel that's sprawled out waiting patiently for me, her eyes are appreciating my body, roaming up and down. I grin when they land on my manhood which is stood up proudly, causing her sapphire gems to grow larger.

Climbing on the bed, my mouth makes its first assault on one of her ankles, kissing, biting and running my tongue all the way up to her inner thigh and because I like to treat things equally, I give the same attention to the other one. I've decided I will torment her a little bit not to be cruel, no. I just love the sounds she makes when my lips connect with her soft smooth skin. As I place tender kisses on both her inner thighs, she pulls at my hair. It never takes me long to get her worked up to her first orgasm. I let her tug a bit more at me while I watch her other hand grip the sheet then my lips crash onto her soft warm mound. My tongue tormenting and tantalizing her nerve endings as my lips leisurely kiss and drink her in. Oh, how I've missed this. In minutes she is squeezing my head between her thighs, moaning and calling out my name. I don't stop until I feel her hand unravel from my hair and she feels limp beneath me. Time to take what's mine. My teeth bite and scrape at her hipbone and I get a whimper from her. Kissing along her bikini line until I reach the other side, I then do the same again. Making my way up her body, I stop at her lower tummy and place a tender kiss and quickly work my way up, twirling my tongue around her hard nipples. I need to get used to sharing those buggers. Face to face, her eyelids are heavy with lust and my cock nudges at her entrance, eager to be home. When I thrust forward into her warmth, her eyes spring open and I can't help but chuckle.

"Miss me?" I whisper into her lips, not waiting for her answer as my body shows her how much I've missed her. Love her. She clings to me as I push further into her, filling her while I kiss and suck on her neck. My thrust quickens when I feel her tighten around me and as she sinks her teeth into my shoulder when her orgasm hits her hard, I see stars. Holly's high goes on for a while as she squeezes me tight, drawing every drop from me. I shake and shiver like I've never done before and as her name roars from my mouth, bouncing off the walls, I collapse at the side of her, both of us panting hard.

I roll us both over so I'm on my back and she's sprawled across me, her face snuggled into my neck. I kiss her hair, inhaling her sweet scent and she lifts her head then places a soft kiss on my shoulder where she has left her teeth mark. "Wow. If I wasn't already pregnant then I'm sure I would be now," she chuckles. "That was…. Intense and very pleasurable," she sits up and kisses my chest. I lay there with my arms behind my head, pleased I've done my job right.

"You're quiet," she says when I just lay there watching her. "Are you sure you're ok?" I nod my head to answer her then I turn to my side, taking her with me.

"There is something," I tell her, tucking a loose strand of hair behind her ear.

"What is it?" her voice is quiet and as she waits for me to speak;

she brings my hand up between us then runs her finger over my knuckles.

"I would have loved to have been there," my other hand comes up and I hold her delicate hand in both of mine. "To hold your hand while we waited for the stick to read positive. That should have been done together."

"I'm sorry, Vlad, I never thought. It was sprung on me so quickly…" I place my finger on her lips, she doesn't need to feel bad about it, I know Holly doesn't have a bad bone in her body and neither do her friends. They couldn't have known that I didn't get to do all the normal things an expectant father gets to do. I only got to go to the hospital visits when Natalia was carrying Lucas because she didn't have a choice.

"We can do another one. Get another one from the shop and watch it together."

"It's fine, Holly, I was just saying it would have been nice. Something special."

"Oh, now I feel bad," she sits up quickly and straddles my waist. "What can I do to make it up to you?" she looks panicked and I didn't want that. I sit up too, placing my hand round the small of her back, holding her to me.

"Holly all I want is to be able to do the normal things a father would do. I want to be there when you visit the doctors, midwife and when you're due any scans. I want to be able to run out in the middle of the night because you're craving twiglets and honey." She giggles and I do because fuck knows where I got twiglets and honey from, but she gets what I'm talking about. I place my hand on her stomach. "I want to feel our baby growing and kicking inside you and I want you to rant at me when nothing fits. So I can go out with you and buy you clothes that do. Together, I want us to decorate the nursery and buy baby clothes, cuddly toys, bottles and…"

"I want that too," she whispers, tears filling her eyes. "Vlad, this is new to me, I don't know what I'm doing. I might have been round a lot of children, but they weren't my own. I want you with me every step of the way doing all those things together. I need you to be that man." I kiss her mouth softly and lay us back down, Holly still attached to my chest. I smile wide, I can't fucking wait.

"Thank you," I breath into her hair. She tilts her head to look up at me and kisses my chin.

"We'll go out later when I've had a nap," yawning on cue. "And get another kit." And just because I want to watch it happen, I nod my head.

Holly soon nods off in my arms and while I'm thinking about which room to turn into a nursery and how I can't wait for Holly to start showing, I drift off as well.

*

"Wake up, lover boy," I hear Nicholas' rough voice breathe against my skin. My eyes flicker open and he's knelt at the side of me, grinning like the idiot he is. He's not on his own, the other three are stood there grinning. It must be fucking catching.

Gently, I lift Holly off my chest, careful not to uncover her then I sit up. "What the fuck are you doing?" My whisper comes out louder than I intended it to, and Holly stirs. They all put their fingers to their lips telling me to shush. Cheeky bastards. "What are you all doing in here?" I quietly ask.

"Nothing," Nicholas answers. "You weren't downstairs. Concerned, we came looking for you and here you are."

"I'm seriously thinking about taking out an injunction. No, I am putting a ban on you all entering my bedroom without my permission. So, fuck off downstairs because I didn't invite you in." They stare at me, still grinning, not taking a blind bit of notice to what I am saying. Holly might want to rethink about having me as a father to our child because I spoil them rotten and they do as they like.

"Aw don't be mean, paps, we just want to congratulate you," Sebastian says while he waves Holly's test strips in the air. I turn to the bedside table then look back at him. Obviously, they're not going to be there because he has them in his hand.

"You lot downstairs now, let me get dressed." This time my tone is not up for challenging. I'm not sure whether Holly wanted anyone knowing yet. I know my sons aren't just anyone and that her friends know already but we haven't discussed when we were going to tell them.

Seb heads out first, chuckling, followed by Daniel then Nicholas leaves. Lucas hangs back and sits down on the bed.

"Sorry, dad. It was my fault," he says quietly. "I came home from school and you weren't downstairs, so I came up here to let you know I was home. I did knock at the door, but you didn't answer." He shrugs his shoulders. "I gave you a nudge to wake you and you were sound asleep that's when I saw them, so I phoned Nicholas." Fucking rent a gob. He'll have phoned his brothers and got them over here. Not at all bothered about invading our privacy. I hope Holly knows what she's let herself in for. Of course she does, she loves that my sons wind me up. All in a bit of fun.

"Don't worry, Lucas, I'm not mad at you," I tell him as I swing my legs out of bed. "Go join your brothers, I'll be down soon."

"Ok," he says, getting off the bed and walking to the door. He turns and looks at me smiling, "I'm glad Holly is back and I'm glad I'm not going to be the youngest anymore," then he leaves.

I look at Holly who's still peacefully asleep, spread out like a starfish, as usual. I stroke her hair, "I'm glad too, Lucas," I whisper then make my way to the shower before I go and deal with my sons.

Chapter 32

Holly

Four weeks later

"I'm not going, nothing fits me anymore," I exaggerate, ranting at the big oath that's smirking at my little tantrum. He gets off the bed and walks up behind me, wrapping his strong arms around my waist, laying his hands on my stomach. I lean into him as we both look in the mirror.

My boobs have suddenly taken on a life of their own and I'm only three months. God knows what they will be like when I'm nearly full term.

"Sweetheart there's nothing wrong with them. If they've grown then it's only slight because they still fit my hands perfectly," there's still that smirk on his face as he slides his hands upwards and cups my boobs. "And you have to go, it's your birthday party," he adds, kissing my neck.

"Yeah well. I don't understand why you thought I needed a party. I'm thirty-eight, it's not a special birthday." He kisses my neck again then spins me around so I'm facing him. His dark blue eyes sparkle with amusement which they do most of the time these days. And that cheeky grin has become a permanent fixture. It can be quite annoying sometimes when I'm trying to be serious. Since finding out I was pregnant, and moving in with him and his family, he's never stopped smiling. Neither have his sons. They're over the moon to be having a baby brother or sister and Vlad's grandchildren can't wait either. Izzy thinks it's hilarious that Vlad's going to have another child and tells me what a big softy he has become since his grandchildren came along and now me. She said he's a different man now to what he was when she first met him. Apparently, he used to scare the shit out of her. I can't imagine why.

"Holly," he pecks my lips then takes a deep breath. "Your family and friends love you." He pecks at my lips again. "You have done so much for them, they just wanted to say thank you by celebrating your birthday altogether." I get another kiss then he lets go of me and saunters off towards the bed, leaning down and grabbing at something underneath it.

"We could have had a party here, you didn't need to close the restaurant for the evening," I say to his bare back while he fumbles with whatever it is he is trying to pick up.

"Shut up woman," he says playfully when he stands and thrust a large box into my hands along with a smaller one that looks like a shoe box and a gift bag that I think might be lingerie.

"Happy birthday, angel," he whispers as he kisses my cheek.

"Vlad you gave me my present this morning," I chastise him. He did. He bought me a beautiful Rolex rose gold watch with a black face. It must have cost a fortune. I'm not good at accepting presents and maybe that's because I've never had that special someone in my life to buy me them. But saying that, over the last month I've been spoilt rotten and I find I get a little giddy when Vlad buys me a gift. It can be anything from flowers, chocolates, sexy undies to a pair of earrings, my smile lights up his face and I love seeing him smile. I do the same for him. He can come home to ties and tiepins, cufflinks, silly boxers and matching socks or just me naked wearing one of his ties. I got that from Pretty Woman. But my man loves it.

"I know but I knew you'd be moaning so I bought you something special for tonight."

"I do not moan," my eyes widen at him and I slap his arm.

"I like spoiling you," he says, twirling me round. "Now open your gifts. Get dressed before we are late for your own party," then he slaps my arse, wanting me to get a move on.

While he is putting on his trousers, I open the box. He has excellent taste in women's clothing and is very good at picking out matching underwear, so I know I'm in for a treat.

When I'm dressed, I check out my appearance in the mirror. The black detailed fish tail dress that stops at the knee fits like glove, highlighting my figure and even though it's off the shoulder, my breasts don't look overly big. Maybe Vlad was right, and I just think they are because I'm pregnant. Smoothing down the dress I stop at my belly, resting my hand there. I'm sure I have a slight bump, just a little swelling. I turn sideways to get a better view and yes, my flat stomach does have a swelling; it's not much but it's there. It makes me smile.

Vlad appears at the doorway fastening up his waistcoat, as ever he looks good enough to eat. Why is he wearing a waistcoat? I don't know. Anyone would think we were attending some swanky posh function. However, it is his restaurant that's hosting my birthday party so maybe he thinks he needs to look the part. "Do you think my stomach has gotten bigger?" I turn to the side again, glancing in the mirror, keeping my hands where they were.

"No," Vlad places his hands over mine, leaning down to kiss my shoulder. "You look as sexy as sin in that dress. How about we stay here and have our own little party?" He kisses my shoulder again then works his way up to my neck. As much as I love his kisses, and I could quite easily take him up on his offer, I know we can't, and he does too. His sons, Izzy and grandchildren are waiting for us downstairs and we need to get moving before they come bursting through the bedroom door. They haven't taken any notice of him when he told them they were banned from walking straight in and had to wait to be invited in. All they do is give a loud knock and shout we're coming in, no privacy at all, but we have started to remember to lock the door just to annoy them.

"Are you sure?" I ask, tilting my head to have another look.

"Yes, I'm sure. Your boobs are the same size as they were and so is your stomach," he pats said stomach then picks up his jacket asking me to hurry up.

"Hmmm," is all I say. I think he just doesn't want to tell me that I'm putting weight on, trying to be nice. It's not going to upset me, I'm pregnant; it's inevitable that I'm going to gain a few pounds. Anyway, I know that I have. All my bras and jeans are feeling tight on me, so I know he's just playing it safe in case I go all nuclear on him, blaming him for my weight gain. What's he going to say when I'm heavily pregnant?

I shake my head at him, and he just smiles and winks at me as we make our way downstairs where everyone waits.

"Wow, you have a little bump already," Izzy says, jumping up from her seat as we make our way into the kitchen. I bloody knew I had. I eye Vlad mimicking, "I told you so," while Izzy gets close and personal with my tummy and she's not on her own. Before I know it, I have several pairs of hands feeling at it, all mumbling about it being a big baby, which gets me thinking.

Vlad's sons are huge except for Lucas, but I know the reason behind that.

"Get your hands off my baby," Vlad tells them as he smacks their hands away playfully. Izzy stands there with her hands on her hips grinning at us both. Vlad has now moved to the back of me with his arms wrapped around my waist, resting his hands on his baby.

"I think you're going to have a big baby, Holly. I was lucky my kids took after me but me thinks yours might take after its daddy," she laughs, and I turn to the man at the back of me who finds this amusing. He soon loses that smirk when I frown at him.

"How much did Sebastian weigh when he was born?" Nicholas chuckles behind me and the look on Vlad's face tells me I'm not going to like his answer.

"Nine pounds three ounces," he says slowly, and I look down at my belly that I know is going to stretch beyond belief.

"What about Nicholas?" I turn to look at Vlad's sons who are all grinning at my questioning.

"He was eight pounds ten," I blow out a breath, thanking God that we're getting smaller.

"And Daniel?" He's the biggest of them all, same build as his father, I dread to think what size he was.

"Holly you've got to understand their mother was a lot taller than you, bigger boned…"

"Just tell me," I say calmly. I'm not really that bothered but it would be helpful to know their size at least I'll know what to expect and, like he said, Natalia was almost six foot according to what Vlad told me, so they were never going to have small babies. Well not when she went full term anyway.

"Ten pounds two…" he gives me a concerned smile then pulls me into him while his sons all let out a low whistle.

"Bloody hell," Izzy says shocked. "It will split you in two," she shocks herself with her last statement and covers her mouth. "Sorry." I'd have thought she'd have known how much they all weighed but maybe she never asked. I move out of Vlad's arms and Lucas is standing behind me.

"I was only tiny," he says, trying comfort me. I place my arm around his shoulders and pull him into me, kissing the top of his head.

"I know, love, you were the cute one."

"Yeah," Nicholas says. "He was like a gorilla with all that dark hair," he nods his head towards Daniel who just shrugs his shoulders.

"Are you worried, Holly?" I can see my questioning and reaction is bothering him and to be truthful I'm not that bothered. Women have big babies all the time, I know this. My friend's babies were not small, they weren't ten pounders but still they were decent weights.

"No, not really," I peck his lips to reassure him and he nods his head when I pull away.

"Good. Anyway, we're having a girl who I know will take after you, and I'm sure you were a beautiful dainty little thing." His smile reaches his eyes, he really wants a girl and I don't blame him. He's got four sons, who are his world, a little baby girl would be the cherry on top of the cake.

"You have your three months scan next week, don't you, Holly?" Izzy says. I nod my head at her knowing it's on Monday, three days away. "Well they'll let you know if the baby is normal size or if you're going to give birth to a giant," Vlad shakes his head at her while we all laugh at her comment, but I can see he's holding back that smirk. He just doing it for my benefit, thinking that I'd worry.

"Come on," Sebastian says. "Enough about babies, I need a drink." He kisses Izzy's head when she narrows her eyes on him. "What? You said I could have a night off… I've been up all week with this one." Ben is fast asleep in his pram, not caring what's going on around him. Joe is sat on the sofa; he too doesn't care, and Rebecca is in her room gathering some toys for her and Megan to play with at the party.

"Ok," she says, kissing his cheek. She knows he's a good dad and husband, running around after his children. Taking and picking them up from school. Helping with the cooking and cleaning then work. He'll get up most nights to feed Benjamin, telling Izzy to go back to sleep. Yeah, he's a good one. "But don't get as bad as you did at your birthday party otherwise your kipping in with him," she nods her head towards Nicholas who just smirks at her.

"We didn't make it to bed that night, from what I can remember, I was cuddling his feet most of the night on the sofa. I woke up thinking I'd pulled until I realised where I was then climbed on to the other one," Nicholas tells us still laughing.

"I hope you weren't sucking my toes…" Sebastian shivers.

"You should be so fucking lucky," his brother tells him.

"Fucking idiots," Vlad mumbles, running his hand threw his hair. "Come on. Shout Rebecca down we need leave," he says as he puts his hand in his waistcoat pocket only to bring it out empty, looking confused. He then taps the pocket of his jacket and his expression changes and that smirk he's been wearing comes back.

"You ok?" I ask him.

"Yep," he winks then takes my hand, leading me outside to the car.

Chapter 33

Vlad

Keeping the news about the baby a secret was never going to happen. What with Olivia and Sarah knowing, there was no way they could keep it from Jack and Nick. Then my sons found out which is like putting an advertisement in the morning paper. Before we knew it, Tom and Mary were round congratulating us, followed by Jay and Ivy who were overjoyed at the news. I do think they came over because they were worried about our relationship but once they saw how happy we both were Jay shook my hand and Ivy gave me a motherly hug, it brought a tear to my eye and to hers.

We were all invited to Jay and Ivy's for Sunday dinner and while we were there, I gained a bit of information that I'm ashamed to say I should have known. Holly's birthday. She knows when mine is, we met on that day, but we've never once discussed hers and I've never asked. Like I said, ashamed of myself.

It was Sarah who informed me about it and when she realised I didn't know, she wasn't surprised. She knows as well as I do that Holly is a selfless person. Happiest doing for others and not one bit bothered about if her birthday was forgotten. Finding out like I did I could have kicked myself and was determined to surprise her with a trip away, but the rest of the clan wanted to celebrate with us, so my plan to take her away for a week was put on hold so we could all be with Holly on her birthday.

We're still going away but we need to wait until after her scan. She doesn't know what I have planned, nor does she know what's burning a hole in my jacket pocket. Just thinking about it has my collar tightening around my neck and as I pull at it, Sebastian catches my eye and nods, giving me a knowing smile. He's aware of what my intentions are tonight, and he knows I'm a nervous wreck. My other three sons know too, I can't keep anything from them. I thought Nicholas would be his usual piss-taking self, but he's surprised me by how adult and grown up about it he's been. They've all been supportive, and I understand why. This is a big thing for me, it's something I've never done and never thought I would do, so in the words of my sons, I'm shitting myself.

"Hey big man," Olivia shouts over the music and chatting. I turn to see her wide smile as her arms come around my neck then she kisses my cheek. I don't stop her, there's no point. "You've done a fantastic job with the room and the food was delicious. The whole night has been amazing. Holly has really enjoyed herself, even if she can't have a drink," she grins, wiggling a glass of wine at me. I didn't really do anything apart from informing Maureen, my restaurant manager, how I wanted the room setting out and what food to have prepared.

"Thank you, but it was the staff that did all the hard work."

"Yeah, but you made it special for her and that means a lot to Holly." My gaze lands on Holly, she's showing Lucy and one of Sarah's sisters the watch I bought her. Olivia's eyes follow mine and she smiles again. "You know, Vlad, I wasn't sure about you at first. I thought that you'd just be a bit of fun Holly needed," I understand what she means. I think they were a few people that thought the same, I thought otherwise. I knew from day one that Holly was special and that I needed her in my life. "But the more Holly spoke about you, the more I realised what you two had was the real thing. It's a shame you didn't meet years ago." I nod my head at her and thank her for her words, but Holly and I know it was the right time for us to meet. Meeting any earlier than we did things might have been different; I don't think Holly would have coped with me and my past.

Holly lifts her head and catches my eye; she laughs when she sees I've got Olivia hanging off my arm and my nerves stretch to snapping point. This place is packed with friends and family who love us both, so I know they will all be delighted to be here when I do the one thing I never thought I'd ever do.

Nicholas breaks my thought when he slaps me on the back and spins Olivia round, tapping his cheek for her to kiss. She obliges as my other three sons join us.

"Are you ok?" Seb asks. When I hear him shout to one of the bar staff to get me a brandy, I know he's picked up that I'm anxious. I haven't had a drink all night. With Holly being pregnant, she isn't drinking so why should I. Although she told me to have a drink, I really want to support her through everything while she's carrying our child and if that means giving up drinking then so be it. When he passes the glass to me, I shake my head and keep my focus on the one person besides my sons that can calm me.

"You can do this, paps. We've got your back," Nicholas says as he takes the glass from Sebastian and offers me it again. As a rule, I have no trouble telling Holly or showing her how I feel but, in a room full of people and with what I want to say, I'm anything but calm. So, taking the brandy from my son, I down it in one, keeping my focus on the woman ahead who holds my heart and hopefully will become my wife.

Walking towards Holly, I can hear the music, people laughing and Olivia questioning my sons on what I am doing. As I get closer, my angel being the centre of my aim, the noise around me ceases. There's just Holly and me and that's all I need to continue. I come to a halt in front of her and her head lifts, eyes meeting mine when she senses I'm close. I put my hand out to her and her friends stand and step to one side as she takes it. Once she's up out of her seat, standing in front of me, I lower to one knee, keeping her hand in mine. Her eyes widen with shock, excitement and nerves. She bites her lip as she tries hard to stop that nervous giggle from exploding out but fails when a little yelp escapes which she covers with her other hand. She knows what I'm about to ask, I can see the happiness spreading through her which calms my nerves, giving me the courage to carry on. I might have been married before, but I didn't get down on one knee to propose or declare my undying love in front of a room full of people.

"Holly you know how much I love you," she nods her head,

smiling as she gives me her other hand, the expression on her face tells me she loves me too. I don't look at our family who are all stood now watching me and Holly, the women all letting out soft sighs. I carry on with what I came to do.

"Sweetheart, I'm not about to give some long-winded speech in front of everyone about how we were meant to be. You know I'd rather show you in the privacy of our home. But I do need to tell you that you are my everything. Everything I didn't know I needed or wanted and now everything I can't be without. It took us a long time to find each other and what we found… is special, something rare." Tears form in Holly's eyes and one rolls down onto her cheek. Standing, I move her hands to my shoulders then wipe away the lone tear, placing my hands on her hip my thumbs stroking over her stomach where she keeps our baby safe.

"You know everything about me, the good, the bad and you still love me. I am truly in awe of you. The kindness and love you give to anybody who is lucky enough to know you." I move one of my hands to wave around at the family and friends that are gathered, with almighty grins on their faces and I can see they agree with me when they all nod at my last statement. "Holly I know we have both been here before, but this time it's you and me. Us. We work. What I'm trying to say is can we make our way through the rest of our lives with our family, friends and our baby as man and wife." She sniffles and I hear a few sobs and 'oh my god' before I kneel again, taking the ring from my pocket. "Holly Spencer will you marry me?"

I don't get to show her the ring before she launches herself into my arms, knocking me off balance and smashing her lips against mine. Sebastian, Nicholas, Daniel and Lucas really do have my back because they stop me from toppling over, taking Holly with me. When she finished attacking me, she places her face in my neck and I do the same, breathing her in. There's whistles and claps as we hold each other tight, my heart pounding out of my chest. Then I realise I haven't heard that one little word.

With us both kneeling on the floor, I take Holly's cheeks in my hands. "Angel was that a yes?" I chuckle. Her blue eyes, her laughter lights up the room, "Yes," she grins then wraps her arms around my neck, her mouth kissing my cheek. "I love you so much, Vlad." This time it's me who kisses her, pouring all my love into it and I couldn't give a fuck who's watching.

    As we stand, I take Holly's left hand in mine, placing the eighteen-carat white gold, solitaire diamond engagement ring on her finger, then brush my lips gently against hers. Again, everyone is cheering and clapping, happy knowing what we have always known. We were meant to be together.

Chapter 34

Vlad

Laughter and singing fill the room as family and friends continue to celebrate Holly's birthday and our engagement. As I watch them, I can see it is not just Holly and me that fit together perfectly; they do too.

All my life I've never had any close friends. Kept myself to myself, never knowing who I could trust except for Dimitri but he left Russia when we were both fourteen. We kept in touch over the years with telephone calls, letters then emails, but I was always careful never giving away too much information. Sasha was the only other person that I was close to, my older brother who would do anything to keep me safe while I was growing up. When Sebastian came along and I was at an age where I could go clubbing, it was Sasha and his friends that I would tag along with, no real mates of my own.

When we came here to England and I took over Dimitri's parent's restaurant, my boys were growing up. I had all that I needed, or so I thought. Little did I know that slowly I was letting other people into my life. People I could trust and call friends.

Dave and Mark, I met through the hospital that Lucas attended regularly and straight away we had things in common. Dave been both Lucas and Mark's daughter's doctor, who were both golfing buddies. When they invited me to join them, I didn't give a second thought in accepting and the nights out that we went on once a month was a welcomed release.

Mr and Mrs White were the housekeeper and gardener of the house that I bought from Dimitri's parents who I kept on. Straight away they took to my sons and were only too happy to help where they could which I was grateful for. Still am. In turn my sons have become very close to them both, treating them like grandparents. They have been with us through so much over the years that I didn't realise until now that they have been nothing short of loving parents towards me.

Izzy exploded into our lives, taking no prisoners. Sebastian fell head over heels for her the moment she barged through the office door and, to be truthful, I found she made me laugh as she kept my eldest on his toes. His brothers took to her like a big sister and when she introduced Joseph into our lives then I couldn't help but be there for her as a father figure. She'd never known hers and neither had Joe, so Seb took pleasure in becoming his adopted daddy and I was only too happy to have gained a daughter in mine.

Turning my head towards the raucous laughter coming from the end of the bar, I watch Frank slam his shot glass on the bar then he raises his arms above his head. Jack, Nick, Dave and Mark follow him as they shout at one of the new bar staff to top them up. Even Zach, my solicitor, is joining in their game, all in high spirits. Again, Frank and Zach have crept into our lives, giving sound advice and support when needed and not just because I pay them their wages.

It's took me over twelve years to realise that we've needed these people in our lives and I'm so glad that we have them.

Then there's Holly's friends that she calls family and I understand why. They have all been there for her when she's needed them, and she's been there for them. Each one of them are special to Holly and in the six months I have known her they have become special to me and my family too.

"Here Vlad, get one of these down your neck," Zach slides a shot glass towards me as he makes his way from the rowdy crowd. "Come on, it's a celebration big man," he says, slapping me on the back. I decline the drink, still taking in everyone around me while I wait for Holly to return from the ladies. God knows why women need to go in packs and take so long. She went in ten minutes ago with Olivia, Sarah and Izzy and not one of them have returned yet.

"You ok?" Zach asks as he picks up the drink he offered me and downs it in one. He knows I won't drink it; I might have had one earlier, needing a bit of Dutch courage, but I'm sticking to what I have said and won't be drinking until after the baby is born.

"Yes. Never been better," I answer. "What about you?" I ask, raising an eyebrow at him. Parties aren't his usual thing; not family parties anyway. On a Friday night, he's normally being assertive in the Dark Rooms which he has shares in. It's known for catering to high class women and men that are into a certain lifestyle. Not my cup of tea but each to their own. I don't judge, they're all consenting adults. "No one to play with tonight?" I ask, chuckling.

"Bored with the same routine," he blows out a breath. "I need something different in my life. Someone that's permanent, I'm getting too old…" he shakes his head chuckling. "Look at us getting all deep and meaningful," I chuckle too because it's not something we would usually talk about but if he needs a shoulder then I'm here.

"Anytime you need to talk then you know where I am, feel free to drop by the office." I tell him as I watch his eyes follow one of my female employees. She feels his stare and looks up, giving him a shy smile and he returns it with one of his own and for a brief moment they're lost in each other. It's quite touching really, or it would be if she wasn't one of my staff in her mid-twenties and he wasn't my solicitor who I know has certain needs.

"Huh," he says, when their spell is broken. He didn't hear a word I said.

"Keep your hands off my staff," I tell him in a diplomatic way just as my angel appears, snaking her hands under my waistcoat. Holly stands in front of me, her arms around me and mine around her as she turns to Zach.

"Listen to him, Zach. Jen doesn't need any distractions in her life," she lays her head on my chest as Zach nods his head at her, but I see the struggle in his eyes as he makes his way back to the end of the bar, trying hard not to look at Jen. Funny how my little minx knows small details about the new staff that have started working here, and I don't even know their names. Saying that, she has taken time over the last few weeks to come in and get to know them, so it's understandable that staff have confided in her with private matters about themselves. With her cheerful approach and caring nature, the employees in all three of my establishments love her.

We stand moulded together as the music plays, while our family and friends laugh, sing, dance and drink, all enjoying themselves. And when the music slows down, I lead Holly onto the small dance floor. We're not on our own as we sway in time with music. Sebastian and Izzy are in a loving embrace, Nicholas has dragged Lucy up. She has her head on his shoulder. He has his face buried in her hair. Jack and Nick have left Frank and Zach at the bar while they cuddle with their wives to the slow seductive sound. Everyone else happy just doing their thing.

While the music still plays, my hands move to Holly cheeks and I place a soft kiss on her lips, "I love you, Holly Spencer," I say into them.

"I love you too, Vladimir Petrov," my angel smiles against my lips and I know life has smiled down on me at last. I have so much to be thankful for. Holly, the light of my life, who is carrying our baby. My sons, Izzy and grandchildren. And, of course, new friends and family, ones I know play hard, love even harder and I know I can trust them.

This is what family is all about.

About the Author

I work full-time as a learning support assistant. I live in Leeds, West Yorkshire, England, which is where I was born. I come from an extremely large family which has two sets of twins, me being the eldest of one of the sets. I am kept exceptionally busy with my job and family commitments where I take care of my elderly mother. I enjoy spending quality time with my partner of thirty years, stepdaughter, two grandchildren, my twin sister and her family. Any spare time I have, I can be found reading a good romance novel, contemporary, erotic or thriller. If not reading I will be using my newly found creative side, writing. When I have the chance to take a holiday, you will find me in the breathtaking province of Alberta, Canada, where I get to take in the scenery, sample all they have to offer and spend time with my older brother and beautiful nieces. This is my second book in the *Ain't Nobody Series*.